Sparks Ignite

Hannah Beth

ISBN 978-1-64299-923-5 (paperback)
ISBN 978-1-64299-925-9 (digital)

Copyright © 2018 by Hannah Beth

All rights reserved. No part of this publication may be reproduced, distributed, or transmitted in any form or by any means, including photocopying, recording, or other electronic or mechanical methods without the prior written permission of the publisher. For permission requests, solicit the publisher via the address below.

Christian Faith Publishing, Inc.
832 Park Avenue
Meadville, PA 16335
www.christianfaithpublishing.com

Printed in the United States of America

To my mom, Melodie Quiring - who always believed I could

And

To my grandma, Louise Quiring - who wouldn't let it go

And

To my husband - who made it possible.

Reader's Note

Countless stories and books have been written on the very real persecution that fellow brothers and sisters in Christ have suffered, throughout the centuries. We are often reminded of the harsh past that Christian believers have suffered, but some do not realize how real the persecution remains in many countries. We are spoiled. The majority of Americans have homes, computers, electricity, televisions, equal rights, and freedom to open our Bibles and worship God openly. We, as American Christians, have become dispassionate and reluctant when it comes to telling others and sharing the very real love that Christ has to offer all.

Not only is Christian persecution age-old accounts, but it is happening now. In India, families are being torn apart for their faith. In the Middle East, men and women who follow Jesus Christ are being tortured, shot, and beheaded. In North Korea, it had been reported that believers who are caught witnessing are sent into labor camps that they rarely come out of alive. The Bible is illegal in some countries and is heavily regulated in many others. Scriptures tell us that in those last days, people will be beheaded once again for their faith. Even here in the United States, Christian freedoms are becoming threatened.

This story is fictional. The native country and people never existed. But the tales and trials of Christians throughout the centuries are hidden within the story of one family. Everything I have written regarding the ways of torture and military rule over people is more significant in some countries than others, but I put them here so you can understand the severity and the solemnity of persecution. I hope this story makes you laugh and cry and examine your own heart. How far would you go to stand up and say, "Christ is mine!"

Part 1

The Beginning

Prologue

December 24, AD 2078

Four siblings stood with their spouses in the cold Colorado cemetery as they said goodbye to their mother for the last time. She would soon rest beside her husband until Jesus returned. They knew that their mom lived a long and full life, but were sad to see her go nonetheless. A few tears escaped the eyes of the youngest, Marie.

The siblings' children and grandchildren stood behind them. The preacher finished his message and invited all mourners to return to the church for refreshments. Blustery wind drove most people back to their heated cars immediately. Marie hesitated longer than her siblings as she said her goodbyes in her heart. Laying her rose down on the casket and turning to follow her family back to the car, she saw her adopted granddaughter, Sophie, waiting for her.

Sophie had been adopted into Marie's daughter's family when she was ten years old. Now seventeen, she had loved her Great-Grandma Safira Banks as much as she loved Marie. Sophie offered her arm to her grandma.

"I wish I could have known Grandma Safira. I've caught comments here and there to know that she was an extraordinary woman."

"Yes, she really was," Marie responded

"Tell me about her."

"I'll show you tonight when we all go back to the big house."

Sophie nodded, accepting her grandma's word. She handed Marie over to her husband and went back to her family's waiting car.

Later that evening, the families gathered around the fireplace. The youngest children slept soundly upstairs, and the older grandchildren played quietly with various electronic gadgets. It had been nearly four years since they were all under the same roof. They were thankful that the family's matron had insisted on purchasing the small mansion so the families were now able to remain together throughout Christmas. Everyone had made plans to be home for Christmas months in advance. Even at Safira's age, having Safira pass away just days before Christmas was a mixed blessing because some of the family would be leaving the country once again in the New Year.

Family members began sharing stories of their mother and grandmother as they sat sipping hot drinks. They laughed and cried remembering her. The grandchildren set their electronics down and listened intently. Many of them had known her and even spent some time with her, but they all wondered about her past. They'd hear stories, but hadn't quite grasped exactly who she had been as a person.

Marie, noticing the looks of interest, decided it was time. Silently slipping out of the room as David told another story, she grabbed the media disk from her room and was back in short order. She picked up the remote and turned on the large television. The family grew silent when a picture of a small red room appeared on the big screen.

"No one else really knew this, but several years back while I was visiting Mom, she asked if I'd help her with something. I agreed, and we went into her favorite room of the house. She'd already purchased the camera and had prepared the room. I was amazed, to be honest, when I saw how much thought she'd put into decorating. So, over the course of that week, I spent time recording her stories. She wanted her great-grandchildren to know her, in her words. She knew she wouldn't get the chance since we are all so spread out. She asked me to show you this video when it was finished, when we were together as a family again."

"Show us?" Sophie questioned.

Marie nodded. She had been so thankful that her education in filmmaking had been useful after all. She'd used some of it by creating videos of Keilron to show others her family's ministry. But she had put a lot of work into this video. She'd had to piece together her mother's stories with her journal to make sure the story was in order.

It had taken time. She clicked the play button and watched the faces of those around her light up at the sight of Safira.

Time had taken its toll on Safira's body, as had many years of service to her heavenly Father. Grandma Banks, Mum-Mum to her family, had been a strong woman all her years. She had been the thread that had woven them together. She'd been the inspiration her children needed and the beginning of a strong generation of believers.

"I was ten years old when I heard my birth story. I was educated, but I was always a restless child. The gods did not satisfy. Riches couldn't fill the void. Being highly favored and loved by my father couldn't curb the emptiness inside me. Only One ever could."

Her entire family glued their eyes to the screen as they listened to the wisdom told from Safira's life. They all loved to hear how their parents met, but Marie knew that what they were going to hear was more detailed than any of them had heard previously.

The camera panned the room as Safira began to speak. Pictures, letters, a Keilronian New Testament, journals, ticket stubs, clothing, and an original Keilronian flag and weapons covered the walls and perched on the shelves behind Safira. She sat in the middle of the small red room in a padded white glider.

"When I was born, women in my country of Keilron were nothing more than breeding stock and slaves. Women were sent from the gods to bear sons and give pleasure to the higher sex of men. Leaders were men. Children were useless until adulthood. Fathers had no use for their children until they were old enough to marry off or put into the military, but for some reason, my father found it within himself to love his only daughter."

Chapter 1

Beginnings and Endings

Late April 1982

Col. Bormak Rofisca stood beside the large office window staring down at the crowded streets. Today was Saturday, and from his perch, the colonel could see down into the busy marketplace. The main market that he was viewing had everything from produce vendors to home wares. Women wore colorful robes that covered them completely with matching veils that left only their eyes exposed. Rofisca's eyes scanned the crowds as he picked out several of the soldiers he recognized by name walking among the merchants with their machine guns slung over their shoulder.

The beasts that clopped along in front of the carts were far too thin to be pulling their heavy loads. The sight of them made Rofisca angry. He was wealthy and able to maintain all his household, including his horses. But most of Keilron was not so lucky. The king of Keilron, Sheikh Jaminic Karshac, was yet another example of how important it was for someone to take a stand against the harshness of the Karshac family. The monarchy had been repressing the country for years with higher and higher taxes that the average Keilronian could no longer pay, just to maintain the living style the royal family was accustomed to. Along with their greed, the Karshacs had become unconcerned about their religion and careless about the strange religions rising up, taking the place of their native gods. The latter was a painful wound for Rofisca and several other military and powerful dignitary leaders. The time was not right for them to attempt a coup, but his small circle was growing, and they would be patient.

Rofisca's heritage had a large bearing on his success in the military. He was only twenty-eight and had managed to win the favor of the sheikh through several military successes. He had been entrusted with his own troops at twenty-three. He was a tall man among his people at five foot eleven inches. His square jaw remained clenched most of the time; few had ever seen the man smile. His military haircut hid the thickness of his black hair. His skin was tan due to his heritage, and the sandy-colored military uniform hid his toned muscles.

Rofisca turned from the window at the sound of the office door opening. He glanced at the clock when he recognized his personal slave. The slave put both hands in front of him as if praying and gave a slight bow. Rofisca gestured with his hand for the man to speak.

"Word has reached me that your wife Kiahra is in labor, sir."

"Thank you, Savai. Saddle my horse," he ordered.

Col. Rofisca had been anticipating the arrival of another child from his first wife, Kiahra, for several days. She was his first wife by title only; in reality, she was his second out of five, but he had made her his favorite. He secured the documents on his desk and met his slave in the courtyard. He took the horse's reins and mounted. Glancing at his watch once more, he slowly made his way through the streets. Although his palace was only fifteen miles from the edge of the city, it would take him two hours to arrive due to the swarms of people he had to maneuver around.

His estate was set back from the main road by a quarter mile. The land had been coveted by many for its irrigation possibilities because of its location near the largest river in Keilron. Keilron was an arid land most of the time, and water for produce could be an expensive amenity. Having the land that was capable of growing produce was worth every gold piece. Boasting an orchard of pomegranates and a vineyard, the home was an oasis for travelers. No expense had been spared on the home. Built by Rofisca's father, the structure was constructed of stucco and marble shipped in from Europe.

Rofisca had replaced the traditional seating cushions with couches, beds, tables, desks, and chairs. He had visited the United States as a younger man and decided he preferred furniture from the Western world.

His arrival caused the household to come alive. He was master here, and his wives and children respected his position. They knew why he was here. He was always present when a new babe was welcomed into the home. Rofisca noticed his young sons peaking around corners and his wives doing their best to drag them out of sight. Rofisca was not a cruel man, but he was driven when on a mission. Today was not the day to visit with his many sons or other wives.

Arriving at Kiahra's chambers, he could hear her voice in agony beyond the thick tapestry hanging in front of her threshold. He waited for only a moment before a midwife presented herself and with downcast eyes and fidgeting hands told him that the birth could take hours before the child was born and that they would send for him immediately when the infant made an appearance.

The midwife's hasty retreat back into the birthing room gave Rofisca an uneasy feeling. He left the women to do their work and moved toward his office on the opposite side of the palace. His heavy steps echoed through the hall as he strode across the marble floors. He spotted his eldest son, Narshac, peaking around one of the large columns as he crossed the second-story porch that connected the two ends of the home. The eyes of father and son met and held as Rofisca came to a stop. The ten-year-old boy hesitantly came out from his hiding spot and stood before his father. He stood shifting his weight from side to side as the silence was prolonged.

"Where are you supposed to be?" Rofisca's question was casual and took the boy by surprise.

"With my brothers," he spoke hesitantly.

Narshac was Kiahra's son. Rofisca's first young wife had not conceived till months after Kiahra. Narshac's birth had been one of the reasons Rofisca had chosen Kiahra as head wife.

"Were you looking for me?" He allowed his voice to soften, seeing the boy's uneasiness. Perhaps, he was as concerned for his mother as Rofisca.

Narshac dropped his eyes and wrung his hands together. Rofisca allowed his eyes to travel over the courtyard and back down the hall looking for any spectators. He took a deep breath and knelt down in front of his son when he saw no one in the vicinity.

"Your mother is in great distress bringing a new sibling to you. Worrying for her will do us no good." He lifted his son's chin so the boy was forced to meet his father's gaze. "It would be better to go pray to Handrel than to lurk behind shadows. Handrel will decide what is to happen today. Pray to him."

Narshac's head bobbed in consent.

Rofisca stood and stretched out his hand in the direction he'd come, giving his son opportunity to go to the worship room. The temple was a large part of the home that Rofisca had made sure was always pristine, a place with the image of Handrel where his family could worship when necessary. He had even employed his own priest. He watched Narshac as he dodged out of sight toward Handrel's presence. He considered following his son for a moment before deciding to take solace in his office with a good brandy.

Three hours later, Rofisca had moved outside on his office's balcony. He stared up at the sky, glass in hand, and took a deep breath. He'd still had no word on his wife's progress. Kiahra had been in labor for far too long; he was aware of that. He was also certain that one or both of them would not make it through the night. If they both made it, it would be a miracle of Bedrale, the god of childbearing. His wives had all been good to him, producing eighteen sons. Kiahra had already given him four sons, which was why the birth of this fifth child was so unexpected. He had observed that the most difficult births were commonly the firstborn.

The stars above sparkled, and the full moon glowed bright yellow. He was about to take another drink when he saw a shooting star. Col. Rofisca abruptly turned. Setting his glass down on his desk, he briskly walked back to Kiahra's chamber. It was written in the prophesies of the gods that if a star fell during a full moon as a child took its first breath, the child would be a leader of many. He heard the wailing of the newborn as he approached the room. The child had to be a son. He smiled as he thought just how blessed he was. It would have been enough that he'd had so many sons, but to have a predicted leader in his home was a sure sign that he had the gods' favor.

"Sir, your wife has delivered a woman child." The maidservant spoke quietly as she exited the private quarters. She had barely spoken the words to him as she continued past him with her arms full of linens.

Rofisca's facial expression remained unreadable. How could the child be a daughter? Could she be a great leader of many? Indeed not. She would be bound to the same fate as all women of Keilron. He would, in due time, marry her off to get the best price or strongest alliance. He could only hope that the gods would be merciful enough to give his daughter beauty.

"Your wife, Col. Rofisca, is in a bad way. She won't live through the night because she has lost too much blood." Another midwife had appeared before him and had spoken matter-of-factly. This woman was in her midfifties and was obviously the more experienced among the three who had helped with Kiahra.

"Come, she does not have long," the midwife said as she lifted the heavy tapestry giving Rofisca entrance. He watched as the third woman laid the small infant beside her mother's breast for her first and last feeding. The feeding was vital to the child's survival, as all Keilronians knew.

Col. Rofisca went to Kiahra's side. He took her hand as she wearily looked up at him. He met her gaze. His face lost its composure when his jaw relaxed and a sad smile played at his lips as he stared down at his beautiful wife. His eyes no longer looked with calculating precision, but rather softened as he took in the last moments with the one woman he had almost loved.

"May the gods be good to you in your hour of death, and may you make yourself worthy of their grace. You've done me right, woman, in every way."

Kiahra turned her gaze from the feeding babe to her husband's stare. She knew she could expect no other word from him. He had experienced no love as a child, and she knew that he'd loved her in his own way. She wished for just a little more time to show him love, but she could tell by the other women's downcast eyes and hesitancy to speak to her that her weariness would soon lapse into death. She wished she had words to comfort her husband, that he would have courage to mourn her. She knew it wouldn't happen, and her death would only help harden his heart more.

Rofisca gently stroked her face one last time before he stood and left the room. Kiahra looked back down at her daughter. She'd always wanted a girl. She closed her eyes taking in the feel of her child. She struggled against the exhaustion she felt and then opened her eyes and looked at her personal slave and constant companion, Aspa.

"Take care of her." She struggled to speak the moment she'd gained Aspa's full attention.

"I promise I will, as long as I'm able," Aspa swore to her mistress.

Drained from her exertions and unable to fight her body any longer, Kiahra looked down at her babe one more time.

"She's beautiful. I always wanted a girl," she confessed as her eyes slid shut again. The head wife of Rofisca took one last breath before her arm went slack.

"Don't worry. Rofisca won't mind a bit if I become your servant now," she smiled and looked down at the innocent child.

A daughter was a daughter. Worthless. Rofisca paced on the other side of the tapestry waiting for the slave to present him with his daughter. Kiahra was dying for the child she held. The anger he began to feel toward the babe replaced any grief he might have felt for Kiahra. She was favored among his wives, and he'd cared for her; her death would be a great loss in his household. It seemed wasteful for such a beautiful and good woman to die so young.

Aspa knew that Rofisca waited outside the room to be introduced to his child, despite her gender. She cradled the infant in her arms and took the few steps out of the bedchamber. Sure enough, Rofisca stood unreadable as ever, his arms stretching out for his newborn.

When he took the girl in his arms and glanced down at her, his whole demeanor changed. The unreadable stone-faced man melted into the image of a loving father. His eyes softened, and the corners of his lips turned up ever so slightly. He took a finger and softly stroked the child's cheek. The contact caused the baby to stir in her sleep.

Her movement caused a miniscule smile to appear on Rofisca's face. Aspa stared at the pair and prayed that somehow the child would reach into Rofisca's heart.

August 1986, Four Years Later

Col. Rofisca had loved his daughter from the moment he had held her in his arms. Whenever he was home, he made a point to tuck his daughter into bed and read her a story. He had named her Safira. Her name meant beautiful. Aspa had shared with him Kiahra's last words, and he'd found his wife's declaration of their daughter's beauty to be fitting.

Rofisca experienced fatherhood in a whole new way. His sons were independent and headstrong. He was grateful for their tenacity and strength. Narshac and three of his other sons who had become of age had followed in their father's footsteps and were already proving to be promising leaders. Safira took after her mother's gentle spirit, and Rofisca found she depended on her father's love and attention in ways his sons had never sought. She loved to get hugs and sit on his lap. She was unafraid of him. Perhaps, his boys had been taught a level of fear for their father by their mothers and women caregivers that Safira had not acquired. Her fearlessness may have been misconstrued as disrespect by outsiders, but the colonel knew this was not the case. The four-year-old girl spoke little in the presence of her father's guests as was expected of women.

Nolisko Shovak, Rofisca's friend since childhood, often visited Rofisca at his palace. Shovak was a very opinionated man. His family came from the priesthood of Handrel. Shovak had embraced the religion wholeheartedly and was driven by the rules and practices of the Keilronian gods. He had been drawn to Rofisca when his mother had come to the temple to sacrifice to Handrel, Rofisca in tow. Neither of the boys had reached their tenth year, and they'd spent all their time together when Rofisca came with his mother.

With adulthood, the two boys had chosen separate paths for their vocation. Rofisca had followed his father's footsteps and entered the military. Shovak had left his father's line of priests and had pursued connections among the dignitaries. Only two years earlier, Shovak had become trusted enough to enter into Rofisca's circle of those waiting to overthrow the Karshac monarchy. Shovak had quickly become a favorite among them and had been chosen to lead them into a new era.

Shovak had seven wives and many children, though he was a year younger than Rofisca. His marriages had been for strong alliances. He didn't give his family personal attention. He was much too busy moving like a snake throughout the Karshac palace listening and waiting for his opportunity to make the move to overthrow the oppressive royal family. His ability to come out victorious was resting on his alliance with Rofisca, the leader among the military supporters. Shovak had no desire to ruffle feathers with the respected colonel, so he kept his own council when it came to Safira's upbringing.

Shovak was visiting Rofisca when they heard Safira's giggles from the hall. Appearing in the doorway moments later, Safira smiled at her papa. Rofisca, as usual, welcomed the interruption. He stepped from behind his desk and invited the child to come forward. He moved to a large chair near the warmth of the fire as she came into the room and proceeded to sit on his lap.

"Have you come to say goodnight?"

Safira bit her lower lip and nodded, refusing to look up at him as she usually did.

"What's wrong, little one?" he gently asked.

Safira glanced over her father's shoulder at Shovak standing by the open balcony, glass of brandy in his hand, staring at them.

Rofisca followed her gaze. Understanding took root as he looked back down at his daughter. He used his finger as a hook and carefully lifted her face to meet his eyes.

"Talk to me, Safira," he quietly ordered. His command was a welcome invitation for her to speak despite her father's guest.

"Aspa says I shouldn't speak to you as I do."

He smiled, "She's right, but I make exceptions for you."

Safira nodded in acknowledgment. Rofisca waited patiently as her eyes looked back down at her hands clasped in front of her. After several heartbeats, she looked back into his face, her eyes inquisitive, and her lips pursed.

"Where do the gods come from?" she asked solemnly. She did not blink as she waited for her answer.

"They don't come from any one place. They are powerful, which is why we must give them respect." Rofisca had no desire for such questions but knew if he did not answer, she would not rest until she'd sorted it all out. She was far too inquisitive for one so young.

She sucked on her lips and stared hard at him. He knew the look meant she wasn't satisfied. But with Shovak only a stone's throw away, he had no desire to pursue the matter further.

"Go to bed, little one. I will be sure no harm comes to you," he replied, putting an end to her inquisition.

She sighed loudly and reached up for a hug and kiss. Rofisca obliged, and she was off his lap, skittering across the office back to Aspa's care.

"Such questions are dangerous for one so young." Shovak spoke quietly as he came to stand by Rofisca.

"Perhaps, but she will grow out of it."

"Your sons, were they so inquisitive?"

"I don't know. They were never given liberties with me."

"Favoritism isn't wise," Shovak cautioned.

"She's a favorite among her brothers. I don't know what's wise or not, but I know that a child predicted to be a leader may become an influential wife," Rofisca defended.

Rofisca had often spoken of the sign he'd seen the night Safira was born. He had been proud to share with all who listened.

"You only speculate now," Shovak said casually. He waited for a moment before changing to a less touchy subject. "Come, have a drink with me. Tomorrow, I leave for Shemna, and you will be with me."

"I'm to leave again?" Rofisca questioned. He was thankful Shovak was willing to let the matter drop.

"Yes. I received word yesterday that our time has come. Shemna is in an uproar, and the citizens are ready for a change. There are still too many Karshac followers for this to be an easy transition. I'm afraid we must gather our followers and begin strategizing our next move. We may have to wait to take Shemna, but perhaps, it's time to begin the uprising."

"Very well," Rofisca willingly obliged. He'd been anticipating and plotting for nearly a decade to bring hope back to his people. He smiled at Shovak as they toasted to the overdue civil uprising.

February 1995

Safira stared out her chamber, watching in dismay as her father left on another journey to Shemna. She knew he'd be gone for several days. At last, Shovak had conquered the monarchy with her father's help. He had officially appointed her father as Keilron's head general. Staring after him, she recalled the last lesson with her history instructor only days earlier.

She left her personal quarters and was led to a study her father had built for her to learn from private instructors. No woman was allowed education in Keilronian schools, so her father made it possible for her to gain all the knowledge she desired.

Her history instructor, Mr. Sheldon, like many of her instructors, had come from an outside country. She'd had a math instructor who had come from Germany. Although the man had spoken very little Keilronian, he'd been able to teach her mathematics. She'd taught him to speak more fluently in her native tongue so their lessons could progress more quickly. Her father and her older brother had made a team effort to teach her to read and write Keilronian. A Mr. Pollson taught geography, and Mr. Larson came from England to teach her science. Mr. Sheldon had been tutoring her for several weeks on her own country's history.

The moment she sat at her desk, he placed a notebook paper on the tabletop. "We've been discussing reasons behind the recent civil war. Now that we've finished discussing the circumstances, I'd like you to write an essay of your own opinion on whether you agree or disagree with Shovak's takeover."

"I haven't formed one yet. You told me facts. I understand what you want from me, but I can't write my thoughts down," she said.

"Why not? I'm not asking you to form a firm opinion if you don't have one. I merely want you to write down your feelings about what you've learned."

"I'm not going to. My opinion is muddled, and I don't feel that any opinion I have to offer would be unbiased. You have taught me much about what my father's war was about. I can't, however, write my personal opinion."

Mr. Sheldon met her gaze for several seconds. He understood what she was saying. Even a confused opinion could be construed incorrectly if read by the wrong person. The general often asked to see her work, and he would definitely be the wrong person. Mr. Sheldon often had difficulty with the restrictions the countrymen had in regard to patriotism and the restrictions they placed on their women.

"All right. Let's see what you remember of our discussions of technology. I told you about computers and explained modern types of travel. I've gone into detail of how much most of the world relies on electricity. I'd like you to write at least three pages on how you think the outside world's technology could benefit and how it could harm your homeland."

"I don't understand, sir. Why do we not use their tools for ourselves?"

"Many of the Keilronians believe that modern technology could destroy this country."

"Do you believe that, Master Sheldon?"

Mr. Sheldon met her gaze. He took a deep breath and exhaled an exasperated sigh as he shrugged his shoulders. He could not give her the answer. He was being well paid to teach the very intelligent young lady, but he also found it increasingly more difficult not to answer her direct questions. He'd been warned when he'd taken the position that he was on a very tight leash. Her questions often left them at this point. She knew now, by the look he gave her, that he was unable to answer the question openly. He watched her turn and lower her eyes to the blank sheets in front of her. She looked back up a moment later.

"Aren't you an American?"

"Yes, Safira, I am."

"Do you have family?"

"No, I don't. Please begin your essay."

Safira sighed and turned her attention back to the task at hand.

Mr. Sheldon had been thoroughly investigated before the position had even been offered to him. He knew, after the general had admitted it, he'd been chosen because he had no family. He'd put himself through college after the foster care system was finished with him. Don Sheldon had learned Keilronian during his second year in college for the credits and the unusualness of the language itself. He'd never married and had no siblings. He was American, and to the Keilronian general, that meant trouble. Once it had been proven that he had no ties to Christian organizations, the general had welcomed him. He found it strange that it was because he'd been brought to Keilron that he'd found interest in Christianity.

A few hours later, Safira's father entered her quarters.

"You will not have lessons any longer," he told her. His voice, usually smooth and relaxed, was harsh. He spat out each word as if cursing at his men. For the first time, he almost frightened her.

"Why?" The moment the word had been spoken she knew questioning him had been a mistake. His eyes flashed with anger, and he growled out his response.

"Your teacher has been found in contempt of Keilronian laws. He is condemned to death for treason against the gods."

Safira lowered her eyes from her father's. Never had she seen him so agitated. She had never thought her father was devoted to the gods, although he'd shown respect toward them. Condemning a man to death for believing in another religion felt wrong. Could even the gods approve of such cruelty? Were they demanding as to force a man to kill another for their sake?

Questions and fears would often enter Safira's mind. She'd voiced those questions to Aspa on several occasions. Her governess usually reproved her for making such inquisitions and gave her no answers. She recalled speaking with her father as a young child, wishing to understand more of her own religion. Her questions were sealed within her mind as she watched her father leave her quarters. She knew that she would never get the answers she longed for. The time had come for her to grow into the woman she was meant to be and accept her heritage as truth. But still, watching her papa ride away, she sat wondering if maybe he was wrong. Then, what? She so desperately wanted truth. Her father's angry voice echoed in her mind. She turned away from the window. She would not provoke his wrath. Not when he'd given her more than any woman could expect. No, it was time to stop questioning and start behaving as the woman she was meant to be.

Chapter 2

Decisions

May 1995
Near Denver, Colorado, United States

The red Camaro shifted into fifth gear as the teenage boy merged onto the highway. He had ten miles of good road to test the new vehicle. A wide grin spread across his face as the speedometer reached ninety. The posted speed limit was seventy, but the car hummed like a kitten, and the open road made the temptation to speed uncontrollable. As he zoomed under the third underpass, blue and red lights flashed behind him. The young man groaned and applied the brakes. He pulled to the side of the road and waited for the state patrolman. Rolling down the window as the officer approached, he grabbed his ID and car information from the glove box.

The officer returned to his car to run Christian Banks' name through the system. Chris groaned again. It was bad luck. He'd gotten his dad to take the younger siblings to school so he could have a chance to drive his grandfather's gift. He hadn't spotted a cop car in nearly three months of driving to his Christian school in his mom's Ford Focus, siblings on board. Today, of all days, the officer had chosen to stake out the highway. There was no denying he'd been speeding, and he knew he deserved the ticket that was coming but wasn't looking forward to explaining the citation to his mother.

Chris Banks pulled the '95 red Camaro into the high school parking lot. Several male classmates trotted over to inspect the prestigious car. He barely had a chance to get out as a dozen fellow seniors surrounded it, touching it with a kind of awed reverence.

"Dude, this is awesome! Did your grandpa buy it for you?" Trent Gorman stroked the shiny hood.

"Yeah, but I don't know yet if I can keep it, pretty sweet though. Drives like you wouldn't believe." His smile was huge just thinking about his earlier experience.

"Why wouldn't you be able to keep it?" James Delaney took his eyes off the car long enough to furrow his brow at Chris's statement.

"What your mom have to say about this?" Blake, Christian's best friend, interjected before Chris could respond to James. Chris knew he could count on Blake to understand the dilemma.

"She wasn't able to convince him otherwise. She tried, but his only response was, 'A boy needs a car, and he's my only grandchild. Like it or not, he'll inherit everything. I'd like to think I can trust him to be responsible with a car.'"

"Typical. Hey guys, back off the car. We got to go to class." Blake led the group of car enthusiasts to the doors of the private Christian school.

*****

Harris Kleren smiled at his wife as he stepped into the kitchen. She had just finished making them both sandwiches and set them on the small kitchen table. He had come home for lunch, as he had been able to do for the last ten years. He owned his own heating, air conditioning, and ventilation company and with the business came certain liberties that he enjoyed. Eating with his wife was one of his privileges.

After they said a brief prayer for their meal and Harris had taken a bite of his food, he watched Fay as she nibbled on a baby carrot.

"I think we should discuss Chris's car situation," he said, taking another bite of his sandwich.

"I don't like that Morris just hands him things like that. A car is a big deal. A Camaro is a little over the top." She dropped the carrot and glared out the kitchen window.

"What's really bothering you?" Harris knew that his wife's opposition to her father-in-law's gift wasn't about the object. He just wanted her to admit that.

"I don't know. JC idolizes his brother, and Kate is already jealous of him at times. Morris has always gone over the top for Chris. We can't compete with his gifts, and it seems unfair to the other two. If we let him keep this gift, I'm afraid Morris will see it as a surrender."

Morris and Fay had been at odds with each other since the accident that had taken her first husband, leaving her a young widow and single mom. Harris had swept in a year after the accident and had been a great help and support to the struggling mom. Morris had tried to take Chris from her only a month after the funeral, she'd refused, and when threatened to be taken to court with the issue, she'd held firm. In the end, Chris had remained with her. Ever since he'd lost, Morris had attempted to override her authority in Chris's life by spoiling his grandson in any way he could. Most of the time, Fay had held firm and refused the gifts. On more than one occasion, Chris had been very disappointed when he'd had to return his toys.

Morris had insisted on being in the boy's life, and Fay had agreed. Her father-in-law had been grooming her son to be the businessman he wanted Chris to be. What Morris hadn't seen was that his grandson had inherited his mother's heart for missions.

Morris was not the kind of grandfather who was often invited to family dinners. The man ignored his daughter-in-law's other children and refused to have anything to do with her choice of husband. Morris' blatant disrespect for her and her family rankled Fay to no end.

Harris interrupted her thoughts. "He could use a good car in Chicago."

"He'll be at a Christian college. He won't really need a car." She turned her eyes back to Harris as he took the last bite of his sandwich.

"Trust me, every boy needs a car. And Morris had a point last night. Chris needs to learn to take care of things on his own. A fancy car is nothing compared to what he'll inherit from Morris and his trust." Harris reasoned.

Fay sat back in her chair. Harris was probably right, much as she hated to admit it. He not only had been a rock for her to depend on but also had shown a lot of wisdom when it came to raising Chris. Harris knew Chris well, and if he thought Chris should keep the car, she wasn't going to naysay him.

Chris picked up his younger siblings from the elementary-middle school and headed home.

"I totally want a car just like this one. Do you think mom will let me have one too?" JC's eyes sparkled as he put his seatbelt on.

"You know, bud, I'm not even sure I'll get to keep the car. Mom's not too happy."

"Dad will make sure you keep it though, right?" JC cocked his head at his brother as the elder glanced in the rearview mirror. Chris smiled at JC's thinking. The young boy acted as if dad had the last say no matter what.

"I'm not sure Dad has final say this time."

"Bummer." His lower lip made an appearance as he pouted.

His eleven-year-old sister seated in the passenger seat just rolled her eyes.

"Good luck with Mom. You know she's not done fighting this one," she said.

Chris ignored her statement knowing anything he said in defense would only cause retaliation from his sister. She wasn't an easy one to get along with lately.

They scattered in various directions the moment they entered the modest suburban home. Chris lagged behind them, hanging up his coat as he shuffled toward the kitchen and dining room area where he could hear his mom preparing dinner in the kitchen.

"Hey, Mom," he said hesitantly. She barely looked up from her position by the sink where she stood peeling potatoes. Chris's face was red, and his lips were pressed together. He was looking over at her through his eyelashes as his head was aimed to the ground.

She sighed. "That's an awful guilty expression."

"Sorry I ran off on you this morning. I wanted a chance to drive it just once before you made me refuse it. I didn't want the kids with me either."

"Your dad took them to school since you left them high and dry. Thanks for the warning note though. They barely got to class in time," She accused. She turned her head slightly to glare at him from across the room.

"So, I guess that means I can't actually keep it."

"After your behavior this morning? Just running off like that, and you have the gall to ask me, with puppy eyes, if you get to keep the car!" She nailed him to the floor with her gaze for a few moments before returning to the sad little potato in front of her. The peeler had long since taken the skin of the vegetable, and it was receiving unnecessary abuse by the cook's mood.

Chris watched his mom's hands move fast and stiff as she attacked the job in front of her. He really didn't want to bring up the speeding ticket now, but since he was already in trouble . . .

"It gets worse," he mumbled. He clenched his fist over the backpack strap still hanging on his shoulder. He took a chance look at his mom, who'd stopped her attack on supper. She pierced him with her eyes. He knew she was waiting for the rest of the confession.

"I kind of got a ticket this morning." His mouth twisted to the right side of his face. He figured he could at least attempt to look cute and innocent. His mom's eyes rolled heavenward as her hands rested against the edge of the sink, knife now in hand.

Fay cocked her right hip up against the sink as the foot relaxed. Looking at her son, she knew exactly why he was pulling that face. He was in big trouble.

"Where were you, and how fast were you going?" she forced her voice to remain calm.

"I was out on the highway. I hit ninety-two when I got pulled over," he admitted grudgingly, still clinging to the shoulder strap of his bag.

Her jaw dropped open, and the knife clamored into the sink.

"First, you will pay for that ticket. Second, you will never, ever, desert your siblings to take a joyride. Third, your actions have consequences. You will be driving my old Focus for two weeks. You can leave your keys on the counter. I don't want to see your face till suppertime. Do I make myself clear?" Her words were spoken with force. Chris knew by the way her hand shook that her tone belied the anger she was withholding.

"Yes, ma'am," he reluctantly dug the keys out of his pocket and relinquished them to the countertop. He was about to take his leave when he realized what she'd said. He swiftly did a one-eighty. "You mean I get to keep the car?"

Fay stared at her son. Unbelievable! She knew he was quick, but after being admonished, she hadn't expected him to catch on so quickly. The sparkle of hope in his eye softened her heart just enough that she was able to relax her face and give him a nod.

"Now get out!" she stressed.

He spun and was out of sight before she took another breath.

Each day, Chris looked up the top stories on his computer for local, national, and world news, a habit created by his grandfather's coaching. It was a Thursday night, and he took advantage of the quiet room he shared with JC since his brother was at the neighbor's for the evening. A small article caught his eye. He'd rarely heard of Keilron, an eastern third-world country, but he hadn't heard much news from that part of the world recently. His heart ached as he read,

> In Shemna, Keilron, a new dictatorship has been established. Dictator Shovak has succeeded in his attempts to overthrow the current government and brings with him tyranny to Christians as Hitler did to the Jews. His harsh and inhumane ways of torture are beyond gas chambers. Besides using guns and modern means of death, he is reviving the ancient ways of torture to be used against those who will not follow the Keilronian gods, such as whips, chains, racks, and guillotines. Keilron looks to their new leader with high hopes of economic growth. Sheikh Jaminic Karshac and his father, the previous sheikh of Keilron, have

drained the country of its riches by overtaxing their people. This new leadership is bittersweet. Time will tell whether this new authoritarian rule will build this poor third-world economic society or if his rule will bring them into a different sort of social crisis due to his unheard of intolerance of Christian beliefs. At this point, Keilron is officially closed to all ministries connected to Christianity. Most American publications have been boycotted. Imports of clothing, most foods, and textiles are still recognized with regard to current trading partners. The people of Keilron hold hope that this new leader will be far less oppressive than that of the previous monarchy. This small country has suffered great injustice over the years. Keilronians cheer and applaud this new leadership despite the new laws banning Christianity.

Chris sat staring at the screen in disbelief. The article went on to say that Shovak had given a grace period of thirty days for all Christian organizations and those under mission visas to vacate the country. If they did not do so, they would be treated as any citizen of Keilron. Many missionaries would be returning home immediately.

He'd never met anyone from Keilron, nor did he know of any missionaries serving there, but he bowed his head and prayed for them. In his world of fancy cars, stylish clothes, and diamond jewelry, a world his grandfather was ushering him into, he would never understand what it would be like for the native believers who were now to be hunted for their faith. He was trying to imagine such sacrifices and fear that those who were being forced to leave were feeling when his mom's voice interrupted his contemplations.

"Honey?"

He turned from his computer to see her standing against his bedroom doorframe.

Her eyes narrowed in concern. "What has you looking so worried?"

"You heard any news on a small country called Keilron?" He asked.

"Um, bits and pieces, why?"

He gestured to the computer screen. She moved in to read the article that was still up. She looked back at her son. She knew right then that her son was probably unaware of his own compassion and where it could take him. She'd seen it in his eyes as he cared for others who were unable to do it themselves. She'd seen his giving spirit, and she thanked God for helping him become so unlike his grandfather.

For some reason, she felt something she hadn't felt before, and uncertainty gripped her heart as tears filled her eyes. It felt as if the Lord Himself were telling her something about her son that she couldn't quite grasp. She patted him on the shoulder, prepared to speak when the phone rang.

Reaching for the cordless phone by the computer, she answered, "Hello?"

Chris saw her concern.

"Yes . . . ," she gasped. "No . . . All right, my son and I will be there as soon as possible."

"What's wrong?" he asked, perceiving her pain the moment she hung up the phone.

"Call your dad. You and I will be at the hospital. JC and Kate are still at their friends' homes. I have to make sure they stay there tonight. Your pappy just had a heart attack, and they don't think he's going to make it through the night."

In the Denver hospital an hour later, Chris sat beside his grandfather and held his hand. The man's breathing was shallow, and Chris worried that he wouldn't get to say his goodbyes. He began wondering if his grandfather had ever understood his son and grandson, if he'd ever accepted Christ as his Savior. Chris hoped for one last chance to witness to his hard-hearted grandfather.

The man lying in the bed seemed old and fragile, nothing like the man Chris remembered. As Chris thought about getting coffee, he felt his grandfather squeeze his hand. He met Pappy's blue eyes, which were identical to Chris's.

"Pappy..." Words failed him as the two men stared at one another.

"I know, they told me earlier. My prognosis didn't look good."

"They want to do surgery, but they don't know if you will survive it."

"I told them to let me be," he said grumpily.

"You don't even want a chance?" Chris's voice was quiet, but his open gaze caused his grandfather to hesitate.

"What difference would it make now? We all do the best we can. We all die." Pappy's voice was strained, but his tone was matter-of-fact.

"Pappy, are you ready to die?" Chris's voice was hesitant. He wasn't sure he could believe his pappy's nonchalant attitude.

"No one is ever ready, but I've lived a good life, and perhaps, I'll see my wife and son again now. And if not, at least, I won't be missing them anymore."

"Pappy, I know my dad's in heaven with Jesus. Will you be meeting him there? Have you ever accepted Christ as your Savior?"

"Now, you sound like your dad. He got all worked up about the Jesus thing when he visited a church with a buddy as a teenager. I still remember when he came home all excited about 'getting saved.' I never did understand, thought it was a phase, but he just wouldn't let it go. He kept going to church and then met your mom. She wasn't what I expected for him, not if he was to keep climbing in society. He died believing that Jesus stuff, even tried to tell me about it a couple of times."

"That 'Jesus stuff' is pretty important right now I'd think, Pappy. You may be meeting your maker very soon, though I wish you weren't. What will you say when you come before the King of Kings, the Almighty God? Can you tell me that you have lived a perfect life, a sinless life?"

"No, I haven't lived that. I know I've made my share of mistakes, first with your grandmother and then your dad... I wasn't the father I should've been. I guess I was trying to make up for it with you."

"Would you like to go before the Almighty with an advocate at your side to defend you, Pappy?"

"What? They even got lawyers in heaven?" Pappy tried to chuckle, but soon, he was coughing.

"In a way, I suppose so. Jesus died on the cross to pay for *your* sins, Pappy. Even if you were the only one, He would have died for you because He loves you that much. He wants to stand with you when you stand before God the Father because only His blood will wash away your sins. You must accept His grace and know that there is nothing you can do to get out of hell, except believe in Jesus's payment, the payment of God the Son. You know of Jesus. Now, I'm asking if you believe in Jesus."

Pappy silently calculated what his grandson had said. It made sense; he'd heard these words from his son years ago. But when he'd heard them last, he thought he was invincible, that he could make up for past wrongs, that somehow being a good person would be good enough. But now staring into the face of death, he knew the truth. Nothing he'd done was going to make up for the evil in his past. He knew that now was his last chance. He felt an ache in his heart as he realized the truth. He believed. He chose to believe and clung to the Savior in his hour of death. His heart ached with regret that although he could have confidence in his Defender in heaven, he would have nothing to show for the selfish life he'd lived.

Pappy nodded, a tear leaking from his eye. Chris held his hand as they prayed together. When they'd finished, he looked at his grandfather again, and a small smile graced the old man's face.

"See you later. I'll say 'hi' to your dad for you, and I'll tell him what a great young man you were when I left."

Chris smiled and told Pappy he loved him before he closed his eyes. Chris thanked God that night when four hours later, his grandfather's heart gave out, and Chris realized that he had seen his grandfather open his eyes for the last time.

Chapter 3

Searching

Shemna, Keilron
September 1997

Safira walked toward the dining hall where she was honored to join her father and Dictator Shovak for an evening meal. The two men acknowledged her as she entered the room and sat down with them at the large dining table. It was a rare occasion for her father to be home, and she was enjoying his presence immensely.

"Safira does well for you, Rofisca," Shovak said as Safira sat down.

"Her name defines her, I suppose."

"She's fifteen, and she isn't wed. Are you saving her for me?" Shovak was teasing Rofisca as he often did.

"No, I just haven't found a man worthy of her beauty."

"Not even I? Well, perhaps your words are a cover up for some flaw you don't want anyone to discover. Speak, then Safira, or are you mute? Is that the reason you aren't wed?" Shovak grinned at the young woman not five feet away. Accustomed to the attention, Safira's smile was partially hidden by the thin green veil she was used to.

"No, my lord, I speak fluently, and you know that very well," Safira replied. Her eyes held those of Shovak. She was not afraid of this friend.

"Bold as well. I believe that's the reason she remains under your household."

"Speak kindly in my home, Shovak. She's my daughter, and she's pleasant to look at. I mean to keep her a bit longer," Rofisca said as the food arrived, and they began to dine.

"You're right, Rofisca. I apologize. I don't wish to offend you." The two friends often bantered in such a manner, but it was always Rofisca who would find a way to turn the conversation from jest to insult. Shovak knew this and often found it interesting to see just how the general could turn words around to suit his fancy.

Safira was used to their conversations and remained silent. Finding their conversation dull, she left their presence after dinner. She had no desire to listen to them bicker and banter tonight. She'd been hoping for a chance to spend some time with her father alone. With the amounts of wine her father had been consuming with Shovak, she knew he wouldn't be seeking her company tonight. She walked out of the main house and into the grassy manicured backyard. The moon lit her way as she crossed the large lawn and began walking into her father's orchard. The tree shadows proved just how bright the moon was. The quiet was pleasant as she listened to the night insects hum.

Breathing in the fresh air, she moved past the rows of trees. She heard movement in a tree to her right. Startled, she backed away from the noise. Looking up into a nearby tree, she saw the shadow of a man. Obviously, he didn't see her, but she heard him bite into the fresh pomegranate. She waited a moment, not sure how to react.

At last, something inside of her prompted her to speak. "Excuse me."

Startled, the intruder lost his balance and grabbed the nearest large branch. After he'd steadied himself, he spoke, but his words were so choppy and accented that she could barely make them out.

She spoke again. "Would you come down so that I might see your face and understand your mumbled tones?"

The shadow in the tree began to move, and the man jumped down from the branch he sat on. The distance to the ground wasn't far. The orchard trees were not tall, and he'd not been very far up.

She stared at him. Obviously in his midteens, he was a large-framed boy with a lopsided smirk on his face. The traditional garb he wore was a poor disguise when matched with the pale tone of his skin and terrible grasp of her language. His gaze shifted from the ground to her face several times as his feet busied themselves digging into the ground nervously. The silence was awkward and tangible.

Safira was the one to break the silence, "What is your name?"

"Shawn Matthews," he said quietly.

He was pale like her English and American tutors had been. "American or English?"

"American," he said looking at her questioningly.

"I'm Safira Rofisca. Why are you here?"

The boy looked confused, so Safira repeated the question much slower.

"I'm visiting my uncle Tim Kindel."

She stared at him, wondering what visiting with his uncle had to do with her question about being in her orchard.

The boy tried again. "He lives in Shemna."

Shemna was slightly over fifteen miles away. Safira crossed her arms in front of her and shifted her weight to her right foot. She raised her eyebrows. She was no fool.

"I was running." His voice was quiet and uncertain.

Her eyes narrowed and traveled up and down his thick frame.

"I left this morning," he said.

This made a little more sense to her. Her eyes softened, and she dropped one arm. She still stood waiting for further explanation. The boy was struggling with his words, and she knew she'd have to be patient while he gathered his thoughts.

"I was hungry and saw the orchard."

Now, she understood. But why was he running, and from whom? She gestured for him to continue with her left hand.

"My uncle is a Christian. He didn't want me to get captured because of him. I was headed home." Shawn had been warned to be careful what he said and to whom, but the pretty teenage girl couldn't be dangerous.

"How old are you?" Safira asked. He looked old enough to be in the Keilron army.

"Sixteen," he announced proudly.

Her brother, fifteen like her, had been in the army for two years, and a sixteen-year-old brother was making negotiations for his first wife. This boy seemed incompetent of even getting proper directions.

"Who are you running from?"

"Soldiers."

"Why?" she asked.

"I am Christian," he said nervously.

Understanding clicked in her mind. Shovak and her father were attempting to rid the land of such evil. She froze because she didn't know what to do. This immature teenager obviously didn't realize who Rofisca was. Having Shovak settled only a few hundred yards away inside the palace created a sense of duty inside her soul. She should call for a guard, have the boy tried, and executed by daybreak. But old questions floated into her mind, questions that she could only have answered by one of these Christians. In the end, curiosity won out.

"I wish to meet your uncle. Can he speak better than you?"

"Yes."

"Then go tell him I want to meet him here day after tomorrow at midnight."

The chubby face nodded, and the young boy began to jog off out of the orchard and toward Shemna. The moment he reached the end of the orchard, he slowed to a walk. His uncle may not be very happy with him. He was supposed to be meeting with the small plane missionary pilot at daybreak. Shawn hadn't expected Keilron to be as hostile as it was. His experience had been cut short by his desire to return home. He knew he wasn't meant to be a missionary as he'd once thought. Shawn's heart told him that he had to return to his uncle and tell him about the girl, even if his return trip was delayed. There were no coincidences.

Later as Safira prepared for bed, her governess whispered quietly to her.

"You should be careful with whom you associate. These days are dangerous with Shovak on the throne."

"Shovak has no quarrel with me."

"Keep it that way my child."

As the governess blew out the candle and left her room, Safira stared blankly after her. What did her maid mean? Was Shovak a dangerous man to her? She hardly thought so.

Shawn burst through the door of his uncle's study.

"Uncle Tim, I met a young girl."

Tim Kindel turned toward his nephew. Pastor Tim was tall and fit, a contrast to his sister's son. Pastor Tim's dark blond hair differed from his nephew's dark hair. Tim's sharp hazel eyes pierced Shawn the moment the older man heard the boy's voice.

"It's dangerous for you to be here. Why did you come back? To tell me you met a girl? Shawn, we're talking about your life. My sister would kill me if anything happened to you." Out of concern, Pastor Kindel spoke sharply to his nephew.

"But see, she wants to meet you. And I didn't know how else to contact you."

"What's her name? How old is she?" He no longer glared at his nephew as his expression changed to interest. His life's work was for the Keilronians, and they had been far from receptive since Shovak had claimed leadership. And he understood the reason—to claim Christ was a death sentence. He was always willing to go to someone who was searching.

"She looks about fifteen or sixteen. Her name is Safira Rofisca."

Pastor Tim stiffened. He knew Safira was Rofisca's only daughter, as did most Keilronians. He stared at his nephew and relaxed, praying and thanking God for keeping Shawn safe.

"It's by God's grace you are even alive. You've been here for two weeks. Don't you know the name Rofisca?"

"No," he replied.

"She is the only daughter of Shovak's number one general. I'm amazed you don't have your head in the guillotine. As a matter of fact, Shovak is spending the next couple of days in Rofisca's palace. He's there now."

Shawn's eyes widened.

"When does she wish to speak with me?" Kindel asked after letting his words soak into his nephew.

"She said tomorrow night, in her father's orchard at midnight."

"Then I must go, but I have a few things I need to do before I leave."

"But you just said . . ."

"It's my job, my calling. I love you boy, but I need to check on my sheep. I'll be back in a couple of hours. I'll contact the pilot and get the new information to him. Hopefully, we will have you back in Tennessee in less than a week."

Shawn nodded and watched as his uncle slipped out the door. He never knew if he'd see Uncle Tim again and had been amazed that his parents allowed him to come, but his Uncle Tim had convinced them that it would be good for him. And it had been.

*****

Safira snuck out of her house and headed toward the orchard. There was a slight breeze, but it was a warm night nonetheless. She kept her eyes open for any unusual movement. At long last, she found what she was looking for. Stepping from the shadows, a man stood before her. He was of a strong countenance, his body toned and strong as a soldier. The lines on his face were the only indication that he was from an older generation. He wore the traditional Keilronian clothing, though his dark blond hair and lighter skin tone gave away his disguise. She spoke not a word waiting for his response.

"May we enter into the shadows where there is less likelihood of being seen?"

Safira nodded, and they moved to the base of a tree.

"What have you called me here for?" he asked her pleasantly.

"I've been taught from a young age. Many things I've heard about other nations, but of the Christian religion, I've been forced to remain ignorant. I am told that the Christians are evil and vile in every way. But yet I am not told why. Of many gods, I've learned, but of your god, I've not."

"You seek me out for an education?" He was astounded that she saw the opportunity to learn. She didn't seem interested in her own soul. She was simply curious. Tim knew that if he taught her of Jesus

Christ, the information could change her life if she let it. He had no qualms about teaching her.

"Yes. Your Keilronian is almost flawless."

"Thank you, but I've lived in this land for a long time."

"What is your god's name?"

"He's called many things, but one of His names is Jehovah."

"Teach me of your Jehovah." She looked at him with curiosity as she leaned against the tree trunk, prepared to hear what the man had to say.

*****

Christian Banks couldn't stop staring at the girl in front of him in college chapel. He'd been working up the courage to ask her out for a couple of weeks. She was a junior like himself, and he'd seen her around the school, but it hadn't been till early September when he'd gotten the chance to actually visit with her. What he'd learned about her had impressed him, and since then, he'd wanted to pursue her. But he soon realized that pursuing her was much more difficult than speaking to her. He hadn't ever felt so preoccupied by one girl before. Every time he tried to ask her out, she had smiled at him, and he'd been unable to form his question. He was finding it difficult to actually pursue instead of being pursued. He breathed deeply as chapel dismissed. She was bubbly and cheerful, and above all else, she was on fire for the Lord.

"Hey, buddy!" Blake Marty, Chris's best friend, slapped him on the back. Christian was not a short man, but his friend still stood three inches taller than his six-foot frame. "Go talk to her. I'll leave you alone," Blake said knowing the direction of Christian's thoughts.

Christian left his friend and approached the willowy brunette.

"Hey, Angie," he said casually, although his heart thudded loudly.

"Hey, Chris. How's it going?" She smiled.

"Good."

"Good," she said staring at him. He stared at her silently for a few awkward seconds.

"I better get going." She gave him a tiny smile.

"Wait. Angie, would you like to go to dinner with me tomorrow night?" he blurted out. He felt his knees buckle for a moment and then . . .

"Sure, what time?" She smiled casually.

"Seven-thirty?"

"Sounds great. Pick me up at the dorm?" she said as she waved goodbye and left the chapel to head to work.

"Was that so hard, Chris?" Blake asked from behind.

"You try it someday and tell me."

"No, no, I'll leave that to you. I'm not much of a dater these days. It just hasn't been the same since Vanessa," he said. He referred to a girl he'd dated since his sophomore year in high school. It had ended abruptly when she made it abundantly clear to him that Jesus wasn't her life's priority.

Chris and Blake headed to their shared apartment nearby. Both men prepared for work and left. Chris's steps were light as he got into his red Camaro. He couldn't wait to see Angie.

Chris tried to hide how nervous he felt when he picked up Angie the following night. She was gorgeous in her printed blouse and blue jeans. He escorted her to his car and played the gentleman by opening her door. She was calm, but he could tell by the blush in her cheeks that she was a little nervous too. When he realized they both felt the same, he relaxed some.

"So tell me, Angie, what kind of food do you like?"

"Would Chinese be okay?" she asked.

"Not a problem. I know of a pretty good place."

He pulled his car out into the Chicago traffic and tried to start a conversation.

"So what do your folks do?" he asked.

"My dad's a Christian school principal, and my mom works at the local nursing home as a CNA."

"CNA?"

"Certified Nurses Aid, she works in our local nursing home."

"Well, that's neat. You grew up around ministry-minded people then, huh? No wonder you're here at Bible College."

"Yes, they had a lot to do with it, but really, I just want to serve God. I feel being in the ministry in whatever aspect he wants would be amazing, especially in a full-time capacity."

"Hmm, sounds like you came to get your MRS degree and help serve with a husband."

What possessed him to be so bold he didn't know, but glancing over at her, he saw her turn bright red as she tried hiding a smile.

"That was uncalled for and a little forward. Are you volunteering?" she said. She hadn't been sure how to take his comment and said the first thing that came to mind. She hoped that her response might break the ice.

It was Chris's turn to blush, and with it, a huge smile lit his face.

"Maybe, but let's take it one date at a time."

"So, tell me, what do your parents do? I mean, I've seen you around campus, and I've definitely taken note of this beautiful car. So I'm curious how you managed to find yourself at Bible College?"

"You don't know who I am?" He questioned her in amazement, but was also thankful for the freshness of the conversation. It was nice to tell someone things without her already having preconceived ideas.

"Except for a few weeks ago, all I knew was that you had a fancy car and a lot of followers. I've seen you around campus, sure, but you always seemed a bit unapproachable, too confident for my liking. But then when we talked, I realized that maybe there was more to you than what I saw."

Chris had never thought of himself from that perspective. He'd have to give it some thought. Perhaps his grandfather's pride had inched its way into his demeanor without his knowledge. This date was going to be amazing if she kept this attitude going.

"Well, then let me enlighten you a little. My dad came from money, and with some of his inheritance, he made a fortune of his own. And when he accepted Christ, he didn't have a desire for ministry, and so he continued to be a light in the business world. He died in a car accident with my Grandma Banks when I was only four, so I don't really remember him. He was an only child, and I was his only child. My grandfather liked to spoil me, as you can see by the car.

And although he had been grooming me to follow in his footsteps, I felt God calling me into ministry. What all that entails, I don't know yet, which is why I'm also majoring in linguistics."

"Wow, that's quite the story. I can't wait to dig into that a little deeper. My life seems so easy and uncomplicated. I think I'll keep my story and my old Chevy Impala."

Chris smiled at her and shook his head as he parked the car in front of the restaurant. He had decided to keep things simple, and the place he'd chosen was a Chinese chain restaurant.

She was pleased by his simple choice. She'd half expected him to pull out all the stops. He obviously didn't fit the poor college kid profile. She liked that he'd kept things easy by choosing something a little more comforting. This was going to be a great date.

February 1998

Pastor Tim had been teaching Safira about Jehovah but had been able to meet her only every other week. Their meetings were often drawn out by Safira's constant questions. He had been patient and had to remind himself that she didn't need to learn all the Bible stories at once, much to Safira's disappointment. He had been skimming through the Bible, touching on the key points. At last, he'd reached the story of Christ, where he'd left her the previous meeting. He could tell she was hungry for more of the story.

"Christ then had a supper with His disciples and went out and prayed in a garden to Jehovah."

"I still don't understand that part. You said He was Jehovah. How then can He be praying to Jehovah?"

"Because They are the same, but They are also separate."

She sighed, "I can't seem to understand."

"It's difficult for a human mind to comprehend. Think of an egg. It has a shell, a white, and a yolk. The parts of the egg are all separate, but they come together. You cannot have one without the other, and the shell will never disagree with the yolk or the white disagree with the shell. The parts do not come separately. They are always together, but they can also be separated."

Safira nodded. She was able to understand the illustration, but it was still a strange idea.

"So Jehovah was Jesus, and Jesus was Jehovah. But yet They are able to separate from each other, even though They are the same," she said trying to clarify.

"Basically, yes."

"Okay, so Jesus was praying to Jehovah." Safira leaned against the tree waiting for more of the story.

"One of His disciples betrayed Jesus for money, and to show the soldiers who Jesus was, he kissed Him. The soldiers came and took Jesus away to prison."

"For what cause?" Safira casually asked.

"They did it for no true cause. They disliked Him for the things He said."

Safira nodded. She understood power. If a powerful man didn't like another person, it would be easy to find guilt even where there was none. She had witnessed these types of injustices within her small world.

"They tried Him the next day, and He was found innocent, but the crowds still wanted Him dead."

"But if He were innocent, why would they want to kill Jesus?"

"Because He had declared Himself Jehovah God, and these were devout men. They did not believe such a lowly teacher could possibly be the Almighty God of heaven."

"Those men were ignorant."

"On the contrary, they just didn't understand yet. They thought the Messiah, the one who was to come and save them, would physically free them from the oppression of those who didn't believe in Jehovah and that the Christ would then establish His kingdom, for those prophecies were the ones they had studied."

Safira's eyes pleaded for more.

"The man in charge of the trial washed his hands as a sign that he was not guilty for the innocent blood the crowd wanted to shed and then allowed the soldiers to crucify Jesus. He was beaten beyond recognition and never once raised His voice against His attackers. He allowed them to place a crown of thorns on His head. He carried His cross on His shoulder up a hill where criminals were put to death." When Pastor Tim saw how riveted Safira was, he handed her a small wooden cross pendant on a nylon string necklace.

"This is what the cross was, except big enough to place in the ground and hang a man on it."

"How did they keep Him on that cross if He was God?"

"He let them. He willingly allowed them for you, Safira, for all the wrongs you did and I did. He allowed them because only His blood would be an acceptable sacrifice for sins. They stretched out His arms and nailed His hands to the cross. They drove a nail through His feet and waited for His death. It didn't take long."

Tears streamed down her face as Safira fingered the cross in her hand. She shook her head slowly, as if in denial of the preacher's words.

Pastor Tim placed a hand on her shoulder. "And to prove that He was the sacrifice for sins and that His sacrifice was acceptable, three days later, He arose from the dead."

Safira's eyes widened at this news. "So where is He? Did He die later? Why did He not establish His kingdom then?"

"He met with many of His followers, including His disciples, over a forty-day period. His disciples watched Him ascend into heaven, where He remains preparing a place for us when we die. When He returns for His children someday, only then will He establish His kingdom."

"Who are His children?"

"I am one of them. You can be too."

"How?"

"By believing that He is Jehovah's son and believing in His payment on that cross for you. If you do not accept what I have told you, then you will go to hell and pay for that sin forever. Remember what happened to the rich man from Jesus's story?"

Safira instantly remembered the story of the rich man burning in hell.

"But if you do believe, Jesus will be walking with you for the rest of your life, because He loves you!"

All the pastor had been teaching over the last months finally came together. And inside, she knew that what he spoke was true.

She had not done the unspeakable evils her father had, but she knew she had sinned against this Jehovah, the One true God.

"Pastor Tim, I want to be His child. He is real. I know He is real. And I want to believe in Jesus. I want to be clean from my sin. I want Him to be with me always as you have said."

Pastor Tim felt his eyes fill with tears of joy as he led her to the cross that night and watched her begin a relationship with Jesus Christ.

Chapter 4

The Call

Colorado

Standing in the large doorway to the kitchen, Chris watched his siblings and Angie. He couldn't help smiling as they made sugar cookies. The trio was covered in flour from rolling out the dough to make heart shapes. Angie and Chris were visiting for the weekend. They often flew home from their Chicago Bible college to visit Chris's family. She was a welcome addition to the intimate group. She always slid right in as if she'd always been a part of his family.

Fay snuck up beside him. Chris gave her a smile before turning his attention back to the bakers.

"She's a keeper, Chris," Fay said quietly as Kate and Angie started dancing to the song on the radio, laughing as they did. JC stole some cookie dough before the distracted girls could stop him.

"I know. I'm going to ask her to marry me this weekend. It's Valentine's Day tomorrow, so I figured I would take the family out and do it then," he said quietly. He knew Angie wouldn't hear him between the radio and Kate.

"What about her family?" Fay asked. "I'm sure they would want to be a part of it."

"I already spoke with her dad. He was thrilled with the idea and said he might miss the proposal but he looked forward to the wedding."

"That's nice of him."

"It would be if I'd let it go at that. But I insisted, so they will be at the Bellford Hotel. They should be getting in late tonight and flying out Sunday with Angie and me."

"Wait. You planned for her family to be there? You are a sweetheart. But why did you wait to tell me?" Fay questioned. She was trying to contain her excitement for her son, with the leading lady just a whisper away. She was proud of him and couldn't be happier over the bride he'd chosen.

He smiled at his mom. She was an amazing woman he greatly respected. "Bigger surprise for everyone I guess." He was grateful he had the money to include everyone in the proposal. "You will be there too." He tacked on. He knew she wanted to be included and was impressed with his plan.

"You have it all planned out?"

"Yup. I think I even know the answer to the question."

"What answer do you have for what question?" Angie asked. The song had ended just as he'd spoken, and his voice had carried. Chris didn't skip a beat as he responded flawlessly.

"To the question of what we're having for supper. I'd like to have steak and potatoes. But I have to run to the store and get the steaks. Hey, Dad, you want to come?" Chris called over his shoulder to the living room. Grabbing the keys from his mom's outstretched hand, he began his way out. Chris's dad, hearing the bit about steak, stood up from the couch where he was watching a Broncos football game and followed Chris out the door.

The next night, the family accompanied Chris to the fine dining restaurant he'd chosen for his event. He had rented the whole restaurant, much to the delight of the staff. Chris had sent Angie and his mom on a shopping trip earlier that day so she'd have something formal for their date. She'd found a V-necked long, turquoise blue dress with sequined trim around the neck and hem that she now wore. Her hair was up, and she was stunning. Chris had thought he was ready for tonight, but one look at her and he questioned his own confidence.

Angie's eyes lit up as she scanned the atmosphere of the elegant five-star restaurant. Chris liked to go all out to impress her. He'd done so often enough, but today, he'd outdone himself. After soaking in the glow of the crystal chandeliers, the white tablecloths, warm red hues on the walls, and dark hardwood floors, she turned her gaze back toward Chris. Her eyes flashed over Chris's shoulder where she was stunned to see her family. Her smile blossomed. The distance between them evaporated quickly as both mother and daughter rushed toward one another. The rest of her family surrounded her and took their turns greeting one another. Even her older sister and younger brother were present. Angie, still holding her mother's hand, turned to question Chris.

Chris was closer than she'd expected. He was smiling down at her only inches away.

"I thought maybe they should be here when you got the news of your graduation."

"My graduation?" she asked, her smile fading and her eyes clouding with confusion.

Chris knelt on one knee and pulled out the beautiful large diamond ring.

"Will you allow me to give you an MRS degree and be mine?"

Tears welled in her eyes. Her smile broadened, a giggle escaped her lips recalling their first date. There was no doubt in her mind that she wanted to be with Chris for the rest of her life. She nodded. Tenderly taking her left hand, Chris slipped the diamond onto her ring finger. He stood to kiss her. Both moms' eyes glistened with happy tears, and the dads stood back smiling. The siblings tried giving the two a moment before they hugged the happy couple. It was a spectacular beginning.

August 1998

Safira continued to meet with Pastor Tim Kindel every two weeks to make it less noticeable that she was being mentored by anyone.

"I have a problem, Pastor," she said when she saw him in the orchard.

"What's that?" He sounded interested.

"How can I worship Jehovah if I am forced to worship gods that don't even exist?"

"What does your conscience say?"

"I can't be sure. I don't even want to pretend I'm worshiping other gods anymore. The Holy Spirit is selfish. I keep telling myself that I'm only doing it when people are watching. I've even tried to believe that I'm praying to Him when I'm kneeling before Handrel. I still feel guilty. But if I don't worship with the others, it could be bad for my health." She said making a sweeping motion with her hand across her neck. "Is going through the actions of worshiping these false gods wrong, if my heart is not worshiping them, and I believe only Jehovah? Does it matter what my body does?"

Pastor Tim understood her dilemma. New converts often voiced the same question. He empathized with them.

"It's a decision you'll have to make. You're the only one who can decide whether to be open about your new faith, but Christ wants you to be open about who you serve. Even faking your worship of other gods is denying to the world that Jesus is your God. Keilron is not a place where open Christianity is possible. Refusing to worship false gods isn't openly professing Christ. Perhaps you should consider evasion rather than a declaration. Finding excuses for not going with your family would be one way."

Safira bobbed her head in understanding. She would have to think on his words, but she didn't feel secure enough to stop her pretend worship. She wasn't ready for the possible consequences yet. Deep down, she would have to make a decision one day, but she refused to do so now.

"I wish I had the scriptures to read for myself," she said. Her voice and mannerism were contemplative. She was obviously soaking in the pastor's words but wanted to read what God had to say for herself.

"I'm still working on it, but it is slow work doing it on my own. I have a few books translated, but I don't know how I'm going to get them printed and distributed yet. I will be leaving for the United States next week, and I'll be gone for several months. I'll send you a message when I do return so we can continue meeting then."

"Why are you leaving?" Her eyes returned to his, and she almost looked panicked.

Pastor Tim knew with all his heart that this sixteen-year-old would do great things for the Lord. Her struggle was like so many others, but her obstacles, if she overcame them, were monumental. She was a deep thinker, always seeking truth. She loved deciphering problems and understanding the scripture.

"I must go to America. I need to give reports to those who support me and try to gain more support. It takes money to print the scriptures," he spoke gently.

"Bring me back something?" She teased.

"We'll see," he smiled.

Safira knew she would miss him while he was gone. He was her only source of information in understanding her Savior. She knew he'd return, and perhaps in the time he was gone, she would be closer to making her decision about kneeling before the image of Handrel.

October 1998

"The call is for you as well. Do not allow yourself to sit back in your comfy chair and think 'that's cool, but God couldn't possible mean me.' He does mean you! Keilronians are in desperate need of men and women willing to teach them of the one true God. Women, don't think you're excluded. We need women to feed and care for the widowed and orphaned children who have been forced underground for safety because of their faith. We need families to reach out with financial support for those who are risking their very lives to be in Keilron."

"There is hope. This past year, I've counseled a young teenager who is close acquaintances with the dictator Shovak himself! And just eight months ago, her name was sealed in glory forever. Men, we need willing workers, those who are willing to learn the language and help teach, preach, disciple, and translate scripture into the Keilronian tongue. Look into your hearts and listen. Do you hear God calling you to this field? I hope you feel a burden to pray for the believers who are in grave danger for choosing to trust in Christ."

Chris listened to Pastor Tim, a special speaker from the mission field of Keilron. His heart burned with tenderness toward the countrymen once again as it had two years earlier the night his grandfather had died, and he felt a pull toward Keilron like he'd never felt.

After the service, he was unable to follow Angie and the crowd as they slowly filed out. A few people lingered around talking, but Chris still felt deep inside that he had to speak with the pastor. First, he needed to pray.

Angie hesitated on her way out when she realized Chris wasn't behind her as usual. She went back to Chris and sat beside him, watching his face carefully. She could tell the message had spoken to him and waited for him to open up. The sanctuary continued to empty, and still, she waited.

"What are you thinking?" she finally asked, taking his hand in hers.

"I was praying. I think I need to speak with Pastor Kindel. Would you mind waiting a few more minutes?"

She shook her head. He would speak to her after he'd spoken to the missionary. Spotting a friend lingering in the lobby, she decided to join her while waiting for Chris.

Chris captured Pastor Tim's attention when he approached and spoke directly, "Pastor Kindel, when do you leave for your next visit?"

"Not until tomorrow evening. Why?"

"I'd like to take you to lunch tomorrow, if I may."

"What's your name?" Pastor Tim felt the urgency from the young man by the way the boy had completely skipped over introductions. Tim was always willing to visit with people interested in the Keilronian ministry. He saw the burning desire in the other man's eyes and began to pray in his heart for the younger man.

"I'm sorry. I'm Christian Banks."

"It's nice to meet you. I'd love to have lunch. Did you have a time in mind?"

They set the time and place, and Christian left to find his fiancé again.

"Angie, let's go for a walk."

Smiling at her friends, she waved goodbye as Chris ushered her out of the building.

"What's on your mind, honey?"

"I can't say for sure, Angie. The Lord is trying to tell me something. I'm probably going to be absentminded today, so maybe we should put our dinner on hold."

"That's fine, but won't you at least try to tell me what's going on in that head?" she pleaded.

He paused, searching for the right way to begin. "Are you willing to give up everything for Christ? I mean *really*?"

"Of course, I'm willing. We've already talked about our desire to work in ministry."

"What if God were to call us to a place like Keilron?"

She was intrigued in his change of heart. "I didn't know you had a desire for foreign missions."

"I didn't know exactly what God wanted. I still don't know what He wants. But I'm considering the possibility my heart is heavy right now because He's trying to tell me something."

"Okay. Well, it would be scary. Just listening to that missionary gave me the chills. Living in that environment would take a lot of faith and strength," she admitted.

"But if God wants us there, would you feel as frightened?"

"We've talked about having children someday. If we were in that kind of country, it would be dangerous to have kids. Not just to raise them, but in those conditions, giving birth would be risky too."

"If we were supposed to be there, God would take care of us."

"Yes. Chris, you've got plenty of money to support us both for years without having to raise support, and now, you're talking about risking our lives in a place like Keilron?"

"Perhaps. I've got some praying to do first, Angie. I want to see where God calls me. Wherever that is, I'll go, but I need you to be aware of what God's doing in my heart."

"I'll pray, Chris," she promised.

He smiled weakly as he opened her car door, kissed her, and watched her drive back to the girls' dorm.

Pastor Tim met Christian at his favorite home-style restaurant the next day. They sat down, and after a few minutes of pleasantries, the waitress came to take their orders. They ordered their food, and then, Chris forged ahead, expressing the reason behind the lunch meeting.

"I heard your message last night, and it struck a nerve. I want to know more."

"I didn't hold much back last night. What more do you want to know?"

"How could I learn the language? How does the paperwork come together as far as even entering a country that's shut down to missionaries?"

"I'm afraid you're getting ahead of yourself, Chris. I must warn you that learning their language isn't easy. You could learn the basics, but in reality, you must be completely immersed into it. There are few people able to teach you the language, and even some of them are a danger to work with if they know your motives."

"Language barriers can be broken, or so I'm learning here. I've been studying linguistics at the college. I know you, which means you can help me learn their language from across the globe. With my training, it shouldn't take long."

"That's easier said than done. There is no Internet there, and phone calls are kept brief. Even if I wanted to add teaching to my list of things to do, it would be very difficult and tedious to teach you the language through letter. I could begin teaching you so you understood some, but to learn the language well, you must be immersed into it. It usually takes missionaries several years to reach their financial support, so it's possible to get you acquainted with the language. As for the paperwork, it would be best for you to find a job as an interpreter or teacher. Often, Keilron needs English teachers or officials to translate between dignitaries. I'm technically a political translator."

"If being immersed is the quickest way to learn, then I'd like to go as soon as possible after graduation. Money isn't a problem for me, Pastor."

"When do you graduate?" Kindel inquired. Chris's declaration had gotten his attention.

"This coming spring," Chris said.

"You could come to the country as a language student to begin with. I can teach you the language, and in time perhaps, we could get you a permanent position on staff somewhere."

Pastor Tim watched the young man's serious expression and the slow nod. He had sent out a call for help in Keilron last night as he often did, but this was a rare conversation. He often tried to scare the young people away because if talk could do that, then often, they weren't meant for the grueling challenges that Keilron would present them. The man before him now looked to be every bit as interested as many others before him, but there was something else in the boy's demeanor that triggered a sincere desire that Chris would join him in the battle to win souls for Christ.

Pastor Tim was trying to tame the excitement in his own heart. For the last two years, he'd been asking the Lord for a partner, someone willing to help him lead in the Keilronian world. Many of the locals had been trained to be ministers to their own people, but Tim wanted and needed another translating partner. In his prayers, he had never specified age, but he'd always pictured someone more mature than the kid before him. God moved in unexpected ways though. While studying Chris, the Holy Spirit planted a thought in his mind.

"Chris, I would love to see you follow Christ to Keilron, but I recall seeing a young lady with you. Is she your wife?"

"No, not yet, but we are planning a wedding right after graduation." Chris smiled to himself at the thought of Angie, but the next words from Pastor Tim wiped it from his face.

"I hope you understand what it would mean if you were to marry her and come to Keilron together. It's dangerous enough for a single man. But to bring a wife would be treacherous. It could be done. Don't get me wrong, but I sincerely hope it would be her desire as well. If she were to marry you only because she loves you and follow you to Keilron where she could not contact her family often, nor find many friendly faces, and discover the harsh reality facing most women there, I'm afraid she would realize love for you wasn't enough. I'd hate to see anyone go through that pain. You must also ask yourself, and her, if this is her calling too. If it is, I'll welcome you both, but if it's not, what will you choose?"

"I'm not sure, but if I find that this is where I need to go, then I won't hesitate to go."

"Pray long and hard Chris. The decision you're facing will change your life forever."

Chris nodded as their food arrived, and the two moved on to lighter conversation for the rest of the meal. Chris asked questions of the young teenage girl Pastor Tim had led to Christ, of the families he'd left behind, and of the men he was teaching to be leaders within the Christian circle.

When they finished, Chris walked the pastor to his car.

"I will stay in correspondence with you as best I can. Mailing is even hard in Keilron because they check nearly everything. If you're dedicated and you can prove to me that this is what you want, then I'll send for you. But learn the language and customs as best you can. Some research can be found here in the United States. The Internet will help with research, and there are a few missionaries who left several years ago that I can put you in contact with. They can also help you." Kindel spoke decidedly.

They exchanged addresses, and Pastor Tim gave Chris a few names to contact.

Chris prayed when he arrived home. He couldn't focus on school or anything else, for that matter. Angie called Monday night, and they spoke briefly. He told her he was still praying and seeking the Lord's will and needed a few days. She told him she loved him and understood. Angie promised to pray for direction as well. It wasn't until Friday morning while reading and praying Chris felt a surety come over him. He knew in those quiet moments as he opened the scriptures that God was calling him to Keilron. The decision was made, but another dilemma faced him, and his heart grew heavy. It was time to speak to his future bride. He prayed right then that no matter what her decision, he would stay true to the Lord. He knew if he had to choose between Keilron and Angie on his own, he would choose her. He loved her.

That night, he met Angie at a nearby park with trails they often walked. She smiled uneasily at him before he had the chance to wrap her in a hug. He loved this woman so much, and he prayed that she'd come to the same conclusion as he had. He took her hand in silence, and they began their walk along the trails.

"I've been praying pretty hard this week. I'm sorry I haven't really felt like talking to you about it. I needed to get it straight in my own heart and mind first. This morning, I felt God encouraging me to take a step of faith and prepare for Keilron."

"I'm glad you had the chance to figure it out for yourself, but honestly, I wasn't sure what to think. We've heard missionaries from all over speak. Why is Keilron the one that got your attention? I even remember some of those mission fields being intriguing to you, but you were never ready to jump into the mission field."

"I know. I never picked an area other than missions and linguistics because I wasn't sure what God wanted me to do. I hadn't even ruled out the business world. But Sunday night, with Pastor Kindel, something clicked. I could see it—the people, the tortures, horrors, and the lost souls crying for help. I'd never seen anything like it, and I had never experienced such helplessness. I wanted to reach out to them. But like you said, it's not exactly the first time I've been drawn toward another country. This was important enough to meet with Pastor Kindel, and then, I needed to pray diligently this past week."

Angie remained silent for a moment. The chilly breeze hinted to the winter coming, and the night was crisp and clean. At last, she spoke.

"This is very hard, Chris. I've been praying too. I knew God touched your heart Sunday. I prayed He would change your mind or soften my heart toward this mission field. Neither has happened. I fervently prayed, and I shed tears because I love you so much. You are the kindest, most generous person I know, and you love the Lord with all of your heart. I thought I did too. So I can't understand why the Keilronians do nothing but terrify me. I think about the lack of communication, the lack of normal amenities like flushing toilets, the persecution, and the way women are treated. I want these souls reached, but I'm also terrified at the idea of following you there."

"We would be protected by God," Chris tried to reason, feeling his own heart aching at what he feared was coming.

"Yes, but Chris, God isn't calling me there. I would love to be a part of a ministry, but I've always thought of domestic ministries.

Foreign fields have never really interested me. I've prayed since I was a child that God would send me a ministry-minded man, and I thought that was you. In some ways, it is you. But I guess I left off the part where He needed to prepare me for whatever came. Do you remember when we were having chapel earlier this year, and the speaker was talking about picking the right partner? He said, 'Mission must match matrimony.' If we were married right now, I would humble my heart before God and follow you because that's what a wife is supposed to do. But we aren't married yet, and I'm wondering if it isn't a blessing that God has chosen now to lay upon your heart the mission He has for you."

"I love you" was all Chris could say. His throat constricted, and he held back tears at what she was saying. He knew she was right. He wished he had words to convince her to join him. He felt ready to let go of Keilron for her. The Lord held Chris's hand as he faced Angie.

"I love you, very dearly." Her voice held the sadness and pain that he felt.

"I don't want to let you go." He whispered the words as a few tears escaped.

"I know. I don't want to leave. But Chris, you just told me that you have never felt surer of anything than you do about going to Keilron. Am I right? That's basically what you meant."

"Yes, it is." He held her hand a little tighter as they stopped their strolling around the park.

"I can't stand in your way, and I will not be a hindrance to what God has called you to do. I will not allow you to choose between me and God because I want you to choose Him over me. You have to, or you're not the man I know. I love you dearly. This is going to hurt us both deeply. I can't go to Keilron with you. God has made it clear to me. I belong here in the States."

They didn't stop holding hands, but neither one could say more at the moment; both had tears streaming down their faces. They were standing at a crossroads, and they knew their lives were going to separate rather than be joined.

Before they drove away from each other that night, they prayed for one another and promised to continue doing so. Chris touched her face one last time. They embraced for several minutes before parting. With the diamond ring in his hand, he watched her drive away. He knew he'd have to see her in school for the rest of the year, and it would be difficult for both of them to know what could have been. But at the same time, they both knew this was God's plan, and they would abide by it.

He flew home the following weekend to tell his family that Angie wasn't going to join the family. As he told his mom about Angie, she could tell how brokenhearted he was. She embraced him and let him cry. He promised her as long as he served Christ in Keilron, he would choose not to marry. He didn't want to bring anyone into a country where death could be imminent at any time. Fay held her son, her heart breaking for him. She recalled the day he'd first read about Keilron and now understood the fear she'd felt. Her heart broke a little more for herself. All too soon, she would be watching him leave home, with no guarantees that he would ever return.

Chapter 5

The Escape

October 1999

Safira entered her quarters and closed the door behind her. She had not gone out of her way to pay homage to Handrel since the pastor had arrived home. If she were forced to go with a group to worship the god, she went begrudgingly through the motions. She wasn't ready to stop altogether and be discovered or questioned by her father. Tonight, she was returning from another meeting with Kindel. He'd given her much to consider yet again.

"You must leave tonight," Aspa admonished. It was unusual for the motherly woman to speak harshly to Safira. Her tone had startled Safira from her contemplations. She eyed the packed bag on the bed before she met Aspa's gaze.

"Why? Where am I going?" Safira was confused at the urgency she heard in Aspa's voice.

"A messenger left this evening to fetch your father. The message speaks of your meetings with a stranger. I told you to be careful! If your father returns to question you, will you have answers to satisfy him?"

Aspa had known for months of Safira's meetings and of her new faith. Safira had even gone so far as to share the gospel with her slave. Aspa had pondered Safira's words. In the end, Aspa had told Safira that she was not allowed to accept any god other than her master's.

Aspa had promised then that she would remain silent, but Safira was to be more cautious. There were guards and even a few male slaves who had begun to wonder about Safira's change in disposition.

"Whoever spotted me couldn't know who I was with or why I was meeting him," said Safira, attempting to defend herself.

"Your father has been lenient to be sure, but when he questions you, will you be able to lie convincingly to him? If you try to say the mysterious man is a lover, he will demand you reveal his name, and you will be not be able to produce someone who doesn't exist! Besides that, you have never been a convincing liar." Aspa spoke as a mother chastening her child.

Safira knew what Aspa said was true. She'd never been able to hide her emotions from her father. She did not, however, want to run away without an explanation.

"Surely, there is another way than to just leave tonight! What will my father think?"

"It is safest for you to go. If your father finds out about the Christian or about what you have been doing, he won't spare you. He could not protect you even if he wanted. Rofisca leads the hunt against Christians, and you would be made an example, proof that he means what he is saying."

Safira heard the wisdom in Aspa's words. She'd wanted to keep the meetings secret from the woman who had been like a mother to her, but hadn't been able to. Aspa, being a slave, was sworn to secrecy and would surely not be questioned. Aspa walked toward Safira and grabbed the bag off the bed. She hung the satchel on Safira's shoulder and adjusted the veil about her face for the last time.

"I pray your new God will protect you. I don't know where you will go. If you hurry, perhaps you will be able to catch your teacher."

Safira nodded and embraced the older woman before spinning on her heels, and while sticking to the shadows, she swiftly moved along the halls and out toward the orchards.

Once she was surrounded by the darkness in the orchard, she began running as hard as she could, tears streaming down her face. She had thought that somehow, Jehovah would work it out so she wouldn't have to leave. Once her father knew, he would protect and spare her from any harm as he had always done. Aspa was right though, with Shovak and Rofisca heading the charge against Christianity, no way could he overlook his daughter's decision. She wondered too, as she ran, if perhaps this was Jehovah's way to force her from her home so she could embrace Him fully in ways she was unable to do from home.

Her heart began to break as she realized that never again would she feel her father's kind eyes on her or feel the protection of his household. Nor would she see her governess and her brothers. She felt shunned from her own people who'd treated her with such respect her entire life. The wind wiped the tears from her eyes as she ran. She left the orchard and joined the road to Shemna. Somehow, she had to find the pastor. Finding Pastor Tim was a life and death matter.

A hand reached out and grabbed her from the darkness. Even her pride could not fight the hand that held her. She was blinded with fear and grief as she felt herself pulled into a gentle embrace.

Soft words reached her ears in comfort, and at last, she opened her eyes and saw Pastor Kindel's gentle face. She let herself relax as he held her.

Pastor Tim had been walking for nearly half an hour when he'd heard footsteps running behind him. Instinctively, he'd crouched in the shadows. He recognized the lone shadowed form as Safira. He didn't ask what was happening. He didn't have to. He knew full well that the time would come for her to turn her back on her family and follow Christ. He just hadn't expected it so soon.

November 1999

"You've been searching for one little girl for nearly a month, and you're telling me she's gone? I don't believe that. I've put out a no fly on her, and her picture was posted at every post exiting this country. She must still be here. Why haven't you found her yet?" General Rofisca barked at one of his captains.

"Sir, the Christians are a tight group. She must be with them, or she would be much easier to find. We have kept our search relatively local, believing that Shemna would be the best place for her to hide. We have put out feelers in the other cities, just in case."

"Keep searching. Leave nothing unturned. We may get lucky and unearth some of these Christian rats. Now, get out of here and find her!"

Shovak walked into Rofisca's office. He understood the situation and knew that Rofisca was concerned for his daughter. He would be as well if his daughter was half as beautiful as Safira.

"Rofisca, I understand your concern, but I am doing all I can. I believe your young captain could be right about the Christians harboring her."

"She's been educated to love and understand our gods. I never allowed her to be anywhere where she could hear about any false religions. I made sure of it."

"She was reported to be meeting secretly with somebody. You don't know how long that might have been going on or with whom she was meeting."

"True, but if she has fallen into the evil teachings of the Christians, then I have no daughter."

"Don't think the worst just yet, friend. Have hope, Rofisca. She may appear. Perhaps, the man she was meeting was only a secret lover, and she found that she'd been spotted, so they ran away together. She'll come home married to some brute."

"Perhaps, Shovak, but even that would have to be dealt with harshly. I'm ashamed of being careless with her. I spoiled her too much, and I regret it now."

"Yes, but coming home after being wed is far less punishment and shame for her than to be discovered among the Christians and put to death. We have many opportunities to question Christian prisoners, so if we're able to get any information from them about your daughter, I shall relay it immediately. If not, we will keep praying she returns soon."

December 1999

"So you see, Safira, that's why so many countries celebrate Christmas. If it wasn't for the birth, there would be no death, and if no death, then no salvation."

"Why do they exchange gifts?"

"Originally, it was to remind us of the gifts the wise men brought to Jesus. I've often thought it symbolized Jesus, the gift to man, but ultimately, it has become a tradition."

Safira was silent, which was, as the pastor had learned, an indication that she understood and was considering his words.

The small meeting house where they were this Christmas was crowded with widows, orphans, and homeless Christians, all of whom needed a good dose of hope. Safira had been a shining light here, though she'd only been at this location for a week. She'd made friends with many of the children and helped the mothers. She was only seventeen, but had been forced to grow into womanhood. The pastor had been blessed to watch her grow by leaps and bounds in her spiritual walk as she interacted with other believers and heard the word of God on a daily basis.

Safira lifted one of the orphans in the shelter onto her lap and began to tell her the story of Christmas. Her storytelling abilities, discovered immediately after entering crowded spaces, drew even the pastor into the timeless truths of God's Word. Today was no different as she began telling the story of Mary and Joseph. She wove it into a beautiful love story filled with a treacherous journey to Bethlehem, where there was no room for the expectant mother. Children gathered around her, and mothers stopped their conversations to listen.

"Pastor," Robert Camp whispered from behind him.

The pastor turned to look at his fellow comrade. Camp nodded to the back of the room where Gamico, one of the men who worked with the pastor on the other side of Shemna, stood by the door. He strode across the room toward the man. As he approached, he could tell that Gamico was nervous and scared. The man gripped Pastor Tim's arm as soon as he was within reach.

"Pastor, I've news from Chris Banks. He's sent me to ask for prayer as he prays for you. Pastor Block has just been captured, and he's to be executed on Friday."

Pastor Block had been working closely with Chris since the younger man arrived over six months ago. Kindel had hoped to do it himself, but found he couldn't help as much as Banks needed. Pastor

Block had volunteered to help tutor him. Banks had progressed splendidly under his tutelage and had begun working on the Bible translation alongside Kindel only a couple of weeks earlier. Pastor Block, the one who first worked with Banks, had begun to distance himself from the duties of mentor as he began helping more needy converts. Legwork among the new believers was always a bit dangerous as people were awarded money for information leading to the capture of any Christian. Kindel knew that despite the last weeks' distance between Block and Banks, the two had created a friendship much like those who served in the military, a brotherly bond.

"What about Banks? Is he all right?"

"Yes. He's okay, but nervous. All of us are. We know what goes on in those prisons, and we fear what happens if Block is forced to talk. Not that any would blame him if he did."

"Thank you. You're welcome to stay here for now. I'll go to Banks."

Pastor Tim glanced over at Safira before he headed out the door and across the city, praying as he did so. He had warned Banks that Christian work in Keilron was dangerous, but this was the first time he'd personally experienced the loss of a friend, and Kindel was determined to offer him strength. Camp, Block, and Kindel had come to Keilron long before Shovak had taken over. Life had not been easy and had grown progressively worse. The younger man must stay because someone needed to continue the ministry after they were gone. Kindel knew Banks was capable of being that man. He could see Chris Banks had the courage it was going to take.

January 2000

Moving stealthily through the old part of the city, Safira weaved through the complicated street patterns flawlessly till she came to the doorway she sought. She took a deep breath and knocked.

The door swung open, and she was quickly swept inside. The family with five children sitting crossed legged on the floor welcomed her.

"Safira?" the woman questioned.

"Yes," she said.

The children sitting on the floor obviously didn't all belong to the young couple. The three older were between twelve and fifteen years. She knew instinctively that the two youngest were the only ones who belonged to the young couple because one was only a toddler and the other around four.

"I was told to come here for a time. I hope I won't be a burden for longer than a week or two. I'd like to help with the children if I could," Safira offered.

"We're glad to have you. The help and company would be nice." The woman smiled gently. Safira immediately felt at ease. "My name is Karmilita."

Safira had been forced to leave the small home the pastor had filled with children and widows. They all knew she couldn't stay in the same place long, or someone would begin to notice her. This was the first family that had volunteered to host her. She could tell by the generosity of this couple that she was blessed to have found such friends.

*****

"Still no news, General. Not enough to find her anyway. Enough, however, to know she is not married, and she is in Shemna. We have several Christian prisoners who have confessed she is among their numbers."

"You are doing well, Captain. Keep looking," Rofisca complimented. "If she remains in Shemna, she can be protected for only so long."

February 2000

Safira felt the dark night close in as she lay her head down in the cramped room that had been built in secret for those who were on the run. She sighed deeply and rolled on her side, trying to sleep. As her eyes shut, her mind became alert to every sound. A tear carved a path down her cheek from pure exhaustion and fear. Many nights, she would cry herself to sleep; it seemed easier than being strong.

The battle Safira fought was much deeper and much more powerful than seen on the outside. She realized that captured Christians were being interrogated with unspeakable tortures about her. This fact alone pained her, but she knew it was much more. She felt no security, no peace, and the only comfort she found was in Christ.

She pled with God as her body shook with sobs. She wanted a way out, but none was in sight. She contemplated turning herself in just to spare her brothers and sisters, but knew that her death would not mean the end of torture for them. There were no alternatives. Not only was being a Christian in Keilron bad enough, but also being the head general's daughter, whose face was known and who had a price on her head, was extremely difficult. She would not be able to avoid her father forever.

Praying in earnest, she sought comfort and clarity. When her tears dried up and words failed her, she simply felt her heart ache. It was in these moments of stillness that she felt the weight of her situation ease. Her heart became less painful, and she felt her Savior's arms wrap around her. It was the most surreal feeling; it was also the most comforting thing she had ever experienced. At the moment, she knew without a doubt He loved her and was going to take care of her. She fell asleep in the Savior's arms and relaxed into the best sleep she'd had since leaving her father's household.

Stonebrook, Colorado

Fay Kleren looked up from her work when her seventeen-year-old daughter walked into the office. Kate's dark hair and green eyes reminded Fay so much of herself. She paused what she was doing and pointed to the comfy chair sitting in the corner.

"What's on your mind, honey?"

"Have you heard from Chris lately, Mom?"

"I haven't gotten anything since the letter three weeks ago."

"I wonder what it's really like in Keilron."

"Difficult I'm sure. He's sent some letters to me about the things going on there, and to be honest, they don't paint a pretty picture. I don't usually read those to you."

"I guess I'm starting to wonder if things are as bad as he makes them out to be. I never really got to know him, Mom. It's like we were raised in different times or something. And now, I want to know him and hang out with this super cool brother, but he's not here."

"You're seven years apart. When he was fourteen and wanting to play baseball, you still wanted him to play tea parties and Barbie. He wasn't real interested in you at that point." Fay smiled at the memory. They were such precious memories now. Chris hadn't been very tolerant of his younger siblings in his early teen years. They were always getting underfoot and embarrassing him in front of his friends. He'd loved pushing all the wrong buttons, with his sister particularly.

"Yeah, I guess, but I don't want to play Barbie anymore. I just want to talk with him, give him a big bear hug, you know?"

"I understand that feeling. He's my baby, and I don't want him over there either, but God does. We must keep praying hard to see him again. You still have JC around, you know. Don't miss your opportunity with him."

Kate sighed heavily. JC, fourteen going on fifteen, was more interested in sports than having grown-up conversations with his older sister. Her mom was probably right, though. She couldn't guarantee what God would have in store for JC

"Chris wrote me a couple of months ago that the pastor he was under was just put to death," Fay said, bringing the conversation back to Chris.

"I think something needs to happen, something only God can do. And I'm hoping it happens before we have to say goodbye to Chris." Kate spoke with her eyes aimed somewhere across the room.

"Just keep praying, Kate, and remember, God has a plan for Chris and the rest of the missionaries over there."

Kate nodded but didn't say any more. Eventually, the younger woman picked up the Bible lying beside her and began to read.

Fay felt a need to pray for her son at that moment. She prayed that he would stay safe, that he would accomplish everything God wanted. She prayed that he'd find the right people to help him. She prayed for the countrymen whom her son loved so much he was willing to risk his own life. And she prayed that someday, he would come home so he could have a glimpse of the adults his younger siblings were becoming by his influence, even from the other side of the world.

Shemna, Keilron

Safira felt the death grip harden on her shoulder. The guard who'd been chasing her for the past twenty minutes had finally caught her. Out of breath and physically drained from the last four months of cramped places, she turned wearily toward him. Her eyes widened as she saw her brother staring down at her. They shared the same mother and were only two years apart. She feared being caught, but this confrontation, facing a dear family member, was worse. Being caught by a random soldier would put her at risk, but being caught by a sibling was sure to result in a face to face with her father. Her stomach twisted in dread.

"Safira, our father has been searching for you for many months now."

She didn't speak. She couldn't. Her veil had come undone, and she was mortified for him to see her unveiled.

"Look at me, sister," he commanded.

Once her eyes met his, he spoke. "Father has given more to you than a woman deserves, but that was his place, not mine. I must give you to him. He has surely found a man for you. I know that many a man desires you for a wife."

"If he were planning on giving my soul away, he'd have done it sometime ago."

"Maybe he was waiting for the right offer or the right alliance. Now that you have been rumored to be among the Christians, it's no surprise why Father wants to find you. He wants to know if those rumors are true. He still wants to believe the best in you. Are you a Christian?"

Safira's chin rose, no longer ashamed to stare into his eyes. "Yes, I am."

"Why? Why risk everything you had to believe in a strange god?"

"Because He risked all for me, He loves me, so I chose Him."

"You talk nonsense."

"How would you know? You are not educated to understand."

"Our gods have been good enough."

"You don't really believe that," she said as she gazed intently into his eyes. Her questioning look spoke volumes. He remembered their conversations as children, when they'd both wondered if the gods were real.

"Go, leave this city and do not return. If ever I see your face again, I shall slit your throat myself," he threatened. She'd pointed out his own weakness—doubt in the gods he served. One thing he did believe in was his role as brother and soldier. This act of mercy was all he could offer his little sister, a chance to get out before their father killed her.

Safira felt his hand release her shoulder, and she wrenched herself from his grasp. Covering her face with her veil once again, she ran toward the west side of Shemna.

Chapter 6

God's Answer

April 2000

Chris had never used the phones in Keilron, mainly because they were monitored, and he had to be cautious when speaking. Over the past week, he'd been experiencing a strong desire to speak with his friend in the States. A phone call was the quickest way to get in touch, and Chris had decided to risk the call.

"Hello," Blake's voice came through casually. The simple greeting caused Chris to smile.

"Hey, buddy. How is everyone?" Chris casually leaned against the phone booth.

"Chris? How are you?" Blake was obviously excited to hear from his friend.

"I'm doing well. I just wanted to ask you a favor."

"Sure. Anything. What's up?"

"You remember Pappy Banks' house near Denver?"

"That old Victorian?" Blake asked. "Yeah, I remember." Blake was attending school for architecture while serving as a youth pastor near the Kleren's home. He'd begun to refer to homes by their style.

"Right. Would you get it cleaned up and have JC help you get it in order? I want it prepared for a tenant."

"Sure. Are you thinking of renting it out?"

"No, I just never know when I'll have to run home. I've got a strange feeling someone may need it. Maybe as a temporary place. Just let me know who you might have there."

"Will do. We miss you here."

"I miss you guys too. Tell my folks 'hi' for me and give Kate and JC my love. I got to go."

Chris's words were barely spoken when Blake heard the click. He got on his cell and called Kate and JC

May 2000

Safira was tired of shifting from one home to another. She possessed only four robes, and those were beginning to wear. Time was against her as she struggled to stay one step ahead of her father.

Being a criminal on the run who had to watch her every step made her grateful for the veil she was forced to wear when she was in the streets. The equalizer for women, the veil had always been a thorn in her side, but since she'd left home, she was thankful for the camouflage. She was lonely and growing weary of the constant changes. In her heart, Safira wished for a place she could be safe, but for her, there was no such haven.

Pastor Tim hurried through the crowded streets of Shemna, the rain began to fall gently on his head. He tightened his hold on the two books wrapped in leather closer to his body. Another glance back couldn't hurt, just to make sure he wasn't followed. Creeping through the city this way was a normal way of life, but today, he was more cautious than usual. The special package tucked in the crook of his left arm had to be delivered safely. Veering into the small alley, he walked several yards before quietly knocking on the door to his right. Moments later, he slipped inside.

Pastor Tim perused the ten runaways who had been hiding in this small alcove behind the tailor's shop. His eyes rested on Safira, and he took a deep breath. The night before, he'd received an idea that must have come from heaven. What he couldn't figure out is why he hadn't thought of it before. It was a long shot on both sides, but he felt he had to offer the idea. Safira would be the easier of the two to sway, as her heritage made her more agreeable; just in case, he had brought a peace offering.

He knelt down to where Safira was sitting. She smiled at him as he offered her the parcel. She took it and removed the brown wrapping. Her smile grew huge when she realized what it was.

"This is part of God's Word!"

"Yes, I have more translated, but this was all I could get printed for you. I hope you will cherish the books of John and of Romans."

"Oh, thank you, Pastor!" Her eyes instantly began to devour the words on the page.

Tim smiled at her. "Safira, before you get to involved, we need to discuss something."

She lay the books aside, giving him her full attention.

"I'm not sure how to begin." He took a deep breath as she waited.

"You need to get out of Shemna. No, you need to leave the country. Your father continues getting closer to your whereabouts. We can't hide you much longer."

"I cannot. You know as well as I, it would be difficult to leave Shemna, but to enter another country would be impossible. No one, no country, would defend me against my father."

"I realize that. Last night, I got an idea, and I decided to approach you first."

"First?" Her eyes narrowed, and her lips formed a straight line.

"Yes. Have you heard of Christian Banks?" he asked hesitantly.

"He's one of the missionary pastors on the other side of Shemna. I've heard his name a time or two. Why?"

"He is one of our pastors, true, but he is also a wealthy American. He has a reputable name and standing within the United States. He could support you there while remaining here."

"Are you suggesting what I think you are?" Safira's eyes widened, and her mouth formed a small "O."

"If the paperwork is in order, we can get you into the United States under your married name. And you will be safe from your father. He would have no more control over you as a married woman." Kindel's eyes searched Safira's face. Her eyes drifted to a spot to the right of the pastor, unable to meet his gaze. She remained silent. Her mouth closed, and her body relaxed. She closed her eyes for several minutes. Pastor Tim patiently waited for her response.

Her lids fluttered open, and she looked straight into the pastor's eyes. "Where did you get such an idea?"

"Last night, the Lord pressed it upon my heart." He spoke honestly, hoping she could read the sincerity as her gaze penetrated to his soul. She must have seen what she needed to because her eyes flipped back to the spot on the wall. Her silence lasted nearly a full minute before she turned her eyes back to him.

"Even if he were crazy enough to marry me, how would I get out? I'm sure my face is plastered all over the airports."

"We have a few private pilots who are willing to fly you out of country. Your paperwork won't be inspected until you land in Greece, where your picture isn't posted. Your new name will give you reason enough to pass through security without problems. From there, you will be flown to the United Kingdom and on to the United States."

"Why would this man choose to marry me when he could have any American woman?"

"He told me he doesn't wish to marry and bring a woman to this land of persecution. He would never ask a girl to come here."

"But I am already here, and I am trying to leave." She wrapped up the situation nicely in her own words. Pastor Tim nodded, letting her know she'd understood correctly.

"Yes, you are. Safira, you need to leave. Go to the United States, and learn how to speak and write English. Perhaps, when it is time, God may call you back here again."

"I am running out of options. I have learned what Jehovah has said about marriage. What He wants is very different from how things are here. If I marry him, I will not be free to marry another."

Pastor Tim nodded solemnly. He had been teaching her many things, as had many of the Christian families she was a part of. He had known that she would realize the finality of this decision.

"You've never met him, and I've yet to speak to him on the matter, but would you be willing to give your name away so quickly?" The question was asked with kindness.

"Is there no other choice?" She asked, looking at the pastor in hope.

"Not that I have been able to find," he responded, his head bent, his eyes looking up at her.

She looked at Pastor Tim, knowing he needed an answer.

With a shaky breath, she spoke. "If this man accepts your request, then I know it is God's will, and I will submit to His authority. Christ has brought me this far. He will give me the strength," she quietly answered.

Pastor Tim looked into the girl's honey brown eyes. At eighteen, she showed the strength and endurance of a warrior. Her servant's heart put his own to shame, and her determination encouraged his older believers to keep trusting. She was an inspiration to them all. He saw in her eyes a fierce fire and knew she meant every word she'd said. Pastor Tim realized at that moment that Safira would make Christian Banks a fine wife someday. He wondered how *that* would come about if she were to go back to the States. He cleared his mind; there was one more person to speak to before he could even begin to hope. God would take care of the rest.

Pastor Tim left Safira shortly after and began to make his way slowly to the other side of the city where he knew he could find Chris. Praying as he went, Pastor Tim strolled toward Chris's dwelling. The younger man welcomed him with a smile and a hug before letting him into the home.

Chris offered Pastor Tim a chair beside the small kitchen table. Tim moved slowly and purposefully as he sat down. Usually, he was relaxed and eager to talk with the younger man, but today, his demeanor was stiff. He'd barely spoken a friendly greeting. Chris felt the older man's eyes boring into his back as he began to prepare tea.

"What brings you my way, Pastor Tim? You look like you have something on your mind." Chris spoke at last as he sat down in the chair across from Kindel.

"I do. I've been praying about something, and last night, the Lord gave me an idea that I'd like to share with you. You've heard of Safira Rofisca, I'm sure."

"Yes, she's General Rofisca's daughter. The military has been after her for a while now," Chris replied. He listened halfheartedly as he organized his own translation work on one side of the kitchen table so that Pastor Tim would have a place to set his cup. Chris poured Pastor Tim some tea and offered it to him. He accepted the cup and gestured for Chris to sit down.

"She is under my protection," Pastor Kindel said. "Do you remember when I was in the States and you heard me preach? During our first lunch, you even asked about the young woman I had led to Christ during that first lunch. The truth is that young woman was Safira. She's a faithful follower of Christ, and it wasn't long after I returned that she was forced to leave her home. Her father had discovered her meetings with me. Since that time, I've seen few as dedicated to Christ as she. Even with the whole country out to get her, she has stayed true to the Word of God, and I've been blessed to watch her grow spiritually. But I fear this is not the place for her just yet."

"What do you mean, 'just yet'?" Chris asked, sitting down across from him.

"I need her to get an education and to return as an American. If she stays here much longer, she will be caught, and that will be the end of the sparks she has ignited. Her acceptance of Christ has encouraged others to believe in Jesus as well. She is very well liked among the people here. Few have ever actually seen her, but she is well-known nonetheless."

"Getting her out of the country is impossible. Even I've been affected by their searches for her."

"I've thought about it a long time and couldn't come up with any solutions. Last night, you came to mind."

"Me?" Chris's eyebrows arched and his eyes widened.

"Chris, Safira needs a new name to be able to go to the States. If the time comes for her to come back, I don't want any suspicion that she is anything but an American. I believe with all my heart that God is going to use her to do great things here, but now is not the time." Pastor Tim's words were urgent.

Chris took a deep breath and leaned back in his chair. He scanned his simple surroundings before meeting the pastor's intent stare. He wasn't ready to accept the insinuation.

Seeing his hesitancy, the pastor decided to continue. "I remembered you telling me you didn't want to get married because you didn't want to worry about a family here. But if you help Safira and give her your name, you wouldn't have to worry about her. She will go to the States, and become the American she needs to be. If she decided to return, you wouldn't need to worry about her. Who could know more about loving this country than a native? I wouldn't have brought this up if I had any doubts it wouldn't work in some way."

"You've given me a weighty decision, Pastor. If I agree, you must understand that my decision would be final, that I'd be true to my vows." Chris's voice was low and intense.

"You are a man of your word. I understood that long ago. If I thought otherwise, I wouldn't have brought this to you. You must know that she is the kind of young lady who measures her words carefully. She has agreed."

"Please give me some time to pray about this. I feel a little bit like I just got hit by a train," Chris said honestly, running a hand through his hair.

"There isn't much time, I'm afraid. The sooner we get her out, the better. The general has been closing in. He must have someone on the inside, so staying ahead of him is increasingly difficult. I don't know how much longer I can do that. I've even used some of the people on this side of the city to harbor her, but that didn't help as much as I'd thought."

"You want me to make a decision *now*?" Chris asked, his eyes widening and his mouth gaping. He could feel the intense urgency resonating from the pastor's words, but found himself automatically rejecting the idea of an arranged marriage.

"Yes, though I do understand the need for prayer and thought." The pastor calmly sat back against his chair and took a sip of tea.

"Well, the verse about not knowing what tomorrow will bring definitely comes to mind. I never would have thought I would be making such a decision today," Chris mumbled as he took a drink from his own teacup. He took a deep breath and began to silently ask for wisdom.

"You say you love these people, and I believe you. What I'm telling you, Chris, is that Safira just might be an important key to helping these people. I don't know how yet, but I know God is going to use her."

Christian stubbornly remained silent. He folded his hands in front of him, elbows on the table, and stared past the man before him. What Pastor Tim was asking was impossible for his mind to comprehend. To marry a complete stranger just to give her his name so she could be rescued was so outside the limits of his own culture. He knew that the Keilronians were a people of arranged marriages, so he understood why the young woman must have agreed to the marriage when it was requested by a male of authority in her life. Chris, on the other hand, had been raised to believe that a love match was the only reason to marry.

Angie came to mind, and he swallowed hard. She had not felt the call or the love for the Keilronians. But this time, the question wasn't if the woman was willing to come to Keilron. It was whether she was willing to come back again someday. If not, how would he handle solitude for the rest of his life? He had made the statement to the pastor and his mother that he hadn't wished to marry, but he knew deep in his heart that he missed having someone special in his life. If he did what Pastor Tim was suggesting, he could lose any future opportunity of finding happiness in a love match. But what was it he had said? Safira was serious about staying true to what she promised. If she didn't return to him, then she too would be losing the hope for a future. Most Keilronian women desired children and a family. Despite her new faith, wouldn't she too be wanting more than a false marriage?

Chris began to pray silently. He felt peace as he accepted the idea and saw the situation from her perspective.

"How old is she?" he asked after ten minutes of silence. He feared the answer. She was the general's only daughter and unwed. She had to be quite young.

"She's eighteen. She is an adult in our society back home. The marriage would be completely legal and accepted there as well," Pastor Tim answered, knowing Chris was calculating and praying about the question.

Chris didn't bat an eye at her age. He remained quiet as the pastor patiently sipped his tea. Several minutes passed as Chris struggled in his heart. Eighteen wasn't so bad. She would be accepted readily back home. The Lord began to play scenes in his mind. The feeling to prepare his home in Colorado and his desire to keep from bringing an American to Keilron. Every step had led to this decision. He exhaled loudly, and a small smile turned up the corners of his mouth. God had been preparing him for an unexpected future.

"All right, I'll do it. I need to make arrangements for her back home, though. Could you give me a week to get everything in order?"

Pastor Tim nodded, and the two discussed a time and place to meet. They prayed earnestly before the pastor departed for the other side of Shemna.

*****

Pastor Tim sent word to Safira that night, and the engagement was settled. She dropped to her knees in prayer and remained there for nearly an hour. She couldn't understand why God was allowing this arrangement, but she did know that it had to be His will. She thanked her Savior and asked for the courage, strength, and determination to stay true to Christ no matter what. She was also consumed with a thankfulness that she would've been betrothed to an unknown man had she not run away, and at least this way, she knew he was a fellow believer. She took great comfort in the thought, and in her praise, she soon found herself praying for Chris's safety.

Chris and Safira prayed for each other the next week before they met at the ceremony on May 26, 2000. Safira tried to be fearless and brave, but it was useless. Her hands shook, and the butterflies in her stomach wouldn't settle down. Along with a few friendly faces, she waited in a separate room of the house for the men to arrive. She knew there were to be a few witnesses, and she was prepared for the quick departure following the ceremony. Everything had been arranged.

When she was told that the men had arrived, she was escorted to the main living room for the ceremony. Her heart nearly stopped when she saw the man next to Pastor Tim. He was several inches taller than she was. She instantly loved his cool blue eyes, and when he tried to give her an assuring smile, her heart fluttered. It would have been a dream to have gotten to know this man. What a shame she wouldn't get the chance. He wasn't at all what she'd expected, though she wasn't sure what she'd expected. He didn't match the image she'd created, but looking at him, she was glad he hadn't.

On the other side of the room, Chris watched as she appeared through the small doorway from what he assumed was a bedroom. Obviously, the woman he'd entrusted had come through and had purchased the new light blue robe trimmed with silver stitching that she now wore. Pastor Tim had warned him that her things were in need of replacing, and although she was leaving her native land for new customs and styles, Chris felt it was appropriate to let her travel in style. Medium height and small framed, she fit the norm for Keilronian women. He could tell she must have taken after her mother because she looked nothing like the general he'd seen. Her eyes, a warm brown, reached into the depths of his soul. Chris was surprised she wasn't wearing the veil today. Her hair, uncovered without the veil and headpiece, was coal black and looked soft and thick. He smiled reassuringly and was rewarded with a small smile in return. She was a beautiful young woman.

When she stood across from him, he reached out and took her hand.

"Safira, it is nice to meet you," his Keilronian was heavily accented.

"Chris, it is good to meet you too."

"I wish the circumstances were different. I want you to understand that I take this seriously, and I feel honored to have you share my name."

"You don't know me." Her voice held bewilderment and her eyebrows narrowed.

"I know of you. Your reputation precedes you." He tried his best to convey his sincerity through his eyes, hoping she would understand he meant her no harm.

She blushed under his gaze.

Pastor Tim smiled as he interrupted their introductions. "We must get on with this. I have a plane waiting for Safira."

It didn't take long for the couple to be officially declared man and wife. Keilronian standards were far different from American weddings. Chris and Safira's was a rare mix between the two cultures. The marriage certificate was not the only document to be signed that day in order for her to enter the United States. As she signed the necessary papers, she knew she was giving her hopes for family away. She looked at the man she'd just given her life to and then looked down and signed the last form before she was taken by the arm and led outside to the waiting missionary plane.

"Wait!" Chris called after her. He caught her before she disappeared with the two men briskly walking with her toward the airfield several miles away. "Here, you'll need this. Everything that's mine back in the United States is now yours too. This folder has everything you'll need to prove you're my wife. All I have is at your disposal, both my family and my home."

Safira climbed into the waiting aircraft two hours later. She thought on the kind words of her new husband before the ceremony and couldn't help but wonder how it would feel to have a man like him actually love her. His touch had almost been her undoing, but at the same time, his gentle way was comforting.

Safira clutched the folder Christian Banks had given her along with the John and Romans translations. Knowing she was leaving Keilron for an undetermined amount of time and understanding the dangers of being a Christian in her homeland gave her no promises that she'd ever know her husband. Even if he did survive, there was no guarantee he would call for her return. No matter the outcome, she had vowed her life to him, and she would keep her word, even from across the sea. With his name, she was allowed an education, and she was rescued from the hardships that remaining in her homeland would cause.

Chris watched her disappear from sight and began to pray for his wife's safe journey. He'd given not only his name to her but also his future. No matter what the cost, he knew he'd done what God wanted. There was still so much to do, but he couldn't help giving one last thought to his new situation. Would he ever get the chance to return to the United States? And if he did, would his bride be waiting? Would it even matter that he'd married a stranger?

The missionary pilot looked over at his charge. She was obviously scared. She was barely eighteen and married, even if only by paper. Adjusting his altitude, he began to pray that in time, Safira would discover what an amazing man had just pledged his life to her. He had known Banks since he'd brought him to Keilron and knew him as a faithful man. Word in the Christian circle regarding Chris was all positive. The stories the pilot had heard of the rich boy gone missionary were enough to convince him that the marriage might be a means to an end, but Chris would keep his commitment to her.

On his lap lay a letter to Chris's best friend, Blake Marty. He knew the letter contained instructions and explanation about Safira. He also understood the importance of getting the letter to Blake before Safira arrived in Colorado. He had been given permission to open the letter and send it via e-mail as soon as he was in Europe.

Chapter 7

New Beginnings

Safira's journey to the United States had been a grueling one. Getting out of Keilron and into London had been nerve-racking enough. Once she'd been safely deposited in London by the pilot, who'd introduced her to a missionary couple. The missionary family willingly hosted her for over a week while she got the rest of her papers in order before flying to the United States.

New York City had been an amazing city to catch a glimpse of. She'd been taught much about the history of the United States and loved looking down on the city where so many immigrants had once passed through for a better life and religious freedom, a reason she could relate to. She followed her instructions and was soon bound for Denver, Colorado. Arriving early Saturday evening in Denver, she took a cab to a local hotel. She reread the letter of information that Chris had given her. One of the tidbits that he'd put in the letter was the name of his home church and when it held services. He'd also given her a large sum of cash for her traveling expenses.

Safira sat quietly in the back of the small country church the next morning. The taxi driver had welcomed the extra cash when he'd delivered her to the small Stonebrook church. The congregation was already singing when she slipped into the back of the white building's meeting room. She couldn't understand the pastor's message, as it was spoken in English. Looking around her, she noticed the variety of families and basked in the warmth she felt from the people seeking after God's words. She felt safe in this house of worship. There were older couples and young families sitting around her. Her husband would've been among the young boys sitting with their families throughout the church several years earlier. What would it have been like to grow up with a Christian family surrounding and supporting you? Was it any wonder Chris was strong in his faith and desire to serve Jehovah?

As the service ended, Safira bowed her head and gave her own thanks to God for His amazing provision as the pastor spoke in the unfamiliar tongue. She wished she had learned English, but her father had forbidden it. She'd learned a few words while staying in the United Kingdom, but her vocabulary was very limited.

A man came forward after the pastor had finished and everyone stood. The organ and piano music mixed with the congregation's voices uplifted her. She'd heard of such things, of course. She'd even learned a few songs from the underground church meetings, but never were they able to sing so loudly and openly. She glanced at her neighbor, a frowning teenage boy not much younger than she, who was mumbling through the song with little enthusiasm. She hummed the unfamiliar tune but couldn't understand the boy's reluctance; maybe he just didn't understand. She'd even sung Christian songs herself, but always quietly and never with accompaniment.

When the song ended, everyone turned to their neighbors and began talking. According to Chris, his family should be within this crowd. How would she be able to find them? She felt a hand touch her shoulder just as she'd decided to leave. Startled, she turned and looked right into the eyes of a tall red-haired man. At a glance, she could tell his eyes were green.

His voice was friendly, but she couldn't understand him. She wanted to converse with this fellow Christian brother, but she knew her words would not help the situation. He stared at her for a moment before saying something she did recognize.

He pointed to himself. "I'm Blake Marty, Christian Banks' friend." She nodded, indicating she understood. One of the few words she did understand was "friend."

Motioning for her to follow him, he guided her through the groups of people. He stopped in front of a small cluster of women. Two of the older women gave hugs to the younger two and walked away. Just as the two women turned toward them, a young man glided in behind the women and leaned on the back of the pew.

"Chris's family," he spoke. "Kate," he touched the young lady on the shoulder. The girl was nearly the same age as Safira. "Fay," he offered as he gestured toward the middle-aged lady. Safira connected the dots in her mind. Fay had to be Chris's mom. "And this is JC" Blake nodded to the teenager leaning on the pew behind the girls. The boy had very few similarities to Chris.

"Hello," she said with a heavy accent.

The family all smiled. Fay looked at her new daughter with understanding. Fay gently took Safira's hand.

Blake had learned Keilronian from Chris in limited conversation and through letter; however, he had little experience actually speaking it. He was the only one who had any communication skills, and although he fumbled through it, he was able to get an invitation extended to Safira to join the family for dinner.

Blake stayed with the Banks family for the afternoon, offering support to Safira and some minimal translation assistance between the new family members. Safira was grateful for the strange red-headed man's help, but she began to feel the exhaustion of her trip catching up with her.

Fay noticed the girl grow more tired. Safira valiantly tried to stay alert to the family around her, but Fay saw that it was time to let her rest.

"When did you arrive in Colorado?" Fay asked.

Safira looked at her in concentration as if she could somehow decipher the language if she thought hard enough. Blake, a patient teacher, pointed at his watch and then gestured to the table as he expressed the question again, rephrasing it so she could understand the keywords that made the question recognizable.

"Yesterday," she responded in Keilronian.

Blake translated her answer and then turned to her, repeating her answer in English. She tried to speak the strange word.

Fay nodded, understanding washing over her. She stood and walked over to Safira and extended her hand. The younger woman took it and followed Fay while the rest of the family remained seated.

"How did you recognize her as Chris's new bride?" Kate inquired.

"Well, the pilot who took her to Europe e-mailed me Chris's letter. I printed the letter for you guys, but the pilot also personally e-mailed me a picture he'd taken of her. He figured she would be delayed in Europe for a bit before she reached us, and he wanted me to have a way to keep my eye out for her."

Kate nodded and took another sip of water. Fay returned to the family only a few minutes later and began to clear the table. JC and Blake headed to the living room as Kate joined her mother.

"I'm home for the summer, so I'll try to see if she wants to go to the community college for some English lessons with me this fall," Kate said to her mother as they washed the dishes.

"She'll need a friend, Kate," Fay said, still amazed that her daughter was headed to her freshmen year of college in a matter of months.

"I know, Mom."

"Try to remember that she's your sister-in-law."

"Only on paper. Chris explained that in his letter."

"Doesn't matter. She still needs a friend more than an instructor," Fay gently reminded.

JC entered the kitchen. "What's for dessert?"

"What do you think of our new member?" asked Fay, ignoring her son's question.

"She seems young, like she should be a senior in high school or something."

"She is eighteen, JC," Fay smiled.

"I think I should take her to school with me," he grinned. At fifteen, Jeremy Caleb was at the top of his freshman class and was popular to boot, even among the upper classman.

Fay shook her head and was about to comment when the backdoor opened, and her husband walked up behind her. Her children knew when it was time to leave. With hurried "later, Mom" and "hi,

Dads," the two skittered out of the kitchen. It wasn't usual for their father to be away on a Sunday, but Grandma Kleren had been failing, and Harris spent time with her as often as possible at the nursing home. Her funeral wouldn't be long in coming, but the grandchildren were uncomfortable staying by her side as her health deteriorated.

"I saw Blake as he was leaving, and he told me he'd met our new daughter."

"As we all did. How is your mother?"

"She's doing as well as can be expected. So what is she like?"

"Safira?"

"No, our other daughter-in-law," he teased, even as he wrapped her in a hug.

"She's petite and young. She speaks only a few words in English, and she is absolutely exhausted from her trip. She's sleeping upstairs in Chris's old room. She only arrived last night. I'm surprised the jet lag didn't get her before today."

"Poor girl. She was probably running on adrenaline."

"I think so, but she is trying so hard. She's more at home than I would have thought possible. Chris must have told her something about us."

"Perhaps. Chris speaks of a country that has harsh restrictions on women, and Christianity is punishable by death. Is it any wonder she'd be more relaxed here? Have you heard from Chris?"

"Nothing except what Blake related to us."

"Maybe we should consider letting her stay here for now. We've got the spare room. I'd think that staying with strangers will be better than being by herself, at least for now."

"I quite agree, Harris Kleren." She smiled at her husband before he kissed her and headed for the shower.

The first week Safira was with the Banks family, the conversations consisted mostly of gestures. Fay had extended her hand of friendship, and the two worked together in the kitchen or the garden. Fay was surprised that these times were not spent in silence. Safira, being a student to the core, kept asking questions both verbally and through gestures. She was constantly asking the name of things she already knew. She asked for the name of foods, utensils, objects, plants, even cars, and clothing. Safira filed the information away quickly and began to speak of the objects in English.

Fay was so mesmerized by Safira's growing knowledge and desire to learn the language to communicate she didn't immediately notice her daughter-in-law's meager wardrobe. The Keilronian robes reminded Fay of the Muslims. She didn't worry about it though, as Safira hadn't expressed any desire for change.

Fay prayed for wisdom in approaching Safira on her wardrobe. In the end, Blake finally handed her the transcribed e-mail the pilot had relayed from Chris. The message indicated that one of the lessons Safira needed to be taught was to blend in. Fay knew of only one way to help. It was time to introduce the girl to the American mall.

Fay entered their nearby mall with Safira and watched as she became instantly overwhelmed by all that surrounded her. Safira was experiencing the stores she'd never seen before, and Fay was going to suggest clothing that would expose her neck, arms, and legs. Taking things one step at a time, Fay breathed a prayed for guidance as they walked toward a large department store.

"Look!" Safira spoke with awe as they passed by an arcade store.

Fay smiled and looped her arm with Safira's. "If you think that's something, wait till we get you some new clothes to wear."

"Bad?" Safira asked, looking down at her clothing. Safira knew her clothes were getting thin, and they certainly didn't help her to blend in. The traditional Keilronian robes made people take a second glance. She'd noticed the stares but thought she could do nothing about it. Her understanding of the English language had grown considerably because she'd been so immersed in it. She felt proud of all she'd come to understand in such a short time.

Fay smiled at Safira.

Inside the store, Safira's eyes opened even wider in awe at all the clothing. Shemna had many venues, but the merchants were specific to one thing. One vendor might sell veils, while another would sell material for new robes, and yet another might be specialized in jewelry. Safira saw so many options and choices, the kind of choices she did not have in her homeland. She looked up at Fay like a five-year-old going to her first birthday party.

"Here?" she asked, her eyes wide and her mouth gapping.

Fay smiled encouragingly. "I'll help."

Safira entered the dressing room with more than a few questionable items of clothing. She hesitated only momentarily before opening the door and showing Fay the jeans and a blue T-shirt. Fay had decided to keep things as easy as possible to begin with.

Fay smiled because she'd half expected to find a tiny figure beneath Safira's Keilron robes, but she had been sorely mistaken. Safira's frame was petite, but her figure was womanly.

"No like?" Safira asked when she'd seen the open stare of her mother-in-law.

"Yes, I like it very much."

To Safira's dismay and Fay's satisfaction, they went to the front after two hours with many new clothes for Safira. Most of Safira's clothing choices included long skirts and high-necked T-shirts and blouses. If Fay knew her daughter, Kate would soon have Safira comfortable in jeans and sleeveless shirts, but they had to start somewhere.

Safira wasn't comfortable with her new clothing choices. But she couldn't refuse her mother-in-law's generosity, so she walked from the store and blushed when Fay took her to the restrooms and asked her to change.

She did so with some regret and felt like the lamb as the lion prepared to pounce on its prey. She said nothing as Fay took her inside another shop. This one was not at all like the first. The first had many racks of clothing, but this shop was open and had lower and upper cabinets along the walls like a kitchen and chairs that were attached to the floor. She watched as one of the workers easily adjusted her client's position by twirling the chair a quarter turn to the right. Fay spoke a few words to a lady sitting at a desk as they walked in. The woman nodded and waved Safira to follow her. Safira sat on the proffered chair and stared ahead at the mirror between the upper and lower cabinets.

Safira heard Fay giving instructions, and before she could protest, her braided hair was undone and fell loose against the back of the chair. Not willing to offend her mother-in-law, she once again accepted what would happen. Her hair had not been cut since she had become a woman and was so long it went just below her knees when she stood up. She felt her hair lifted and heard the snip of the scissors. Safira wanted to cry out with dismay. In Keilron, a woman's hair was her best attribute, but now, it was four inches below her shoulders. She felt herself leaning backward toward a sink where the woman who cut off her precious hair washed what was left.

The entire process was soon over. Her hair was dried with the use of a handheld machine that blew hot air. The lady gave her a mirror, and she gasped at the stranger looking back at her. She was no longer a Keilronian woman, but a young American lady. She looked at Fay and realized what she'd been doing. She could never return to Keilron as she'd been. She'd have been recognized and imprisoned despite her new name. But returning as an American would be possible. No one would guess that the American woman was one of their own. Safira resolved to learn the English language and to adopt it as her own.

"Yes, you are American now, Safira. And you are my daughter," Fay said as she stepped behind Safira. She couldn't understand all the words, but she understood enough.

Safira nodded. She had no English words to express her emotions. She understood the clothes and realized as she glanced around the mall that they were plain and modest. She would just need to grow accustomed to the change. Her hair looked beautiful, and she appreciated the input her new mother had given.

She gave Fay the only words she knew. "Thank you," she whispered as a tear of joy slipped down her cheek.

Part 2

Safira Banks

Chapter 8

The Dove

Shemna, Keilron
July 2000

"Have you found my daughter?" Rofisca's voice was calm. He didn't look up from his desk when the reporting officer entered the general's headquarters.

"I've seen her," the voice said casually.

Rofisca's head looked up, his eyes glazed, ready to chastise the soldier for insubordination only to find the eyes of his eldest son calmly staring back.

"Narshac, what are you doing here?" Rofisca sighed.

"Your interest in my sister also interests me."

"What does she have to do with you?" Rofisca sighed.

Narshac stared at his father as Rofisca returned his attention to the papers on his desk. Narshac looked down at his hands and then back to his father.

"I've seen her. Several months ago, here in Shemna," Narshac admitted.

"She's not here anymore." Rofisca didn't even lift his gaze.

"How do you know that?"

"I closed off the borders and put out a red flag on her name and image. There is no way she could have escaped, but my findings have revealed scarcely anything. According to sources, she is outside our borders, perhaps in Europe or the States. I'm not sure finding her is in our power at the moment."

"You will give up then?" Narshac almost hoped his father would let her go.

Rofisca glared at his son. "No, I will not. If she gets away with this, then others will attempt the same."

Narshac accepted the criticism with outward humility, but inwardly, he seethed. "I must go, Father. May the gods help you in your search. I hope to see my sister again."

Rofisca's gaze immediately turned back to his work. Narshac turned and left his father's office with a clenched jaw. He dearly loved his sister, but his father's unnatural attachment to her had always baffled him. With Safira out of the picture, he'd hoped that his father would recognize his accomplishments. He knew better now.

*****

"Pull it tighter," Narshac commanded as missionary Brandon Moore let out a scream from the pain. "Do you know where Safira Rofisca is?" He repeated his original question.

Sweat streamed off the man's nose, "I . . . I've seen her only once and heard her name a dozen times. But I don't know what has become of her. I haven't heard anything in months."

Narshac turned from his captive and spoke sharply to the young soldier awaiting orders.

"Send him to the guillotine at dawn, unless of course"—Narshac turned toward Brandon—"you desire to denounce your Jehovah and bow before our gods?"

Brandon's tormented eyes stared back at his assailant. "Would you deny a friend who died in your place?"

"Gods are not friends, you imbecile. They are to be worshiped and feared." Narshac's jaw clenched as he spat out the words before the infidel.

"My God is sufficient for me. He is my friend, my Savior from hell. You may torment, mutilate, and kill this body, but my soul is safe."

"What peace you Christians have, all foolish notions," Narshac's voice was subdued.

"Why, then, do you stay to hear my final words?"

"Someone must be here for you to confess your sins to." Narshac nodded to the men operating the rack. They pulled a little more on the ropes, sending Moore into shouts of pain once again.

Narshac dismissed his guard. "Leave me."

"You say you have heard the name of Safira Rofisca. Is her faith in this Christ?"

"Yes," he gasped.

Narshac's voice was sad. "Then in time, I must ask the gods to spare her life."

"Why ask mercy for someone other than yourself?"

"She is my beloved sister. She has found favor with many," he reasoned.

"Have you found favor with Christ?"

"I don't know what you mean. How do you desire to die? I shall honor your request."

"Why do you offer me mercy now?"

Narshac took a step forward and raised his eyebrows at the older man. "I stand here asking you how you wish to die, and you consider that a kindness?"

"Why not? This earth is a hard journey. If you kill me, my worries will be over, and I'll be held in the arms of my Savior, the only one who can forgive sins."

"Then be at peace. I shall deliver you into the hands of your god. Only pray He is merciful."

"I wish to die quickly, if you will not let me go. But please let me tell you my God's story."

"Blasphemy," Narshac's voice sounded noncommittal. He was no longer sure it was blasphemy. Did his gods really live? He knew he would not suffer death for his gods. What, then, possessed these Christians to be so willing to die?

Narshac refused to dwell on his own uncertainties. He was a soldier, and it was his duty to satisfy his commanders.

He left the room and spoke to the missionary's executioners. "Let him die quickly."

Both men nodded without question. They both knew that Narshac was General Rofisca's heir and favored of Shovak. Unless the Christian man withheld information, there was no need to further torture the poor soul. The men understood Narshac was a man of both mercy and justice. They were loyal to him to a fault and often discussed the possibilities for their country when Rofisca eventually handed things down to Narshac. Any man who worked under Narshac knew that the country would be in capable hands when the general resigned.

*****

Chris knew he couldn't mail a letter to his family without it being intercepted by the government. He felt eyes watching him every time he stepped out of the house. Because he was an American, he was automatically suspect. The moment Safira's trail had gone cold, the general had begun turning over every rock, seeking Christians. Chris knew every foreigner was being spied on and that it was not under suspicion of Christianity, but rather aiding and abetting a fugitive. He'd been careful with his job and had poured more into it than before, just to divert interest from himself. Thanks to Pastor Tim, he'd become a Keilronian translator for the government. Translating between English-speaking dignitaries and Keilronian officials was common, but so was translating government letters, treaties, and foreign policies from Keilronian to English and vice versa. He was doing his job, but he was also translating the forbidden. Pastor Kindel and he were finishing the book of Mark, and both men were becoming more and more aware of the eyes following them. Chris bowed his head and prayed once again for his family and wife back in the states. At last, he chose to write a letter, but it had to be coded in some way. He needed to write a letter because otherwise, the government would notice the lack of communication to his family. Any suspicion of him had to be dealt with as easily and quickly as possible. So he wrote, trying to keep the letter as uninteresting as he could.

*****

Dear Mom,

I'm okay. The translation work is much harder and more challenging than I thought. It's been a while since I've written, but I've been preoccupied with work. Just wanted to know how the family is doing and if Kate has been taking care of my Dove. I'll try to let you know how I'm doing every couple of months or so, but time seems to be slipping by quickly. I shall return home whenever my time here is done. I hope to see you soon. Don't bother to write. I really am only making sure that you are watching over my Dove. Someday, I'd like to see her again. I'll try to come home before she is too old.

Christian Banks

"Reseal it, and send it. There's nothing there even remotely stating he is in anyway associated with the Christians or Safira. A pet dove. Now, I didn't see that coming," the guard said as he handed the letter back to the mail carrier.

"I told you, sire, he's just what he says he is." The man stuffed the letter back into his bag and shrugged at the soldier.

"You're probably right. I think it's time we ease up a little bit."

"Yes, sir," the mail carrier said as he walked down the street to finish his route.

Stonebrook, Colorado
October 2000

Kate exploded into the living room where her mom was stretched out on the coach watching the local news. "Mom, I got a letter from Chris!" Fay reached for the remote and muted the television.

"As did I, what's yours say?" Fay asked as she pulled her legs out of the way for Kate to sit on the sofa with her.

"I've read it four times and can't figure it out." Kate opened the letter up and began to read. "Kate, I'm checking to see how you are and asking about my dove. I just wanted to make sure you're keeping an eye on her. She's young, and I was a little concerned about her when I left. Poor thing, she's too young to have a broken wing. Tell me about college. Have you found any cute boys to bring home yet?"

"I got a similar letter. He's trying to ask about Safira, I think. In Shemna, he's still known as a translator. If they suspect him of anything, it's the government's right to read the letters he sends out. He cannot call her by name and must seem oblivious to Safira's departure. He's protecting himself."

"I understand." Kate stared at the letter in her hands. Her eyes were moist when she looked up at her mom. "It's just now dawning on me. When I said goodbye to him, it might have been final goodbye."

Tears sparkled in Fay's eyes as she nodded in agreement. "That's why it was so hard."

Kate scooted across the sofa and leaned into her mom's side. She looked young and vulnerable to Fay.

Safira was in her room when she heard Kate's voice. Eager to show her sister the college application she'd gotten earlier that day, she bounded down the stairs. When she hit the last step, she could hear mother and daughter talking in soft, almost sad, tones. She held her breath and leaned against the wall. Safira knew eavesdropping wasn't right, but she still felt like an outsider sometimes and often wondered if they were put out by her presence. As she listened, she picked up bits and pieces, and from what she understand, she sighed quietly. These two wonderful women were concerned, it seemed, for Christian.

Safira closed her eyes and let her head rest against the wall. She clutched the application in her hand and let herself feel, if only for a moment, the aloneness she often felt. Most times, she was able to push it to the back of her mind. Every day, she smiled and asked questions to better acquaint herself with the American language and culture, hoping that by doing so, she would somehow earn the right to be a part of this wonderful, welcoming family. They were always kind to her. But she could not shake the feeling of isolation.

Safira lifted her heart to the heavens, praying that Jesus would keep her husband safe. She did not know him, but she could tell by his family that he was a good man. The family photos and the obvious love the women of his family had for him and for each other was evidence enough for Safira. She wanted to know her husband!

Safira tiptoed back upstairs, unwilling to disturb her adopted family. She entered her room and shut the door as softly as a whisper. Going to her bed, she reached for her pillow and hugged it to her chest. Try as she might to hold herself together and be brave, she couldn't hold her tears back any longer. She wanted to be emotionally strong, but the truth was, her heart was still breaking. Even when she thought it could shatter no more, she felt it crack. Alone now with no one near to hear, she brought her legs up on the bed, lay down, still clutching the pillow, and wept for the family she could no longer see, the husband she could not know, and the family she would never feel she belonged to.

Later that evening, Safira sat cross-legged on her bed facing Kate, who held the college application and a pen. They'd been trying for the last half hour to fill it out. The college offered English as a second language classes, and Safira was anxious to take them, along with a few college math classes. The application was a little more complicated since Safira was not yet an American citizen. The information and paperwork confused her, and Kate was growing impatient.

Safira sat with a false peace, trying her best to understand the information Kate wanted from her. The two young women were at a standoff since neither knew how to communicate further. Kate's growing frustration at her inability to explain and Safira's own lack of English understanding forced the two into silence. Safira had learned enough English to communicate most of the time. Over the last five months, she'd come a long way with her English, but her understanding of government documents and protocols that would allow her into the school was inadequate. A wave of relief swept over Safira when the phone rang. Kate jumped up to answer.

"Hello," she paused, "Safira?" she questioned the speaker. "Yes, hold on." Kate handed the cordless phone to Safira.

"Hello?" She answered. Her eyes knit together. Who would call her?

Safira's eyes widened, and a smile stretched across her face the moment she heard the Keilronian greeting. She bounced off the bed and began to pace.

"Tim! It's so good to hear from you." Safira knew that his calls might have been monitored so she did her best to hide his identity as a Christian.

"I wanted to see how you are doing."

Safira heard the concern in his voice and knew he was sincere. Several minutes passed as she briefly brought him up to date. To speak her own language and be understood lifted her spirits. Knowing he wouldn't be able to speak at great length with her, she tried to keep her enthusiasm and stories short. If the pastor was able, why couldn't Chris? The pleasure of speaking with Pastor Tim would have to be enough. There was no doubt in Safira's mind that there were reasons Chris couldn't call and Pastor Tim could. Calls were often monitored, particularly if a person was under suspicion. She had no way of knowing what was going on at the moment and knew better than to ask.

Kate watched in awe as Safira became animated. She had suddenly come to life in a way that was unfamiliar to Kate. Usually, Safira was reserved and watchful, soaking in everything she could. Kate got the impression that Safira had a meek and quiet spirit. She had to admit that perhaps she didn't know her sister-in-law as well as she thought.

"Tim, I can't understand. Kate is trying her best to help, but my English is still so limited. I'm becoming quite frustrated," Safira admitted as she closed her brief explanation of the last five months.

Pastor Tim chuckled kindly on the other end. "It sounds like you have been learning a lot. Perhaps I can help with this problem while I'm on the line. Give the phone to Kate."

Safira offered Kate the phone. After listening to the pastor for a brief moment, she put the phone on speaker. With the pastor's help, Kate was relieved to finally get the answers she needed to help Safira finish the application. When the job was done, Kate handed the phone back to Safira, and Kate slipped out the door.

Kate had been thankful for the pastor's interpretation. She knew she'd have Safira in college soon, and things were going to work out. But still she wondered, with a slight smile, how long it would be before she and her sister-in-law could actually get to know each other.

Safira was surprised that the pastor stayed on the line for another fifteen minutes with her. She knew the forty-minute phone call would cost him dearly. As she said goodbye, tears trailed down her cheeks. The phone still in her hand, she let out a deep sigh. His words of encouragement still soothed her aching heart. She smiled and sent a prayer of thanks to God for the gesture of love she'd just experienced. Setting the phone back into its cradle and heading downstairs to join the family, she wondered, briefly, what had possessed Pastor Kindel to call her in the first place. He had mostly listened, offering only the briefest advice and counsel.

Shemna, Keilron

Shovak walked into Rofisca's office and found him sitting at his desk.

"I've something interesting to show you, Rofisca. Come into my office," Shovak said.

Rofisca was rarely invited into Shovak's personal space and knew that something was happening. He followed Shovak and noticed a strange box on Shovak's desk.

"You've heard of the computer. The Americans have them, as do most of the world. I decided to try it first before I begin to update some of our government buildings or at least parts of them."

Rofisca was greatly interested as Shovak began to show him how to work the Internet.

"What I don't know, I have hired an expert to help us learn. He's at your disposal as well," Shovak said, handing him a phone number. "Your computer will be here in a few days and will be installed in your office immediately."

From everything Rofisca had heard of the Internet and computer technology, he knew there was nearly unlimited access to the rest of the world through their use. His mind began to turn, *Maybe there was a way to track her down after all.*

*****

Pastor Tim felt the grip on his arm the moment he stepped into Chris's home.

"Did you speak with her? How is she doing? Is she adjusting? Is she with my family? Are they treating her well?"

The older man chuckled and placed a hand on the young man's shoulder. Meeting his gaze, he replied, "She is doing well. Lonely to some degree, I think, but she is adjusting. She is with your family for now, has been since she arrived. I get the feeling she won't be for long. She was applying for a college somewhere closer to Denver and will probably have to move closer. She misses her people. Kate was the one helping her get into the college."

A smile played at Chris's mouth as he stared at the wall over the pastor's shoulder. "That sounds like Kate."

"Maybe you should consider visiting for a couple of weeks."

"No, I'm needed here. Perhaps next summer."

"Maybe you should consider writing to them all more frequently. Kate asked about you before she got off."

"Probably right. I just have a hard time knowing how to write them when it's obvious the government checks my mail."

The pastor nodded in understanding. "I need to keep moving. I've several people I'm meeting with this evening and have an appointment to keep in the government building." The two shook hands, and Chris was soon left alone in his small abode.

He sat down and sipped his cold tea. The pastor was right. But how was he going to send letters to his family without being able to ask the questions that he so wished to express?

Chapter 9

Becoming American

Safira smiled as she glided the steps and met Kate. She wore her favorite pair of jeans and forest green blouse that Kate had purchased for her on one of their shopping sprees.

Safira grinned, "Let's go."

Kate noticed Safira's command of the English language was improving dramatically.

"It's a bit chilly outside. You may want a coat," Kate advised, knowing that Safira was not used to the Colorado chill.

Safira took a moment to grab her coat as she walked out the door. Kate had been giving Safira driving lessons for weeks, and Safira was going to take her driving test today.

Waiting in the office by the licensing building some time later, Kate glanced at her phone to check the time. She thought about her sister's look of excitement every time she got in a vehicle. Safira had never driven or ridden anything other than horses. Safira wasn't back yet, but she figured that was a good sign. Kate knew she would pass because she was a good driver; still, she remained nervous for her friend.

Safira put the car in park and smiled sweetly at her male instructor. He was younger, probably in his late twenties, with black hair and blue eyes.

He looked stern as he reviewed her scores.

"You are a good driver. There are, however, a few things you need to keep in mind."

Safira's heart sank to her stomach as the instructor began naming off mistakes from her driving.

"All in all, you did very well. I'm going to pass you."

Safira's heart once again found its rightful place as she let out a deep breath. She thanked him, and after taking the paper from him and hearing his instructions, she exited the car. She nearly skipped back to the building where Kate waited.

Kate smiled as Safira came to her, grinning from ear to ear.

"I pass," she said.

Later that evening as the family gathered around the living room fireplace and entertainment center, Safira surprised them all.

"I learn to read well, yes?"

"Yes, you have," Fay encouraged as she curled up to Harris on the couch. He automatically wrapped his arm around her as he took a drink from his mug of hot coffee. Safira was becoming accustomed to her parents-in-law's acts, but it still made her feel uneasy, sad even, knowing that she would not feel the tenderness of her husband, even if she did see his face again. Safira knew full well the dangers of Keilron.

"When I left Shemna, my husband gave me folder. I was not able to read then. I can now. I understand what he was trying to tell me. He told me everything that is his is mine. Last night, I found folder, and I open it. I read the documents. I understand I have a house not far from my college." Safira scanned the room, briefly meeting each family member's gaze briefly. The folder she spoke of lay on her lap.

"Yes, you do," Harris said matter-of-factly. He felt his wife tense up. She obviously was unprepared for this conversation.

"I want to go there. I have driver's license. Drive would be quick," she explained, looking at Harris. She glanced at Fay and over to Kate's stunned expression. "I come here on weekends for visit," she quickly added. She wouldn't want them to think she was leaving permanently. The long drive to classes was tiring, and she had considered moving to the dorms before she'd found the folder.

"Don't you need a car first?" JC asked.

"I have one," she said, pulling out a car title from the folder. She offered it to Harris, but he held his hand up indicating he didn't need the evidence. JC may have asked the question, but to Safira's understanding, it would be up to Harris to approve her move.

"You're right. You do have a car, Chris's old one," Harris confirmed.

JC's eyes moved to his dad. "I thought he sold it."

"No, it's been hiding in Blake's garage," Harris replied.

"Man, how'd I miss that opportunity?" JC sighed.

Harris and Fay chuckled in unison at their son. Safira's head cocked to one side as her eyes shifted between JC and his parents.

"Chris's car is an American sports car. JC wishes he'd had the opportunity to drive it around," Fay graciously explained.

Safira nodded in understanding, and her eyes softened as she sat waiting for her own questions to be answered.

"Safira, let me contact Blake and see what he's willing to do. Could you maybe wait till after Christmas to move to Chris's place?" Harris asked.

Safira nodded and relaxed as JC loaded his metal hanger with marshmallows and stuck them into the fire.

> Dear Chris,
>
> How are you? I've been keeping an eye on your dove. Her wing is healing nicely. She's even beginning to sing. Marty has been keeping his eye on her. I love your dove. She's ready to begin flying again, although we are taking it slowly.
>
> I miss your letters and hope you are doing well. I know you are very busy. Kate is doing well with school, but she hasn't brought any boys home yet. You would be proud of your little sister. JC was quite disappointed to discover that Blake has been hiding the Camaro in his garage rather than allowing JC to drive it. Otherwise, he joined the basketball team and is doing well. Your dad misses you and sends his love.
>
> By the time you receive this letter, I'm afraid your grandma Kleren will have passed. She lived

a good long life: don't mourn her. But rejoice, she is no longer suffering. Keep safe, my dear. Please write soon. I love you.

Love, Mom

Fay set her pen down and folded the paper. A tear fell down her cheek as she thought about her son in a land where Christianity was outlawed. The tears continued to fall as she folded her hands in silent prayer. She'd worried and fretted over him for more than a year since he'd gone to Keilron, but that day, she finally laid her son in the Savior's hands knowing full well that she may never see him on earth again.

Harris stood in the doorway watching her before he sat down beside her on the bed where she'd been writing. He held her hand and waited. The look on her face told him she was struggling through something on her mind, and it probably had something to do with her oldest son.

Harris spoke quietly, opening the subject up for her to bare her heart to him. "Chris is not my son by blood, but since I've married you, he's been as much my son as yours. I love him dearly. I too fear for his life."

"I've just given him to Christ. I hadn't really done that before," she confessed.

Harris wrapped his arms around his wife and let her cry. They both knew the dangers Chris was facing, and once Fay's tears ceased, Harris prayed with her for their son.

December 2000

Safira walked to the mailbox and began flipping through the letters as she briskly walked back to the warm house. Her heart almost stopped when she saw the letter from Keilron. The return address was unknown, and she feared the content of the letter, but it was addressed to D.S. Banks. Who was that?

She handed the mail to Fay as she held onto the envelope, somehow hoping it was for her.

"Fay? This letter is addressed to a D.S. Banks. Do you know who that might be? It's from Keilron," she said.

"I have my suspicions that might be you. Open it and find out. I don't know who else it might mean."

Safira moved to the living room, curled up in her favorite spot on the sofa, and tore open the letter. She scanned the contents and instantly knew that the letter must be for her because it was written in Keilronian.

> *Dear D.S.,*
>
> *You may wonder at the context of this letter. You may not understand why I have addressed you now. I've been thinking a lot about our last meeting and realized that I would hate for that to be the last time we had contact. My colleague, Tim Kindel, is most encouraging that I take every opportunity to get to know all of my family. I agree with him, and consequently, I find myself writing you this letter. I understood you were interested in Keilron, so I have written to you in the language. I will try to keep you informed of any developments that are not broadcasted on the air. I'm not sure that you will immediately accept my attempts to make amends, but I'm hoping you will at least consider corresponding with me.*
>
> *I hope my friend Blake Marty has befriended you. I meant what I said when we last met. I'm pleased to hear that you have accepted my word and have now made yourself at ease. Please write me back. I will continue to write to you.*
>
> *Yours, Chris Banks*

Safira reread the words a few more times before setting the letter down. She prayed for God's guidance. It was unbelievable that her husband had written her. Even though she knew the letter was nondescript and that he could have been writing to a cousin, her heart filled with joy at the notion that her husband willingly took the risk of writing her.

She tried to calm her heart and let herself remember she was his wife, but only on paper. In Keilron, a woman was lucky to find herself married to the man she loved, and even then, she'd have to share him with other wives. Only God's grace would allow her to see his face again. She jumped up, ran up to her room, and grabbed a pen and paper. She sat at her desk and began to write.

*****

Christmas break was exciting for Safira. The Kleren family included her in all their holiday preparations and activities. She was in awe when the family went to a place where they sold trees with needles, referred to by JC as Christmas trees. Her excitement built as she watched the family drag their chosen tree into the house, set it into a stand that held it upright, and began decorating the tree with lights, popcorn strings, and ornaments of all kinds.

As Christmas got closer, she watched in anticipation as more gifts were added under the tree every day.

She smiled at Kate walking into her room on Christmas morning.

"Merry Christmas, Saf!" she exclaimed excitedly.

Safira grinned and pushed herself from bed, grabbed her robe, and headed downstairs with Kate. The night before, Kate had told children's tales about Santa Clause and the giving of gifts.

She had seen the number of gifts beneath the tree the night before, but now, she could only gasp at the bottom of the tree. Gifts piled high were wrapped in shiny, colorful paper. Pastor Tim had explained these traditions to her the year before, but she found it fascinating. Willingly, she'd purchased gifts for her new family and wrapped them herself. The fire was lit, giving extra warmth to the room; and on the mantle, five stockings hung, stuffed to the brim.

Harris smiled as he entered the living room with a steaming cup of coffee in one hand and his wife at his side. Fay smiled at the scene. Like a child, Safira's eyes sparkled with joy.

"Go ahead, Safira, see what's under that tree for you," Harris suggested.

Safira got down on her knees and began to hand everyone their gifts.

*****

Chris opened his Bible early Christmas morning. He read the Christmas story and once more marveled at how the Creator of the world would come to save mankind. Leaning back in his chair, he closed his eyes in prayer for a moment before thoughts of home began to overwhelm him. He knew the streets downtown would be covered in lights and nativity scenes.

Thinking of the differences between his two beloved countries, he thought of his young wife. *Wife*, now that was a concept he still had difficulty comprehending. She must be overwhelmed by all the outward celebrations of Christ's birth as well as traditions previously unknown to her. He must have been foolish to send the gifts to his homeland, but he hadn't been able to resist.

He prayed a while more that his family and his wife back in the states would have a wonderful Christmas. He stood and left his house, weaving his way through the streets to Pastor Tim's small gathering.

*****

After the gifts were unwrapped and the contents of the stockings had been revealed, the Klerens all seemed to disappear for a moment, leaving Safira to think. She smiled and prayed for the Klerens and for Chris spending his Christmas away from his family. She couldn't imagine how he must feel after she experienced the excitement at the Kleren's home.

The family members returned, each holding a Bible. They opened the Bibles to Luke 2 and began reading the Christmas story. Safira closed her eyes and listened. She never could get over the words of the Bible now that she could understand the English language. How beautiful the words were to her ears.

At that moment, she realized how important it would be for her people to read and hear the word of God. And her husband was doing all he could to accomplish just that. The room grew silent when the story ended. Safira opened her eyes and spoke.

"I want to pray for my father, Shovak, my brother who let me go, and my other brother Narshac. They have always shown me mercy." Giving Fay a sheepish look, she said, "And my husband's safety."

The family nodded, and their joyous occasion turned into a time of prayer for those in Keilron who were not allowed to enjoy Christmas this year.

Blake gently tapped on the door before he entered the house as he'd done many times before. In his arms, he carried a large box. Blake smiled at the scene before him as he entered the living room. Every one of them was bowed in prayer over their Bibles, with wrapping paper strewn all over. Once Harris closed his prayer, Blake announced himself.

"Good news! You guys are not done with Christmas yet."

Kate and the others smiled at him as he set the large box down.

"Last night, a rather large package was delivered to my home. I believe it is from a man in Keilron."

Smiles broadened as Blake took out his pocketknife and opened the box. He immediately began handing carefully wrapped packages to each person.

Blake smiled gently at Safira as he handed her a box. "He wouldn't forget you, dear," he whispered to her.

Safira unwrapped the small box. Inside, she found a shiny silver dove pendant with its wings outstretched dangling from a silver chain. She felt a tear slide down her face. Her estranged husband gave her a gift from across the sea. She knew his kindness must stem from his love of Christ. He didn't even know her. What other reason would he have bestowed such a gift to her? The family around her had each received a small, but thoughtful gift.

Knowing her thoughts, Blake smiled.

"You are his wife. One way or another, he would not forget that," Blake whispered to her as the family moved from the living room to the kitchen for the scrumptious Christmas breakfast Fay had prepared.

"He does not know me, and I've seen his face only once," she reasoned as she put on the necklace.

"In his eyes, you are his responsibility, and that alone is reason enough for him to love you."

"He must be a man of great honor, if he thinks of a wife he does not know."

"You are a Keilronian who has sacrificed everything for Christ. What more does he need to know?"

Safira continued to shake her head in protest.

Blake rested a hand on her shoulder till she looked up at him. "Saf, you are special, even if you don't see that."

"Thank you, Blake. You are good friend."

Today was a happy day, and Blake knew it was time to move on. He shifted his gaze above Safira's head and sniffed the air. "Let's go get some breakfast. Smells like Fay's outdone herself."

"Where your family?" Safira asked as she stood and began to follow him.

"My parents live in Europe. They're missionaries to Ireland, and I see them once every other year or so."

"That long?"

"I've made my life here, and they belong there. We do have phones and e-mail."

Safira blushed; she'd forgotten that the American luxuries of communication were also in Europe.

Her mind moved back to family as the feast was set before them on the dining room table. The aroma of eggs, bacon, and cinnamon rolls tempted her nostrils as she sat down and enjoyed the fellowship with her new family. Occasionally, her mind would wander back to the Keilronian Christians who were this day celebrating in hidden walls and spaces throughout Shemna's neighborhoods.

*****

After the New Year, Blake was helpful in getting Safira set up in Chris's home and willingly handed her keys to the Camaro. Though her new home was only an hour away from the Kleren's, they were sad to see her go. They gave her hugs, wished her good luck, and made promises to see each other the next Sunday for church.

Once her few things were moved into the fully furnished Victorian-style house, Blake, who'd been the caretaker of Chris's belongings, now prepared Safira to take the job.

"I'll arrange for the car insurance and other bills to be sent here. The house has been paid off for years, so you won't have that to worry about. But water, heat, and electricity are a few things you'll have to pay."

"How do I pay?"

Blake realized then that she didn't have a checking account, and without Chris here, he couldn't add her to his. He thought for a moment before asking for the folder Chris had given her.

His jaw dropped at the figures shown. He knew that Chris was well off, but he hadn't been aware of how rich. Scanning the papers, he found something that made him smile. Chris always did have a knack for planning ahead. He pulled out the paper and closed the folder.

"Safira, we need to take a trip to the bank."

*****

The banker was helpful enough, and with very little effort, Safira Banks was added to Christian Banks' account.

Safira was proud of herself as she walked from the bank with a small checkbook.

The banker told her that her debit card would arrive in two weeks. Blake smiled at Safira. Had she not married Chris, he would definitely have considered dating this beautiful young lady. He made a mental note to write Chris about his new wife, but realized that it would not be well received. Chris had enough dangers surrounding him; he didn't need news about Safira.

*****

When Safira started her first semester of college, she was introduced to the world in a new way. She found the classes and learning with other students pleasantly challenging. She also experienced firsthand what Kate had tried to warn her about, the boys and girls outside the church. The girls often wore clothing that either exposed much of their flesh or brought attention to certain areas of the body that got the boys' attention. The male student body was preoccupied by the fairer sex rather than their studies. Now, she understood what Kate and Fay had taught her about personal wardrobe choices and accepted that she was dressing quite modestly in comparison.

The boys flirted with her mercilessly, and she did her best to deter them. She was married and not interested in seeking out a boyfriend like many of the girls seemed to be doing. It was no wonder Kate had wanted Safira to go to school with her. Safira had insisted, however, that she preferred the college near her own home. Her choice to strike out on her own was the right one. She was learning more and studying harder than perhaps she could've had her fun-loving sister, Kate, been attending the same school. Safira also came to understand that while America had its freedoms and women were treated with respect, some students were more popular than others; and sadly, much of it had to do with appearances rather than intelligence. Often, students tried to hang out with her, but her motives for being in school were scholastic; and she often, unintentionally, put off advances to befriend her from both sexes.

Kimberly Shelton was one of the small community college's most beautiful and popular girls. Her long, silky blonde hair and bright blue eyes drew people like a magnet. Wherever she went, eyes were directed toward her. She'd decided to befriend new students and make them feel included before she began using them for her own purposes. Safira Banks was no exception.

Safira was what Kimberly Shelton would call incorrigible. No matter what Kimberly did to gain her trust and, therefore, control over her, Safira would only smile and gently ask to be excused from Kimberly's invitation. Her excuses for not wanting to be friends usually involved her need to study.

Safira's heavy accent and sweet disposition also had a negative effect on Kimberly. She couldn't stand Safira's gentle ways that seemed to draw attention away from her. The boys flocked around her, but Safira would only smile and politely respond to their inquiries.

Kimberly watched Safira enter the classroom and seat herself beside Craig Nelson, one of her own ex-boyfriends. She watched as he hopelessly tried to flirt with Safira in class, but failed miserably as she smiled at him, but largely ignored his comments.

Kimberly stared at her. There had to be something she could do to get the girl under her influence. She thought about Safira's accent, and she realized that she needed more information before she could research.

"Safira, boring lecture wasn't it?" Kimberly called as she fell in step with Safira Banks after class.

"Not bad. I appreciate his knowledge."

"So, where are you from? You have such a beautiful heavy accent."

"Keilron."

"Interesting. So, what's it like, Keilron, I mean."

"Women are property. No cars. No Internet. Things are as you would say, third-world country."

"Huh. Say, I need to book it out of here, but it was nice talking to you." Kimberly flashed one of her friendliest smiles before disappearing down another hallway.

Safira shook her head. She never would understand the popular Kimberly Shelton. One moment the girl was friendly and kind, and the next she acted like she had a much more important place to be.

*****

Kimberly moved the computer mouse to the search engine and typed in "Keilron." She kept looking over her shoulder, as if Safira herself were watching.

Kimberly began opening sites that told of the country's conditions, economy, government, population, and on the list went. She was about to give up when a Christian website came up, and she began to read the dangers of living in an anti-Christian country.

Keilron is far from a free nation. Women are no more than slaves and used to produce children. The gods of their country are idols of many kinds. The more spiritual people pray six times a day for their souls to be delivered from hell. Any missionary who enters this country to share the good news of Jesus Christ is on a dangerous mission. Such instruments as the guillotine, the rack, gas chambers, physical beatings, and many other torture devices from past centuries are still in use to torture and kill Christian missionaries, as well as any who are affiliated with them.

Kimberly's mouth gapped open. She couldn't believe that such countries existed. From what she found, Keilron was under a modern-day Hitler; the only difference was they were out to get Christians, not Jews. And the country was in the throes of a personal religious war that did not seemingly extend outside their borders.

One more website caught her eye, and her mouth turned upward as she read.

*****

Rofisca read his e-mail and replied immediately to the inquiry about the general's long lost daughter Safira. He couldn't believe his good luck. He replied to the e-mail, trying to sound interested but not desperate.

Perhaps, he had at last found the lead he needed. He leaned back in his chair and crossed his arms over his chest in victory, a satisfied smirk on his face.

"No one can run from me now," he whispered in the empty office. "Your new god cannot save you now, my dearest child. I have the gods on my side."

He stood, walked to the window, and put his hands behind his back as he stared at the busy city below. She had escaped Shemna and Keilron, but she would never escape from his power.

*****

Safira smiled sweetly as Kimberly fell in step with her.

Kimberly took Safira by the elbow and led her to the side of the hallway and whispered to her quietly. "I did some research this weekend. Is your name, your real name, Safira Rofisca?"

"No, my name is Safira Banks."

"Banks is not a Keilronian name."

"I'm married. My name is Banks."

"But you were first a Rofisca. I know I've found everything about you. You are a criminal, a wanted criminal in Keilron."

Safira's heart stopped. If Kimberly knew, then the whole school could know in a matter of hours. She let her heart calm down, knowing that Christ was her protector. "What do you want from me, Kimberly?" she pleaded.

"I just want you to realize that you are nothing here, no matter how many guys fall at your feet. I know what I want, and you are getting in the way."

Safira felt her mind twist and turn in different directions, but still could not figure out what Kimberly wanted. When at last she thought she understood, she spoke. "I am married. I've no interest in your men."

Kimberly scowled at her. "Keep it that way. Or I will tell your father where you are," she said before flipping her blonde hair over her shoulder and strutting down the hall.

*****

Rofisca sneered as he received the information needed. He'd demanded that the e-mail address from the inquiry be tracked down to find an address for the person who had written the e-mail. All he'd been able to get was a general area. He e-mailed back to the person named Kimberly Shelton.

Kimberly sat down at her computer and her heart began to panic as she read the e-mail from the man she'd e-mailed nearly two weeks ago. She felt a shiver go up her spine as she read the chopped English.

> *Kimberly, yes, I know you name. I respond again because I know you live in Colorado, and I know you will do my wish. If you refuse, do not think I do not have connection in United States. What is Safira's alias in America? I need more information. I want you to name me names of people Safira knew in Keilron. Her criminal actions must be stopped, as does the people she is connected with. Her crime is one of the worst imaginable. The people she worked with here are a danger to the government and must be stopped. If you do not wish to give me her name, at least give me the name of her accomplices to begin. This is your mission. If I don't receive my information, then you shall fear your life.*

Kimberly's stomach plummeted. The e-mail was not signed. She looked at the address, BeshanRofisca@Keilron.gov. She felt real fear for the first time in her young life. She shut the computer down and dashed from the library. Her heart pounded faster with every step to her car. She turned the ignition key and took a deep breath. He was requiring information from her. She dialed her phone and heard Safira's voice.

"Hey, Safira. I thought we could go to lunch. I want to apologize for my behavior earlier. I really would like to be your friend."

Chapter 10

Be Strong and of Good Courage

March 2001

Safira and Kimberly sat across from one another, finishing their lunch. Kimberly was on her best behavior. She'd even been rewarded with several smiles and friendly banter. They had settled in at their table with two trays of hamburgers and fries. Kimberly hadn't expected the young middle-east lady to be so friendly after she'd threatened her. The comradery they now shared was disconcerting to Kimberly. She was actually beginning to like Safira, but the e-mail flashed through her mind.

Kimberly set her fork down and leaned back. "What was your family like?" She had grown accustomed to Safira's choppy words and hesitations over the last hour. She'd even begun to think her speech endearing. Often, Safira would look to her right in search of the correct words. But considering she'd been in the United States for less than a year, Kimberly thought she was communicating well.

"Father was soldier. Many old brothers to boss me." Safira smiled as her mind drifted home. "Mother died giving birth. Slave taught me like mother. I learn, other woman could not. I get education."

"I take it Keilron doesn't educate women?"

"Correct," Safira confirmed.

"You mentioned you were married to a Banks?"

"Yes, Christian Banks." Safira supplied as she bit into another fry.

"Where is he?" she asked casually, taking a sip from her soda.

"Keilron. He need stay."

Kimberly took mental notes as they continued their meal. Noticing Safira's growing discomfort at being the center of attention, Kimberly changed the subject to school. After lunch, the two girls went shopping. When they said goodbye, Kimberly felt she'd made some progress. She'd learned Safira's husband's name. Surely, her contact in Shemna would consider that sufficient.

Kimberly's computer buzzed to life the moment she returned to her dorm. Getting the information out was crucial. She believed her contact when he threatened her, and she wasn't going to take any chances.

*****

The loud pounding on the door caused Chris to jump. He'd been drifting in and out of sleep the last half hour while trying to finish the chapter he'd been translating. Glancing down at the work in front of him, he swiftly gathered the papers and hid them under the large, loose floor stone. Efficiency and speed had become his friends while in Keilron. He allowed the government translation to remain scattered on the table as usual. Before he took his second step toward the door, it burst open and several soldiers barged in. Two soldiers grabbed Chris by the shoulders and pushed him down to his knees. The men shouted insults and threatened their prisoner with semiautomatic machine guns. Chris had feared this day would come and had tried to prepare himself, but no preparation would have been enough. The two men standing over him yanked his arms behind his back and bound them. After lifting him to his feet, they thrust him forward and out the door. He moved with them willingly enough, knowing that to struggle would be futile. How had they discovered him?

Chris realized he was marching toward the Christian prison near the center of the city.

His captors dragged him through a courtyard and several hallways before entering a large office. Chris's guards forced him to the ground.

General Rofisca strode from behind his desk and glared at the prisoner. The man was young and strong. Rarely did Rofisca allow a prisoner into his office. He could count on his one hand how often he'd spoken to captives directly. Rofisca eyed the guard approaching him with the orders of detainment. Glancing at the paperwork, he understood. An uncontrollable anger rose up within.

Chris's blue eyes drifted upward until he met General Rofisca's dark, furious gaze.

Hatred shot from the commander's eyes. He waited for retaliation from Banks. The silence in the office was stifling. "You are Christian Banks."

Chris felt the Lord cautioning him to be silent.

"Send him to Granshamila. I want him tortured, but keep him alive. Death is too easy for this one. Make sure Narshac is aware of my orders and this man's identity. Now, get him out of my office. I never want to see him again!"

With an air of authority, the general turned his back on Chris, who was jerked to his feet and dragged from the office. He prayed as he was shoved into a waiting prison wagon. At Granshamila Prison, he would need strength beyond his own in the very imminent future. He'd heard stories from the locals of the inhumane way inmates were treated there. The tales caused him to shudder. Being sent to Granshamila, where Narshac Rofisca was the top authority, was wholly unexpected. Normally, the prison housed murderers, defilers, adulterers, kidnappers, thieves, and traitors. Chris recalled Pastor Tim calming his fears; Christians had never been sent to Granshamila.

Arriving at the stronghold of the prison, he marveled at the structure. A nineteenth-century U.S. Civil War fort may have looked similar. The buildings were built close together in a U-shape with only one gate leading in and out. The center courtyard floor and execution block staged in the center of the space was comprised of large, square stones. The execution platform was an ancient guillotine with an extremely sharp and shiny blade gleaming in the sun. Where they unloaded him, Chris saw the blood-stained stones surrounding the contraption, and his gut wrenched. The platform had a pole protruding from beside the guillotine. A man hung on the pole with his hands tied above his head. Christian cringed for the man; the sun was beating down, and the temperature had to be well into the hundreds.

Chris was rushed into one of the dark openings, down a flight of stairs, and thrust into a filthy cell. A shadow moved in the corner. It took several moments for his eyes to adjust to the darkness. When they did, he saw a desk set up in the cell with a single sheet of paper and a pen. The shadow he'd seen moved again, and this time when Chris's eyes flashed into the corner, he made out the form of a man, not much older than himself.

"Write to my sister and tell her what has happened. She must come home now. You are no longer important to her, do you understand?" Narshac's voice echoed in the emptiness.

Chris held Narshac's gaze. His eyes belied the harsh tone he'd used. Chris understood. The letter wasn't about getting her home at all. Narshac was giving him a chance to say goodbye.

Chris wanted to ask why he'd been given the olive branch, but he knew he couldn't. Narshac was the authority at this prison. Chris had to play the game if he wanted to contact home for the last time.

*****

Safira's meeting with Kimberly had become a custom, but Kimberly noticed Safira's mind was elsewhere. Aside from trying to protect her life by drawing information out of Safira, her façade of friendship was becoming more real than she'd anticipated.

When they pulled out from the college parking lot in Safira's car, Kimberly asked, "What's wrong, Saf?"

"I not hear from my husband. I'm concerned. Over two months, I received letters from him. One every two weeks, but I not hear in six weeks. Family hear nothing too."

Kimberly felt herself drawn to Safira as never before. Putting her mental notebook away, she wanted to know the truth. The man on the other side of the world had made it clear Safira was a fugitive, but he'd never told her why.

"Why did you run from your country?"

Safira took a deep breath. Perhaps the time had come to tell her new friend about Jesus. "I refused worship Keilronian gods. I chose Christ. Father kills Christians. I run."

"That's why you're wanted?" Kimberly asked in disbelief. She felt her pulse race. How could she have not put two and two together before now?

"Yes. My husband translates Bible for my people to read."

"Your own father wants you dead because you chose to believe in Christianity?"

Safira nodded as she stopped at a red light.

"Wouldn't it be easier to bow to the gods?"

"No." Safira's voice was firm. How could she explain to Kimberly in her limited English that a Keilronian believer would rather die than fall victim to unfaithfulness before the Savior of heaven? It would be a terrible fate to stand before the King of Kings and be accused of being unfaithful. She pulled over into an empty parking lot and stopped the car and then turned to her friend.

"Jesus died for me. He is God. I have chosen Him. How could I bow to dead gods? My heart and mind must be good when I die and stand in front of Him." Safira had gestured her way through her statement, trying to help Kimberly understand what she was trying to say. She'd put one hand on her heart and one pointing to her head.

"You mean your conscience must be clear," Kimberly clarified.

Safira nodded. She'd heard the phrase before and understood it. She just hadn't been able to find the words. She tried the phrase, and when Kimberly nodded encouragingly, she stored it into her memory bank for future use.

"There are so many different types of churches. I'm surprised to hear that they can all succeed in a place like Keilron."

"No." Safira shook her head. Kimberly looked interested, though slightly confused. Safira was frustrated with her limited language skills. "One church, Christians hide together. They believe Bible. They believe same things. My English, not so good. I memorize English Bible to help learn."

Kimberly believed that the Bible was the Word of God but had little time for it, and she certainly had not thought of it to be as special as Safira made it sound.

"'For all have sinned and come short of the glory of God' (Romans 3:23). We all bad inside. 'For by grace are ye saved through faith, and that not of yourselves, it is the gift of God. Not of works lest any man should boast' (Ephesians 2:8–9). We cannot be good. God gave us gift of Jesus. Jesus died for me. Jesus died for you. He rose from death. He lives. 'For God so loved the world' . . . me and you," she explained. "'That he gave his only begotten son' . . . Jesus. 'That whosoever' . . . anybody, 'Believeth in him' . . . He paid for sins . . . 'should not perish' . . . You won't pay for own sins, 'but have everlasting life.' Go be with Jesus always."

Kimberly lowered her eyes from Safira's gaze. Safira was not wanted in Keilron for a crime worthy of the deception Kimberly was leading her into. She let Safira's words sink into her heart and mind. She nodded in understanding, tears reaching her eyes. She'd deceived Safira; she had deceived many of her classmates. Kimberly knew at that moment what she had done was wrong. Safira made sense. She had heard the gospel before, but this was the first time she understood its application to her personally. She understood now that Jesus loved her. That she had sinned. Having heard Safira tell of a people who would die for their faith, she'd been interested enough to truly listen. Having accepted the fact, she intentionally disobeyed and failed God; she knew why Jesus was so important. She knew Christ had died for her. She accepted the truth and put her future into the hands of Jesus Christ. He loved her, and now she loved Him too.

"I believe. I trust Christ's sacrifice will get me into heaven." Kimberly meant every word as the tears flowed down her face. She felt Safira reach for her. They hugged until Kimberly pulled away, wiping the tears from her eyes. They prayed together and decided to skip their shopping trip and visit Kate instead.

*****

Kimberly turned on the lights in her dorm room. Her roommate would be gone the rest of the weekend, so she decided to fire up the computer. Safira's influence had been good for her. She wanted to follow Jesus like Safira and knew exactly where to start. Logging in to her e-mail account, she wrote to Rofisca.

> *Sir, I've given you as much information as I can. I won't be a rat anymore. I can't deceive such an honorable person. I have found her Light and have claimed it as my own. I understand. I've been wrong. Your words cannot scare me any longer. Fear for your own soul. Mine is in the hands of an awesome God I now know. Safira is a woman of honor. Her testimony cannot be stopped by any one man.*

Kimberly immediately wrote Safira a letter of encouragement. The words spilled out as her pen scratched against the paper. Words had always come easily to Kimberly, and she bared her emotions in the letter. She encouraged Safira to finish her linguistic degree and to never stop telling the world about Jesus. Her heart of gratitude emerged as she thanked Safira for sharing with her the message of eternal life.

After finishing her homework and grabbing her coat two hours later, she headed outside. It was a nice night for a walk. As she made her way off campus, she slipped the letter to Safira in the mailbox and breathed in the evening air. A small smile touched her lips as she strolled down the street. She often walked this route and had never felt nervous doing so. The sidewalks were well lit, and the streets were usually busy enough to keep sinister characters away. Her sixth sense kicked in when she noticed the streetlights were out for two blocks. Her stride slowed, and her eyes darted from side to side.

Somewhere on her right, a man's hand wrapped over her mouth, and she was dragged backward into a dark alley. She kicked out and fought against him, but to no avail. Tears ran down her face as she realized there were two of them.

"Bad idea to say 'no' to Rofisca, Kimberly. Really bad idea. And now we get the privilege and authority to harm you how we see fit."

"If you think we'll get caught, you are mistaken. Even if they traced the meager evidence to us, we have diplomatic immunity. Your authorities can't touch us." The man standing to her left smirked. Panic overtook her as she fought against the large man behind her.

"She sure is pretty, prettiest thing I've ever seen," her captor sneered as his tongue lapped at her earlobe. Muffling her screams, he laughed at her useless struggle.

"Well, you're welcome to her, but I want my turn too," the man who seemed to be in charge of this assault ceded. Evil permeated from both men, and Kimberly's gagged and taped mouth silenced her sobs. She felt the pain after the sharp knife slit one of her arms. Aware that this was going to be the end, she wept all the harder and continued praying heavenward.

*****

JC strolled into the house and threw his book bag down on the couch before flipping on the TV. Home for the weekend, Safira passed by the living room and paused to watch the evening news with her little brother.

"Tonight's story," the newsman announced, "is about the murder of a student from one of Colorado's small community colleges. She was found dead this evening in an alley. Police have claimed that the girl was raped, tortured, and shot. More on that story tonight at seven."

Not wanting to hear more, Safira flipped the television off, handed JC his book bag, and suggested he do his chores. Excitement washed over Safira when she saw the letter for her on the kitchen table as she went to see if Fay needed help with supper. The letter was from Chris. All thoughts of helping her mother-in-law died as she slit the envelope open; however, her excitement was short lived.

Dear Safira,
　For the first time, I can spell your name on paper. I don't have much space to write, and I can write to you only. Your father wants you home.

Narshac Rofisca beckons you to return. I am not afraid. I don't know what message you should pass on to my family. Be merciful. It will not be easy for them. I love them. I have no regrets. Tell Kate to be strong. I need prayer. I know God is still in control, and my race isn't done. I have accomplished much here and do not regret my decision to come, nor my decision to marry you. If my accomplishments for Him are finished, so be it. Pray without ceasing. "Be strong and of good courage, fear not, nor be afraid of them, for HE it is that doth go before you."

Chris

The date was nearly two months ago, and the location was Granshamila, the well-known prison. She faked a smile to Fay as she walked up to her room. Her stomach was in knots, and the tears welled up in her eyes. She grabbed a pillow on her bed and hugged it. As Chris had declared, prayer was the only help he could receive now, so she prayed for several minutes. What could she tell the family? Should she tell them anything? It was a miracle she'd received a letter. Agony gripped her heart. The letters between them had only begun, and she'd anticipated each one. But now, he'd been captured. What more did her father know about her, and how had he discovered Chris? She reread the end of the letter.

Be strong and of good courage. She couldn't believe his words. She knew what danger he faced, and yet he'd written to encourage her. She knew the words were from the Bible because she had just read them in her devotions. She prayed for the courage to do what needed to be done in the States for Chris.

"Fear not, nor be afraid of them." She didn't need to fear. Her father and his army could do nothing to her, "For He it is that doth go before thee." Christ was with her. She needn't fear. She felt at peace. Her last name was connected with a man who had a great love for the Lord.

She ate dinner with the Klerens that evening but couldn't bring herself to say a word about the letter. She looked at Fay with compassion. What would she do if she knew that her son was in one of the harshest prisons in Keilron? Safira knew she'd have to talk with the family about him, but she couldn't bring herself to tell them just yet. Wanting to wait till after the meal, she tried to act normal. Surely, no one would be able to eat once the news was out. She didn't feel like eating either, but forced the food down.

JC shoveled down his food and beelined it back to the television.

"Come here. You got to hear this, Safira. It's about someone from your school!" JC hollered across the house. The rest of the family rolled their eyes, even as Safira rose to join JC

"Saf, are you okay, dear? You seem out of sorts." Fay stopped her with a gentle hand as she voiced her concerns. Glancing over to Harris, she saw the question reflected in his eyes.

The phone rang before Safira could respond. Fay answered it and quickly handed the phone off to Safira.

"Hello?"

"Safira Banks?"

"Yes," she said not recognizing the troubled voice. The woman on the other end of the phone began to weep.

"She's dead. She's gone. You were one of her best friends."

"Who?" Safira asked gently.

"Kimberly, my dear Kimberly!"

"I come quickly," Safira said. After taking down the address, she hung up the phone. "Kimberly is dead," she said in disbelief to Fay, who was standing close by.

"Go. Her mother wants you," Fay said.

Safira nodded, grabbed her purse, and hurried out the door.

Fay turned toward JC who had entered the kitchen and had overheard everything.

"Kimberly is the girl they found in the alley. She was unrecognizable; only her purse showed her I.D. She was raped too, but the cause of death was a bullet. Whoever did this has no sense of humanity. I think we should pray for Safira."

Fay stared at her son in disbelief. Safira was about to walk into a very fragile situation. JC muted the television and took a moment to pray with his parents. When they finished, JC turned the news back on. Fay sat on the coach with him, but her mind continued to plead for the family who had just lost their daughter in such a tragic way. She also prayed that the Lord would give her strength if Chris never came home and that Chris would have the courage to endure what he must.

*****

The Shelton family held Kimberly's funeral on Monday. Safira comforted the family the best she could and tried to remain loving and kind. Desiring to offer them hope, she told the family of Kimberly's recent decision. They were not ready to hear her words; no merciful God would allow their daughter to be taken so tragically.

At the Kleren's home after the funeral, she sat down on the front porch swing and stared out across the yard. She'd been told how Kimberly died and couldn't fathom the pain the family was going through or what suffering Kimberly experienced before her death. She didn't notice when Blake sat beside her. Not until Blake's arm wrapped gently around her did she let the tears flow unchecked. The pain and exhaustion from the last couple of days washed over her. Amidst her tears, she thanked the Lord that Kimberly had come to know Him before her death. Once she regained her composure, she spent ten minutes convincing Blake she'd be okay to drive home. She wanted to be alone; she wanted space to grieve.

Blake's car trailed her all the way home. He obviously hadn't taken her at her word. They waved to one another when she got out of her car and walked to the mailbox. Blake continued past her house and toward his Denver school. She hadn't been home since she'd last been with Kimberly. Flipping through the letters as she went into the house, her heart jumped. Kimberley's handwriting stared up at her from the blue envelope. Safira opened it using the letter opener on her desk. She read the two pages of longhand before the tears began blurring her vision.

Tell your story to the world. They need to know about Keilron. I hope that someday you will meet your husband again. But until that day comes, speak to all who will listen. Keilron can be touched by the freedom your message brings, but our nation needs to hear the same message. My only wish is that you finish your linguistic degree and go tell our nation of your heritage, your story. I'll always cheer you on, supporting you in the background. I cannot express the gratitude in my heart for you, for leading me to the truth of Christ.

*In Christ,
Kimberly Shelton*

    Tears dripped on the paper as she read Kimberly's last message. Bowing her head, she prayed for an hour on Kimberley's words. She'd always assumed she would return to her country when she received her degree, so Kimberly's advice touched her heart. She opened her Bible and began to read in Mark, Chapter 15.

    "Go into all the world and preach the gospel to every creature . . ." She slowly read the words out loud and smiled. Her answer was in front of her. Kimberly hadn't known it, but her message was the same one God had for Safira. She would tell her story.

    Safira spent much of her time after the funeral with her studies and also began writing specific churches, asking if they were willing to have her share her story with them. People were hesitant, and she was only able to book a few engagements. She began taking speech classes and immersed herself with the Stonebrook church's women's Bible studies, library book clubs, and any group willing to help her grow in her communication skills.

    Postponing the news of Chris to his family still wore on her, and she could tell that Fay was growing more concerned. Finally, she decided it was time to speak with them. She phoned Blake and asked him to come down to the Kleren's on Friday afternoon. She had news and wanted to say it only once. Blake was a great ally and like another brother in the family. She felt he should also be aware of Chris's situation. Once the last family member settled into a chair, she took a deep breath and plunged in.

"I got a letter from Chris when Kimberly died. I could not tell you then because much was happening in my life. I didn't want to tell you what he said. It was bad news."

Fay sat up straighter, her heart sinking in dread. Why had Safira been the one contacted and not her? She knew, of course, that Chris had been corresponding with his wife, but he would automatically convey any real news to her. Her feelings were certainly irrational, and she knew it, but she still couldn't help the small amount of jealousy that crept into her emotions.

"The letter came from bad prison. It is not Christian prison. Christians are tortured and killed quickly. I do not understand why he is in Granshamila. This prison is for murderers, thieves, traitors, and bad men. It is meant for repeat torture."

"What is 'repeat torture'?" JC quietly asked, intrigued that the letter had come from such a place. If this were about Chris being in prison, they wouldn't have allowed him to write, at least as he understood it.

Safira wondered how she would describe to JC what she knew. Her English had improved dramatically in the last month, and she hoped her words would satisfy the family.

"They torture until people are ready to die. They let them rest, feed them, heal them, and torture again. No mercy, no rest, and no peace. Bones get reset and are allowed to heal. It is . . . ouch . . . hurt . . ."

"Painful," Blake supplied.

Nodding, she continued, "Painful to rebreak bone over and over before it is all healed."

JC cringed at the thought.

"I will say no more. I do not want you to have bad dreams. I do, because I hear much stories of prison and what they do in detail when my father and Shovak first took it."

"You got a letter from Chris, from this prison?" Harris asked, placing a comforting hand around his wife. "What did it say?"

Safira pulled out the letter and translated it into English for them. The letter was of no comfort to the family. When she finished reading Chris's words, she looked at the faces around her.

Fay's eyes filled with tears as her shoulders shook, and she put her face in her hands to hide the sobs. Harris held her tightly and tried to be strong for his family as he clenched his jaw several times. Kate was shell-shocked for several heartbeats before her emotions overwhelmed her, and she began to cry. Seated beside Kate, Blake wrapped his arms around the hurting young woman, allowing her to turn into his shoulder and soak his shirt with her tears. Blake stared out the window while dealing with the reality in his own way. JC sat unmoving for several minutes before he stood up and simply left the house. His pain would be dealt with on his own. Safira opted to follow JC, as the news was not new to her, and she had no one to mourn with. Before she left the room, she heard Harris's husky voice.

"Is he dead?"

She helplessly shrugged. "I do not think so, but I do not know. They do not kill men for years. He has not been there long time." Her words were laced with hope, but the despair was obvious.

She left the house and found JC standing on the front porch, staring across the street with his hands in his front pockets. He didn't look like he wanted to go back in. Looping her arm through his, she led him forward.

"We go for walk," she said as they stepped down from the porch and walked toward the street. He easily matched her slow step.

JC split the silence, "You know Chris is a lot older than me."

Safira nodded and hoped the boy would open up to her.

"I've suspected for some time that something was amiss. You haven't been your usual self. At first, I chalked it up to Kimberly's death, but then after the funeral, you just about disappeared on us. You used to call us, especially Kate, all the time. She loves that you know and actually tries to rub it in my face, like I care. And then I heard from our pastor's wife that you had decided to speak to churches and women's groups about Keilron, something that wasn't an issue for you when you came. You began to come only for Sunday dinners, and even then, you wouldn't open up like you used to."

"You see things others don't."

"I'm just observant I guess."

"Observant?"

"Like you said. I see things. I notice everything."

"We do not give you as much credit as you deserve."

Smiling, he teased her. "So you don't understand observant, but you understand credit?"

Safira rolled her eyes. "Credit I understand. I do pay own bills."

"Saf, why would Chris be willing to sacrifice so much for people he doesn't know? He hasn't been there much more than eighteen months, and he's put in prison. How is that fair? I mean, how did he get discovered when he's been so careful? Pastor Kindel has been there for over two decades and has never been imprisoned!"

"Yes. But Christianity is illegal only since Shovak is leader. Many Keilronians ignore God's people before Shovak. When Shovak became leader, he wanted Christians dead. Pastor Tim has been there before, during, and after war. He's old foreigner, not suspect. Chris come eighteen months ago and was suspect from first day. What I not know is why he not killed."

"Maybe they know he married you. How angry was your family when you ran away?"

"I had brother threaten to kill me. Father wanted to marry me off, so I stay out of trouble. What do you think?"

"I think that Chris was as careful as they come when it came to his safety. I think there was another force behind this. If what I've heard you say is true, if being a Christian was his only crime, they would have put him to death, and Pastor Kindel would have written a letter of condolence to my family. So I still don't understand why they have put him in this torture trap. I hate to even imagine what he might be going through."

"You blame me?" Safira's voice was quiet and shaky. She feared what the family would feel toward her if they believed that Chris's imprisonment was her fault. Clearly, JC had made the connection; perhaps, the other family would too, eventually.

"I couldn't hate you, Saf, and I don't blame you. You may be the reason he's still alive."

"It would be better, perhaps, if he weren't."

"There is a chance he will come home. Under different circumstances, we would be praying for comfort, not salvation."

"Thank you."

He smiled down at her. "Did I ever tell you how I came to Jesus Christ?"

She shook her head.

"It was Chris. He came home from a Christian camp one year. I guess they'd been teaching about witnessing and being strong in the faith because he came home all happy. Being so much older than I was, I worshiped him, and I was excited that he was back. I figured he wouldn't mind playing some tricks like we used to. We were silly boys, and I suppose my childishness mixed with his cleverness gave my dad a lot of headaches." JC remembered and chuckled to himself.

"I had this idea to play a dirty trick on one of our older neighbors. I can't even remember what it was I wanted to pull, but Chris wouldn't play along this time. I didn't understand why. He explained to me that it wasn't something Jesus would approve of. I remember that conversation because I was overwhelmed with guilt and sadness for making Jesus unhappy with me after all He'd done for me. My brother led me to Christ that day. Instead of playing a dirty trick, we played a fun game with the elderly lady. Her garden stayed weed-free the rest of the summer. She figured it was a miracle because she never spotted us since we did it in the evening after she went to bed."

Safira smiled. She liked hearing stories like this one. She loved to know more about the man she'd married. Who knew? Perhaps she would be a widow before she'd get the chance to meet him again.

When they returned from their walk, the family had scattered from the living room. Blake waited on the front porch. JC nodded at him and went into the house. She heard him mention something about lemonade.

"Blake, I . . ."

"Safira, they won't blame you, but you can't just leave them on their own."

"JC needed to talk. Did you know Chris led him to Christ?"

Blake smiled, nodding at the memory.

"I helped keep that garden weed-free. Chris was all excited after summer camp. He told me then he wanted to live for God wholeheartedly. He said keeping the garden beautiful was helping him remember to keep the weeds in his heart cleaned out."

"That's very . . . good of him." In Keilronian, she would have said "poetic," but she didn't know the English translation.

"He was thirteen. Perhaps, it was. But it worked. He stayed out of trouble that summer, which wasn't exactly like him. He was smart, but I think he liked to rebel because it flustered his grandpa Banks almost more than his folks."

Just as she sat down on the porch swing with Blake, JC walked out with three glasses of lemonade.

The young man chuckled. "Yeah, didn't last though as I recall."

"Nope, he found himself getting into some trouble all through that school year. It's hard being a boy, so much trouble to be had," Blake winked.

"Try being girl in Keilron," she said quietly, a smile playing at her lips.

The birds chirped as the sun beat down. It was the perfect spring day.

"I heard you were trying to spread the word about Keilron, trying to get an audience," Blake said after taking a sip of lemonade.

"Who would tell you that?" she asked, looking directly at JC with a smile.

JC grinned unrepentant.

"Is it true?" Blake asked.

"Yes, but I can't find people who want to hear. I've thought to write book, but that not work well. I read English. I can speak, mostly speak it. But writing English is hard."

"Yes, well I have an idea that might launch you into things a little faster."

"Oh?" she asked, genuinely curious.

"Did you know that Chris was a pretty popular guy here in the United States?"

She shook her head.

"Well, he was, is. Very little is mentioned about him these days. Going into a third-world country will do that to you. Even the paparazzi don't want to hunt you down in those conditions. Before he left, he made it a point to make a big deal about his departure. Every once in a while, he would send a picture and a small article of information to a publication here or there. Smart, he didn't want the public to forget his face or name. Considering what he's worth, it's good publicity. He's very careful about what he allowed in the articles, especially the name of the country, of course. But perhaps if we spin this our way and declare you his wife publicly, then perhaps we can get those churches lined up a little more easily."

"I don't want to cause him trouble."

"He's already in the worst prison imaginable from what you just told us," Blake said.

"Yes, but how do I know what are good churches? I understand not all churches are the same here. I do not want some churches."

"Agreed, I can help you with that. So can JC I know he's still in high school. But between the two of us, we might be able to get this rolling."

Inside, Fay washed her face and went to the kitchen. Maybe getting supper ready would help her focus on something else. She understood now why Chris had written Safira. The letter was written from prison. He was probably asked to write her. Fay's hands shook as she peeled the potatoes. Her oldest son wasn't going to come home. And she would never get to say goodbye, never get to see him with children, and never watch him fall in love with his wife. Tears threatened behind her eyes again, but this time, she forced them back. She had other children to think about. She had a God bigger than her problems. Setting the knife down momentarily and taking a deep breath, she prayed for Chris's safe return.

The whole family started praying daily for Chris and faithfully hoped for a miracle. Blake and JC helped launch Safira into the pages of church society. Three months from the time they'd sat on the front porch, she began to speak at colleges, churches, camps, and retreats. Every time, she left more people behind who were willing to join them in prayer for Chris. Fay encouraged her and continued being there for her family. Blake, along with helping book events for Safira, returned to his final year in school. Kate received her associates degree in business and often traveled with Safira to her engagements. She also began a secretarial position at a nearby manufacturing company. Time passed, sometimes quickly and sometimes slowly. But no one was willing to give up hope for Chris.

Chapter 11

Pray without Ceasing

Two Years Later
April 30, 2003

Christian's hair fell into his eyes as he sat on his mat in the corner of the tiny cell. His hair had grown back in the last six months since the guards last shaved his head, a consistent way of torture because the soldier nearly scalped him in the process. The best he could tell, every six months or so, he was subjected to "barber" visits. He was grateful for the hair length since it covered the scars on his scalp. His clothes, originally a grayish blue, a universal color and clothe for all inmates, was now saturated in dirt, sweat, and dried blood. Only once had he received another "uniform." The one he wore could have been mistaken for a grease rag. The brown mat he sat on served as his bed. The two-inch-thick mat was his only protection against the stone floor. By his bare feet lay a crumpled-up gray blanket that served as Chris's only source of warmth against the cool nights.

The cold from the floor soaked into his bones, and Chris couldn't even remember what warm felt like. His breathing was labored as he let out a hard cough. He had been battling with his lungs since the yearly rains had begun, and though the rains had passed, the infection had not.

The waste buckets inside each cell reeked from use, and the odor penetrated throughout the prison. Most of the time, the buckets were emptied daily, but were never washed. Sound echoed through the ancient stone and stucco building, leaving little to be unheard when men were tortured throughout the day and weeks.

Chris was weak. His body ached from bruising, torn muscles, broken bones, and untended abrasions that he'd received. His bones had been set and were healing; lacerations were stitched if necessary and left to heal on their own, leaving scars. The man who could run for miles and carry heavy loads through the Shemna streets was now a distant memory.

His skin sagged over conspicuous bones. The clothing he wore hung on his frame. He found it hard to stand when he rolled off the rough, flat mat. He fell to his knees as he tried to take the food when a guard let out a grunt and slid the food closer to Chris.

He wasn't sure if he could handle any more torture. He'd even gone so far as to pray for an end to the suffering. Often, he'd contemplated ways to trick the guard into killing him, but he turned to scripture and prayer until he could go on, whispering words to his Savior once again asking for strength. His mind often strayed, wondering if it was all for naught. Was there really a Savior he was serving, or was it all a fantasy? He pushed such notions away quickly and tried to focus on the truth he knew.

The food was edible, but rarely did Chris think about the taste. His sense of taste was no longer the same. Starvation changes a person's thinking on what is worth eating. Normally, he received very little in the way of food, but the amount had increased over the last several days. His captors were hoping his wounds would heal rapidly. Chris decided he'd rather be in continuous pain than to feel the agony Narshac had in store for him. Eating only half his ration was his own act of defiance, praying he wouldn't heal quickly. He'd tried starvation as a means of escape, but hadn't had the will power.

"You'll be expecting company this afternoon," the guard said gruffly.

Chris found it difficult to focus on the guard outside his door with the lantern. Dwelling on the upcoming visitation was out of the question. Company usually insinuated further suffering. He didn't even want to think about the pain to come. Scripture scrolled through his mind as he shoved the remainder of his food back toward the door.

The marks against the wall he'd scratched out with a loose rock indicated the days since his arrival. The time wasn't exact, since there were days or weeks missing when he was unconscious. But with the marks, he estimated his time to be somewhere near two years. He closed his eyes, and his mind drifted through his time in this hole. When he'd first arrived, he was sure that he could handle anything with the Lord. He'd been strong, even cocky. It took less than a month for him to realize just what type of prison he was in. Not only were the prisoners actual criminals, but also the endless torture and humiliation were more than any man could take for long.

He'd discovered a Christian friend for a brief spell, but as always with the Christians, the man who had been across the hall from him had not lived long. At first, Chris had wondered at the reasoning for his own imprisonment. He assumed his imprisonment had to do with Christianity, but soon learned, it was about his connection to the general's daughter.

Today, as he sat against the wall, he cringed at the painful memories. He diligently prayed that somehow, God would end this torture and hoped his family in the States would not mourn his death for long. He thought maybe the distance he'd put between them over the years would dull their pain. On the other hand, perhaps, they'd already mourned him; he'd been gone a long time. Not even Pastor Tim knew where he was. Safira could move on with her life and never have to feel trapped inside a loveless and unorthodox marriage to a complete stranger. He had no intention of claiming her as a groom ought. He had made the decision while corresponding with her that he wasn't going to bring her back to Keilron. How could he? He'd left Angie behind in the States to pursue his calling. To marry another woman and bring her into Keilron, whether it had been her home or not, was a double standard to him.

His mind began to fog. Sleep was inevitable, and he couldn't keep himself awake for more contemplation, nor did he want to. The pain in his body would numb while he slept, but he couldn't avoid the isolation he felt.

*****

Narshac's order for the prisoner to be brought outside to the smaller courtyard of the prison was quickly obeyed. The sun beat down against the commander's face. He stood enjoying the warmth and brightness of the late spring day. A prisoner would not be as appreciative of the light as he would the warmth. Narshac knew the prison cells were cool and damp from the heavy rains that accompanied the spring season. But he had chosen the courtyard for the discomfort it would bring his captive, since the sun would be blinding for someone accustomed to darkness.

Two soldiers dragged the tall skeleton to the center of the courtyard. When they let go of Chris, he fell to his knees. The man was slightly younger than Narshac, but he had no strength left. Narshac almost pitied Chris as he slumped in front of the strong commandant. Narshac saw there was nothing left but skin and bones. The lack of food and absence of exercise over the past three months had taken their toll on the missionary. Records indicated the man had been with them for two years, and frankly, with the conditions the man had endured, Narshac was impressed he was still alive. By now, he'd expected the scoundrel to have attempted suicide, either assisted or self-inflicted, but the man had remained persistent. Narshac had recently ordered that he be fed more rations and left to heal for a time. Narshac had every intention of abusing the prisoner further, but the man before him didn't appear to have received extra food. Frankly, he didn't believe Banks could survive another six weeks, with or without further torment.

Narshac disliked his job at times. As he stared down at the gaunt man, a sense of pity entered his heart. Unaccustomed to the feeling, Narshac plunged into his duty and dismissed his heart's reaction.

"You've been here for two years?"

Chris looked at the commanding officer. Answering a question the man knew the answer to was a waste of energy. Narshac had personally overseen most of his agony, and Chris knew this was a personal vendetta. Was it for the men standing behind him that Narshac would make such a declaration?

"Do you know your crime?"

Chris mustered up the energy to answer quietly, "I'm a Christian. I helped someone escape."

"It's the 'who' that has always irritated me."

"Safira," Chris muttered.

"My sister, Safira Rofisca, is your wife, no?" The question had been asked many times and had always incurred the same answer. Why Narshac staged the question yet again, Chris couldn't fathom.

"Yes," Chris broke the prolonged silence.

"I must ask you. Have you dishonored my sister?"

"No," Chris sighed. He was weary of this particular line of questioning.

"Where is she now?"

"Safe from harm," his words came out a hoarse whisper as his coughing began. He somehow knew that Keilron would have its sources in the United States, and though he was physically weak, he never told anyone where she was. It was important. Perhaps today, the keeping of this secret would end his suffering.

Angered by his obstinance, Narshac no longer cared whether Chris lived or died. "Send him to Room 205. He has rested enough. I shall meet you there shortly," Narshac commanded his guards. The two soldiers lifted Chris to his feet and dragged him back down into his personal abyss. Narshac gave a self-satisfied smile. The two new recruits who had brought Chris out had not heard Narshac's line of questioning, and the last response gave him cause to torture the man one last time. He'd already decided it was time for a good old-fashioned execution in the morning.

California, United States

Safira looked at the women before her. There were nearly four hundred ladies at this retreat. The last day had arrived quickly. She had been asked to speak about Keilron, to give her testimony, and share her ministry. Having spoken many times over the past two years she was becoming rather well-known for her message. Her heavy accent charmed and drew the ladies' attention when she traveled to different retreats. Her words would fill the room as the microphone amplified her voice.

*****

The pain in his limbs caused Chris such agony the tears fell freely down his face. Ropes pulled his arms out of socket; he could feel the sticky wetness on his back from the beatings he'd received earlier. No shouts of pain. No words of anger. He could barely moan as he grew weaker. Narshac enjoyed a strange satisfaction from watching the suffering of the American.

"I loved my sister. She could have lived to be a wealthy and influential wife, but no, you had to get your dirty little American hands involved," Narshac spat at the pitiful man.

Chris was helpless. His voice failed as his body wrenched with pain.

"Can you speak?" Narshac mocked him.

Narshac didn't expect an answer as the body suspended in the air by ropes was half dead. The soldier's footsteps echoed as he turned his back on the inmate and was about to walk out when a noise behind brought him to a halt. The voice was quiet, barely above a whisper, but he'd heard the words. The missionary's question reached into his heart.

"Why do you torture yourself?" Chris hadn't been sure the voice had even come from him. He hadn't known that he could speak. He thanked God that Narshac had heard his hoarse voice. Chris could only hope his voice would hold out.

Narshac had tortured and killed many men. Christian and criminal alike. Criminals were convinced they were innocent, and Christians tried to convert their captors with powerful persuasion. But the question that had stopped him in his tracks was unlike any plea he'd encountered. Banks had spoken of the Christ God during his early torture, but today, his words were different. His words showed concern toward the very man responsible for his predicament.

Narshac stared at him for a moment before dismissing the guard who was accustomed to this action and suspected nothing out of the ordinary.

"You lay in pain barely able to speak, and you ask after me?" Narshac questioned.

"Why are you bitter?" Chris's weak, husky voice asked.

"You took my sister from me!" Narshac shouted, taking a step closer to Chris.

"No, I didn't meet your sister until May of 2000, long after she left your safekeeping. But you already knew that. It's not me you are angry with. What are you searching for, Narshac?" Chris was in awe, his voice growing stronger as he spoke.

If someone would have kicked him in the gut, it wouldn't have surprised Narshac more. The man was dying from lack of food and injury, and yet he was concerned for his captor. He grunted and tried to harden his heart. But it didn't obey as quickly as it used to.

"You know of Christ. You interrogate missionary after missionary. Each one tells you the same thing. You know the truth, and yet you won't let it set you free. Narshac, you hear the call of the living God. Answer it." The last words were spoken with compassion. Chris felt the brief surge of strength evaporate from both mind and body. He barely glimpsed Narshac's retreating form before all went dark.

Narshac left the room. He didn't want to hear more. Every time Christians spoke, he felt curiosity grew. He didn't want that at all.

"We use the guillotine at dawn," he demanded as he passed the two soldiers guarding the door.

*****

"I challenge you, ladies, to pray for the men and women in Keilron because each day may be someone's last. On a more personal note, I ask you to be in prayer for my husband. Although we've only met once, I know he is a man of strong faith. Before he was captured, he was translating scripture into the Keilronian tongue so that others could hear God's Word. I believe he is still alive." Safira looked into the faces of her audience. She thanked them and the hostess before returning to her seat, allowing the director of the retreat to take over.

"We've heard Safira's amazing story. Tonight, there is a basket at the front of the church for anyone willing to give to Safira's cause."

Safira glanced up, her lips gapping slightly. She'd told the hostess that she didn't need offerings. But she watched in silent amazement as the pianist began playing, and the women came forward and gave money to the Keilronian ministry. Once the music had stopped and all were seated again, Mrs. Olson, the hostess, stepped forward again.

"We've given to the cause, but I think we all know the most important thing is to pray. For those of you who feel you couldn't give, or if you feel you didn't give enough, let me challenge you to divide into groups and spend a few minutes praying for the Keilronian missionaries and Christians, particularly for the protection of Safira's husband."

Safira watched as Mrs. Olson dismissed the crowd. To Safira's surprise, no one in the room left. Groups of three or four joined together in prayer for her people. Tears welled in her eyes as she realized that Kimberly was rooting for her. This was what she had wanted.

*****

The voice on the other end of the phone surprised Fay. She hadn't expected to hear from Safira for another hour or two. Her daughter-in-law often called after her speaking engagements so they could pray together for Chris and the other persecuted believers. Safira explained she'd felt the need to pray earlier tonight. She told Fay about the women praying in the auditorium and felt the urgency to join them.

"I've been praying a lot for Chris. I keep hoping he will come home." Fay responded.

"We mustn't give up. He must still live."

Fay and Safira began to pray together, not knowing that JC had joined them on the phone in the kitchen. Kate and Blake sat on the steps outside reminiscing on things they'd done with Chris. Their stories had led to prayer over their missing brother. Blake took Kate's hands and bowing his head, began praying with her.

*****

Chris was lifted from the rough cot he'd been occupying in the medical wing. Every movement caused excruciating pain, and he was too weak to cry out. The soldiers roughly dragged him outside and hung his body up on the pole in the center of the courtyard. The first rays of sunlight lightened the sky. His eyes adjusted easily, and for the first time in a long time, he appreciated the beauty of the sunrise. The horizon was barely lit and the sun just beginning to appear. A warm breeze brushed the strands of hair from his eyes, and he felt a peace in his soul that he'd not known. The sun splashed colors of gold, brilliant pinks, purples, and soft blues across the sky. He watched the sixty or so men, maybe more, doing their daily chores. He breathed in the fresh air as the pain intensified. The birds began chirping. He felt the gentle wind caress his exposed and torn flesh. The peace had to be a sign that he'd join his Savior soon.

The sun finally peaked from its hiding place and lit the sky. One of the men marched up the three steps to stand beside the pole Chris hung on. He cut the ropes that suspended Chris and dragged him to the guillotine. The soldier let him fall to his knees, and his head was positioned for the blade to sever his head. His eyes stared down. The stains from the blood of many before glared at him. The rough wood choked him.

Lord, protect this people, show them the truth, and keep my dove safe. Thank you for giving me courage to endure. He prayed as he waited for the guillotine to come down and with it, the end of his life.

There was an unsettling stillness that had come over the courtyard. Several moments passed before Chris puzzled over the peculiar silence. No one moved. Men who'd been doing chores earlier were suddenly frozen in place. There was no shifting, no footsteps, no clank of buckets. A horse pounded impatiently at his stall door, but otherwise, all was still. Was this the peace God was giving him, or something else? Chris waited, but nothing happened.

He heard Narshac's soft command. "Release him. Get him out of here." The words were spoken as if someone had him by the throat.

The soldier beside Chris shook uncontrollably as he lifted Chris from the guillotine and cut the rope that had bound his hands. Opening his eyes, Chris found every man unmoving, watching him. No one objected as the guard led him out the gate about fifty yards. The soldier was nervous, eyes shifting right and left. He let go of Chris's shoulder and bolted back toward the compound.

"Leave us and never come back. We want none of that here!" Narshac yelled as the gates closed, and Chris found himself looking into the brilliant sunrise. Ahead of him, he saw the road. He couldn't believe his eyes. He lifted his praise to God. The exhaustion lifted. He forced himself to stand erect and begin a weak shuffle down the road. His pace was slow, yet he trudged painfully toward Shemna with a renewed strength he couldn't explain and a heart filled with wonder.

*****

Safira hung up the phone. Something inside told her that Chris was alive. She sighed as she returned to the retreat. The women were beginning to break up, and Safira thanked them for taking the time to pray.

When Fay and JC hung up, they felt the peace of God. He was working in ways unknown to them. Blake and Kate finished praying, and Blake gave Kate a comforting hug, assuring her that Chris was in God's hands.

*****

Inside the Keilronian prison, Narshac was still standing, frozen in place. Had his eyes deceived him? Was he going insane? Turning to the soldier beside him, he asked, "Did you see them?"

"Yes, sir, we all did."

"One of them spoke to me."

"I saw, sir, what did he say?"

Narshac's glare sent him on his way without a response.

Narshac briskly walked back inside to his office. He had much to sort through. No one in his command could offer any suggestions. His heart gave a little more as he remembered Chris's last words to him. Could this Jehovah have sent the man help? Whoever or whatever it was he had just witnessed was definitely a display of power. Was their God real? The evidence was in front of him, but it was easier to think he was going mad or that it had been witchcraft than to accept the facts. Narshac began comparing his gods to that of the Christians.

*****

Pastor Tim jumped when he heard the thud on his door. Cautiously, he stood from his desk to open the door and caught Chris as he slid toward the pastor. The other young man standing with Chris had been unable to sustain Chris's weight any longer.

"Chris? Lord, you are merciful!" Pastor Tim exclaimed. "Shoseph, how did you come across him?"

"I was coming to Shemna for supplies and found him curled up in a ditch about two miles out. He told me his name, and I knew he was connected with you."

"He talked to you?"

"Other than telling me his name, no. I just helped him get here. I don't think he could've made it without help. I'm glad to see you recognize him. You will take it from here? I must get to my business because my master will be upset if I'm too late in my errands."

"Of course. Thank you again, Shoseph," Pastor Tim replied to the Christian slave before closing the door behind him.

He shook his head in disbelief while helping Chris toward the spare bed in the corner of the small apartment. Once Chris was lying on the bed, he visually scanned the younger man for injuries. He could tell that Chris would be in pain when he woke. Leaving Chris to rest, Pastor Tim reached for the radio and immediately prepared the way for Chris to return to the States. He glanced toward the corner and sighed; the sooner Chris got home, the better. He looked like he'd crawled from the grave.

Part 3

The Americans

Chapter 12

Welcome Home

May 10, 2003
Colorado, United States

A taxi pulled up beside the man leaning against one of the canopy poles beneath the airport drop-off zone. The middle-aged driver got out of the car to load the man's two bags into the trunk. The driver couldn't help noticing how the man shuffled forward and carefully lowered himself down into the backseat. If it hadn't been for the long brown hair, the man would have thought the tall stranger an old man. The driver did his best to divert his gaze as he got in and asked for directions.

The man handed him a piece of paper with an address for south of Denver.

"That's like an hour drive. I don't usually go that far. You got the cash for something like that?" the driver challenged. The young man looked like a homeless man, and despite the long sleeves and baggy clothes, he could tell by the sunken cheeks and bony hands that the man was clearly malnourished. The passenger nodded and handed him a hundred dollar bill.

"All right, then," he smiled and pulled out into the 3:00 a.m. Denver traffic. He glanced in his mirror several minutes later to speak with his fare as he often did, but the man was asleep. He shook his head and turned the radio on quietly.

Chris's eyes were closed, but he was not sleeping. He heard the music come on and was slightly surprised the station was a local Christian broadcast. He let his mind drift back to one of his last conversations with Pastor Tim.

"You need to go back to the States. You can barely walk, and the doctors here aren't trustworthy. I'm sure you have broken ribs. I set your arm, but it may need more than I can do. I can't see all your wounds. But as much as I want you to fly home, you can't leave here in your condition either, so what are we going to do? I've arranged for you to return home, but I'm beginning to think you should stay and gain some strength."

"I want to leave as soon as possible. Forget about doctors. I can make it home. I will worry about medical help then. Besides, they can help more if the wounds are fresh."

"Have you looked at a mirror? Son, you look worse than a corpse that's been dead for a week. You can barely walk, and you want me to let you fly out of here on your own?"

"I've got to go home now. I'll be back again."

"I have no doubts that you will, Chris. I love you, and I think it's a good time for you to recover your strength and report to our supporting churches. Are you sure you want to leave immediately? I could postpone the trip for a couple of weeks."

Chris had nodded. The older man could see right through him, and Chris knew it. The way Pastor Tim's gaze penetrated his heart worried him. He wasn't completely sure he would be back. Perhaps the best thing for him would be to raise support in the States and get to know his family again and get acquainted with his wife. He could support the mission field without having to return. In his heart, he knew his emotions were shaky at best, and he could not make hard decisions yet. But he doubted his own return, even as he'd all but promised to do so.

He opened his eyes and sighed deeply as he stared into the dark morning sky.

The driver had heard the man stir, and when he looked into his mirror, he realized the man was awake.

"Where you fly from?" He casually posed the question.

"Keilron."

"That's an uncommon place to be. Were you there on business?"

"I'm a missionary there."

"Not a safe place to be a missionary right now from what I've heard."

"No, and it's not for the faint of heart." Chris acknowledged.

"Coming home or visiting?"

"I'm going home for a while."

*****

It was nearly five in the morning when Chris made it up the front steps of his Victorian-style home. Using the key hidden under the flowerpot, he unlocked the door. The moment he stepped inside, he knew his body was too tired to climb the stairs to his familiar room. He took his two duffel bags and laid them inside the living room before he plopped on the couch. The blanket lying beside the couch welcomed him. He picked it up and spread it over himself. The softness of the couch and the pillow under his head were pure bliss. He relaxed for the first time in years, not just his body, but his mind. There would be no more torture, and he knew he'd be left in peace. He'd told Pastor Tim he would go to the hospital when he returned to Denver, but he didn't have the patience to deal with the emergency room, and no energy to attempt any such feat. He decided he'd survived two years without proper medical attention. What were a few extra days? This was his last thought before his mind drifted into a dreamless slumber.

*****

Safira woke early Friday morning. She groaned when she heard the alarm and hit the off switch. She'd love to have the luxury to just sleep until she woke, but today would not be that day. Another women's retreat that she would have to catch a plane for was scheduled at a camp in Missouri. Thankful she'd packed her bag the night before, she put her feet on the floor and headed for the shower. The alarm clock warned that she had twenty minutes before she had to leave the house. When she got back to her room and dressed, she quickly made her bed; it had become a ritual when she left for the weekends to do so. It was welcoming to come home to a tidy bed. Grabbing a granola bar from the kitchen, she glanced out the front dining room window; sure enough, Kate's car was waiting for her. At the door, she picked up her single duffle bag and slipped on her shoes. She hesitated at the door glancing around the empty house. A sudden awareness that something was off struck her. The horn beeped outside from the small bug that Kate drove, pulling Safira from her uneasiness. Taking a deep breath, she shrugged and dashed out the door, making sure it was locked behind her.

When Chris woke, he felt his stomach growl and found his way to the kitchen. He'd asked Blake to prepare the house in case someone needed it. He discovered the cabinets nearly bare, but he'd expected as much. A few cans of soup and vegetables would have to be enough for now. He opened a can of soup and heated it before eating. The mess was cleaned up with a paper towel before he grabbed one of his duffel bags and headed for the shower.

The shower had been pure heaven. Fresh scents tickled his nose as he toweled off and slipped into comfortable sweats. He stood looking at himself in the mirror. The man looking back at him was unfamiliar and hollow. Exhaustion washed over him. Pain he'd been ignoring became unbearable as his body begged for more rest. He stumbled from the bathroom into his bedroom and collapsed on his bed. Before sleep claimed him, he knew that with the pain so intense, it was vital he get to a doctor soon.

The Kansas City airport buzzed with activity as Safira waited for her connecting flight. Her family bore heavily on her mind. Taking from her bag the letter JC had given her the night before, she recalled their awkward conversation.

"What's wrong, JC?" Knowing that something wasn't right with her brother-in-law, Safira had finally voiced her question. He'd been acting strange all evening, almost standoffish, which was unusual for the normally outgoing boy. She'd followed him out onto the front porch swing hoping he'd confess.

"Nothing."

Silence drifted between them, but JC remained close-lipped. At last, he'd spoken.

"I want to give you a letter because I can't seem to say what I want to say. It just won't come out right. I wrote it the other night but haven't had the chance to give it to you. I thought I could just talk to you. We're usually good buddies, but it's too hard."

"Of course, I'll read it," she promised.

"Okay, but you have to promise me to wait until you're traveling tomorrow."

She'd promised, and now sitting in the airport, she opened the envelope he'd given to her. Easing the paper open, she read the small missive.

Safira, I've been praying for Chris. I've been hoping for two years that he will come back to us. But I'm tired of hurting, of wondering, of hoping. I don't think he'll ever come back. Pastor Kindel hasn't had any news to offer us. You're my sister. I never want that to change. But don't you think it's time we acknowledge that Chris isn't coming back?

Safira raised her eyes and looked out at the airplane tarmac. She'd met Chris once under dire circumstances. She knew nothing about the man except that he was willing to lay down his life for Jehovah and that his family adored him. She could only wish that she would have the chance to know him herself. JC was obviously hurting and wanted to make the pain ease by allowing himself to heal. He couldn't do that as long as they held onto even a shard of hope. But was he right? Was it only hopeful thinking that Chris was alive? They had heard nothing. The times Pastor Tim called her he'd had no news or hope for Chris.

*****

Fay's smile broadened as Harris whipped a towel at JC, who laughed as the towel completely missed his thigh. Now a senior in high school, JC was no longer the straggly boy he'd been at fifteen. He was built bigger than his father and surpassed him in strength.

Fay felt an intense pang as she thought about Chris. He'd also been his father's pride and joy until the accident took Joshua Banks from their lives. She could almost see her dear Chris laughing at his stepdad and younger brother as they did the dishes. Chris had been overjoyed to go serve the Lord in a country that didn't welcome the Good News. Tears formed in her eyes as she thought that now, he may have gone home to be with the Lord. She left the kitchen when she felt her heart ache. Picking up the letter in her hope chest at the end of her bed, she read once again the letter she received from Pastor Tim nearly two weeks ago.

> *Dear Mrs. Kleren,*
> *It is with great regret that I write this letter. I'm writing in regard to your son, Christian Banks. I watched as the soldiers took him away. If he is alive it would be better if he were dead. It's been a little over two years, and at last, I find myself having little hope that your son still lives. But know this, Mrs. Kleren, your son was one of our greatest men here. He accomplished a great many things and was such a ray of hope for so many. I hope that someday I will be able to thank you for giving your son up so willingly to the Lord. If not in this life, I hope in Heaven.*
>
> *Love, Pastor Tim Kindel*

Fay still couldn't believe that her son was in heaven. Tears began to roll down her face. She prayed, as she often did, for her son. She hadn't shown Safira the letter because Fay didn't believe that he was gone. Two years of no communication, and yet her heart still said he was alive.

Harris strolled into their bedroom, knelt beside her, and wrapped her in a hug.

"Fay, darling, won't you let him go? He's in God's hands."

A weak smile gave way to a flood of tears. He held her as she wept. Several minutes passed before she composed herself enough to speak. "I won't believe that he's dead, and I know Kate doesn't think so either. Safira keeps him in her prayers as do many women around the United States because of her. With all that prayer, he can't be gone, can he?"

"What if he is?"

"I won't believe it," she said stubbornly. She stared up into her husband's eyes.

Harris gave a sigh and held her close. He knew she'd been writing to Chris. The unsent letters were stored in a shoebox on top of her desk. To lose their son would be difficult, but not knowing whether they were to pray for him or grieve over him was a heavy burden. As his wife cried, he allowed a few tears of his own to fall.

*****

Chris groaned as he rolled from bed. It was Sunday, and the alarm clock read 5:28 p.m. How could he have slept so much? He knew the time change would throw him off a bit, but twelve hours at a time? He'd rise long enough to eat, but after his meal, he'd be exhausted again. He was disappointed with his body. He was planning a trip to the hospital on Monday rather than deal with the emergency room.

He ate, trudged back to his room, and slept for at least eight-hour increments before he woke and started the routine again. Part of his planned trip to the hospital would have to include a shopping trip. He was running out of food.

He rose and trudged to the shower. Warm water helped with the pain, if only briefly. Ten minutes later, he felt his body relax back into the cozy bed. Still not used to having electricity again, he'd yet to turn the lights on in his home. Before he drifted off, he saw the alarm clock's red numbers read 7:15 p.m.

*****

Safira loudly exhaled as she plopped in the front seat beside Fay. The women's retreat had been delightful, but exhausting. She looked over at Fay, who sat studying her.

"What are you thinking?" Safira asked.

"How extraordinary you are. Your English is almost flawless, and your computer skills are increasing. If someone had told me that the little eighteen-year-old girl who was at my doorstep three years ago would be traveling all over the States as a guest speaker, I wouldn't have believed them."

Safira smiled. She reached over and squeezed Fay's hand.

"Since its 10 o'clock, where do you want to go, my home or yours?" Fay asked.

"I'd prefer being in my own bed tonight, if you don't mind."

"No, of course not," Fay said, pulling away from the curb.

Safira waved over her shoulder at Fay as she pushed the door open to her home. Fay pulled away when she knew Safira was safe. Her bags were dropped in the entryway. She was too tired to drag them both upstairs tonight. She just wanted to get some sleep.

Safira trudged up the stairs and pushed open her bedroom door. After turning on her light, she shuffled toward her dresser. Before she got there, her steps were halted by a movement from the bed. Panic ran through her veins at what she saw. A man lay in her bed! She backed against the wall near the door. As she did, she accidentally knocked a picture down, and when it hit the ground, the man in her bed sat straight up. The couple was frozen as they stared at each other.

"Who are you?" she demanded as her body shook. Unknowingly, her words were not her carefully learned English, but rather her native tongue.

"I could ask you the same thing," the man in the bed responded in Keilronian.

The silence was suffocating as their eyes locked. She took a deep breath and spoke in English. "I own this house."

Amazed at her switch to English, he followed suit. "No, this is my home."

"I'm Safira Banks, and my husband is away right now, but when he finds that you claim his home as your own, he will be irate," she said trying to scare him.

Chris blinked several times and wiped his face with his hand. His eyes softened as he stared at her. This was his wife? She was far from the scared young woman he'd met in Keilron. Her eyes were the same honey brown, but they were confident. And her shiny black hair rested a little below her shoulders. He began to chuckle at the situation. Here was the woman he'd married, his own wife, and yet neither one recognized the other.

"This is no laughing matter!" she retorted, angry at his mocking.

"Safira Banks, it's a pleasure to meet you again. You don't recognize me," he said beginning to sober.

Safira's eyes narrowed as she studied him. The man's long hair, sunken cheeks, and unshaved face was unfamiliar.

"My name is Christian Banks, and this is *our* house."

Safira couldn't believe that this was the same man she'd married in Keilron.

"You are Christian Banks?"

Chapter 13

Accepting Change

The alarm clock emitted enough light for Safira to watch the fan spinning above her bed. She'd been praying for his return, but she'd never thought it would happen like this. It was supposed to be a joyous occasion with the whole family welcoming him back. The surprise so late at night had truly rattled her, and sleep wasn't coming easily. Insisting she have her own room, he moved his things and took up residence in one of the spare rooms for the night. His appearance had shaken her when he'd weakly stood and shuffled to the spare room. She suggested that they go to the hospital and have him checked out. As he winced from pain, she'd cringed inwardly. What had he endured? She wanted to drag him to the car and drive to the hospital immediately, but he again insisted they could wait until morning.

The night dragged on as she tossed and turned. When she glanced at the red alarm clock numbers for what felt like the hundredth time, she decided that despite the glaring 5:16, she had to get up. Throwing on her bathrobe and blue fuzzy slippers, she quietly crept downstairs.

Flipping on the switch to the kitchen, she made herself a cup of coffee and went to the front living room. She clicked on the table lamp and curled up on one end of the couch before picking up the Bible lying on the end table. She didn't know where to look for wisdom on this one. She read a few verses in Psalms, Proverbs, Mark, and into James. Nothing spoke to her as she wanted. Safira sighed and closed the book. Her cup of coffee cradled in both hands, she sat enjoying the smell before taking a sip. The French vanilla flavor that mingled in her brew warmed her. The quiet was calming.

The cough from above her, where Chris was sleeping, instantly brought the awkward situation to the forefront of her mind. The coffee was nearly gone when she set it down on the coffee table and began to pray. As she did, she closed her eyes to rest in her conversation with God.

Sleep won the battle at some point, and Safira was startled, not only by the sunlight from the window but also from the knock on the door. She didn't want anyone to catch her in a robe and slippers. Quickly, she tried to slip upstairs to change, but the visitor was persistent. The knock grew louder. One glimpse out the window revealed a familiar vehicle in her driveway. Now was not an ideal time for an impromptu visit from her friend, but it seemed a mercy nonetheless.

She opened the door wide and invited her guest in. "Good morning, would you like some coffee?" she asked pleasantly.

Blake shook his head. "Where is he?"

Safira's eyebrows rose in surprise. "Upstairs. Did you know he was coming?"

"No. I've been away from my computer all weekend, and when I checked it this morning, I found a couple of important messages. A contact in the U.K. e-mailed me to say Chris was with him. He was expected to fly out Sunday night, and I should meet him. He didn't want to alarm the family unnecessarily, but Chris is in very bad shape. He refused to see a doctor until he was stateside, and much to their dismay, they couldn't convince him otherwise. The second message was from the same person saying Chris found an earlier flight and would be arriving Friday or Saturday. And by the deer-in-headlights look on your face, I assume he beat me here."

"Yes," she yawned. "He's upstairs sleeping. What time is it?"

Blake glanced at his watch, "A little after seven thirty."

"He promised to let me take him to the hospital today, but I'd hate to wake him. He looks awful and sounds worse. So I'm going to offer that cup of coffee again. It may be a long day."

Blake accepted this time. "I'll make us a pot. I think I remember where everything is. Why don't you get dressed? I'm sorry for interrupting your morning."

"Okay, but don't feel bad. I'm actually a little relieved because I don't know Chris at all. I'm at a loss, and I don't want to be alone telling the family."

Blake nodded as he headed for the kitchen, allowing her to escape upstairs.

Blake and Safira sipped coffee and chatted until nine. He finally volunteered to wake his friend, and Safira gratefully acquiesced. She had not been looking forward to being the one to do so. Rinsing out the coffee pot and cups, she stared out the kitchen window toward the backyard.

Blake quietly entered Chris's bedroom and stared at his sleeping friend. He could tell his friend had changed, even covered with a blanket. There was a rattle in Chris's breathing, and if that wasn't bad enough, the small bulge beneath the quilt hinted at how thin he'd become. Blake understood why Safira hadn't wanted to wake him. But if the e-mail and Safira's personal account were accurate, then Chris needed a doctor.

He took three easy steps across the room and touched his friend's shoulder. The reflexive response startled both of them. Chris jumped both up and away from the hand that had woken him. His breathing went from a baby's rattle to hyperventilating. It took several heartbeats for Chris's eyes to focus on his friend. When they did, Chris raked his hands through his hair, pushing it out of his eyes. A smile spread across his face.

Blake didn't let Chris move before reaching out and embracing his best friend. The extreme thinness of Chris caused a lump to form in Blake's throat, but he quickly brought his emotions under control. The baggy clothes Chris wore hid how bad he really was. Blake never knew Chris to be anything but healthy, strong, and muscular. The hug confirmed how vital it was to get him to the doctors.

"I'm sorry I wasn't there to greet you. I didn't get the heads up that you were even coming home until this morning. I was thrilled you were alive, but to be honest, you don't look like I pictured you," Blake finally said as he released Chris and sat on the edge of the bed.

"I wanted to get home so badly. But now that I am, now that I see you here, well, I think it's time I do get to the hospital. I hurt a lot, and I thought the sleep would take care of most of the pain. I've been sleeping all weekend, and I swear I'm getting worse. I'd love to get some pain meds."

"I want to hear about what happened from you, but I think we better get you dressed and moving. Safira is waiting for us downstairs."

"That's another thing. I don't know why it never occurred to me that she'd be living here. I think Pastor Kindel even mentioned it at some point. I feel awful about last night. I hope I didn't scare her too badly."

"I don't think so. She's unsure about the situation, not you. You just wait and see. I bet you are going to find it difficult to not fall in love with your wife. She's extremely independent, humorous at times, but compassionate. She doesn't take things for granted like many of us do. That's for sure."

"No one from Keilron would take things for granted, not when you've lived there for so long. But Blake," Chris tried to smirk, "did you fall in love with my wife?"

Blake laughed. "No, not in love with her, but I do love her, like I've loved all of your family. She's a sister."

"Kate's not your sister," Chris said smiling to himself.

"What's that supposed to mean?"

Blake's look of bewilderment caused a short chuckle to escape Chris. The laugh didn't last long as pain ran through his body. "Nothing. Now, are you going to help me or waste my energy talking?"

"I haven't seen you in years, and you're already getting bossy."

"We will have time to talk, plenty of time now," Chris said soberly as Blake helped him.

Getting to the hospital hadn't been challenging, convincing Chris to stay awake enough to go to the nurse's station had been. The hospital had offered him a wheelchair, which he accepted, and paperwork was filed. A doctor Walker, who'd stopped at the nurse's station to hand off some paperwork, took one look at Chris from across the room and told the nurse he wanted to see him next.

Chris was immediately admitted into the hospital. Two hours later, Blake and Safira were waiting for him to return from x-rays when Dr. Walker entered the room.

His eyes were tender as he looked straight at Safira. "Your husband is in serious shape. Aside from the pneumonia in his lungs, he's also very malnourished and dehydrated. You said he's been home all weekend by himself, and he even admitted to sleeping most of the time. We've x-rayed him thoroughly, and I'm amazed he's held up this long. His arm will have to be rebroken and set correctly. The left leg is barely healed, which could be a good thing since it was set wrong and really needs surgery as well. Walking on his leg is causing some of his pain. Very few ribs haven't been broken or cracked, and even now, he has three that haven't healed. I'm going to admit him. We want to take care of him. He may have internal bleeding if the rest of his body is any indication, and with the kind of torture he's been through, I'd like to keep a close eye on him for a while to make sure we've diagnosed everything. After that, it depends on how he heals and how quickly his body can recover."

Dr. Walker had never witnessed this kind of brutality in his ten years as a physician, and his patient's serious condition from the prison had rattled him. The look on Safira's face was unreadable. She was not surprised by the diagnosis. That much was clear. Her friend, on the other hand, swallowed several times as he stared at an empty wall.

Safira met the doctor's gaze. "When will he be back to the room?"

"We'll move him into ICU for at least two days for monitoring. We will go from there. I'd wager he's been close to death several times, and his body is struggling to fight. If what you told me is true, Mrs. Banks, I'm glad he's young. It's the only way he's got a chance of making a full recovery. The level of malnourishment is very serious, his other injuries aside. I just wanted to give you a heads up."

Safira thanked him and watched him disappear out the door and down the hall.

Blake put a hand on her shoulder and turned her to face him. "You don't look surprised."

"Honestly, the only thing I'm surprised at is that he is alive and that somehow, despite his medical conditions, he's made it back home."

*****

Safira and Blake left Chris sleeping after promising to tell his family. They'd decided the sooner, the better. Pulling up in front of the farm-style home, Safira didn't immediately vacate Blake's Jeep. They both stared straight ahead.

"I knew he looked bad, but I had no idea," Blake said softly. "How do we prepare them? How do we tell them?"

"I don't know. I'm amazed he found a way to come all the way home. If he's going to make it, he can't quit fighting. I know how they treat prisoners. It's not just torture, Blake. The mind is just as easily hurt as the body when you know where to prod."

Blake stared at her. From the hours of conversations, he knew she'd been privy to many of the talks between Shovak and Rofisca, but he hadn't given thought to what that meant. She was obviously not shaken by the fact the stranger was her husband, but rather that the stranger had survived at all. Perhaps, she saw Chris as a survivor who needed to heal. Blake prayed she'd find out how important it was for Chris to grow strong again. He prayed she would experience the joy of discovering for herself the kind of man she'd married. He knew them both and knew that if given the chance, there would be no better person for his best friend than the strong woman beside him.

Blake broke the silence. "I texted Kate and JC and told them there was an emergency, and they were needed at home. From the looks of it, both of them got the message." Blake nodded toward the two cars parked on the street. "Harris and Fay are already home."

Safira took a deep breath and opened her door. Blake matched her step as they trudged toward the house and up the porch steps.

The screen door flung open and JC demanded, "He's gone isn't he? That's what this is about, right?"

"No, that's not what this is about. Let's go inside." Safira's voice was subdued, and JC was immediately suspicious. He followed her into the house where the rest of the family anxiously waited.

The faces of her family showed mixed emotions. Harris sat beside Fay, his face expressionless. Fay fidgeted beside him. Kate was sprawled on the couch, her face twisted as she looked into Safira's serious gaze. JC wouldn't stop staring as he positioned himself on the ottoman. The last time she'd called a meeting had not been pleasant. This was good news; it just had a minor glitch.

"Last night, I was surprised by a visitor," Safira began. She watched her father-in-law's eyes narrow.

"This is good news," she was quick to reassure. "But it's like a rose. It has a few thorns. I found Chris in my bed last night."

Every jaw in the room dropped. Safira allowed the shock to settle in. Fay stood up, unable to get her words out, but the questions filled her eyes.

Safira raised her hand to stay any questions.

"Blake helped me get him to the hospital in Denver this morning. He's in bad condition. He's in the ICU and has requested that you all meet him there. But . . ."

Fay grabbed her husband's arm. "We have to go, now!" she interrupted Safira.

Blake spoke loudly, demanding attention. "Mom, the truth is, when we say tough shape, you have to prepare yourself. I wasn't prepared when Saf told me this morning. I went to see him and nearly cried. He looks like he stepped out of a holocaust video. We aren't even sure if we've found all his injuries yet. When you go see him, you will find it difficult to accept. It's best you don't react to his condition."

"He's *my* son, and I don't care how he looks. I've been on the verge of mourning him for too long. Today, I rejoice in whatever condition I find him," Fay declared.

Blake nodded and gestured toward the garage. The gesture was all it took for the whole family to scramble toward the minivan.

*****

At the hospital, Safira led Fay into the ICU. Only three visitors were allowed at a time, and Fay had requested Safira to show her where Chris was. The moment they entered Chris's curtained domain, Fay's hand flew to her mouth, covering her gasp. Chris was sleeping and was spared her initial reaction. Reaching for Safira's hand, Fay clutched at her for several minutes, just watching Chris breathe. Eventually, Fay's hand relaxed, and the silent tears trickling down her face eased. She wiped tears away before she approached her son.

"Chris," she spoke softly as she reached for his hand.

"Hey," Chris opened his eyes before she'd touched him. His face relaxed, and he tried a smile.

"Two years and all you can say is, 'Hey'!" Fay smiled down at her son. Leaning forward, she kissed his forehead. The hand that reached for her was frail. She felt the weak pressure as he squeezed her hand.

"Sorry, I was preoccupied. It's wonderful to see you again, Mom. I thought of you often, and I cried for what you must be going through. I've missed you."

"And I you. Safira shared a little with me on our way up here, but I think she was holding back. I wonder, how is it that you are here in my arms again?"

"I don't know. Sit down, Mom. I'll tell you what I know, if you really want."

Fay reached for the corner chair and brought it closer to his bed. She reclaimed his hand and waited. All she could see was the child he'd previously been needing care once again. But the story he began to weave told her he was no longer a child, and he'd seen and experienced things that no one ever should. The tears couldn't be helped. Seeing those tears, he skipped past the harsher details and shifted quickly toward his rescue.

"I don't understand what happened the moments before my release. I was prepared to die. I figured after two years, you and the family would've mourned me already. I was at peace. I was looking forward to heaven and painlessness. But God has other plans. Suddenly, I realized the courtyard had become deathly still, as if every soldier was paralyzed. Next thing I know, I'm getting dragged out of the compound and thrown onto the road leading back to Shemna. God gave me strength to come home, Mama," he said, allowing her to cry as she clung to his hand.

Now that she knew, her heart was breaking and suffering with him.

"I'm here now. Don't be sad. We have time together now." He mumbled as sleep claimed him.

*****

"They are giving him something for the pain. He was sleeping a lot before, but now, it's almost constant. He comes and goes, but he's never awake for long. Come, you must let him rest," Safira said, encouraging her mom to leave the room.

"No, I won't leave him, not yet. I just want to stay here. You could send the rest one by one, but I'm not leaving him," Fay said stubbornly.

The scene was touching. The family needed to see their brother and son. Turning from the mother and son, she slipped out to invite the others. After giving directions to Chris's room and watching Kate and Harris disappear up the hospital wing, she turned to leave.

"Safira, you wouldn't be trying to leave, would you?" Blake's voice came from slightly behind her.

"I need rest, Blake, and they need their time with him."

"You will be back for supper, or I'm coming after you," he teased with a raised eyebrow.

Safira smirked at him. She knew he was teasing, and yet she understood that he would come for her if she didn't show. She'd grown accustomed to him over the years and found him fun and endearing, something she'd never thought a man could be. Safira really did hope that Kate was right and that the two of them would indeed get married. She smiled at that thought as she agreed to his stipulations so he would let her pass.

Several weeks ago, Kate had confided in Safira that she was a hundred percent positive she was going to marry Blake someday. It just might take *him* a while to realize it; after all, guys were pretty oblivious to the obvious, she'd said. Yes, Safira had agreed with her, even though her own experience was limited.

    The bed welcomed Safira when she returned home. She knew she could prolong her absence from the hospital for only so long before Blake would make good on his promise. The alarm was quickly set before she collapsed onto the bed and drew the covers up. She dreaded going back. Hanging around the hospital was not a thrilling idea, but she knew that she was part of this family, and one way or another, she was needed for encouragement.

Chapter 14

Healing

After three days, Chris was moved from ICU to his own room two floors down. At first, the family had taken turns sitting with him, but at last, they believed that Chris was going to be okay. The healing would take time, but it was happening. Even Fay conceded Chris's improvement and was persuaded to go home and get some rest. The siblings left with promises to visit when they got the chance. Their jobs and responsibilities had been on hold long enough. Safira promised Fay she was staying with Chris and would report any changes.

Now that Chris was stable, his leg and arm surgeries were scheduled. He would go under the knife twice within the week. The first surgery was scheduled for Friday morning, and Safira would remain with him.

Thursday evening, an hour after the family had said goodbye, Safira sat in Chris's room scanning e-mail on her Blackberry. She'd sent out e-mails canceling many of her speaking engagements and was now receiving confirmation of those cancellations. She'd explained the situation with Chris's return, and as she read through the responses, she was overwhelmed by the words of encouragement and prayer pledges. Word spread quickly, and those she'd contacted weren't the only ones sending her e-mails. Churches, camps, missionaries, and people she'd only briefly met were sending her words of encouragement that she desperately needed. Until she'd scrolled through some of the messages, she'd inwardly been giving herself a pity party. The kind words from brothers and sisters in Christ reminded her of the larger family she was a part of. She prayed and asked forgiveness for her own poor attitude and praised God for His goodness.

Looking out the window, the feeling of loneliness dissipated. She knew she had the Lord to carry her through this ordeal, but she'd wanted physical arms to hold her as well. The words she'd just read wrapped around her heart and gave her the comfort she needed. Hugs from the family expressed their overwhelming joy, but they were not meant to console her. Their joy was understandable, but they couldn't fathom her uncertainty. She could not begrudge them their joy because she was happy as well. It was a miracle for this servant to have made it back home. Clinging to the words of love that had been sent to her, she took a deep breath and relaxed her head against the chair.

"That's a big sigh," a soft voice spoke.

A weak smile played at her mouth as she tried to meet Chris's eyes, but was unable to do so comfortably. She looked down at her phone, seeking a distraction. Chris's intense gaze was hard to meet. She blushed under his scrutiny, her eyes vacillating between him and the phone several times.

"You've done just what Pastor Tim wanted. You've become American," he stated as he nodded toward her phone.

"Yes, I suppose I have," she replied, finally getting enough nerve to set the phone aside and look into his face. He'd gotten some color back, but his body would take some time to recover the fat and muscle it had lost.

He smiled, "Let me guess. Phones aren't the only thing you know how to use now."

"No, I know enough about a computer to get by most of the time. I've done a lot of traveling. I've seen remarkable things, to be honest. The United States is fascinating."

"Compared to Keilron, I suppose it's like stepping into the future. You travel often?" He asked casually.

"I speak at many different events. I've been to camps, mission conferences, and ladies' retreats mostly."

"You speak about Keilron?" he deducted carefully.

"Yes. I give my testimony and explain your situation."

Chris remained silent. Pastor Tim was right about her. She was definitely on fire for the Lord and was doing all she could. His opinion of her rose a little more.

"You have been crusading for us. Do you have many close friends?"

"Honestly, I don't know. Kate is about the closest to me. I have many decent people who talk with me, but I don't really have that many friends. I'm too busy."

Chris glanced down at his hands, realizing by her twisting hands that she was uncomfortable. He'd chosen small talk just to grow more acquainted with her. Her answers were direct and to the point, but he didn't feel like he was getting anywhere with her. Honey brown eyes still looked at him when he raised his gaze back to her. His heart softened at her open expression, and he realized there was only one question that mattered.

"Are you happy?" he asked in all sincerity.

She sucked on her lower lip, and her eyes knit together as she thought for several moments on his question. "I'm content, but to be honest, I miss my home."

"There wasn't much for you there. How can you miss it?" His question was honest, but it was not only an inquisition for her but reflected back onto his own conscience. Safira's eyes bored into his, and Chris knew that somehow she saw through him.

"My family, the one's I had to flee from, are the ones I loved dearly. I played games and talked with them. I enjoyed the different festivals. I ate with the other children and wives. Even if your family did not accept your decision and disowned you, would you disown them or would you pray that they too would come to the truth?"

"So you miss them, or rather you miss the familiarity. I can understand that."

Safira didn't understand his conclusion. The look on Chris's face passed from inquisitive to contemplative. Safira felt she had to say more. He seemed too resigned, too encouraged by her words somehow.

"I miss the people too. The Christians who harbored me and the meetings held in secret. We Christians are on edge there. Anything could happen. At any moment, one of us could disappear because we have been discovered. Widows and orphans abounded in our circle. It's unjust, if you look at it from the American way of life. Justice for all."

Chris held her gaze intently as she leaned toward him.

"But there is great joy to be found in Keilron. Here, we may be safe from physical harm, but we are in danger of something serious. The first time I witnessed church services, I was in awe. No one was threatening these Christians with harm, and yet they acted as if they were in hiding. They sang the songs, but often only halfheartedly. They spoke kindly to one another, but I didn't see or feel the same wholehearted desire to lift each other up. I wonder sometimes, when I'm at a meeting or retreat, how many of these believers truly believe what they are hearing. Perhaps, they do. But if they were under the same oppression as my people, I wonder if they would better understand what it truly means to pick up the cross. I'm grateful I came here. I learned the grass isn't always greener on the other side. I'd rather die in Keilron for Christ than stay here and die an old woman who has helped bring much awareness about Keilron. That would be good, but I miss home. I miss our brothers and sisters there."

She saw his Adam's apple bob as he swallowed. He'd held her gaze throughout her speech, and she could tell by the look in his eye that her words had touched him. It was time to let him think. She stood and stretched.

"I'm going for some coffee, maybe a snack. I'll be back in a while."

Safira reached for her handbag and left the room quietly. Chris acknowledged he'd heard her and gratefully watched her leave the room. He'd been afraid to speak. Her words had caused the conflict inside him to wage stronger. Besides, he'd not known how to respond.

Picking up his Bible resting on the bedside, he opened its pages. His mom left it with him, but he hadn't picked it up. The struggle within himself since he'd returned to the States had kept him from reading the Word. Having been without the Bible for so long and knowing the conviction it might hold, he'd avoided opening its pages. He understood the error of that decision now. No inner struggle could be settled without God's help. The struggle of whether he'd been meant for Keilron or not had been haunting him for months. Maybe he'd just wanted so much to make a difference that he'd jumped in too fast. Perhaps he'd done his work there and accomplished all he could, and it was time to come home. Somehow, Safira had hit at the core of his thoughts. Surely, she didn't know him well enough to have read his heart so easily. He knew she'd been standoffish because she didn't know him and was only staying nearby to appease his mom. But the fire in her soul for the homeland that had so horribly turned on her had definitely caused a stir in his heart.

Safira was a blessing already. As two strangers in the military who can speak easily with each other and can feel each other's pain, Chris felt Safira was the only one who could even remotely understand. For the first time in two years, he opened the scriptures and read the Word. *"Take no thought for your life, what ye shall eat; neither for the body, what ye shall put on."*

Chris bowed his head and surrendered his will to the Father's. His mission in Keilron wasn't done; he knew that deep down. The time had come to rest, but it wasn't quitting time. He closed his eyes and surrendered to the promises he'd been unwilling to hear before. A race still lay before him, and he couldn't quit because he was treading difficult waters. As he confessed his faults to the Savior, he felt his mind and heart relax into the peace the Father offers His children.

*****

The difference in Chris was obvious to Blake when he came to visit his friend Sunday afternoon. He'd been worried about Chris earlier, but hadn't found the words to describe why. But today, the smile on Chris's face when his friend walked into the hospital room was enough for him to know his concern had been unwarranted.

The private hospital room was filled with visitors. Kate, JC, Fay, and Harris weren't the only ones popping in to visit today. Blake recognized the pastor and his wife from their home church in

Stonebrook and a couple of other men who were taking up Chris's time when he arrived. Chris's family sat on the fringes of the main conversation looking on with pride at how well Chris was doing. Blake was pleased at the small assembly coming to show support, but wondered at Safira's absence.

"Blake, it's good to see you, man!" Chris exclaimed as he reached for Blake's hand.

Blake smiled. "You are popular today."

"Word is out I'm home. Turns out, Sunday is a popular day to visit invalids."

Fay opened her mouth to support him, but Chris waved her off with a chuckle, letting her know he hadn't been serious.

"Blake, I'd like to introduce you to these two fine gentlemen. These men are Lyle Huston and Grant O'Malley. The press has finally gotten wind of my return, thanks to a tip I had to call in myself."

"Newspaper guys, huh? It is a pleasure to meet you gentlemen."

"And you. We were just about to leave though, so perhaps we will have the opportunity another time," Lyle said while shaking Blake's hand. Grant didn't say anything just shook Blake's hand and followed Lyle out.

"A little early to be calling in the hounds, isn't it?" Blake asked as he sat down on an empty chair.

Fay shook her head and smiled. "That's what I said."

"I figured they get a couple of pictures of me looking like this, and I'm well on my way to positive press, and Keilron is going to get some pressure about the way they deal with Americans. That kind of press could save lives," Chris defended.

"Your life is all that matters right now," his mom said, patting his shoulder.

"No, Mom. It isn't." Chris's eyes turned serious as he looked up at his mom.

Fay was shocked and looked shamed by her comment. Chris patted her arm reassuringly and turned his attention back to Blake.

"When are you going to be able to bust your way out of here?" Blake asked, breaking the awkward silence.

"Well, the doctors are satisfied with Friday's surgery and want to operate again tomorrow afternoon. They're pleased with my progress. They are hoping to discharge me by Wednesday or Thursday. As long as I promise to go where someone can keep an eye on me."

"You are welcome back home," Fay assured.

"I appreciate that and will consider the offer, but I do have a home of my own."

"Safira lives there. You can't live in the same house," Kate said from by the window where she'd been silent until now.

"Technically, little sis, we're married. It's my house, and I can go live there. She wouldn't put up a fight," he responded logically.

"Why? Because she's Keilronian? Well, you're wrong. She's American, and although she might not fight you coming to live with her, I will. You will ruin any chance you have at becoming familiar, or even friendly, with her if you do that. Besides, I don't think she should have to cancel all of her engagements just because her absentee husband walked into her life," Kate responded firmly.

Chris raised an eyebrow at her. "When did you become her lawyer?" His voice taunted his little sister.

Arms crossed, she stood her ground glaring down at him. "I'm not. I'm her friend, and I'm telling you going home is out of the question."

"We can discuss it later, but you're welcome to bunk with me. I can't do the whole twenty-four hour watch thing, but at least, I'd be checking up on you a couple of times a day. I'm usually home by six and don't leave till 7:00 a.m.," Blake offered.

"Well, that's feasible," Chris said.

"You need more care than that," Fay interjected.

Chris ended the discussion. "We'll discuss it later after we know exactly when I can bust out. I've been told I've no dietary restrictions until midnight, and I'd love to taste a cheesy pizza and order some soda."

Everyone laughed and followed his instructions. JC picked up the pizza. After everyone had eaten, it was getting late. Chris's family said goodbye and promised to visit after his next surgery. Blake didn't leave with the others since he had a shorter drive.

"I wanted to speak with you a bit before I headed home. You seem more relaxed than before," Blake said when the room grew quiet and the main lights were switched off. A lamp by Chris's bed gave a soft glow to the room.

"I'm feeling better, and while I'm dealing with a few things psychologically, I'm ready to be challenged again."

"Posttraumatic stress?" Blake questioned.

"Some, at least that's what they're calling it. I nearly stabbed a nurse with her own needle Friday night when she'd startled me."

"Yup, I remember you almost hitting me when I woke you the other day."

"I'm feeling good, Blake. Safira reminded me of why I love Keilron, why I need to go back."

"I'm glad to hear she's being helpful so soon. Kate's right you know. You can't bombard her."

"I won't. I was rather hoping you'd offer, which you did. I love my mom, but she's a little overbearing right now."

"I could tell. Where is Safira anyway?"

"I'm told she had things to do at home. She's headed on a weeklong camping trip. I promised her before she left yesterday I wouldn't be in her home when she got back."

"You were counting on my offer then."

"Yes, I was. I will be on crutches for a while, so I'm considering staying with Mom for a bit. But honestly, if I managed at home for a weekend, I'm sure I'll manage with a roommate checking in on me."

"We'll make it work, and if we decide you need extra help, someone can step in to help. You have the money."

"Which I will use and take advantage of instead of going to Mom's. I do have to pretend this is a tough decision," Chris smirked.

Blake grinned and chuckled a bit. "I'm going to head out then. See you soon, Chris. Oh, and Chris, you may want to think about how all this is going to affect Safira. I know you've been decent to each other, but be nice, think about courting her."

"I would if I thought it would make a difference, but honestly, I know I'm going back to Keilron. I can't ask her to return."

"She's not Angie. Think about that."

Chapter 15

Reaching Out

The following Sunday morning dawned with blue skies. Safira hadn't attended the Colorado home church in nearly a month because of Chris's arrival and her speaking engagements. She'd been looking forward to attending her church all week. She was pleased to be present today. Chris had left the hospital on Thursday and was planning to make his first appearance. Knowing he'd be there slightly dampened her spirits. Her relationship with Chris was tenuous at best.

When the sports car glided into the parking lot, she saw Blake's car and the Kleren minivan. Parking the car, she took a few deep breaths as she stared at the white building. Her purse and Bible were in her hands before she opened the door and headed toward the church. She arrived a few minutes early, hoping to avoid the family until after services. Smiles met her as she slipped into the back pew. One elderly woman reached out with her hand, and Safira instinctively took it as the woman welcomed her home. Music began filling the auditorium almost as soon as she'd found her spot, and as she'd anticipated, no one was afforded the chance to speak with her. She needed to focus her mind on spiritual things before she got whisked into the whirlwind again.

The message was especially good for Safira as she listened to the preacher's words. His message was based on God's plan for the believer. She listened as he spoke of allowing God to work through situations because everything we see is only a crumb of the delicious pie God sees. He taught about never being afraid of facing challenges because Jesus loves us and wants good things for His children. In Luke, Christ teaches us how the Father wishes to give good things to His children. In Jeremiah, God has a plan for peace for those who follow Him. All we have to do is ask and seek after His heart.

Safira closed her eyes when she realized she hadn't taken her situation with Chris to God in prayer. She'd prayed about it, but only to complain or ask for the situation to just work out somehow. But she hadn't been praying for Him to work in it, to give her peace, or to help her see the lesson and perfect plan He had in mind. She prayed for wisdom after her confession, and when she finished her prayer, she was finally ready to face Chris and the family with her Savior holding her hand.

When the message ended, Safira was ready to accept and move forward with her family and her own situation. Remaining seated after the service was over, she watched people's reactions to Chris's presence. Occasionally, her observation was interrupted when she was greeted by interested friends. Chris smiled, shook hands, hugged, and talked with older members, some of whom had watched him grow up among them. Families that had loved him for years were obviously ecstatic to see him. Newer members acted almost afraid of the frail man and stood apart, giving sidelong glances and quietly asking older members who the man was. It took several churchgoers a few minutes of staring and thought before realizing the weak man was Chris Banks. He smiled and spoke to everyone who came to speak with him. Safira could imagine the effort it took for him to smile and converse at length with many well-wishers. She was aware that despite his release, he was still very weak.

The Klerens took nearly an hour exiting the church. With the many questions surrounding Chris, the family wasn't going to leave the building until he was ready to go. Once outside, they saw how tired Chris had become again and decided to wait a couple of hours before serving the Sunday dinner to give Chris a chance to rest.

Within fifteen minutes of arriving at the Kleren's home, Chris had gone to his old familiar room and collapsed on the bed. Almost three hours later, he opened his eyes and peaked at the alarm clock.

The clock read three o'clock. By the delicious smell drifting into his room, dinner was right on time. He lay in bed for a while thinking about Safira. They'd accepted each other as a reality in the hospital. She'd been helpful and civil to him. But the relationship, if it could be called that, was complicated. They'd connected as war veterans, not as people, and certainly not as a married couple. When it was time to return to Keilron, would he leave her behind? If she was to stay, perhaps it'd be better if he didn't try to cultivate any type of intimacy, especially if he had no intention of following through and bringing her with him. Until he could make up his mind, until he had prayed more thoroughly about it, he didn't want to make a decision one way or the other. Safira had, however, done a remarkable job being his partner on behalf of Keilron. He couldn't throw that away.

The message from the morning's service came to mind. God had a plan and a purpose for everything. The whole picture wasn't visible right now, but that wasn't to say He wasn't creating a masterpiece. Chris prayed for several minutes regarding a move forward with Safira, how to befriend her without falling for her, as everyone was determined would happen or, worse, having her fall for him only to have her heart broken when he returned to Keilron.

He knew by the time he sat up from bed that he had to pursue a personal tie with his wife. Grabbing the crutches by his bed, he stood and hobbled to the dining room where the family was gathering for dinner.

Dinner lasted for over an hour because of pleasant conversation and a loving atmosphere.

Fay glanced at her watch and sighed. "Time to get a move on. I've got choir tonight at five thirty."

"I think I'll stay home. I don't feel up to handling more people," Chris spoke up as Fay cleared his plate from the table.

"I understand. I know you are planning on moving in with Blake tomorrow, but if one morning service can wear you down, are you sure it's such a good idea?"

"Yes. I don't want to socialize anymore today. It's an exhausting adventure, and I want to stay awake longer this evening. I need to start pushing myself a little."

Fay nodded, though her look said she didn't agree. She disappeared up the stairs to get ready to leave. Safira hadn't changed from the morning's services. She finished clearing the table as Chris watched. In quick succession, the family descended and said goodbye to Chris as they left the house. Safira walked back into the dining room and found herself completely alone with Chris. Awkwardness washed over her, and she gnawed on her lower lip.

"Are you sure you won't join us?" Safira asked. Shifting her weight from one foot to the other, she was ready to bolt.

"Actually, I'm hoping you might join me out on the front porch. I can't go far, but I haven't quite gotten used to the idea of being alone again, not after . . . ," he hesitated, hoping she'd understand the aloneness that had kept him company in prison still haunted him.

Safira glanced down at the empty table for a few heartbeats before looking straight into his eyes. Locking gazes for several heartbeats, Chris tried communicating with his eyes what he wasn't ready to say. Safira saw something in his gaze that calmed her. Her eyes softened, and she nodded.

Chris struggled to stand and shuffled toward the sunny front porch where he planned on claiming the swing. A few minutes passed before Safira followed with two glasses of iced tea. Offering him one of the two glasses, she sat in the chair near the swing.

The silence was not unpleasant, but neither was it comforting. Chris knew by the way she stared at him that Safira had questions. It was time to level the field.

"I'm told I have a wife who is outstandingly kind and finds the nicest things to say to people when they are hurting." He glanced toward her and saw her blush and stare into her glass. "She never backs down from a challenge, is remarkably intelligent, and speaks her second language fluently. I have a hard time with some of these statements. You say so little to me."

Safira met his gaze with a smile playing at her lips. He had her attention.

"I'd love to know this remarkable woman who shares my name. But you seem to stay on the edges of activity, like you're on the outside looking in. Kate was sending you looks all evening, so I assume that you are normally more talkative."

Her eyes glanced across the street and then back to him. "It feels strange to talk to you alone. When I'm with the family, it's even stranger because these people that I've learned to call my own now have their son and brother back. I'm no longer their connection to you. I mean we're married, sort of, and this is your family. But you and I are complete strangers. How do you expect me to act? What do you expect me to say?"

"I see where you are coming from. You should've seen Kate last week though. I got her a little riled up because I mentioned moving into my home, well our home. She was quick to defend you, telling me I wouldn't dare and threatening me if I tried."

Safira smiled at the scene in her mind. Kate truly was a dear friend, and there was proof in this big brother's eyes that he'd been entertained by the idea of his kid sister standing up to him.

"You'd already told me at that point you were going to Blake's."

"She didn't know that, and Blake hadn't technically asked me yet. I was getting myself invited."

"By threatening to move in with me?" she asked, her eyebrow furrowed in confusion.

"I know Blake better than he knows himself. When I first saw Kate, I figured he couldn't be oblivious of her. I also knew he'd been hanging around my family the entire time I was away. He'd do anything to appease Kate by the way he looks at her. I doubt he realizes it himself yet, but those two are head over heels in love, and I'm looking forward to the day he realizes it."

Safira smiled. Blushing, she stared back into her tea. He was right about the last part. His information on warranting an invitation had also amused her. He was witty. She hadn't seen that in their letters. She'd assumed he was a very serious person and took everything to heart. He'd obviously manipulated the situation to fit his liking, but the way he'd done it had taken some thought, and there was definitely a light side to it as well.

"I do have a question for you," she ventured.

"Shoot."

"There are many wealthy men in the States, but not all of them get media attention. Blake was the one to help me get going with the tours and speaking engagements, and he was able to do so by using my connection with you. Why are you of interest? I've seen the bank account, obviously, and I've never had to think about the money aspect here. What sets you apart from other wealthy men?"

"My grandfather started the legacy. He came from nothing and became a very successful businessman. His first companies made him a lot of money for many years. He lived in New York City and invested in Broadway, movies, and other such things that put him in the spotlight here and there. His company merged with an even more successful company, allowing my grandfather to do as he pleased."

"At that time, my father was supposed to take over the company, or rather the companies, and manage them while Grandpa played golf. The problem was that my father wasn't interested in moving his new family to New York City. I was only months old, and he wanted to raise me in church. He knew that the distractions of managing a large company weren't worth the risk of losing his family and his soul. He'd given his heart to Jesus, while my grandfather hadn't. They had a mild falling out, but in the end, when I was introduced to him for the first time, my grandfather understood and continued to manage the company himself. He even expanded and bought out several other companies, one of which was in Denver. My dad was handed the keys to that one."

"My father died in a car accident when I was four years old. My grandfather flew into Minneapolis where we were living at the time, and the media followed him. The money in the account I gave you is only the tip of the iceberg. I have several other accounts and investments all over. My grandfather left everything to me. When he retired and handed his firm over to several very capable CEOs, he began to groom me to be the man my father didn't want to be. Thankfully, my mom met and married Harris, and I became exactly the kind of man my dad would have been proud of. I think my grandfather would be too."

"Wealthy doesn't cover what you are then?" she asked, surprised that he'd laid everything on the line. Some of his story she'd heard from Fay, but was grateful Chris was opening up to her.

"No, but it's of little consequence. The media is interested in me because I'm a wealthy legacy. They thought I'd become like my grandfather. When I chose a different path, they decided to wait for me to fail. They don't believe it's possible for someone like me to give it all up."

"That's why you aren't afraid of the media. They've always been there, haven't they?"

Chris nodded. "That is enough about me though. Let's get back to you. I know you are the daughter of Rofisca, which actually makes you more of a mystery. Kindel said that you were able to get your GED and enter college in rather quick succession."

She understood why he was puzzled. "My father allowed for my education. Math, history, and science mostly. I got to study some linguistics, but those classes were short-lived. My father didn't want me to know English. I suppose it kept me out of trouble, since he'd not chosen to give my hand away."

"He doesn't sound like he's such a bad guy when you speak of him."

"I was his family, not his enemy. He loved me in his own way. He grew up hating Christians, and when the time came for him to rule, he was happy to rid our land of them. I understood his zeal, but couldn't understand why gods as powerful as ours needed the blood of unbelievers. It was Pastor Kindel who taught me what I wanted to know, and God's Word spoke truth to me."

Chris didn't reply. He still had a hard time reconciling the hateful man he knew as a loving father.

Chris studied her. She stared across the street, her eyes not seeing the neighbor's house. He shifted his foot, but she remained still. Her lips turned in a slight smile at what she must have been recalling. Had they been complete strangers and met under different circumstances, or through family friends, the situation might have been very different. Safira was beautiful with the evening sun touching her face. Angie's face flashed across his mind. He hadn't felt the companionship he now felt toward Safira with the woman from his past. How did he speak to a wife he didn't know? They were bound together and yet set apart from one another. Nothing could be so foreign. He didn't have a clue how to make her feel at ease with him. Time, he supposed, would be the only cure. He still wasn't willing to follow through with the courtship idea, but he didn't want to break her heart. She was obviously too precious for that.

"Are you staying here or going back? Last time we spoke, I had a feeling you were considering your options," Safira said in reference to Keilron. He realized she'd turned back to face him.

"You helped me through my confusion, and I'm grateful. I was willing to stay, talking myself into it really. My time wasn't pleasant, as you can well imagine, and convincing myself that I could do more here was a lie I told myself so I wouldn't have to face the music. Truth is, I have to go back. It's where God's called me. Once my strength returns, I'll be traveling the United States to gather support. I'm returning to Keilron as soon as I'm able."

"Where does that leave *us*, Chris? Maybe the better question is where does that leave me?"

"I don't know. I wish I had the answers. I made a promise once that I would never bring a family into Keilron. I lost a woman once who I'd planned on marrying. She wasn't willing to go, and I understood why. The risk is extremely high for me and even higher if there were any children. But I also don't want us to be complete strangers. I want to be partners. We are both seeking God's will, and we've both been doing our parts. I think we should pray about this more. It's too soon for either of us to make any decisions."

"I'm your wife, like it or not. I should go with you."

"I can't agree to that, especially now that I know exactly how dangerous it really is."

"But . . ."

"If you stay here, you could continue to bless the ministry by bringing awareness."

Safira remained silent. She disagreed strongly, but had no way of arguing with him. He was determined. Her mind sought a solution. She would love to go home without fear of her father. He wouldn't recognize her, even if he came face to face with her. She'd love to see how the church had grown and hear the songs of praise sung in her native tongue. How could Chris not understand how badly she wanted to go home where she belonged?

Safira stood, setting her glass down on the patio table.

"I do want to go home now and pray. I assume you will be okay by yourself until everyone gets back?"

"I'm sure I will. The way Mom has been acting, you would think I'm going to keel over and die any moment." He rolled his eyes. When she giggled at his antics, he smiled. Obviously, Fay's attention hadn't been lost on her. "But before you go, I would like to pray with you."

Safira sat down beside him and bowed her head. She was slightly taken aback when she felt him take her hand.

Chris bowed his head and began to pray. Safira lowered her head as if by instinct as she listened to Chris's deep tenor voice praying for her and the situation in which they found themselves.

A few minutes later, she started toward the Camaro but paused. "Chris, I want you to know I won't be seeing you this week. I have two separate engagements, but they will be my last for a while. I need a slowdown for at least as long as it takes for you to be without that cane."

"I look forward to seeing you then." He smiled as he watched her leave. He had to admit he liked the way she looked in his red Camaro.

*****

Angie Koch Randriguez entered the large, quiet sanctuary. She'd come to the youth retreat as she had for the past two years with her husband's youth group. The kids usually loved the music and were all challenged by the different speakers. This particular retreat had scheduled one session for the sexes to be separated and spoken to by separate missionary speakers. The one who had caught her interest was Safira Banks.

The surname Banks had immediately caught her attention, and after a few inquiries, she'd discovered that not only was Safira Banks a native to the country she represented, but also the country was Keilron. A few more well-placed questions, and the story was explained. The woman's husband was indeed her old flame, Christian Banks. Angie anticipated the hour or so before the service. The teens were playing a few last-minute games before heading to the showers to prepare for the evening's speakers and worship time. She'd told her husband she needed to meet the guest speaker and had made the arrangements to arrive early to do so. The church secretary was happy to inform her of the speaker's whereabouts. It pleased Angie to find Safira seated in the back of the large church sanctuary where she'd be speaking in a little over an hour.

"May I join you?" she asked.

The woman was clearly startled, but smiled and motioned to the seat next to her.

"I don't mind the company," she responded in heavily accented, fluent English. Angie would have expected a woman who'd only been learning English for such a limited time to speak more brokenly.

"My name is Angie. Are you Safira Banks?"

"I am. I was just taking time to breathe, pray, taking it all in. It's different tonight. I've spoken at lots of conferences, camps, churches, and retreats. But I rarely present to only young women."

"Don't fret over it. These kids will give you their attention. It's up to the Spirit whether they obtain and soak up anything valuable for their own lives through this," Angie encouraged.

"But I'm still praying for each of them. It's easy to hear and understand the message, but then go home and do nothing about it. I want these girls to have the courage to do something about what they learn."

"I pray for the same thing every day. I love these girls. Twenty-two of them are from our youth group. We love coming every year, and each year, they all leave home excited. It's up to us to try to channel their enthusiasm and keep the fire burning."

"You work with these girls?"

"My husband is the youth pastor in our home church."

"Then I trust that what I am saying will be recalled at another time when needed."

"Of course," Angie reached out and held the woman's hand. Safira looked into the eyes of the woman not so much older than herself and found a kindred spirit looking back.

"How is Chris?" Angie asked timidly.

"You know my husband?" puzzled Safira.

"Yes, we went to school together." Angie had decided to be cautious with introducing her connection.

"Wow, that's wonderful. Imagine running into you here."

"I was surprised as well. He told me he wouldn't marry. Especially after . . ." Angie looked down as her cheeks flushed.

Safira reached for Angie's hand that had gone back to rest in the woman's lap.

"You were the woman he almost married?" she asked.

Surprised by her perception, Angie met Safira's gaze and nodded.

"You are happy now, though?" she asked with genuine interest.

"Yes. I have a daughter who's happily enjoying her grandparents the next couple of days. Chris and I just weren't moving in the same directions. I loved him. Ending it was rough for both of us, but we knew it wouldn't work, not with his heart so full of your homeland. But I am curious how it is that you convinced him to marry. He swore he would never take a family to Keilron after I voiced my concerns."

"You will hear that story this evening, so I will leave you in suspense as to the details until then. The truth is, we may be married, but we don't have a marriage."

"I'm so sorry to hear that. I'm truly surprised," she said, shocked that Chris would allow his marriage to fall apart.

"No. You don't understand. How do I say this?" She thought for a moment, looking down at their clasped hands, and then looked up again. "He married me so I could have his name, so I could come to the United States. We do not know each other."

Angie relaxed. That sounded more like the Chris she remembered, always trying to play the knight in shining armor.

"I heard he's back. You have a chance now." Angie squeezed Safira's hand.

"Yes, he is back. But I don't know for how long. He is planning on returning as soon as his health returns. I won't hurt you by trying to explain what horrible condition he was in when he returned home, but he's on the mend. He has no intention of bringing me with him. So how am I supposed to get to know a man that is only in my life for a short time? I don't want to grow attached to him if he is only to leave me here alone again."

"Chris is stubborn, always has been, probably always will be. The truth is that's one of the reasons why I think God is using him in a land so full of turmoil. But I'm also looking at you, Safira. Keilron is your home. I would never want to be ripped from my family or my homeland even if they sought after me. You can't tell me you don't want to return. Or do you prefer this side of the great pond?"

"My heart yearns for my people. I can't deny it. I keep telling myself I'm yearning for what used to be there. I remember the expensive palace and vineyard I grew up in, and I miss it. I remember the small secret gatherings and want to cry for the hurting ones. But I also remember the pain, both physical and emotional, and the grief we all bore. I wonder why I would yearn for that strife again when life here is so pleasant, and God is using me here."

"You will have to decide for yourself, but it sounds to me like your heart is just as burdened as Chris's for these people. It sounds to me as if you are willing to give it all up in a way that I wasn't. If you decide that God wants you to return, you can't let Chris stop you. I let go of Chris because my calling wasn't for your people, and I knew I wouldn't make it there. Safira, these are your people. Don't let Chris boss you off the island if you know you are supposed to go." She smiled at the giggle that Safira let escape from her last comment.

"You are amazing, Angie. Thank you for your words of encouragement. I will think and pray about this. You have a point." Safira's smile grew.

Silence lingered for several minutes before Angie volunteered to pray for her new friend. They did so before hugging and exchanging addresses and e-mails. Angie excused herself to go make sure her troops arrived on time.

Angie walked toward the rooms the church was allowing her girls to use for the overnight teen extravaganza. She smiled to herself. Chris had been an amazing boyfriend and attentive fiancé. He had been a gem, and her mother hadn't understood why her daughter would let him go. Angie had been heartbroken for months, but knew in her heart she'd made the right decision when she thought back to how things had turned out.

Angie had gone home after graduating with her biblical studies degree and had met Todd Randriguez, who'd been chosen to intern with the pastor of her home church. He'd helped her past her broken heart and had brought laughter back to her life. She loved Todd with her whole heart.

Safira had impressed her, and Angie now understood that Safira and Chris had a long ways to go before they might be truly happy in their union. She also had seen what Safira wouldn't be able to. Christian Banks was going to fall head over heels for his sweet wife and would be amazed at just how much God cared for him by providing a helpmate in his chosen field. Obviously, Chris hadn't been looking for a partner or helpmate, but God had seen fit to provide him with a companion who would be a great asset and help in his ministry, the way Angie felt she was to her husband's ministry. It was exciting to see that God had blessed both their lives for choosing Him instead of themselves.

Chapter 16

The Date

Startled awake from his dreams, Chris took a deep breath as his eyes took in the comfort of Blake's spare bedroom. With his body healing and the drugs beginning to recede from his system, memories surfaced in his sleep. Sleep was mentally uncomfortable, and often, he woke feeling exhausted. Every time he closed his eyes, he relived the torture. He felt his body being dragged across the stone and could hear the screams of the tortured souls he'd left behind. Returning to his family was a relief, but he still felt the regret of leaving so many behind. He swung his legs over the side of the bed and stood shakily. The cast had been removed only two days ago, and he still felt unsure on his leg without a crutch. He walked carefully out of the main floor bedroom and into the kitchen where he poured a glass of water. He stared out the picture window facing the line of trees that divided Blake's property from his neighbor. Light gradually stretched across the horizon, while the sun began shedding rays of gold through the trees as it peeked out from its hiding place.

This time of morning reminded him of the strange occurrences surrounding his hasty prison release. What caused Comdt. Narshac to release him so suddenly? And what had caused his other captors to turn into frozen toy soldiers?

Chris's body was recovering quickly, and his schedule was filling with speaking engagements. He'd been told by the doctors that due to the extent of injuries, he had to be careful about doing too much too quickly. They had advised him to proceed slowly and recommended that he give it another month before he began any serious traveling and speaking engagements. Since he felt better, it was difficult to rest, even for a limited time. Despite the delay in reaching the churches that supported the Keilronian ministry, each day brought more people wanting to hear from him. Many of the churches and camps that wanted to hear him speak were from Safira's travels.

He took one more gulp of water before going to the living room to rest on the couch. No sooner had he plopped down, he heard Blake's voice from the hall as he entered the small living space.

"Hey," Chris murmured in response.

"Still having trouble sleeping?" Blake asked.

"I slept longer tonight than most nights. My mind won't concede that I'm home. When I started backing off the painkillers, I began getting more and more dreams, or memories, I'd rather forget. I want to talk with these churches. I want to get going so I can go back home to Keilron to help."

"What about Safira? Do you even know what a gem you've got?"

"I spoke with her Sunday evening. Neither of us is sure how to proceed right now. I'm not convinced I should do anything. I don't want her coming back with me, but there is something extraordinary about her. I have caught glimpses of what everyone is talking about, but I don't really know what to do. She's got me thinking about having her tag along, but I know she has enjoyed her work here."

Blake raised an eyebrow in hope. "You do like her, then?"

"She's pleasant, from what I've experienced. But I don't know what to do about her. She doesn't know me any more than I know her."

"Well, if you are going to be traveling together, it would make sense that you move back home. You can do things on your own at this point, so you really don't need me anymore."

"It would be awkward for us both if I lived there. You know that."

"Wasn't it you who told me women in Keilron are sold to the highest bidder? I doubt that they're given much of an option. Would it be so wrong for you to live in the same house?"

"Are you getting that sick of me?" Chris tried to tease.

"No. But dude, as much as I like having the whole 'guy only' thing, I think the only way you're going to get to know her is to spend time with her. If you don't want to move in, you could consider dating her. Church and family dinners aren't going to be enough. Besides, you are planning on bringing her to the speaking engagements."

"I've thought about it, but I haven't broached the topic with her yet."

"If she does go with you, and I know her, so I'm going to say that she's going to be more than receptive to the idea. You will be spending an awful lot of time alone with her."

"Which will be awkward unless we get to know each other," Chris clarified that he understood where his friend was going with his comment.

"Exactly!" Blake said smiling.

"I'll think about it," Chris said. He closed his eyes, ending the conversation.

*****

After walking in late at church Wednesday evening, Safira saw Chris seated on stage waiting for the pastor's introduction. His presence didn't surprise her because Kate had texted her Sunday night letting her know Chris had been asked to speak. As the congregation finished its last song, the pastor turned the meeting over to Chris. Safira was struck again at how fast he was recovering. He was still thin, but his cheeks were no longer hollow. The limp was pronounced when he took a step toward the preacher and shook hands, but he no longer needed the walking boot. He laid his Bible on the podium and used both hands to steady himself. Taking a deep breath, he spoke.

"This will be kept brief as I'm still a little weak."

Safira felt proud of Chris as he began his story for the congregation. Her brother Narshac was an intimidating man, and yet Chris had stood up to him. Chris had survived the physical torture, mental frustration, spiritual battles, and emotional roller coasters. Halfway through his story, Chris began to lean heavily against the pulpit as his strength drained. He wrapped up his story and finished with his thoughts before giving the audience back to the pastor. The message and testimony had been short, but the congregation now understood the reason for the changes in him.

Safira watched with concern as he carefully stepped down and sat in the front row. Was she really married to this man? Once again, she thought of how little they knew of one another. Did he really want her only as a friend? Was it possible that she could fall for him as many had intimated? There was a small part of her that hoped their friends were right, but she was a long way from being at ease with him. She loved who he was and respected him the same way she respected Pastor Tim. Respect was a stepping stone toward having the kind of marriage she witnessed with Fay and Harris. She wanted a loving relationship, but if she had to settle for a friendship, that wasn't all bad.

Safira bowed her head as the preacher closed the meeting in prayer, but her prayer differed from the pastor's.

"Lord, I give everything to you once again. You've called me to follow my husband. I know we understand very little about each other, but I know you want me to follow him. Thank you for your grace in allowing us this chance to know one another. Allow me to return home with Chris. Give me strength and courage to follow You. Help me return to my countrymen and give of myself that they might hear of You," she prayed silently.

The meeting dismissed, and Chris was soon surrounded by young men and women. Safira remained seated as she watched Chris with those who had questions. A few friends stopped to speak with her on their way out the door, but she was left mostly to observe. When the group of interested people at last left, Chris slowly limped up the isle toward her, gripping each pew end as he did so. When he saw Safira still seated at the edge of her pew, he stopped near her row.

"What's wrong, Safira?" he asked gently.

Safira stared up into his kind eyes. Knowing where he stood on the issue weighing on her heart, she wondered how he would respond. "I know I must go with you to Keilron," she spoke matter-of-factly, her eyes searching his.

"Safira," he once again spoke her name with such gentility her heart fluttered. It was a good thing she was seated. Chris sat in the pew in front of her and met her gaze. He'd thought and prayed a lot earlier that day on this very issue. He'd come to only one conclusion, and her willingness to declare her desires made it easy to give her what she wanted to hear.

"If you've decided it's God's will for you to follow me, I won't stop you. I have vowed to protect you, and if you join me, I cannot do that on my own. The only way we have God's protection is if we are both one hundred percent sure we are there for the right reasons."

Her eyes lit with hope. "Do you mean that, Chris?"

"Yes." The finality in his voice caused a smile to touch her lips and hope to light her eyes. The sincere look of excitement that lit her face brought a lightness to Chris that he couldn't quite explain. Her joyful expression was stunning. Perhaps he should try lifting her spirits more often.

"I was afraid you would refuse allowing me to go home," she confessed.

"When we last spoke of this, I was confused. I prayed long and hard today about you, and God showed me that this is your decision. I shouldn't get in your way, whatever your decision. If God wants you in Keilron, then I will not argue with Him. But I'm going to ask you to continue in prayer over this until the day we leave. If you have any doubts, I want you to stay here."

"I have no doubts, but I will pray. God will not change my mind any more than he will change yours. I believe God has put us together for a reason. I will trust that reason even if we can't see the whole picture yet."

Chris smiled at her mention of the sermon several weeks ago. She smiled back at him.

"I have events scheduled throughout this fall. Will you join me in spreading the word?" he asked.

Her smile widened as she nodded. "We will be a good team."

Her full smile made Chris's heart skip. This was the first genuine smile he'd seen that was directed toward him. It was much more beautiful than he'd imagined. He couldn't have agreed more; it was definitely going to be a beautiful partnership.

Safira saw something different shining in his eyes, an agreement, a new beginning for both of them. His gaze told her she could trust him. He glanced down at his hands for only a second, breaking the spell of comradery. Safira was instantly aware of the exhaustion he was trying so hard to hide. She stood and offered to help him up.

He took her hand until they were in the main aisle. The moment he released his grip, a sense of loneliness swept over her. When she moved ahead of him, Chris put his hand on her shoulder and she turned. He gazed down at her for a moment before reaching down and brushing a stray hair back in place.

"I look forward to working with you, Safira." He spoke softly, offering her his arm. Once Safira accepted it, they walked out of the church and to her car. Both knew that their commitment to God and Keilron would keep them together no matter what. Neither one expected their future to be anything less than living sacrifices for the Almighty.

*****

The yellow Lamborghini gleamed. It was impressive and flashy. Normally, Chris wouldn't have even considered driving such an ostentatious vehicle. But for once, he wanted to feel the power under the hood. The vehicle would draw attention from any passerby, but today, he didn't care. He'd spent the last couple of years inside one of the world's harshest prisons. Most of his life, he'd spent hiding his wealth, and for once, he wanted to show off.

Chris smiled at the salesman and nodded. The man was quick to bring the paperwork. Chris was planning on renting the vehicle only for the weekend, but he felt the adrenaline coursing through him.

He wondered what Safira would say. Would she even understand how elaborate this car was? Admittedly, there was a corner of his heart that had chosen the car based on his desire to impress his wife.

*****

Safira heard the phone ring but didn't look up from her sewing machine. She'd only recently learned how to use it and was still quite enchanted by its work. The phone rang a second time, and Safira sighed. She set the material down and reached for the cell phone.

"Hello, Safira. It's Chris."

Glancing at her unfinished project, she hesitated before taking a deep breath. "Hi. Just let me grab my calendar so I can correlate with you."

Safira and Chris had been speaking on a near daily basis over the past two weeks to make sure their schedules were up to date. She was a little surprised to hear from him now, however, since they'd spoken earlier that morning.

He spoke nervously. "Actually, I didn't call about schedules. I was wondering, would you like to go to dinner this evening with me?"

"Are you asking me on what they call a date?"

"Yes. I figure we will be together for quite some time, and I think it would be nice to spend time getting to know each other without the stress of scheduled responsibilities."

Safira momentarily took time to check herself. He was right—there was absolutely nothing wrong with going on a date with her husband. The idea was strange to her because she hadn't even thought about such a move and certainly hadn't expected him to make one when he obviously wanted her to stay stateside. Had he given into the idea that she was going with him? She should be grateful he was interested in her instead of reading too much into it. Women in Keilron, as well as some American women, didn't have the kindness in their husbands that Chris displayed. Mentally, she thanked God for His goodness before agreeing.

"Great. I'll pick you up at about seven?"

"Sounds good, Chris. Thank you."

"You're welcome. I'm planning on taking you somewhere classy, so dress for the occasion. I look forward to it."

His voice was smooth, and she believed him. Her stomach broke out with butterflies when she hung up the phone. Blushing as she stared at the sewing machine, she let the moment sink in and felt tingles down to her toes.

She shut the machine down, and her thoughts of bliss quickly turned to panic when she opened her closet door. Finally, she was actually glad Kate had taken her shopping so often, but she still didn't know what to put together. The date wasn't going to be for a couple of hours yet, so she decided it was a good time to shower and prep before choosing an outfit. Perhaps by the time she looked into her closet again, something would pop out then. She thought back to his comment about dressing classy and wondered what that exactly meant. She decided to think about it after showering.

An hour later, Kate rang the doorbell. She'd come to bring Safira some groceries, knowing she'd been too busy to do it herself. No answer. The Camaro sat in its normal spot under the carport, so Safira was home. Kate used her key and entered the house.

"Saf?" Kate called when she entered the house. She heard a clamor from upstairs and followed the noise to the master suite. It didn't take her but one glance to see chaos had hit the room. Normally, Safira kept a clean house, and her bedroom looked like something from a magazine. However, today, clothes were spread across the bed in heaps. Safira was nowhere to be seen, but the noise coming from the walk-in closet was a definite indication.

"Safira, what in the world is going on?" Kate asked with a small smile touching her lips as another article of clothing flew out of the closet.

"Hi, Kate. I'm so glad you're here! What should I wear on a date with my husband? And what, exactly, does 'dress classy' mean?" Safira emerged from the closet looking frantic.

"Chris?" Kate's eyebrows rose and her mouth parted slightly.

"No, the other husband," Safira quipped, disappearing back into the closet.

Kate rolled her eyes and walked over to the bed.

"I'm so sorry I explained sarcasm to you. You've learned to use it way too well." Staring at the pile of jeans and tops, Kate met her sister in the closet. Safira had already gone through many of her skirts and tops, but Kate was determined to see her in the dress she'd bought her sister months ago. It was time to convince Safira it was exactly what she needed.

"Okay. Do you remember this dress?" Kate pulled out the simple cotton green wrap dress. It had loose cap sleeves and a V-neckline. When Safira put it on the first time in the store, she had argued about the length, but Kate finally convinced her that the hemline that ended just above her knees was modest, yet flirtatious. Safira had still not given the dress a chance.

Safira glanced at the dress and frowned.

"Come on. You're a knockout in this dress, and just wait until we accessorize!"

Kate smiled and rolled her eyes. "Put it on. I'll show you."

Though not thoroughly convinced, Safira did as she was told, and before long, Kate proved her point by choosing a white pearl necklace and dangling earrings. Kate also pulled out a pair of heeled pearl white shoes that matched the dress perfectly. After she helped with Safira's makeup, Kate at last showed the end result.

"That's me?" Safira said in awe at her reflection in the mirror.

"That's you, princess," Kate smiled.

"I'm not Safira Rofisca anymore," Safira said quietly. She was impressed with the woman before her, but a tear fell for the Safira of long ago. The girl of no cares, the girl who'd ruled her house, and the girl who could turn even her father's decision to please her no longer stared back. No, indeed. She didn't look like the Safira from Keilron. Her black hair lay thick down her back in a long ponytail clasped by a barrette.

"Safira, you are beautiful, and God is already using you. Why do I see a tear on such a wonderful night?"

"I was only thinking of home."

"I'm sorry. I often forget. I never think of anything but that you were happy to have left. I never thought about what you left behind—your traditions, your styles, everything familiar. Forgive me for being so ignorant."

"No, no. Don't say such things. Without you, I wouldn't be here looking like this. Thank you, Kate."

Kate smiled as the two stared into the mirror at the American Safira.

The sound of the doorbell broke the stillness, and Kate grinned.

"Let's have some fun. You've never been on a date, and I want to make sure this guy is suitable for you."

"Kate, he's your brother," Safira said confused.

"Just play along. Don't come down until I call you." Kate's mischievous grin spoke volumes. She was up to no good, but Safira chose to be a good sport.

Kate disappeared, and moments later, Safira heard the door open.

"You must be Christian Banks," Kate said in a mock motherly tone.

"Very funny, Kate. Where is my"—he hesitated unsure of what to call Safira, and he finally settled on the safe side—"date."

"Well, she's not ready yet. While we wait, I have a few questions for you."

Chris rolled his eyes, "Kate, please."

She cast a glance down at his leg, "Are you able to drive?"

"Of course, pipsqueak," he smiled.

"You have your own car?" she said, ignoring his jibe at the old irritating pet name.

"Yup," he said as he pointed out the window at the rented vehicle. Kate's mouth dropped and her eyes popped.

"Since when do you drive something like that?" She was in awe. For him to drive something so elaborate was completely out of character for him.

"I have a date, and I wanted it to be a good one."

Safira, who'd been listening upstairs, had had enough of Kate's play. She began her descent down the stairs, ending their rivalry.

Chris's eyes immediately latched onto her. She looked good, really good. Kate must've had a hand in it. Safira was usually much more modest. His kid sister had a great eye for fashion, and he was grateful she'd helped. He was going to make this night memorable for Safira and him. Safira made him feel things that his heart had refused to allow him. He stopped his straying mind before it could get him in trouble, but he would have to ponder the emotions later. The discovery that his wife was attractive to him was encouraging.

"You are stunning," he finally voiced, ignoring his sister's presence. Safira bashfully took his extended arm. Safira glanced over at Kate with a mischievous look.

"Goodnight, Kate. Lock up when you leave?" she asked even as Chris led her out of the house and toward his waiting car.

"You can drive again?" Safira inquired.

"Yes, ma'am, and you may be new around here, so let me introduce you to your classy ride this evening." He drew her attention to the bright yellow Lamborghini. Recognition flashed in her eyes. He was grateful she appreciated the sports ride. The significance of the brand was lost on her, but she was impressed by the expensive-looking vehicle she'd seen rich people in movies drive. Opening her door, he let her in before joining her in the vehicle.

"You've been in America for over three years. What's your favorite food?"

She smiled, "I thought you were planning this adventure."

"I am. I'm just hoping I chose correctly, so enlighten me."

"Nothing compares to Keilronian food, but as far as diversity, I think Italian has become my favorite."

"I was right. Besides, I haven't met anyone yet who didn't like Italian food." Chris smiled and started the car. The car hummed beautifully, and he couldn't help but feel like a teenager again. He loved the power of a good engine. With the way the car drove, he was looking forward to his trip back toward Stonebrook after their evening.

They arrived at the restaurant, and to Safira's surprise, Chris parked the car by the front entrance and got out. He handed the keys to a man standing nearby and opened her door, extending his hand to help her. He was nothing but a gentleman to her. Smiling at him as she allowed him to help her out, she decided she was intrigued by his mannerisms. This version of Chris was fascinating—confident, cool, and relaxed like he'd done this a hundred times. The square shoulders and easy smile toward everyone gave evidence of his confidence despite the slight limp. He was showing off just a little, and she knew it.

A man standing by the entrance immediately stood up when he saw Chris and grinned when he saw the pair walking toward the restaurant. He snapped a photo of the young woman on Chris's arm as she smiled up at him. Chris's easy smile when he looked down at his wife was priceless. He'd looked down at his wife for only a second, but that's all it took for the picture to capture the moment. Chris smiled at the cameraman and stopped to shake his hand.

"Grant, it's nice to see you hanging around your favorite haunts."

"Hanging around? You asked me to show up. Thanks for the insider."

"True. And you're welcome. I wanted you to get a good picture of my wife and me."

"So this is the beautiful Mrs. Banks." The man smiled and offered a handshake.

Safira accepted the gesture before turning her gaze to Chris for answers.

"Well, we are on a date, so I won't let you take any more of our time. I'll send you some hot tips later this evening via e-mail."

"I'd appreciate that."

Grant smiled and took a step back, allowing them to enter the stylish establishment.

*****

As they walked in, a waiter ushered them toward a back corner of the restaurant. It was quiet and semiremote. The waiter handed them menus, took their drink orders, and left with a promise to return shortly. Looking down at the menu, Safira's brow knit together as she tried to pronounce the words. The menu was quickly discarded as she stared across at Chris, who was easily scanning the menu.

"Chris, I've been to some Italian places, but never one whose menu I can't actually read. I'm assuming, because I cannot read it, that it's Italian."

He peaked over his menu with a sheepish grin. "What do you like?"

"Chicken, fish, beef. I'm not really picky when it comes to food."

Chris smiled and laid his menu down. "I'll order us some chicken." He smiled as he raised his hand just a moment. The waiter came back and took the order. Chris pronounced the Italian just beautifully to Safira's ears.

"Where did you learn to speak Italian?" she asked, her mouth nearly hanging open.

Chris chuckled. "While my grandfather was trying to 'groom' me, I benefited from the wealthy culture. Part of my study with him was to learn French and Italian. I learned basic Spanish in high school, though I've rarely used it."

"And then Keilronian, of course. Language must come easily for you," she observed.

"Yes, I was blessed with a good mind for languages," he admitted.

"You're showing off tonight I think," she teased him.

"A little. But I wanted the chance to show you that I'm not all about the ministry in Keilron. This"—he gestured around him—"is part of who I am as well. You see me, I suppose, as the prisoner who was freed. You see the self-sacrificing missionary who married you so you could be free. There's more to the story than you've seen. And I want you to see the rest of the story."

"You want me to know you," she said quietly.

"I suppose I do. I don't want you to think of me as just the poor missionary in Keilron. I serve our Savior wholeheartedly, but I also love this part of life as well. Walking away from this country to be in Keilron isn't easy for me."

"It wasn't easy for me to leave my father's house either. You know my father as a harsh, cruel, and unforgiving man. The truth is that he is good to his family, protects them, and spoils them. We had rich fabrics, smooth stone, and marble floors to walk on with our bare feet or sandals. Rugs were absolutely beautiful, many of which were made by his household. He gave us anything we wanted, and he laughed often."

"I'm beginning to see that you and I are not as different as we both would like to think."

"No, we're not. You're right, though. I never dreamed of you as the man who could enjoy such luxuries."

"I loved this world. I also loved to work with financials. You know, I never stopped investing in the firms and with the money I was left. It's fun for me. Keilron had no problem with my business transactions. As a matter of fact, I'm pretty sure they stole some of my ideas while looking for proof that I was a Christian."

Safira giggled at the idea though she understood that it was a possibility.

"You realize, of course, that if you stayed, anything at all could be at your disposal. You could live in luxury. In Keilron, I've tried to live on what they pay me, to live modestly. You won't have luxury there."

"But we would never have to worry about money. I would be helping my people and my friends. You will find that I'm quite stubborn." She took a sip of water. The couple stared at one another. Their food arrived, and she was grateful for the interruption.

"It's nice that the house is this close to Denver. One of the reasons you chose to move there I suppose," Chris said after praying for their food.

"Yes, but I also didn't want to take advantage of your family."

"You could never do that," he said sincerely.

"Perhaps not, but the house was located closer to the school I wanted, and if I'm completely honest, I needed the space from your mother." She blushed.

He laughed. "I know exactly what you mean. Remember, I'm the one who orchestrated my getaway to Blake's house."

The reminder succeeded in getting her to laugh.

They spent the evening in laughter and easy conversation. Chris couldn't help but look for ways to make her smile. Her smile transformed her face into the most beautiful vision. When the evening ended and they said their goodbyes, both had memories to make their future together easy and more natural.

Chapter 17

The Road

Two Weeks Later

Their first speaking engagement was scheduled in San Francisco. Blake chauffeured the couple to the Denver airport where they got on a direct flight to California. Safira was relaxed and casual around Chris. Her husband's easy smile and playful attitude had helped ease any reservations on Safira's part. Even the sudden detour to Phoenix due to weather hadn't dampened their spirits.

They had made the decision that, for the most part, no one else needed to know of their unconventional relationship. It was unnecessary to divulge private information to those who were not involved. Safira had no desire to talk about such intimate details of her life to people she barely knew. She did wonder, though she would never voice the question, how Chris was planning on handling sleeping arrangements. More often than not, people would wish to host them in their homes. She knew he had planned on several of their upcoming trips to hold hotel reservations. This trip was not among them.

They landed at 8:30 p.m. and hailed a cab. Pastor Brody and his wife Kari were hosting them, but, due to the Banks' plane delays, were unable to meet them at the airport personally. But the pastor had promised to be home by the time they arrived.

Once the taxi driver had unloaded their bags from the trunk, Chris handed him a large cash tip. By the time they turned toward the house, Pastor Brody and Kari were gliding down their front steps to greet them. Brody offered a warm handshake to Chris, while his wife went directly to Safira.

Kari hugged her. "Welcome, I'm so glad you guys finally got here safe." Kari took a step back and offered to take the small suitcase from her guest. "You are probably exhausted. Come in, come in," she said, leading the way inside the large farm-style house. "Your room has its own bathroom, so you won't have to worry about sharing with us."

Kari offered them something to eat, which they both declined as they walked past the kitchen. But they sat and visited with their hosts for half an hour in the small living room beside the staircase. With it being late Friday evening and with a men's meeting the following morning, Chris and Safira were shown to their room and left to themselves.

Looking around the large bedroom, Safira immediately wrapped one arm around her middle and peaked up at Chris. The room itself was beautiful with neutral colors and a gold and brown bed spread on the queen-sized bed. One dresser, two chairs, and an oak chest at the end of the bed welcomed visitors. The bathroom was small, but efficient, and was closed off from the bedroom by a narrow wooden door.

The moment the door was shut, he spoke quietly. "I'll be sleeping on the floor, and you can take the bed." He moved toward the two chairs to set their luggage down

So that was how he planned to make it work. She sighed. The day had been longer than anticipated with the four-hour delay in Arizona. His solution was obvious, but she wasn't sure she agreed. She spoke softly, "Perhaps, I should be the one to take the floor. You still need your rest."

A small smile touched his lips when he turned back toward her. She still stood by the door looking at him with concern. She was not opposed to the arrangements, as he assumed she wouldn't be, but rather concerned for his welfare. Chris closed the distance between them. He put his hands on her shoulders and looked down into her eyes.

"My dear, I will be fine. This carpet is very soft, and I have slept in harsher environments. Besides, I wouldn't feel right if my wife was sleeping on the floor. I promise, I will still sleep well."

He watched her eyes soften slightly as she nodded in compliance. His heart leapt at the small smile that barely touched her lips. Leaning forward, he placed a soft kiss on her forehead. "We will get through this, you and I." He pulled her into a hug and loved the way she fit into his arms. They still had a lot to learn about one another, but God was definitely working.

Pulling out of his embrace, Safira moved toward her suitcase. "I think I'd like to shower." She picked up her small suitcase and went into the bathroom, making it a point not to look at him.

Chris heard the pastor and his wife in the kitchen and opted to go back downstairs to visit for a few minutes. Half an hour later, he returned and found Safira in bed fast asleep. Closing the door softly, he tiptoed to the edge of the bed. His face softened as he gazed down at his sleeping wife. Had she known his thoughts as he watched her, she would've kicked him out of the room, but as it were, she lay oblivious to him.

Chris ran his hand through his hair and sighed deeply. Turning to the bathroom with his own bag in hand, he left her side. When she'd left Keilron, he'd prayed for her. Now that he saw what Pastor Tim had seen from the beginning, his heart was opening up.

*****

Waking up the next morning, Safira shot a glance to Chris's spot on the floor but discovered him gone; his blankets were folded nicely on the chair, as if he'd never been there. The bathroom door was open; and she quickly removed the covers, picked up her bag, and made a beeline for the door. She had no need to worry about her privacy as she prepared for the day since Chris was walking the suburbian neighborhood.

With his strength returning, he began to prepare his body for the hard labor of the mission work. Glancing at his watch, he realized he'd been walking for nearly thirty minutes. Before prison, he'd been able to walk all day had he needed to, but now, the thirty-minute walk was as much as he could handle. He hadn't been cleared for running and had been told to take it easy. The only way to improve was to push himself a little more every day, although he was obeying his instructions.

By the time Chris was ready to shower and prepare for the day's events, Safira had finished with the bedroom and resigned herself to the living room. She was seated with her legs tucked beneath her on the far end of the couch with her Bible. When she heard Chris enter the sunroom on his way to their temporary quarters, she looked up and smiled.

Her voice stopped him. "What have you been up to?"

"I went for a walk. I find walking is helping to bring back energy and strength throughout the day, and I'm hoping it's strengthening my leg faster so I can be cleared to run again."

"You think you'll be able to return to Keilron, Chris?" she asked, more serious now.

Chris crossed the living room and sat on the other side of the couch where she was curled up with her Bible. "Yes, of course, when the time is right."

"How long?" she asked.

"I don't know. I'm still healing. I won't return until I've been given a complete bill of health. In the meantime, we will raise more awareness for those in Keilron. I've plenty to support us for our lifetimes and enough if we had ten children living with us. I've often had opportunities to help our fellow laborers, but from my experience, I know that money cannot buy everything. We need prayer more than anything. How can people pray for us if they don't know of the persecution we suffer?"

"I knew we were going to tell our story. I thought we were doing it only to bring more support and possibly bring more men to join with us."

"That might happen too. American currency goes a long way back home, and I won't stop anyone who wants to give, but we aren't asking for the support."

"Home," she said, her voice soft as if drifting into the past.

"Yes, Safira, home. I wouldn't think of it any other way." He put his hand over hers. Somehow, in that moment, he understood in his heart that she really would be going with him. Obviously, she'd been hoping and longing to return to her homeland.

Tears began to slide down her face. "I haven't been home in so long. I feel like my memories are failing me."

"What do you miss, running?" he asked, his eyebrows knit together as he concentrated on her. There were still some aspects of her return he couldn't understand. But, then again, was he not also returning to a people who had hunted him?

"No, *my* home," Safira stressed.

He scooted closer to her and wrapped his arm over her shoulders. He didn't know what to say, so opted for silence. She accepted his comfort and leaned into him while the tears fell for several minutes.

Pastor Brody and Kari didn't come into the sunny living room until it was time for breakfast. By the time they joined the younger couple, Safira was prepared to face others. Chris took the opportunity to slip upstairs for a shower and get ready for the men's meeting. Grabbing a pop tart as they slipped out the door, the two men left the women to do some San Francisco exploration.

Sunday morning services encouraged the missionary couple. So many people welcomed them with open arms and offered their support through prayer. Chris's message had been challenging and inspirational. Safira was reminded again just how special it was to be in the heavenly Father's family. Chris and Safira took a late-night flight to Colorado Sunday evening after services. They would be spending most of the week there for the last summer week of senior high camp.

Monday night, they enjoyed fraternizing with the kids, playing games, and roasting marshmallows over a campfire. During morning chapel on Tuesday, they introduced themselves formally as speakers for the camp. Chris and Safira were young enough to connect with many of the teenagers and wizened enough to give counsel.

While observing the antics of the teens during a game of field capture the flag, Chris was struck with an idea that he'd need his wife's help with. He approached her, and the two removed themselves from the games and teenagers until suppertime.

The camp director noticed their disappearance and became curious. Chris had confided in him about their relationship and living circumstance earlier to explain why he'd requested they be placed in cabins among the kids, rather than to share quarters. So their absence was unexplained and caused him great curiosity.

"What do you have up your sleeve?" Craig, the camp director, asked during the meal.

Chris grinned. "Something that will definitely get the campers attention. Today has all been about awareness, right? They were made aware of who Safira and I are, why we are here, and they learned camp rules. Even the morning devotion was about being aware of others and not just ourselves. So tonight, we are planning on driving home that point."

He grinned as he rubbed his hands together. "I look forward to chapel then." Craig had been intrigued with these two since hearing about them and loved them immediately. Their hearts were obviously focused on the Lord, and Craig couldn't wait to see how they would touch the lives of the young adults.

Safira was looking forward to the evening as well. Chris had come to her with an idea; then, the two of them had teamed up their creative minds and come up with a plan. She was excited to see how it played out. Chris had hit the nail on the head with his idea, and she'd enjoyed the comradery with her husband. They'd come up with an act that would, hopefully, get the point across. A smile played at her lips as she thought about how much fun they had planning that afternoon. He truly was a unique individual, and she was thrilled to know him.

Chris wore his traditional Keilronian attire for chapel that evening. The long robe looked much like the robes seen in pictures of the apostles, though slightly more ornamental. His attire caused quite a stir with the senior high group as they assembled in the chapel. Safira and Chris's campers were herded in by other counselors. Many of the girls' eyes scanned the building for Safira, but eventually gave up, believing she would soon join them.

Chris stood nearby as the music team led the campers in the fun and uplifting songs that have been enjoyed by campers for generations. The team finished, and Chris stepped on stage. He could see the crowd of just over a hundred campers who were still settling in. Just as he'd asked the song leader, they had finished with a lively song, and the kids were still smiling and whispering to each other. He stood, arms crossed, solemnly waiting to catch their attention with his stillness.

It didn't take long, and just as he'd anticipated, the snickers from the boys about his wardrobe were not completely silenced.

"Safira!" he called out loudly and angrily. The room instantly silenced at his tone. Everyone stiffened and glanced at each other with uncertainty. The side door to the chapel banged open and Safira, with tiny steps, rushed to the stage, head bowed in submission and hands clasped in front of her. She wore a long, red Keilronian tunic with the familiar headdress and thin veil covering her chin and mouth. The only skin exposed was her hands and upper face. The girls' astonished looks at her change of disposition cut off any further conversation. Silence dominated the room. The only sound was Safira's scurrying feet as she made her way to stand before Chris.

She curtsied before him. He looked at her in a domineering way as she stared down at her feet.

"You are to be wed tomorrow. I have already instructed the wives to make you presentable. Go. Prepare yourself. This marriage will bring me great wealth."

Safira curtsied again and disappeared out the side door the moment he turned away from the audience toward the wall. Counting to ten before dropping his arms and facing the microphone, his kind and open demeanor returned.

"How many of you women would appreciate your own fathers, brothers, or uncles give you such orders tomorrow?"

Many of the girls shook their heads, and a few commented how they would never allow anyone to tell them what to do.

"Ah, so you think she was too submissive? That things would have been different had she stood up for herself?"

"Yes!" Several cried out.

"Duh!"

"No way would I let anyone talk to me like that."

"Let's try it your way then, shall we?" Chris turned his back to the crowd and waited to compose his features again. He turned to look out over the crowd.

"Safira!" he shouted. Again Safira entered the room, head bent in respect.

"Tomorrow you will marry. Go. Prepare yourself. I have much to gain from this arrangement."

Safira's head snapped up and her look of defiance had the girls smiling. A few shouted out with encouragement, but Safira ignored her audience.

"I won't!" she declared. She crossed her arms over her chest and glared at Chris, her eyes flashy with anger.

Chris raised his hand as if to slap her. She took the fake slap just right. The back rows might have thought he actually had slapped her. Someone offstage had slapped his knee at the moment of impact to give the sound effect needed. A gasp rose throughout the young audience. Safira glared harder at him.

"I will not. No matter what you do. It isn't your right to give me away. I want to marry for love!"

"That's not your choice. It's mine. You better accept your fate, or a new fate will be far less kind."

"I'd rather die!" She spat at him. Her arms went backward slightly as she stood to her full height and took a half step toward him, trying to meet him eye for eye defiantly.

"Then I have no daughter." Chris spun away from her and faced the back wall. Suddenly, two of the counselors from the front row stood and grabbed her arms, dragging her out of the chapel through the side door as she struggled and called out insults and then pleas toward her unmoving "father."

Chris paused for several seconds for impact. When he regained his normal composure, he turned back to the young crowd.

"I see your shock, ladies. The truth is what you saw is exactly what would happen if any woman defied her father's orders. Once she is married, the same fate would occur if she refused her husband's commands at any point. The women are subject to their men's desires. The master of her household must be obeyed, or death is the penalty for her insolence. This is how it is in the country of Keilron."

He continued, "Gentleman, you have it easy there. You can demand the women in your life to please you in any way you see fit. This also means you would never be loved, never find a woman who wants to stand by your side. Most women would rather see their husbands dead. Men are also given the responsibility for their households. Women remain at home. Men are the ones with jobs or trades. One of the most respectable jobs is being a soldier. That isn't so awful, you might think. But to become a soldier, the men must be inducted when they are thirteen, the age of adulthood. Most of you guys are older than that. In Keilron, many of you would be married once, if not two or three times by now. You would be giving homage to the different gods while climbing the military ladder or improving whatever trade you were born into."

"Ask yourself—would you be willing to let your father speak to your mother, aunts, sisters, or friends in the way I just spoke to Mrs. B?"

Many heads went from grinning and nodding at his descriptions to hanging in consideration of his words. The situation was different when he made it personal. Chris continued to describe the culture of Keilron and its history before he brought his point home. By the end of the week, Chris had a plan to help these kids have a clear understanding of missions and of salvation and what it would mean to follow Christ. For tonight, he had planned only to introduce Keilron and what missions looked like in his field of service.

"Conditions for people are not ideal, as you can see. Among all this bondage is yet another, larger, imperfection. Christianity is outlawed. There is no freedom for anyone—no freedom to choose what you believe, no right to preach the gospel, and no right to meet openly to worship Christ."

"The one thing that could provide personal freedom is banned. It isn't just getting a slap on the wrist if you believe, meet, or express Christian views. No. The penalty for expressing or even being suspected of Christianity is death—not swift death, but rather a long, awful, and painful death. I've been tortured myself while imprisoned. I was stretched out on a rack. My bones were broken. My captors even experimented with electrical shock. They would nearly drown me. They even attempted beheading me, but that's a story for another night." He took a deep breath, trying to recover from the sudden flashbacks.

Safira stood in the back and met his gaze. The sorrowful look on his face told her he was seeing it all again. With understanding and encouragement, she nodded at him to go on. Chris encouraged the group of teenagers to begin examining their hearts and see if they were truly pure before God. He challenged them to seek His face and determine if they truly believed in Jesus Christ.

That night as the musicians gathered on the platform and Chris invited anyone to come forward to get their hearts right with God, several came forward to pray. Counselors came and led a couple of the teens outside to talk. The music continued for several minutes until everyone had returned to their seats. Chris closed the meeting in prayer, and the camp director dismissed the group for evening snacks, with instructions to go to chow hall for night games in twenty minutes.

Chapter 18

General's Daughter

Chapel resumed after breakfast the next day. Chris didn't waste time with theatrics, but rather gave a moving challenge on what it meant to follow God's will. He acknowledged that many of them would be looking at colleges soon, and many were also contending with peer pressure. Chris talked about God's principles, and when they were faced with a choice between doing what God wants and what the crowd wanted, the Bible was the voice to obey. He told them God's will starts by doing the things He instructed, like obeying parents, following the Ten Commandments, praying, forgiving, and loving others. Chris also mentioned following God's word on things to avoid like drunkenness and being involved with the wrong crowd.

When chapel dismissed, Chris and Safira discovered that their cabins were combined for a hike into the woods. They were instructed to follow the path and guidelines posted so they wouldn't get lost. With Safira's eight lively girls and Chris's seven rowdy boys, they began the trek with a promise from the older teens that they would love the view at the top of the highest hill on campus. Safira and Chris trailed the group so they could keep an eye on the teens.

"How are you enjoying camp so far?" Chris asked.

Safira smiled. "I love the girls. They are very rambunctious."

"I'd wager that my boys got the girls beat." He laughed. He then told her of the incident earlier that morning. The boys had been bonding by playing harmless jokes on one another, and the prank that morning had Safira laughing.

Chris loved her laugh. He was beginning to theorize that she was most relaxed when around children or, at the very least, while she was involved with ministry.

"Do you have any fun that you need my help with tonight?" Her quiet voice was full of mischief.

"Actually, I'm using my cabin boys tonight. But don't think you're out of the woods yet."

Fifteen minutes later, they found that the older teens had been right. The hike was worth the view. The trail opened up and then dead ended. They were standing at the edge of a cliff that plummeted some hundred feet down into a quiet reservoir of water. The waterfall cascading down into the calm pool below was directly across from them. Lush, green trees surrounded them, and the way the bird songs echoing off the rocks sounded like an Amazon rain forest. A few of the kids began to follow a narrow path that looked more like a deer trail than an actual path. Neither Chris nor Safira saw a sign posting to stay on the trails, so they followed the fifteen older teens and again were not disappointed as they followed the ledge of the cliff and found themselves beside the falls.

Safira had grown up where there was a rainy season for the plains and the almost desertlike world. The falls were captivating for someone who'd never seen such a sight. The teens were soon ready to go back for their next group activity, but it took Chris to bring Safira back to reality from her trance.

"We can come back later while they are playing games right before supper."

"I'd love that," she said. She still didn't move until Chris reached out and gently touched her arm. She looked at him and smiled. The feeling that had coursed through her system from that simple gesture was enough to make her follow him. Her mind puzzled over her reaction for quite a while on their walk back toward camp.

Chris made good on his promise and whisked her away from the camp games. Telling the director not to expect them back until chapel time, he requested and received a picnic lunch from the kitchen. They made it back to the falls, and Chris laid out the supper on the rock surface beside the cascading water.

"Wow, this is amazing," she said. She was appreciative of the effort he'd taken to give her time to take it all in. "Until this morning, I never knew such places even existed. I mean, I've seen pictures, but I've never experienced it like this."

"It is nice, isn't it?" He took a bite out of the apple he'd brought and glanced around at his surroundings.

His eyes returned to her, and he observed her look of wonder. Finally, he asked, "How are you doing, really?"

"I'm doing really well. I did have fun last night."

He smiled. "Me, too."

"Got their attention."

"It did. Skits always worked on me as a teen. Actually, I was thinking you could pick out a few girls for us to use tonight. I can give them a brief explanation of their roles. I'm sure they will understand as we go."

"I can think of a few for you. Speaking of these girls, it seems they are facing things at home that I've no understanding of. I'm having a hard time knowing what to say to them."

"Pastor Tim didn't experience the things you did. How did he encourage you?"

"With words from scripture or stories of men or women from the Bible."

"From my understanding, you have studied a lot of Bible since you've been here."

"Yes, but . . ."

"But what? All we can tell them is what the Bible says, but we can pray for them and trust God to work in their hearts. I'll be praying for you that the Lord brings to mind the things you need."

A small smile played at her mouth. "You have faith in me."

"Yes, as a matter of fact, I do. You accepted Jesus Christ despite the consequences. I remember a teenage girl who ran from home to save her own life. You are the woman whose father still wants to kill you. You are the woman brave enough to have come to the United States on your own and met people you only a vaguely understood. You are still the woman who educated herself and went out to tell the world that Keilron exists, and missionaries need much prayer. Yes, I have faith you will be able to give these girls wise counsel to deal with their families and situations based on what you learned on your own journey."

She stared at him in awe. He held such a high regard for her. He was no longer a stranger. He was a friend and confidant. Reaching out, she touched his hand. They gazed into one another's eyes. No longer did he see apprehension, but rather trust. He squeezed her hand in his. She was offering him a gift of companionship, and in his heart, he knew now that he wanted more. The friendship they had now wasn't going away, and it was no longer a fragile thread, but had somehow become a rope that God was weaving together. Her hand felt so right in his; he never wanted to let go.

That night in chapel, Chris's cabin did an excellent job portraying the brutality that Christians face. The boys perhaps were having too much fun tying each other up and faking torture. But they also portrayed their characters well and got the attention of every boy and girl. The girls who had been chosen to help in the demonstration and did their part well as they watched the men and children they loved being "tortured and killed."

Chris once again challenged the teens to examine their hearts and ask themselves if they would take up the cross of Jesus in their homes and schools. He showed them not only through the skit but also in his words just how easy it was for them to speak and be a witness before their family and friends. The worst that could happen to them was being mocked. How was that so horrifying when so many believers around the world were being murdered for their faith? Unbelievers were encouraged to experience the love and freedom of Christ by accepting Him as their Savior. More came forward that night; two were saved, and five committed their lives to God's plan for their lives.

After the services, the program director stood and declared the evening's night game was capture the flag. The room erupted with cheers.

"We do have a few new twists to the game this year. Counselors, you will not be excluded, but will be divided up between the teams. We are going to do girls vs. boys this year. Boundaries are as follows . . ." The director explained their guidelines and rules. "Oh, and that other twist I was talking about? You don't just have to get the flag, you have to take it back across your line. I know in years past, just getting the flag has been a challenge. This new twist is in honor of our missionaries who have to do a lot of smuggling where they live. I'm going to blow this whistle, and when I do, both teams have five minutes to hide your flags before I blow the whistle again, and all is fair game."

The room filled with anticipation as every camper was ready to bolt for the door.

"Wait, I'm forgetting something. Ah! We need captains for this game. Girls?"

Several names were called out before a chant started and was accepted as a great idea.

"Mrs. B! Mrs. B! Mrs. B!"

Safira stood up and grinned, taking the flag from the director like a good sport.

"Well, then, that's a first. But we can have fun with this. Boys, how about we vote on Mr. B?" The director led the boys into a chant of their own. Chris stood and took the flag waving it above his head and starting a chant like a football player. The rest of the boys joined in.

"Are you ready? Get set!" The whistle blew, and the entire chapel was vacated in minutes. The camp director, program director, and several other staff took a deep breath of temporary relief from the noise.

"Chris and Safira sure are a young couple to have gone through what they have. You would think they've had enough trouble in their lives," Craig's wife, Liz, said to one of the cooks seated beside her. The woman, Halie, nodded.

"Yes, I got to pack supper for him tonight. He said that he wanted to take her up to the falls. Apparently, she was very entranced by it. I was privileged to hear her speak last year while Chris was still overseas. She is a wonderful speaker in her own right. She told us a great deal about her people, and I've been burdened to pray for them ever since. It was such a surprise to hear Chris was back alive."

"I know Chris's mom from way back, and we've stayed connected over the years. I was surprised when I heard he was joining us for camp. Fay made it sound like he was on death's door when he arrived in April, or was it May? Anyway, look at him now. He appears to be doing well," Bonnie, the camp's nurse, chimed in.

"Unless you'd known him before, which I did"—Craig broke in—"he looked more like a football player than a soccer player."

The ladies pondered that thought before Liz changed the subject.

"They are a very good-looking couple, though. I can't wait to see what their children might look like."

Craig gave her a look to silence her. He'd confided in her earlier about the nature of their relationship.

"Don't give me that look, Craig. He is falling head over heels for her, and it won't be long before she figures it out too."

Charles, the program director, chuckled. "I'm more interested in how tonight might turn out. I would love to be a mouse in the corner on this one!"

Had he seen just how things were going down in the camp grounds, he would have been absolutely right.

Safira was sneaking through the trees quietly when she spotted the flag, and the guard was none other than Chris. She waited, trying to think of a way to get him away. Seeing the rock at her feet, she bit her lower lip and picked it up. She threw the stone to her left. Chris turned his back to her and faced the direction of the noise. He took several steps in the opposite direction, and Safira was ready to bolt for the flag when one of the girls beat her to it. Chris was quick on his feet, and the girl wasn't able to get far before he touched her shoulder. She groaned in disappointment as she dropped the flag. Completely distracted by his captive, Chris didn't even notice Safira creep up behind him and take the flag. He turned toward her and saw that she was back peddling as quietly as she could toward the dark woods. She'd covered at least twenty-five feet by the time he'd glimpsed her.

He grinned, "Why, you little sneak!"

"I was on the run a long time. I learned to be sneaky. That's why I knew I could beat you." Her full smile was dazzling, and her eyes sparkled with delight.

"So was I, and you haven't beat me yet."

"You got caught. I escaped," she sassed.

He gave light chuckle, "Only because I helped you."

"True, just like you did now."

"What?" he asked confused.

"I could make a break for it, and you wouldn't be able to catch me. I know your limitations."

"So does my team, which is why I'm not here alone. Now who's got who?" He grinned when he saw the boy behind her touch her shoulder. She'd been caught fair and square.

"I'm just a martyr. I'm not the prize. And I've been stalling." She grinned, revealing her empty hands from behind her back. The flag was gone. Just then, the whistle echoed throughout camp, signaling someone had won.

Chris stared at her unbelievingly for a moment, and the teen boy groaned in frustration. The look of success on Safira's face, however, was enough for Chris to take it in good humor as he laughed.

"I underestimated you, Mrs. B. Never again!"

The kids had all darted away the moment the whistle blew, and Chris draped an arm around her shoulder as they walked back toward the camp.

"Good job. But how did you pass it off without us seeing another person?" he asked.

"You were busy with the first decoy, and your partner was busy spotting me and being sneaky about not letting me see him, so what you both missed was little Gina hiding still as could be right where I'd been hiding earlier. All I had to do was drop the flag and take a few steps to the side, just enough to get your attention."

"You are a strategist," he said.

"I did grow up with a general." She was obviously pleased with herself. She was also quite aware of the arm around her shoulders, and somehow, it felt right for him to touch her so casually.

The next two days, Chris and Safira settled into a pattern. They went to the waterfall every evening for supper before chapel and enjoyed the time to talk about the day and any problems either of them faced. They started depending on each other for support. Every time Chris touched her, Safira felt her nerves jump into overdrive. And those subtle touches were becoming more frequent as the camp days passed. A touch on the arm, gentle pressure on her back as he ushered her through a door, or even a casual arm wrapped around her shoulders was all it took for her nerves to tingle.

The last day of camp, Chris gave his testimony and asked Safira to do the same. Rather than holding the evening service in the well-lit chapel, Chris and Safira had requested a bonfire down river from the falls. It was quiet and peaceful as the campers arrived. Several of the counselors and a couple of campers brought their guitars and were quietly playing *Softly and Tenderly* as the campers gathered around the fire. The kids sat in a semicircle by the fire, but as instructed earlier by the counselors, they approached quietly.

Safira's openhearted testimony touched hearts. She gave her story with honesty about her feelings and emotions through it all. After all, she'd been the same age as many of the girls when she'd been asked to go through the trials that tested her faith. Many of the girls were already crying, and a few had grabbed a counselor and gone to talk when she'd finished and turned the floor over to Chris.

Chris began his testimony, and Safira's own heart broke at the thought of what Chris had gone through. She'd known, of course, that it had been rough. She'd seen the scars, but that was when she didn't know him, and he was only a survivor. This was different.

"I'm not sure what happened to me that morning, but I guarantee it had something to do with prayer. I may never truly know why I was asked to endure such trials, only to be let go and forced to endure the pain of healing. I often thought it would have been easier to end my life, than to survive. I thank God today that I couldn't bring myself to do it. I praise God for His plan to let me go. We are all given a special role in life, and only He can decide when it's done."

"Tonight is your last chance to get things settled with God before you head home to lives and circumstances that, for some of you, will not be easy to endure. But with God, all things are possible. He will never give you more than you can handle, and better yet, He will walk with you every step of the way."

Seven kids accepted Christ that night, bringing the weekly total to twelve. Over thirty committed their lives to follow God in His ways when they returned home. Three others, two boys and a girl, committed their lives to foreign missions.

It was difficult for many of the young counselors to watch as the newly committed Christians climbed back into their church buses and vans to head home, where many of them would face hardships. It had been an encouragement to see the three who had committed to missions exchange information so that they'd be able to keep each other accountable. One of the boys was a senior and wouldn't be returning the following summer.

Safira and Chris were silent on their way to the airport Saturday afternoon. They were flying to Florida for the remainder of the weekend. Neither knew how to express the mixture of joy and sorrow in their hearts. Once they were seated on the plane, Chris finally looked at her and realized just how much she too was bearing and took her hand in his. When she looked at him, he watched her lips turn upward ever so slightly. Taking a deep breath, she relaxed and closed her eyes as the plane took off.

As Chris looked at her, feeling her hand in his, he knew at that moment he would do everything he could to show her just what she meant to him. She was a gift from heaven, and God had really outdone Himself with her. Hope rose inside him that someday, she would look at him as more than just a friend.

Chapter 19

Love Visits

Safira gradually became comfortable sharing a room with her husband, and his presence was reassuring. He never came in until she was in bed and was always gone by the time she got up, allowing her some privacy. Guilt crept in several times as she lay in the comfortable bed with Chris lying on the floor. She voiced her feelings once, but he'd dismissed her concerns with a smile.

The beginning of October brought good news for Chris; he was officially declared healed enough to return to normal activities. Immediately, he began to push his body. Running and muscle toning became a regular practice again. He often grimaced during normal activities, but Safira knew it was from his workout routine and had to do with muscle soreness, not residual pain. She learned to ignore his struggle since she could do nothing to help him.

By mid-October, the couple welcomed the sight of the Denver airport and the entire Kleren clan as the family picked them up on a Saturday afternoon. Chris and Safira had rarely touched down in Denver for two months; and the sight of Harris, Fay, Kate, and JC was welcoming. After they warmly greeted one another, the men loaded the car with the luggage as the ladies climbed in. A few minutes later, they were on the road and headed to the Kleren's home.

"You both look wiped out," JC commented as they pulled into traffic.

"Thanks," Chris responded sarcastically while giving JC a fake punch on the shoulder.

"You look great," Fay countered as she glanced at her son from the rearview mirror.

Safira followed Fay's gaze and really looked at Chris. The transformation had been occurring so slowly that his improvements hadn't really registered to her before now, but it was true. Chris was filling out nicely again and getting closer to the man she remembered in Keilron.

Feeling her gaze, Chris turned to look at Safira. Her face instantly turned red, and she glanced down at her hands before diverting her gaze out the window.

Chris smirked at her reaction. Taking her hand was very tempting, but he resisted. *Patience*, he reminded himself.

"When do you fly out again?" Harris interrupted the silent emotional exchange.

"Not for a week. I decided that we need some rest from the airports," Chris answered.

Harris glanced over at his wife and caught her eye. They smiled at one another. Harris wondered if Chris knew his own heart. The stolen glances at Safira made it obvious to the older couple that something had changed.

After dinner that night, Kate and Safira went for a walk. The two friends hadn't taken time to talk in quite a while and were both relieved to be able to open their hearts to each other.

"Tell me. How is it with you and Chris these days?" Kate asked.

"Things are improved. I enjoy his company now, and I trust his judgment."

Kate smiled as she rolled her eyes. "That's real romantic."

"Well, I thought we might be working toward the right idea when we were in Colorado in August, but then things went crazy. We haven't had much more time like that. We've been to one other camp, but the setup was so different we weren't really around each other. We fly together and get to talk then, but I'm not sure either of us are ready to add romance."

"He's in love with you, you know," Kate said seriously.

Safira blushed and looked down at her feet for a moment. "You can't know that." She looked back at Kate.

"I can too. He's my brother. The question is, how do you feel about him?" Kate spoke sincerely.

Safira paused for a moment before responding. "I'm not sure. I'm not even certain what this love is that you Americans talk about. All I've ever known between men and women in Keilron was the fear women felt toward men. They used women for producing sons and didn't care how it affected the women. I shudder just thinking of how it could have been for me. When I met your mom and dad, I saw a whole different way, and I began to imagine a different kind of relationship. In Keilron, only poor men understood what it was to have one wife. I respect Chris. I trust him. I want to see him happy. But love? Aside from Christ and what I've seen between your parents, I'm not even sure what that is."

"Maybe you should take some time and read some romance novels. They can help you understand what love feels like, but really, it comes down to you. How do *you* feel?"

"Romance novels?" Safira smiled up at Kate, who stood four inches taller than her. "That's the best you can do? How about Blake? I don't see him swooning over you."

Kate sighed. "He will. Someday. But that's not up for discussion. Trust me, Chris loves you. So what are you going to do about it?"

Safira had no answer for Kate, because she wasn't entirely sure she agreed that Chris felt anything but friendship toward her. Chris never flirted with her, nor had he tried to get physical with her in anyway. They spoke of their dreams for Keilron, but hadn't broached the subject of a future family. How could she know he loved her?

Saturday morning breakfast was a casual affair, although Fay made pancakes and sausage. The whole family gathered in the kitchen dining area, including Blake, to plan a day together. Glancing over to Chris several times, Safira had caught his eyes on her. Now that she was conscious of his gaze, she felt her face burn every time their eyes met.

"I was thinking about calling up some of our church friends and seeing if we could get them together for a picnic this afternoon," Harris suggested before shoveling another mouthful of pancake into his mouth.

Playing games and eating with friends was a great idea, and they all agreed. Within the hour, Fay had called many of their friends, and several accepted the invitation. Including the Klerens, Fay estimated about thirty people would be showing up. Quickly coming up with a shopping list, she rallied the girls into helping her with the preparations. Harris volunteered himself and JC to finish the dishes before they headed outside to do some yardwork that had been long neglected. Blake and Chris relaxed on the front porch swing sipping on coffee.

"How are you and Safira doing?" Blake's voice was sincere.

"Better. We had a fabulous time in Colorado at the end of August. But, truthfully, we've become comfortable with each other, as friends."

Blake had always been direct. "You don't look at her like a friend."

"I don't want to scare her away. Honestly, I think she's amazing, and I'm not afraid of her joining me in Keilron, but rather, I'm looking forward to it." Chris bared his heart with his friend. He took another sip of coffee and stared across the street.

"You have to make the first move."

"When I do make that move, I don't want her to be receptive just because she feels obligated to."

"Culture thing?" Blake questioned, staring intently at his friend.

"Yes."

"She's an American. Far as I can tell, she's never been afraid to speak her mind. She's not some delicate flower."

Chris's gaze snapped back to his friend's. "But . . ."

"No 'buts.' I'm telling you, she's no different than Angie. Accepting you will be on her terms, based on *her* heart."

"I'm not sure that's helpful."

"I know how you feel about her. Anyone with eyes can tell. You've been awfully quiet to her about your feelings. Don't you think she would reciprocate if you would give her the chance? Kate was telling me she just might. You've been friends with her long enough, and it's time to decide what you want. Pursue her. She may be your wife, she is going to be your partner in Keilron, and if you want her as your love, you better get a move on. I've never seen Safira wear a ring. Chris, come on, she's your wife. Treat her as such. You're a wealthy man, and your wife doesn't have so much as a gold band. Show her and tell her how much she means to you. You will never be able to move forward unless you make a move."

The black liquid no longer held any appeal. Pushing the cup away from him, Chris wiped his face with both hands. "You're probably right. I can always depend on you to be honest."

Enough had been said, and both men knew it.

*****

The remainder of the weekend flew by. Park festivities went on without a hitch, and Sunday was spent relaxing with the family one last day. Monday morning, Safira and Chris found themselves outbound for Pennsylvania. Safira closed her eyes as she laid her head back against the seat on the airplane.

"I miss them too," Chris said from beside her.

She didn't open her eyes but sighed in agreement. "Traveling is getting tiring," she admitted.

The flight attendant quickly went through her safety routine, and the plane was soon airborne.

"I'm glad I get to travel with you," Chris said quietly beside her.

Her eyes opened, and she rolled her head to the side to face him. He met her gaze warmly, but didn't elaborate. Reaching across the armrest, he took her hand and brought it to his lips. The gesture was so strange to her that she could do nothing but stare openly at him. A small smile played at her lips the moment his kiss touched her hand, and she felt her nerves tingle from head to toe. What was he doing? Perhaps, it was time to take Kate's advice and find a romance novel. Whatever this gesture was, she liked it. He released her hand

and turned away from her. She still stared at him in awe. Hope of catching a nap during the flight died instantly.

Over the next two weeks, Safira became more physically aware of Chris. At every opportunity, he would touch her in some casual way that awakened feelings in her heart she didn't know existed. Several times, he'd even held her hand while strolling through the airport.

An early November snowstorm raged outside the Chicago airport, so Chris and Safira's flight was delayed. They were headed to Colorado Springs from their New York interview with the media and their church engagement.

Chris had gone to speak to the airport staff and left Safira seated near their gate. When he returned, his look was grim.

"Looks like it's going to be a long night," he said when he sat down beside her. "We could try to find a hotel nearby. But from what I'm told, most traffic is stopped, and with it being close to Thanksgiving, most hotels are booked. What do you think?"

Safira's voice was strained. "I'd rather stay put. There will be too many people and no guarantee we find anything decent available. I've never seen a storm like this."

The day had been long already, and they were both tired. Chris saw the exhaustion written on her face and used his hand to gently lay her head on his shoulder. To his delight, she didn't pull away, but rather relaxed in his comfort.

Safira took a deep breath; she felt safe, like she was ten years old in her father's house. Allowing her eyes to close, she listened to the sound of Chris breathing.

One glance down at his wife told him she'd fallen asleep. He kissed the top of her head and smiled. The feeling of her nestled in the crook of his arm was the best feeling he could wish for.

Slipping the small velvet box from his coat pocket, he smiled. Initially, she'd been hesitant to go back to the camp outside Colorado Springs where they'd shared their first week together, but he'd promised her they'd be back to the Kleren's by Saturday afternoon. She'd asked why it was so important, but he avoided the question, so she finally just agreed.

Dir. Craig had been more than happy to help Chris arrange the time to be with Safira. Chris put the small box back in his pocket and took one of Safira's hands in his. She didn't stir. It had been nearly three weeks since they'd seen home, and the constant travel was exhausting.

They arrived in Colorado Springs twelve hours late, but it hadn't made that big a difference in their plans. A parked blue Trailblazer waited for them in the airport garage. The lock was a keypad, and after entering the code, he opened the door for Safira. The keys were stashed in the glove box, and Chris soon had the car's heater running while he lifted the two suitcases into the back.

Chicago's blizzard had no bearings here. The chill in the air was mild, and the landscape, although barren, gave no indication of wintery weather ahead. The couple was soon on the road. It was early evening when they arrived at the camp and were welcomed by Dir. Craig and his wife, Liz. After serving them dinner, the director introduced them to their lodgings before leaving the couple.

"Chris, what are we doing here?" Safira asked point blank. "There is no one here this time of year."

"Get some rest, and I'll explain in the morning." Chris touched her shoulder and kissed her forehead. He'd enjoyed giving her such gestures, and her response encouraged his plan of action in the morning.

She caved. "All right. Goodnight." She moseyed to her room within the two-bedroom cabin and shut the door.

The next morning, Safira was met with a steaming cup of coffee and a smiling Chris.

"It's a beautiful day for a walk. I hope you'll join me. I thought maybe we'd make our way to the waterfall."

"Okay, but will there be anything to see this time of year?" Her brow knit together in curiosity as she clasped the mug with both hands. The beige sweater sleeves were long enough to act as mittens while she held the mug.

"You'd be surprised," he said alluringly.

After grabbing a granola bar, she went to her room to switch from sweats to jeans. She put on her hiking boots and met Chris at the door.

They enjoyed the crisp morning as the sun shone down. Dry leaves beneath their feet crunched as they trekked uphill. Chris casually took her hand, as he often did, and simply enjoyed their time in silence. Safira had tried to get him to tell her what this was all about, but he'd been adamant about enjoying the moment.

When they reached the top, Safira caught her breath. The falls were enchanting. The echo of the falling water broke the stillness that seemed to engulf nearly everything else. Water was flowing, though not as strongly as it had last summer. Safira was grateful Chris had suggested she bring a jacket. Several minutes passed before she felt Chris pull her toward the beaten trail that led to the top of the falls. She willingly followed him as they circled around to stand beside the cascading water. They stood gazing at the world around and below, just taking it all in. Chris at last turned to her.

"Safira, I brought you here because I wanted a chance to be alone with you, away from all the distractions. My family is wonderful, but it seems that every time we are home, I don't get a chance to just talk with you. When we travel, we are rarely alone. And obviously, when we're at speaking engagements, we don't get much time." He took a deep breath and gazed into her brown eyes. His words had softened her expression.

"That week we spent here gave me hope and renewed my spirit as nothing else has. I've spent many nights now thinking about the most amazing woman I met here—you."

She could hear his voice above the falls, but it was soft and filled with passion. Knowing he wasn't finished, she remained silent. She sucked on her lower lip as tears shone in her eyes at what he was saying.

"Safira Rofisca Banks"—his eyes filling with hope as he clasped both her hands in his and asked—"will you marry me?"

"I already did," she whispered, a small smile tugged at her lips.

"When we were in Keilron, we had a wedding ceremony so you could come to America. Now that I know you, and you know me, I want to ask you."

He pulled out a small velvet box and knelt on one knee. "Will you marry me again, Safira Banks?"

She saw the large diamond, and her hand flew to her mouth as she gasped. Reality sunk in. He was proposing. When she spoke, she was surprised at her own first thought. "An actual wedding, an American wedding?"

"Yes."

Doubt entered her mind. "Are you sure you want me?" How could he? He was handsome, rich, and godly. Why would he want to have her as a real wife for life?

"Yes. No one else will do."

"In all ways?" she asked shakily.

"Yes. Did you not hear me? I love you." He stood and kissed her temple.

"Yes, yes, Christian Banks, I will," she answered with a huge smile spreading across her face. He hugged her close and lifted her off her feet, spinning her around as they stood above a two-hundred-foot drop.

He gently touched her cheek. They were both still smiling when he set her back on her feet. Her smile welcomed him, and so he leaned toward her slowly, cupping her face in his hands, and his lips touched hers. He kissed her with all the love and tenderness he had in his heart.

He ended the kiss and gave her a small peck on the lips before lifting the ring from the box and placing it on her left hand, where it would stay for the rest of their lives.

"Safira, I give you this ring as a token of our new life, of our love, and so all who see us will know that you are mine."

She knew the significance of a diamond ring and felt a tear find its way down her cheek as she looked at the beautiful stone, the one her loving husband had just given her. She looked up at him, and this time, she kissed him.

*****

"When is the wedding?" Kate asked excitedly as she stared at the ring on her sister-in-law's hand two days later.

"I want a Christmas wedding with our close friends and family. I want to keep it small, but I do want a white dress. I want red and white roses."

"That gives us six weeks. We should have enough time. We will make it happen. Is there any kind of Keilronian traditions you might like to add?" Fay asked. She was tickled that Chris and Safira had chosen to go through the motions of putting a wedding together. Chris was happy, and she praised God for blessing her son.

"It's not really much of a ceremony. There is only a priest, from whichever god you choose, and he is present when the purchase occurs. If the man desires a woman to wife, he pays the priest a fee, and the priest puts their hands together and says, 'Go in unto her, and make her your wife.' Many times, a great celebration occurs, especially when the union is also a contract that will bring wealth to both parties."

"Just what every woman dreams of," Kate added sarcastically.

Bringing the conversation back to the wedding planning, Safira asked, "Kate, would you be my maid of honor? From what I understand, she's the one who helps the bride the most?"

"Yes!" Kate squealed giving Safira a big hug.

Wedding plans were not easy due to the speaking engagements that kept the couple busy and away from the ceremony location. Safira and Chris chose the colors, the flowers, the people to be involved, the clothes, and the preacher. The couple had decided that since Pastor Tim had the honor of legally declaring them husband and wife, the only person for this new commitment before God and family should be the pastor from Stonebrook, Pastor Garston. Between Fay and Kate, the wedding was pulled together wonderfully, despite the bride and groom's speaking engagement interruptions. The wedding was scheduled for December 24.

With the wedding fast approaching, Safira and Chris chose to seek hotel reservations while attending speaking engagements rather than being hosted. Chris felt it prudent to remain chaste until they declared themselves husband and wife before God and family.

Christmas Eve morning dawned bright, beautiful, and chilly. The Kleren family gathered around the Christmas tree for gifts and time together before the day's activities. Chris and Safira had made plans to go on a five-day honeymoon and would not be with them the next day, so celebrating a little early was the best option.

Kate grinned at her brother, seated on the floor, who had wrapped his arms around his small wife beside him.

"This is the first, and possibly our last, Christmas together in a long time. Christian, would you be so kind as to read the Christmas story?" Fay asked.

The family opened their Bibles and followed along as Chris recited from memory the birth story of Jesus in Luke 2. Looking to Safira, Kate requested hearing the familiar story again in Keilronian.

The words sounded like music as they rolled gracefully from her tongue. The room was filled with thoughtful silence when she finished. Harris closed his Bible and bowed his head. The family understood his actions and followed his example before he began to pray.

"Dear Father, I thank you for this time together. I thank you for the gift you gave us that first Christmas. I'm so grateful to have my family gathered here this morning and for the wedding we will witness this afternoon. Protect and bless Chris and Safira as they begin their journey together, wherever it takes them. Guide the rest of us as we seek You here at home. Amen."

JC rose from his position in the large recliner to distribute the gifts. Each member received a handmade gift from Safira, who had been taught how to make many crafts while under her governess in Keilron, while Chris gave gifts of entertainment and luxury. To his mom, he gave a diamond necklace with each of her children's birthstones surrounding the solitaire stone. Kate received a five-day spa getaway for herself and a friend. The big screen TV for Harris had already been set up and ready for use that morning as a surprise, and JC was ecstatic about the keys to his nearly new Ford Mustang.

The family enjoyed the morning talking and eating. Time slipped away, and before long, the family scattered to prepare for the wedding. Safira knew her time with Chris was limited when Kate disappeared up the stairs.

"When do we go home?" Safira asked.

"I haven't told the family yet, but we're going to leave in May."

"I'm glad. I really miss home."

"Together, I think it'll be a much better experience." He kissed the top of her head. She snuggled a little closer to him, feeling at ease as she listened to his heartbeat.

Kate did, indeed, interrupt them moments later.

"Come on, it's time to head to the church," Kate grinned as she pulled her sister up from the couch.

The husband and wife sighed.

He smiled, "See you there."

Safira simply nodded at him as Kate handed her her coat.

The hustle and bustle of the wedding swept Safira off her feet. Kate did her hair and a friend from the Stonebrook church painted her nails; and then, with Fay present, she put her dress on. Safira gasped when she looked in the full-length mirror.

The dress cascaded to the floor in yards of silk. Her arms and shoulders were draped in vintage-style lace that also trimmed much of the bodice. The veil, attached to her hair, gracefully fell to the middle of her back. The tiara she wore sparkled like diamonds, though they could not contend with the genuine diamond earrings and necklace Chris had given her for the occasion. Her hair was piled on the back of her head in curls. Safira's eyes were bright and confident. Even she had to admit that Kate and Fay had transformed her into a beautiful bride.

Wedding music started, and the small procession began its way to the front. Kate, the only one to stand up for Safira, began her walk down the church aisle. Church members were invited with close family and friends, but the church was only half full. Taking a deep breath, Safira stepped into the sanctuary, alone. Harris had offered to give her away, but she'd turned him down. The Lord had put her into Chris's hands long ago, and it was Jesus who would be walking her down the aisle today. Chris's eyes popped and his mouth gaped as he watched Safira walking toward him.

Handing her large white and red rose bouquet to Kate, Safira accepted Chris's hand, and the wedding ceremony began. So different from their first ceremony, Chris pledged to love her, honor her, and protect her all the days of his life with a heart full of love. She vowed the same to him, and this time, feelings of love shone in her eyes.

"I now pronounce you husband and wife. Chris, you may now kiss your bride."

And so he did. With this kiss, Safira knew without a doubt God had given her all she needed. As the pastor announced them Mr. and Mrs. Christian Banks, Safira smiled at all the friends and family, and her heart praised the Lord for his goodness.

Part 4

The Keilronians

Chapter 20

What Is Truth?

March 2005
Shemna, Keilron

Narshac stood outside the women's quarters waiting for his first wife, Kalita, to deliver her child. He watched as the sun set, throwing brilliant colors across the sky. For the first time in months, Narshac thought of his sister.

Safira would've been a mother several times over had she wed at the appropriate age. He had doubts that Safira had known her husband. Recalling her fiery spirit, he sighed. She'd been the only daughter of many sons, so she'd been spoiled. Narshac made sure his household was treated equally.

A midwife interrupted his thoughts. "It's a woman child, sire."

Narshac followed her into his wife's birthing room.

Kalita smiled up at her husband. "What shall we name her?"

This was her first daughter out of the five children she'd presented him. Narshac knelt by the bed. A new birth always brought a sense of awe and love to Narshac. He often wondered how his father could have been so cold toward his wives. Narshac found a love for each woman and child she bore him.

"I was outside thinking of my only sister. She caused many problems and brought hardness in my father that haunts him still. It's been five years since she deserted us. Yet I still find myself loving the young child from my memories. I want to name our daughter after Safira."

She smiled adoringly at the babe nestled in her arms. "We will pray the gods make this child more obedient."

Narshac smiled at his wife and daughter. He stroked the little one's face and looked into Kalita's adoring gaze. He stood, kissed them both, and left his Kalita and their child to rest.

*****

Shovak's focus on the documents in his hand was interrupted the moment the office door cracked open. Setting the papers aside, Shovak leaned back in his chair and sighed deeply. He gestured with his hand for the interloper to enter.

"Sir, Narshac has arrived."

Shovak spoke briskly. "Send him in." The man disappeared, and a moment, later Narshac strolled into the office.

"Narshac, it's good to see what a strapping young man you've become."

"Thank you, sir."

"Please be seated. Relax."

Narshac glanced at the chairs but declined the invitation. "You called for me, Shovak?" Narshac wanted to come to the point.

"You've done well for me, Narshac. I think your father is proud of you. He's come a long way to being back to normal since Safira."

Narshac silently met Shovak's eyes.

"I have orders for your new post. You will be posted here, in Shemna. You've done an excellent job in your previous posts. And you've certainly not lost your knack for the Christians, as some have."

"I do as I'm ordered."

"I am placing you as head of the Shemna prison. This, of course, will come with a promotion, Col. Narshac."

"Thank you, sir. I will need a place for my family."

"How many are in your family, Narshac?"

"I have seven wives and thirty children, but I was hoping to bring only a select number of them here. The rest may remain in my estate."

"The position does come with a few perks. One of which is a home that I'm sure will accommodate you."

"I appreciate this opportunity."

"Will you join your father and me for dinner this evening?"

Narshac bowed his head in respect. "I'd be honored. Thank you."

*****

Lounging on the bed with Kalita, Narshac took in the sight of his newborn daughter as she nursed. "Did I ever tell you about an American named Christian Banks?" Narshac asked her.

"No. Won't you tell us?" she spoke softly.

Narshac did his best to keep favoritism from his household, but this wife had always held a special place in his heart. She was not the oldest of his wives, but he had placed her above all others, not only because of his feelings for her but also because she'd shown remarkable peacekeeping and diplomatic qualities that were necessary to run a household, or perhaps even two.

"I was posted at a prison camp, one of many in which Christians are kept. There was an American by the name of Christian Banks, and can you believe it, he was my sister's husband. He'd been there for over two years when I finally gave the orders for his execution. As he put his head in the guillotine, hundreds of men dressed in white appeared. One stood by every soldier, each holding on to a great sword. No one could move. I felt a fear rush through me as never before when the one by my side spoke. 'Let that man go,' he told me. I had no choice, and no one questioned my orders as the American was thrown out of the camp. And when the man was out of our hands, the men in white disappeared as quickly as they'd appeared."

"What a story!"

"Every word is true. I often wonder at the fear that gripped me that day. It was unlike fear for my life."

"You question the gods?" Her voice was thoughtful. "After that night, you were never the same, even I saw it. You no longer took pleasure in killing Christians. Do you question your faith?"

"I'd only admit this to you, Kalita, but I do question sometimes. I don't know about their Jehovah, God, but I do know that I've never witnessed such power by our gods."

"You must search for the truth, my dearest husband. Put your mind to rest, one way or another. One should not be confused on spiritual matters."

"Yes, you're right. But how do I go about something like that? I've much to consider." Narshac caressed her cheek with his hand. "We will be moving much of the household into Shemna within the month," he informed her. "I've been promoted to oversee Capitol Prison, and I will give you a list of those who will join us."

"Us? Does that mean I am to join you?" her eyes shone brightly.

"Yes. For a time, you must remain here with the new baby, but I would like you to join me as soon as you feel it appropriate."

*****

Shovak often felt the need to visit the prisons, and tonight was one of those times. When he was struggling with state affairs, he felt the need to justify what he was doing, and going to the prisons where his soldiers had been collecting the Christian filth did just that. No matter how much pressure he received from outside countries, returning to the scum reminded him of why it was so important to pursue the unbelievers.

Narshac, who'd accepted his duties only days earlier, guided him through the passage ways. They entered the torture chamber per Shovak's request. Shovak came face to face with a man suspended in midair by several ropes. The man's wife and three children were shackled against the wall nearby.

"You Christians are vermin in my sight!" Shovak spat at the man, feeling the familiar rage and righteous indignation.

The man's hoarse voice responded. "I'm Keilronian, same as you, but I believe in the Jehovah God who saved me from my sin."

Shovak stared at the man. He signaled for the ropes to be loosened.

"What of the gods of our world? Do you wish to be cursed by them?"

"Sir, they've shown me no mercy, given me no forgiveness. They've lost my confidence because I've seen what Jehovah God can do. He's shown me mercy, forgiveness, power, and love."

"Blasphemy," Shovak replied with confidence. Nothing else was said as the ropes were tightened again. The man shrieked from the pain. His small family against the wall wept as they helplessly watched.

Shovak turned to Narshac. "Are all the Christians of this same mind?"

"Yes, sir."

"Can you say that you see what these men see? Understand what strangeness they speak of? Do you know what makes them turn to this god?"

"No. I know nothing of it. Our gods have always been enough for me. I've seen this God's power with my own eyes. I am still not sure if I saw a god's power or some sort of sorcery, but of his mercy and forgiveness, I know nothing, nor have I seen anything." Narshac answered the master as he was questioned, but as he responded, he realized he was wrong. The Jehovah God had shown mercy toward one of His own followers.

"Narshac, you believe in our gods, do you not?"

"I do sir. Ask any soldier. I give my dues to them."

"I believe you. Do as you please with this man. I must be returning to my work."

Narshac nodded, motioning for a guard to follow Shovak back. He turned toward the man on the rack and eyed his wife and three children.

"Your wife is very beautiful, and your children look strong. Tell me their ages."

"The two girls are fourteen and ten, and my boy is six, sir."

"You only have one wife, and yet their ages are far apart." Narshac raised his eyebrows questioningly. Usually, a man with only one wife would have several children very close in age.

Narshac stared at the helpless man and then looked back at the man's family. Shovak had given him a large house for his family, large enough that he could expand.

"Bring me the woman," Narshac demanded. Instantly, a soldier grabbed the woman by her elbow and hoisted her to her feet. Immediately, the woman rebelled and cried out, but the soldier held her firmly, giving her no other option but to obey. Narshac circled her, taking in her figure and the tearful face, searching for the beauty beneath the dirt and tear-stained cheeks. At last, he smirked and nodded to the guard who led her away. The man pleaded with Narshac not to take her, begging for mercy on behalf of his wife. Narshac could hear her protests as she left. Both were already hysterical at the idea of being permanently separated. The guards instantly understood what Narshac was doing and were pleased with his tactics.

Narshac signaled for the older girl, and the scene with shed tears and pleas of mercy was repeated. He circled her menacingly, taking in every curve he could beneath her thin Keilronian robe. He allowed the father to weep when he touched the girl's shoulder, and her strong exterior dissolved into tears. The girl looked into his eyes, pleading with him for a moment. He experienced a moment of kindness toward her. He stroked her cheek gently like a lover and smiled kindly at her, while the father fought his ropes to no avail. Narshac nodded to the guard who led her out of the room and away from her father's eyes. The father began to beg and plead, but he was helpless against the crimes that would no doubt be committed against his wife and daughter.

"Bring the younger two children to my household. The boy will make a good soldier, and the girl is quite beautiful. Perhaps in a few years, she too may have the honor of joining my household." Narshac's smile looked like a serpent about to eat its dinner. "As for the man, I have an idea that will torture him worse than the stocks ever could. Cut the man down and take him to his cell. I truly hope you are right about your God. You will soon be meeting him, and your household has just become mine. I also hope you have said your goodbyes."

Narshac left the chamber and stared at the guards holding the family.

"I'll take the wife, but send the others to my household. I believe there is a holding place in the base of the house."

After waiting long enough for the man to have been sent back to his cell, Narshac grabbed the woman by the arm. She fought him as they entered the chambers where the man was shackled to the wall.

"Your wife is most beautiful," Narshac said, breathing on the woman's neck. "Tell me your name."

"What difference does it make?" she asked, her shaky voice growing stronger in her anger.

"I like to be able to use the names of my new wives."

"I'd rather die than defile myself."

"You haven't the choice to die, my dear Lonika." Narshac smirked at her surprise. He'd known her by name for many months while the soldiers tracked her and her husband.

"Don't lay a hand on her, I beg you." The man implored his captor.

"Markilsko, you believe you have an option?"

Narshac set the lantern down on a bench and lit the torches on the wall. Then, he slid his hands gently down Lonika's arms. She jerked away from him, but was restricted in her movements. Her hands chained in front of her and the irons around her ankles connected by another chain to her hands hindered her retaliation.

Narshac whispered into her ear. "If you want me to leave you alone, you know what you must do."

"I cannot denounce my God! I've pledged my allegiance to Him, no matter the cost," Lonika answered.

Narshac's attention turned to Markilsko, "And you, her husband, will you sacrifice even your wife?"

"I've made the same pledge to Jehovah," Markilsko gasped.

"Interesting. I, however, would not take your wife without your death first. You see, I've morals as well. Your daughter, on the other hand, is not your wife. I have no problem taking her to my bed."

"She's only a child."

"No, you said you are Keilronian. If this is true, then you know very well that she is no longer a child."

"You cared for your sister. She was not wed at such an early age."

"What do you know of my sister?" Narshac suddenly spoke fiercely.

"I met her four, maybe five, years ago, not long after she ran from home. She was one of the most beautiful girls I've ever seen."

Lonika was forgotten because Narshac was drawn to the man's words. "Tell me more," Narshac entreated.

"She was afraid and alone, yet she was sustained by Jehovah God." The man offered this information, knowing no harm could come to her anymore by the hand of any Keilronian.

"Is she here?" Narshac's voice was hard.

"If rumor be trusted, she married a missionary man and flew to the United States. I know nothing else."

"That is all anyone knows," Narshac spat out. He grabbed Lonika by the arm. "Thank you, for your information and for giving me such beautiful brides."

"No!" the man screamed as the cell door was shut behind him.

Narshac turned toward the guard. "I want him dead by morning. Send for Bovak. He'll do the honors."

The guard gave a nasty grin and went to do as bid. Narshac waited with the woman until Bovak came.

Lonika gasped when she saw the huge six-foot-four-inch frame of a man enter her husband's chambers. She heard his screams of torment. Tears streamed from her eyes as she was dragged down the hallway, her husband's voice silenced. They'd known the cost of giving their lives for Jehovah, but she always thought they'd be somehow protected. She knew she could not fall apart yet, not until she knew her children were safe.

"I'm taking the rest of the day off," Narshac told the captain standing nearby before dragging Lonika to the waiting carriage. "I've got two brides to entertain this evening."

*****

Pastor Tim opened the letter with satisfaction. He hadn't heard from anyone in America in more weeks than he could remember. He scanned the letter, and a smile crossed his face when he read the news of Chris and Safira. They'd been married according to American tradition. Overjoyed by their upcoming return, he set the paper down and raised his eyes to praise his heavenly Father.

There was much to prepare for the Banks' arrival. He hummed as he began his journey through the streets to meet with his people and begin preparations.

Chapter 21

Home to Stay

May 2005

The men unloaded the luggage as Fay and Safira hugged.

"Take care, and please come home safely," Fay said.

"Oh, Fay, Mom, the Lord is watching out for us. Everything is for His glory."

Fay's tears flowed easily. "I know dear, but I love you both, and I hate to think that this is our last day on earth together."

Safira wrapped an arm around the only mother she'd ever known.

"We're all set," Chris called.

Seeing his mom's tears, Chris wrapped her in a big hug. The rest of the family exchanged hugs with Safira and then Chris.

"We'll write when we can," Safira promised Fay.

Harris reached for his wife's hand and then Safira's. The family held hands as they formed a circle. The busy airport faded into the background as Fay, JC, Kate, and Blake took the time to pray for the Banks. They cherished the silence for several moments before Harris began his prayer.

"Dear Lord, bless these two and protect them as they journey so far from here to spread your gospel. Continue to give them strength and courage like you always have. Grant our family strength while we wait to hear from them. Give us faith. Let everyone whom Chris and Safira have touched remember these two in prayer. Lord, bless all they do," Harris prayed earnestly.

Cameras flashed as the wealthy Banks couple headed back to a land most Americans could never understand. Why would someone with the wealth of the Banks desire to go to a land where they could easily be killed? The family never looked up from their circle. A photographer's perfect moment, one that would no doubt be sent through e-mail to thousands of Christians praying for the family. The Klerens and Blake watched as Safira and Chris grabbed hands and disappeared into the airport.

*****

It was providential that Chris and Safira had grown accustomed to traveling, or their trip may have done them in with a two-hour flight from Denver to Miami, followed by an eight-and-a-half-hour flight to London. Chris had known that getting into Keilron from London was going to take some maneuvering and a lot of cash. He was able to bribe a small plane owner to fly them within two hundred miles of the Keilronian border. Within their two-day layover in the small country bordering Keilron, Chris was able to contact the missionary pilot who often helped Pastor Tim and his people. Among their belongings, Chris had the forged paperwork necessary to remain in Keilron if they were ever questioned, but he had decided against using them to enter Keilron through their airports.

The landing strip outside of Shemna was obscure and rarely used, but it did the job. Waiting for them at the end of the runway was Pastor Tim in an old beat-up jeep.

His smile was a welcome sight for the weary travelers. "Chris, you look better than I've ever seen you." The pastor embraced him. Turning to Safira, he took her hand, "Safira, it has been many years. You have changed a great deal, for the better, I'd dare say." The pastor couldn't keep the delight from his voice. He knew their return was dangerous, but it was also a small burden lifted from him to have them both back to share the responsibilities of ministering to the Keilronians.

"Yes, Pastor. It has," Safira spoke the English words to Pastor Tim.

"Why, you're speaking English much better!"

"I've learned many things in the States."

"The journey into Shemna shouldn't be long with this old beast, but let's be off. As you can see, the money you raised has been put to good use. I've been using this jeep to get to some of our new believers who live outside Shemna." The little jeep was loaded with all of their things. Pastor Tim started it up and steered toward the city.

"How is the church?" Chris asked.

"They're fearing for their lives, but our numbers continue to increase. Some will never be open about their new faith. Those who are open suffer greatly. They have been captured, and many of their homes have been destroyed. The support you've raised is greatly needed. Many officials are beginning to choose Christ, but have decided to remain anonymous. Shovak and Rofisca are still as strong as ever. I'm sure you have been keeping up with the news, but what you may not have heard is that Safira's brother is now head of the Shemna prison."

"Which brother?" Safira asked.

"Narshac. He's doing a very good job as far as Shovak is concerned. What Shovak doesn't know won't hurt him." Pastor Tim chuckled. At the confused look exchanged between Safira and Chris, he continued, "While it's true that Narshac is a horrid person to capture believers, he is not as heartless as we first thought."

"What do you mean?" Safira asked.

Chris's look of shock prompted Pastor Tim to continue.

"Do you remember a man by the name of Markilsko?"

"Yes, he and his wife Lonika sheltered me for a season," Safira piped up.

"Right. The entire family was captured a couple of months ago under Narshac. He tortured Markilsko and took the wife and oldest daughter to be his wives. The two youngest were brought into his household as servants, or so he told the soldiers. Lonika heard the death cries of her husband before Narshac led her away to his home."

"That's horrible, so tell me again why he's not heartless?" Chris said, his voice holding a slight edge. Forgiving his tormenter hadn't been easy, and there was still a piece of him that hated Narshac for what he'd done.

Pastor Tim grinned and held up a finger. "Here's the hitch. He took them to his house, but then released the two youngest and told them they should know who to go to. He turned his back on them and diverted his attention to his own duties. Two days later, the children came to me."

"What of Lonika and her daughter? What was the girl's name?" Safira asked, trying to remember.

"Lonika is the mother and her daughter Lomina. As it was, Narshac sold Lonika to a man known for strange dealings, meaning he's under suspicion for having dealings with Christians. A week after her husband's death, Lonika found her way to my circle. She was a devastated, sorrowful mess. Finding two of her children helped, but still Lomina and her husband are lost. She is doing much better and is helping with the orphaned children in our circles. Lomina, the poor child, has not been heard from yet. I fear Narshac did take her to wife." Pastor Tim shook his head sorrowfully at his last statement.

"Yes, he probably did. He has to save face. If he sold a used woman, he is still okay. And if two small children went missing who were not his own, again, no issue. But Lomina was a virgin, and as I remember, a very pretty girl. If he allowed her to leave, he'd have much to face up to."

"You are correct, Safira, but the girl was not yet fifteen," Pastor Tim reasoned.

"Most women are married at thirteen to men much older than Narshac. Lomina is lucky to have been forced to marry Narshac. He's a good man," Safira defended.

Chris looked at her in astonishment of her logic. She would never cease to amaze him. "Tell that to her mother," said Chris.

"He had to kill the husband and take the young girl to be able to save the rest of the family." Safira explained. "You certainly understand that, Pastor?"

"I'm trying, dear. I've been here for more years than I can remember and still don't really understand. Chris, it is a good thing what happened with you and Safira. We foreign missionaries need women like her."

Chris's expression softened. "I quite agree, Pastor." He smiled and kissed the top of Safira's head. "Coming from stateside, however, the transition back into this harsh culture may take a few days. I'm glad I have Safira to explain how silly my American ideals are."

"I didn't mean that," Safira stiffened at his words, but relaxed when she caught the mischief in his eyes and quickly switched gears back to the pastor. "Do we have any other accounts such as this about my eldest brother?"

"No, this was a first. In the past, he has been a feared captor."

"Is it possible that more is going on in the hearts of our leaders than we know?"

"I believe so. Boy, I do. Safira, were you very close to Narshac?"

"More than many of my siblings. He is my father's oldest son and my mother's child. He had a responsibility toward me, and he didn't take that lightly. There was much on his shoulders, but he also had a tender heart. I remember when he would come home and always play with me for at least a little while. If anyone in my family can be reached, I hope it's him." She sighed.

*****

Narshac stared out his second-story bedroom window. The door behind him opened, but he didn't turn to see which of his wives had come to deliver water.

"Send for the young wife."

"Yes, sir." The wife who'd come was of little interest to him at present, and her voice held an edge of anger. Once the door was shut, he turned and poured some water into the porcelain cup from the matching pitcher. The weather was sultry this time of year, even with night approaching. He knew calling for Lomina so often wasn't earning the girl any favors among the wives, but his curiosity was of more import than trivial spats between his wives.

Not more than fifteen minutes had passed when Lomina timidly opened the door and entered his quarters. She didn't speak as she closed the door behind her and leaned up against it. Protocol demanded he be the first to speak.

"Lomina, I hope you're learning there is nothing to fear from me." He spoke kindly as he waited for her eyes to meet his.

"Yes, sir. I've learned many things."

"As have I, with you being here." Narshac sat down on the bed, patting the spot beside him. Lomina met his gaze and smiled slightly as she accepted the seat he offered. She positioned herself so her back rested against the head board. Narshac leaned against the baseboard, facing her, his legs stretched across the bed.

Narshac felt so at peace around her. She was relaxed in this room, more so than anywhere else in the house, because in this room, she was given equality to a man most of the country knew to be a harsh commander and cruel warden of many prisons throughout Shemna. Lomina learned that although he was indeed a vicious man in the war against Christianity, he was also inquisitive about his enemy; she knew God was using her in a way no one else could be. Perhaps in the midst of her grief, God was going to get the glory after all. She was thankful to share the truth with Narshac since it gave meaning for the loss she now felt. Narshac offered her protection while in his presence, protected against the harsh wives in Narshac's household and protected against further pain resulting from her faith. At his nod, she continued her commentary from two nights ago.

Lonika looked up as Pastor Tim entered the small house with a young couple behind him.

She stared at the younger woman. As beautiful as the last time she'd seen her, Lonika immediately recognized Safira. The two women grinned at one another. Sweeping across the room, Lonika flung herself into Safira's arms.

"It is good to see you again, Safira," she said enthusiastically.

"Lonika, I'm sorry for your losses," Safira said.

"It should have been much worse. Col. Narshac is changing, I think."

"Even after serving here for as long as I have, I still can't comprehend how you can see things so positively, Lonika. Narshac just executed your husband and took your daughter to wife. How could his heart be softening?" Chris once again looked as awed as he felt by such positivity in the face of adversity.

"You must be Christian Banks. Well, you see, he normally would have tortured us all, killed my whole family, but he didn't. He spared those he could."

"I pray he is changing. I'm sorry about Lomina, but I'm well aware that he couldn't have let her go," Chris acknowledged once he was in the study with the pastor and away from the two chatty women in the other room.

"Times are going to get rough around here. Sad thing is he may be inquiring, but that's no guarantee he will change, and it's no guarantee things will get better for us. It is getting more difficult to hide, and with more Christians being taken, people are hesitating to put their trust in Him because they fear for their lives more than for their souls."

"We are here now, Pastor, to help. I also know that you are about done with the New Testament, yes?"

"Correct. With your help, we should be done in a matter of months. And with the funds you raised, I'm also hoping we can begin smuggling copies of said translation. People want the Word in their hands."

"We have the starting money to pursue this project quickly. But smuggling isn't going to be easy."

"It never is, my boy. It never is, which is what will make bringing the Word to the people so exciting."

"What are we? Kids playing double-o-seven?" Chris smirked.

Pastor Tim lifted his brow. "It's more fun to think of it that way, isn't it?"

Chris smiled and shook his head at the zealous preacher.

Meanwhile in the living room, the women continued to chat over a cup of tea.

Lonika sighed. "I know there was no other way, but I pray that she won't forget who she really is."

"A child of the King," Safira replied with a smile.

"Yes, and I see good things have happened to you and your husband."

Safira smiled and nodded.

"Welcome home, my dear," she said and embraced her friend.

"Thank you. Is there somewhere I can start, someone we can help?"

"There is so much pain, so much suffering in the streets right now. It's hard to know where to begin, but I have a list in my mind."

"Then we should begin to write those names down so we can not only help them but also pray for them as well."

Lonika looked surprised. "You can write?"

"And read. I have learned much in the United States, and I've learned to help in every way. Perhaps even begin educating our women so when the time comes, they too can read the Word of God."

Lonika smiled as she embraced her new friend enthusiastically. "We would be more than grateful for such a privilege!"

"You and I can work toward that end. Lonika, I believe with all the work that needs to be done, I would appreciate having someone at home to help keep us going. Fixing meals and keeping things clean and ready for any refugees we send home. Would you be willing to do that for us? Of course, we would keep you in our home, as soon as we establish one."

Tears welled up in the older woman's eyes as she nodded her thankfulness.

"It would be my honor to serve you, my lady."

Safira smiled at the respect the woman had just paid her and grasped her hand reassuringly. "I am not your mistress. I am your friend, your colaborer in Christ. When you serve with me, we are serving Christ."

*****

Narshac paced his room. Lomina had departed nearly two hours earlier, but his restlessness remained. Tortured by her words, he ran a hand through his hair. He had refused to believe the Christian ways, and yet the information Lomina was revealing burdened his soul. The God she spoke of was more powerful than any he'd heard of. Shaking his head at the thought, he sat down on the chest by his bed. He didn't want to believe in this God at all. If Jehovah was all-powerful, then what he had been doing to believers of this God would doom him forever. But then again, this so-called all-powerful God hadn't struck him dead, at least not yet, for the crimes against the believers. He couldn't be any more powerful than the Keilronian deities.

He stood up and trudged to the water basin to splash water on his face. He walked onto his balcony that overlooked the city. He braced himself against the rail with his hands, while his eyes roamed the city below. Reasoning his way through the inner struggle was getting him nowhere.

Many Christians would be sneaking through the city at this hour, holding onto the Jehovah God they cannot see. They willingly laid down their lives for Him. Many like his sister had fled for their lives. As he dwelled on Safira, his mind traveled to another time and place.

*****

"Narshac, can I ride the horse with you?" a five-year-old Safira asked.

Narshac had just returned from a long journey and wanted nothing more than a cool drink and soft bed, but her pleading eyes and cute smile were irresistible. He swooped her up with one arm and settled her in front of him on his horse. A single touch of his heel urged the horse forward. Her giggle of delight warmed his heart, and he smiled.

The horse circled the courtyard twice before Narshac dismounted and reached up for Safira. She rested her hands on his shoulders as he easily lifted her off the saddle and carried her to the house as the first rain poured from the sky.

"We wouldn't want you getting a fever, little one."

"How long will you be here?"

"Not long, Safira. I have responsibilities of my own to tend to."

"Why did you come here then?" Her lower lip protruded in a childish pout.

"To see my precious jewel."

Her pout turned into a grin. "Me!" she said proudly.

"You," he smiled and touched her nose with his free hand before kissing her on the cheek.

Safira giggled as she wiggled out of his embrace and sprinted toward the door where her governess awaited.

"I will see you at dinner, brother!" she said. Glancing back one last time, she waved and flashed him a sweet smile

He had just enough time to return the gesture before she disappeared inside his father's house.

*****

Narshac exhaled loudly and walked from the balcony to his bed. He lay down, trying to remember the last time he'd seen Safira. She'd been so young, close to fifteen. Her sweetness and innocence still touched his heart. If anything could keep him from accepting the Christian's God, it was the way his sister betrayed them. He brushed the pleasant memories from his mind and quickly succumbed to the anger built inside of him until he was able to take a deep breath and relax against the wall he'd built against the soft emotions that often plagued him. He tried falling asleep the only way he knew how, by hardening his heart. But he was unable to squelch the face of a five-year-old girl from years ago as he fell into dreams from days gone by.

Chapter 22

In His Arms

Lomina's hands hurt as she scrubbed the stained blue sheets. The older wives kept her busy with mundane chores, and any woman remotely close to her own age refused to meet her gaze. She felt the weight of their jealousy in the constant labor and chores thrust upon her. And the loneliness she experienced by their alienation was unbearable.

The wives detested her because *he* called for her so often. She felt the brunt of their cruelty through their words. They told her in no uncertain terms the master would grow tired of his new bride soon enough and that she had best learn her place now. Others claimed he'd fallen in love with this woman child and that she would soon succeed Kalita as head wife, but no one suspected what truly happened. He had not touched her physically but had requested her presence on a regular basis as a teacher. Lomina almost wished he had made her his wife in every sense. At least then, she could potentially conceive a child. But as he had not actually touched her, Lomina also dealt with cruel comments that she was barren. Even a casual conversation would break the feeling of complete isolation she felt. She stayed in a continued state of prayer to keep herself from falling into a depression.

She sighed and looked down at her red, rough hands. A salve would be necessary to help them heal. She tried not to let her weariness show, but today's chores hadn't been light or easy because the whole household was preparing for a spectacular visitor, and everything must be cleaned till it shined. Lomina was unaware of who the honored guest was since she was shunned from the women's talk.

"Narshac wants you," the older wife spat down at her. She was the head of Narshac's city household and was determined to undermine Lomina in every way, including giving her the most demeaning household chores. Obviously, the woman wasn't pleased to have Lomina called away again.

"I haven't finished, my lady." She had determined long ago to be respectful and had achieved success. Often, other wives didn't know what to do with her gentle spirit. But the hesitation never lasted long.

"I'll have Felmina finish. When the master calls, you go." The woman glared at her as if she had missed the obvious.

Lomina lowered her head in respect. "Yes, my lady."

She sighed in relief as she climbed the stairs. Talking would be a relief from the day's labor, though weary as she felt, even the idea of teaching the master was exhausting. The other wives had no compassion for her. In fact, they tried their hardest to make her useless to Narshac. He, however, was interested only in her mind.

She knocked on the master's door, and upon hearing his reply, she entered.

Once she entered, Narshac spun to face her, prepared to fire away his usual rapid inquisitions. He often had questions lined up from their previous sessions. One look at Lomina, and compassion overwhelmed him. While it was not uncommon for a man of his age, and men much older, to take young brides, he was beginning to feel kindness rather than lust toward the younger wives. Lomina was no exception. She was clearly exhausted from her assigned household chores. The women were no doubt unaware that Narshac knew all the workings of his household and was apprised of Lomina's situation among his family. He instantly thought of his two daughters near her age and knew he wouldn't stand to see them overworked.

"You look exhausted, Lomina," he spoke softly.

She didn't try to hide it. She took a deep sigh, and her shoulders slumped. "I suppose I am."

He extended his arm, offering her the bed.

"Thank you, my lord, but I don't think you've sent for me to rest."

"True."

"My lord, ask what you will."

He ignored her gentle invitation. "I know that you work harder than any other woman in my house, and still you've delighted me with stories and answers to my inquiries. When I ask you to come, even late at night, you have never complained. You've pleased me a great deal."

Her mind reeled. Who would have had the kindness to tell him that she worked harder than most of the women? She could think of no one. There were six wives. The first wife, by designation, was treated much like the wife of a single man rather than another servant. In this case, her name was Kalita. Lomina had not seen Kalita because she was treated more like the queen of the palace. Kalita was not the oldest of the women, but she was the favored one. She was also the only one of the women from Narshac's household Lomina had not met; hence, she was the only one who had not shown Lomina condescension. Kalita made her home in the estate outside of Shemna. Lomina brought her mind to the present. She needed to be with Narshac right now.

"What story, what truth did I end with last time I was with you?" she asked.

"You spoke of a man named Joshua, who'd been chosen by Jehovah to finish what Moses had begun."

"This is one of my favorites because it shows God's deliverance, even in impossible situations." She at last accepted the spot on the bed and leaned her head against the wall before she dove into the story. "You see, Joshua was to lead the people into battle against a big city, Jericho. The walls were too tall and too thick for Israel's small army to penetrate. But instead of taking the easy way out as their ancestors had, Joshua determined to do the impossible. Jehovah sent an angel to instruct Joshua . . ."

Lomina continued her story. When she'd finished with the walls crumbling to the ground, she looked at Narshac who stood looking out at the city.

"How can it be that such a mighty wall could fall simply because they blew horns, shouted, and walked around the city?"

"Jehovah is all-powerful. He's done much greater things than that, or haven't you been listening? He created the entire universe, and He destroyed those walls with no more effort than breathing is for us."

"Why do these great things not happen today?"

"Because the prophesies about the Savior have been fulfilled."

"What of this Savior? When does he come to save His people? From what does He save them?"

"He saves them from their sins."

Narshac turned from the window, his expression curious. "How?"

"By dying on the cross and rising from the dead to prove that He was the last and Perfect Sacrifice." Her eyes were dropping, and although she'd answered his questions, she was doing so with difficulty. He wanted more answers, but Narshac was patient, and he was willing to give Lomina a break for now.

"Rest now, Lomina. You need to rest," he said gently. He walked back to the bed and placed his hands on her shoulders, gently easing her down so she was lying flat on the bed. Then, he placed a pillow under her head. She was so young. Had he really taken women of her age to his bed? While he thought of his sister, an unfamiliar compassion overwhelmed him. He pulled a blanket from the linen chest and laid it over her before returning to his perch on the balcony.

Narshac moved to his writing desk in the corner of his room and wrote a message. When his personal messenger arrived, he handed the missive to the lad.

"You must remain completely silent on this, or I will have your head," Narshac threatened the thirteen-year-old.

The boy replied with wide eyes, "Yes, sir. You know you can count on me."

*****

Safira strode down the streets toward the market. A contact there often had messages for her, and she planned to check in with him. The merchant was discreet and nearly undetectable. Having a marketplace drop was convenient for many within their circle. She smiled as she stopped at the small merchant's booth. Picking up a small piece of pottery, she handed him paper money. The clerk didn't immediately recognize her uncovered face. Often, she would don her Keilronian dress since it was easy to disguise herself, but tonight, she was approaching as an American tourist unfamiliar with the bartering system. The man opened the wad of bills and saw the small message tucked inside. He counted the money and glared at Safira.

"You didn't give me enough for the pot!" the man pulled a disappearing act and the note she'd delivered disappeared. He waved his fist that still clutched the bills at her. "I need at least four more," he declared grabbing the vessel from her and holding it close to his side.

"I already gave you five! You are asking an outrageous amount of money for a small pot. I will give you two more, but that's it," she said firmly.

"Fine. But you are robbing me. Only because you're a beautiful woman will I accept that amount."

Safira smiled as she handed him two more bills. His hand barely skimmed the top of the clay handmade pot as he handed it to her.

She shopped for several other items from different vendors before trudging the half mile back home with her items. Once she was past the busy part of the market and knew she wasn't being followed, she looked into the pot, hoping to find the missive. When she reached inside, her fingers brushed against the paper at the bottom of the pot. Using her index and middle fingers, she fished out the note, then glanced both ways just to be sure no one else was interested in her before reading the short note.

Lomina is all right. No harm has or will come to her. She remains pure.

~From a Friend

A friend? She asked herself curiously. Most Christian circles were unafraid to give their names.

"Don't move," a voice sounded behind her. When she felt the knife dig into her back, she tried to calm herself and breathe normally.

"I'm not here for trouble," she whispered.

"Show me the note, now." Safira handed it to the man immediately.

"What is this? Who are you?" The man demanded

"I could ask you the same thing. I'm obviously heading home from shopping, and you have assaulted me," she answered with a confidence she did not feel.

"American women are scum, thinking you have any rights at all in my country!"

"Well, I have a few more rights than your poor misled women."

Her forceful voice stunned the attacker, but only momentarily, "Turn and face me."

She did as asked, but the surprise was on her. Rather than flee, she faced her brother, hoping he wouldn't recognize her. Her hope was in vain.

"Safira?" The man gasped. The knife went down immediately, and Marvok stumbled back as if he'd been hit.

Marvok had been her closest brother because they'd grown up together. They had played together and kept secrets from their father when they often played games she was normally not allowed to play. It had been a sad day for both after they'd been separated by adulthood.

He stared at her. "What's happened to you? Where have you been? I have prayed to the gods on your behalf."

"I married an American." She reached into her purse and showed him a passport. She never opened it, but she allowed him to see that it was American.

"You've been gone for five years. You've been in America all this time?"

"No," she confessed.

Marvok didn't want to ask more questions. His father's assumptions were obviously true, but Marvok felt it was his right to deny knowing anything of the kind as long as she didn't say the truth out loud.

"You look well, sister. I've no reason to keep you. The note looks safe enough. Go your way. Go to your husband."

Safira bowed in Keilronian fashion before disappearing up the street.

She entered her home, thankful for the moment that Chris was not home to catch her before she had the chance to calm her racing heart. Lonika smiled at her from the main living space as she set her reading lessons aside. She stood, out of concern, when she glimpsed Safira's face.

"Are you all right?"

Safira took a deep breath and nodded and then exhaled loudly before speaking. "I'm fine, just a little out of breath. I have a note for you."

"For me?" Lonika looked surprised.

Safira read the small missive to her friend and watched as the woman reached for the nearby chair and sat down. She had been learning to read but hadn't been taking lessons long enough to read the note herself. She took the note from Safira and stared at the words anyway.

"She's alive, and she is okay." Lonika looked up at Safira and beamed. They both felt the joy the message brought, and Lonika stood to embrace the younger woman.

Supper that night was exhilarating because Lonika outdid herself in her enthusiasm. The meal was more of a celebration than an everyday affair. Chris, when he'd returned from across the city for dinner, had quickly been told of the news and gladly allowed all other worries to be set aside for a little good news. It wasn't until later that night when they slipped into bed that Safira had the chance to really speak with him.

"How was your day?" she asked as she settled next to him with his arm wrapped around her.

"Kindel has his hands full with those mourning their losses. His side of the city seems to be hit worse than ours, which bothers me some. Why aren't we getting detained and persecuted as relentlessly on this side?"

"We are being watched. You should probably find a way to tell your messenger in the market that he needs to lay low for a bit, and we need to find another carrier. I was detained momentarily after I met with him."

Safira felt Chris tense immediately at her words and knew she needed to hasten through her explanation.

"My brother Marvok, as it turns out, stopped me and demanded I show him the merchant's note. I did, not knowing what it was. I realize we code things often, but sometimes, our contacts don't because they trust in our system too much. Well, gratefully, as you read this evening, it wasn't anything incriminating. He asked about what had happened to me, and I showed him the American passport. I didn't have to open it, and he didn't ask for it. God protected me today. The soldier watching the market could have been anyone."

"But it wasn't," he finished as he relaxed again. He hugged her closer and kissed the top of her head, thanking God that he had yet another night to hold her.

"He didn't put two and two together? You being American, accepting notes in secret from merchants?"

"I don't think he wanted to. I chose not to tell him the details, and he chose not to ask the right questions. He and I were best friends growing up. I don't think he wants to see me hurt and certainly wouldn't want to be responsible if I were."

"We are being watched, then. Our time for persecution may come soon. Perhaps, we are being watched by those who aren't sure they want to destroy us. We certainly need to be more careful with our interactions."

"We will just have to change venues for our mail and be more careful how we meet people on the street. Lonika is protected. She's officially our housekeeper. You are the one who needs to be careful because you are on the watch list." Safira spoke every word with concern.

"I know. Bribery can get me only so far."

"It got us back here. Marvok seemed disinterested in you. I'm not sure if he was avoiding the topic so he wouldn't have information he didn't want or if you are flying low enough below radar."

"I promise to be more careful, if you do," he said.

She could tell he was smiling in the dark, and she couldn't help but smile and nod against his chest in response.

Chapter 23

Hearts so Tender

Kalita knelt down on the stone floor to pick up the rattle her baby dropped. The child was nearly four months old and had rarely left Kalita's sight. Her gaze drifted toward Lomina who sat over the washtub scrubbing the last of the dirty sheets. Handing the rattle to the baby, she carried on her back, she glided across the small deserted courtyard and placed a gentle hand on Lomina's shoulder.

Lomina flinched from the physical touch. The eyes of the younger woman stared up at Kalita, unsmiling with wide eyes.

Kalita felt compassion and spoke tenderly. "I'm Kalita. I've arrived from our other home outside of Shemna only a week ago. I've heard much about you from the other women."

Lomina's eyes softened at Kalita's voice. She knew who Kalita was. The household had been preparing for her arrival for some time. Protocol for younger wives left Lomina no more than a servant in the household. Being so lowly among the other wives made the chances of befriending the head wife slim, making Kalita's approach so unexpected.

"If you've heard of me, my lady, I wonder why you would speak with me," Lomina said humbly. She lowered her gaze back to the sheet still in her wet hands.

"True. The other women despise you," Kalita answered matter-of-factly. She bent at the waist and spoke quietly into Lomina's ear. "But our lord speaks openly with me."

Lomina's head quickly spun toward Kalita. Seeing the half smile gracing the lady's face and the sparkling eyes, Lomina gasped. Their eyes held for several heartbeats before Kalita averted her gaze and stood erect. Her eyes scanned the courtyard for probing eyes or ears. She spotted one of the slave women walking along the opposite end of the courtyard.

"Solina!" Kalita spoke with authority, summoning the woman. "Come and finish the wash." The woman obeyed grudgingly. Kalita offered her hand to help Lomina up. The city estate boasted beautiful gardens, and once Lomina stood beside her, Kalita linked their arms and led her toward them.

The gardens were pampered and manicured to perfection by three or four slaves who were kept specifically for that purpose. Lomina passed by them only occasionally because she'd never had the time to actually enjoy them. The garden was deserted, aside from the two women. Kalita led them to the center of the peaceful scene and sat down on an elaborate wooden bench.

"Narshac confided much to me by letter. I'm intrigued by what he's told me about you. Would you share with me what you have been sharing with him all this time? I too wish to know about this Jehovah God. From what I hear, you could use a friend, so let me be that friend. The more I know, the more I can keep you out of trouble, if trouble comes of this." Kalita's voice was low so as not to be overheard.

Lomina's voice was subdued. "I was under the impression that I am safe here."

"Unless he converts to your Jehovah, or at least finds enough information to curb his curiosity without igniting his fury, you are in as much danger as you ever were. He has not yet decided how he feels about your lessons. From my understanding, he is puzzled. It is not a good position for you to be in. As long as he is unsure, he could turn on you in an instant. I am intrigued by your knowledge. I want to know what he knows. If what you know is all untruths, I know

Narshac would have stopped your lessons immediately. However, that's not been the case. Truth is powerful, and I think your lessons hold truth."

*****

"I heard you have been busy today." Narshac smiled at his wife leaning against the headboard holding their child. "You have been visiting with Lomina. I appreciate what you are doing for her. It hasn't been easy for her, as I'm sure you have already discovered. I've been the only one to show her even an ounce of courtesy, and in that, I am limited as you can imagine. I would have said something to the others, but that would have made things worse. I think she's still having a hard time dealing with the death of her father."

"She's a sweet girl, Narshac." Kalita spoke openly to him like she'd always done. She knew he had other wives, but was comforted in that she was the only confidant among them. She accepted and used her position often enough to gain the upper hand for those she favored. Choosing to favor Lomina had been an easy choice, and she was grateful that Narshac applauded her decision. It was a good sign that perhaps Lomina wasn't in as much danger as she'd inferred. "She's won more than my favoritism. She's gained my friendship. Honestly, it is refreshing to have a friend who does not share my husband's bed."

"Kalita . . . ," he warned.

"I know how things are, and I have accepted them. She's very young and, in ways, reminds me of what our daughter may become one day. I get a new friend, and she receives a protector. I believe it will be beneficial relationship." She smiled to reassure him that her comment had not meant to wound or overstep.

He sat on the bed beside her and caressed her face. "Kalita, wife, you are my treasure. You're so precious to me. You've born me sons and now a beautiful daughter. I do love you. Even though I have responsibilities toward others, you are my only love."

She saw the tender look in his eyes and read his intentions accurately. "I would not refuse you, my lord, but the child is still young."

He smiled and motioned toward the corner of the room. "I had a cradle brought in here this afternoon. Highly unusual, I understand, by the slave's look." She hadn't noticed the new piece of furniture, but he could tell by the light in her eyes that he'd won her favor. "Allow the child to rest and come to me. Tonight, I want only you."

Kalita gently placed the child in the waiting cradle and expectantly returned to the bed. He didn't reach for her in the way she'd come to accept, but rather lay on his side and pulled her back against his chest. He wrapped his arm around her and held her hand. He made no further move. Kalita couldn't resist his tender actions. Relaxing against his protective embrace, she closed her eyes in bliss. Her husband was showing gentleness in a way he'd never done before.

"Narshac, how is your heart toward the Jehovah God?" she asked quietly.

"Learning of his power versus our gods is hard to take in and goes against everything I know. But the stories Lomina shares do not contradict my knowledge of history. And you know, I've studied a great deal in that field."

"Your heart has thawed some to this God?"

"I don't know yet how I feel toward Him. He demands perfection that can never be obtained and allows families to be separated and torn apart by their faith in Him. He demands their loyalty and allegiance to the death, if need be. I have not finished my lessons with Lomina, but I think there is more to the story than what I know now. There has to be. If what she says is true, why would not this great God destroy mankind for our horrific ways?"

"Do not all gods want you to dedicate yourself to them?"

"Our gods will rain down punishments if we do not sacrifice to them. They don't care what is in our hearts as long as we fulfill our duties to them. The God that Lomina speaks of is so different from any I've known."

"Will you grant your blessing to me, if I too desire to find out the truth about this Jehovah?"

"You may continue your search. Speak with Lomina. She is wise beyond her years, and she will help you understand, as she is doing with me. Perhaps in time, we will be able to consider these matters together. It will be good to speak about it with someone who understands."

"Thank you, my love," she whispered.

Narshac was touched by her loving words. They did not always see eye to eye nor speak heart to heart. Often, he allowed his pride to deny them the intimacy of baring their thoughts to one another. But while he'd been listening to Lomina's stories, some things made sense. He was willing to try a different way with his family, particularly the part that he held in his arms. She had been the best decision of his life, and he hadn't even known it at the time. Holding her close and giving kindness to her rather than taking was such a good feeling that he would have to find ways of keeping her in his bed more often. He gently kissed the top of her head before they both fell into a comforting sleep.

*****

Shovak's gaze followed Rofisca's movement the moment the office door opened. He'd been waiting for several minutes in the overstuffed leather chair near the fireplace inside Rofisca's office. Rofisca's stride was long and sure before he halted at his desk and set several papers down. Rofisca had obviously not seen Shovak since he was intently reading the paper in his hand.

Shovak smirked, "This is how we won the war?" His voice was playful.

Rofisca jumped and spun on his heel toward the waiting leader who sat calmly, his legs crossed and a glass in one hand.

Rofisca slapped the last of the papers in his hand down on his desk. "You caught me off guard is all. What can I do for you? It's not often you visit me these days." His voice was stiff.

It was true. Shovak had made fewer visits to the general because matters of state and politics consumed most of his time. Shovak was growing weary of fighting off the political onslaught he was receiving from many nations for his anti-Christian perspectives. He had held them off thus far through his own political prowess, but was growing tired of the game and needed a side stop.

"Your son Narshac is doing very well for me. He is the oldest of your household, no?"

Rofisca's eyes narrowed in suspicion. "Yes, he is the heir to all I have," he replied coolly.

"He is wealthy on his own merit as well. He's been head of my prison for five months now, and he's shown great strength. We've put more Christians in the pits than we ever did with Jarlishko as guard."

Rofisca heaved a sigh and spoke with no emotion. "Yes, he is doing well."

"I just came to see how you were doing. Is there anything I need to be aware of?"

"No, all is pretty quiet in the need-to-know field." Rofisca's tone grew defensive, and the change in disposition was not lost on Shovak.

"Good. Well, I need to get back to work," Shovak conceded. He'd learned what he needed from the short conversation, although the answers were disappointing.

Rofisca nodded in respect as Shovak left his office. Puzzled by the strangeness of Shovak's intrusion, Rofisca quickly shook the peculiar visit from his mind. And it was soon forgotten altogether when he immersed himself in his work.

What Rofisca didn't know was that he wasn't the only one withholding information. Shovak was pleased with himself as he strode down the large halls. Taking over as ruler had been one thing, maintaining power had become a chess game. Rofisca was not as loyal as he once was. He'd allowed his hate for the Christians to increase to such a degree that nothing, not even direct orders, would get in his way. Spies and loyal officers had since warned Shovak that Rofisca considered himself the authority and no longer obeyed Shovak's orders if they didn't agree with his own.

Shovak sadly shook his head at the betrayal. Nothing could be done about it; the people revered Rofisca. But someday, the opportunity would present itself, and Narshac would replace his father.

Shovak entered his office and looked out the window. Staring down into the markets, his mind switched gears. How could the Christians be so obstinate? They held to their Jehovah God so tightly.

Families were torn apart because even children would die for Him. What did this God have that the others didn't?

Shovak thought back to Narshac's story. What had happened to the man who had been at the guillotine? What had happened to Safira? He was aware that the Christian man Narshac had nearly beheaded was Safira's husband, and he was back in the country, but he simply didn't care. The man was keeping a low profile and only occasionally poked his head out enough to be caught by the surveillance team camera before disappearing for weeks at a time. Safira's husband had bribed his way back into the country, and that left Shovak believing he was a wealthy man with some influence. If the American newspapers were to be believed, Christian Banks should be left alone. He knew Safira was in the country with Banks, but again, he didn't care. He was more interested in the Christian circles that were spreading than the seemingly private couple.

Rofisca had been left completely in the dark regarding the information on Chris and Safira for good reason. The general was the best at his job, but Shovak knew the man was slightly insane regarding his daughter, and he'd rather have the general focus on the more important matters of national security.

Shovak went back to his original thought, and he pondered the general's family. What had happened to Safira? She'd been raised to respect the gods. He'd witnessed it while he'd watched her grow up. What was it about this strange new God that had her so willing to give up everything she'd known? What was it that transformed any of the Christians into freaks who would die rather than reclaim their old faiths?

He turned from the window and sat down at his desk. He began filing through the papers, but he was unable to discern them because his mind was obviously elsewhere. He leaned back in his chair and folded his hands across his chest. What was it that the Christians had that made them so strong? How could he break them and make them see the error of their decisions? He knew, tough and hardened as he was, that he wouldn't have withstood the tortures that Narshac put them through when they crossed his path. Why did they grip so tightly? What was it about this God that gave them courage outside the realm of possibility?

Shovak's mind remained troubled for the rest of the day, so he paced his palace domain. He received no answers because his mind went in circles. Perhaps, Narshac was getting closer to some answers.

*****

"Sir, I was not expecting you today," Narshac said as he greeted the dictator with respect the moment he saw him enter the prison.

"Have you any man who is capable of speaking?"

"This way, sir. We have one who's not yet been put through the testing."

Narshac lit the lamp inside a small, damp cell. Shovak's eyes adjusted to the dim light; he studied the middle-aged man. His hands were chained above his head against the back wall as he slumped against the wall, his legs tucked beneath him.

"What is your age?" he asked causally.

"I'm fifty-two, sir." The man obviously recognized him from the plastered posters, paintings, and statues throughout the city.

"Why do you put yourself through this mayhem at such a late time in your life? Surely, you have wives and children, perhaps grandchildren? Why allow yourself to remain here rather than to simply deny this god and return home?"

"My Lord, my Jehovah, shed his pure blood for me. I cannot reject Him." The man answered confidently and respectfully.

"Shed His blood for you? Why?" Shovak spoke with genuine curiosity.

"To pay for my sins, sir."

"Is that not why we make sacrifices? When you sacrifice your goods and animals to the gods, is that not for their favor?" Shovak was shocked that this man believed a god would pay for his sin.

"There is but one God and only one sacrifice that He would accept for our sins, the death of His own perfect Son."

"You've heard this plea before, my lord." Narshac spoke quietly from behind Shovak.

Narshac's words silenced the man standing before them. Shovak continued to look puzzled by the man's words, but his face soon masked the feelings into a look of disinterest. He shook his head in disappointment and left the scene, entering the hallway. Outside, he turned toward Narshac.

"I'm beginning to question my reasons for killing these men. I have always believed in the gods my father raised me to believe in. When I hear these men speak of a god I don't know or understand, my blood used to boil, but now, I wonder. I see the courage these people display as they are tortured and killed. I see the looks of pity and forgiveness, and I wonder, what it is that we are missing? Perhaps, things are not as black and white as I once believed."

"I wonder too. I've seen more than you can imagine as your head of Prison," Narshac confessed. "But I follow your orders. My loyalty is with you, sir." Narshac held a glimmer of hope that he would be given an order to stop the senseless killing. He had no righteous indignation toward these men. Truthfully, the looks of pity were driving him into a pit of guilt as if he were striking down innocents, and perhaps, he was. He would not be held in contempt, however, against direct orders. He'd been trained as a good soldier.

"Tell no one I've spoken to you on this. Do not kill any on the guillotine any longer. If they die from the tortures, fine, but I want to see how much they will take before confessing our gods. No more easy deaths. I want to see what they do under real pressure when death is no longer an option."

"I'll do as you say." Narshac knew he'd been given a two-edged sword and was uncertain how he felt. He would not have to be the one to give death orders any longer, and those who would die under excruciating pain had a chance at any time to escape their fate without the threat of an immediate death penalty. But that also meant more torture than before.

"One more thing. Americans and Europeans who come to our country are to be given grace. If they are caught preaching Jehovah, they must be punished, but they will not be tortured. If, after they are disciplined, they refuse to be silent, they will be deported, not beheaded. We're getting too much attention from the United States and its allies. We need to be sure no American or European life is taken, especially the United Sates, which is a large country with the power to destroy us quickly. Do not draw American blood."

"Yes, sir. I understand. Will you be writing that statement up so as I have written orders."

"Of course, I will have the orders to you by the end of the week, but as your commanding officer, I want you to begin following these verbal commands at once."

Narshac saluted as the leader left the prison, "Yes, sir!"

*****

Chris watched Safira move gracefully in the kitchen. She used the old kitchen tools easily and cooked expertly on the fire hearth they used for a stove.

"You're watching me." Safira smiled, her back to him.

A small smile touched his lips. "How would you know?"

"Because I don't hear your pen scratching anymore." She turned toward him and gave him a quick wink.

Chris slid his chair out from the table and walked over to his wife. Wrapping his arms around her waist, he kissed her cheek. Lonika had taken the last couple of days off because she'd wanted to be with her children and spend some much needed personal time with them. Chris and Safira agreed wholeheartedly and were enjoying complete privacy in their home for a few more days.

"Every day, I count it a blessing that I married you. Every day we're running and trying to remain safe, I thank God that we're together. Every night, I'm blessed to lie beside you. I praise the Lord we're both safe," Chris whispered in her ear.

"We're all safe," Safira corrected. She smiled broadly and turned in his arms to face him.

"All? Are you telling me that you're, that we're . . . ," he stammered, unable to put his emotions into words.

She giggled. "Yes, Chris. You're going to be a father." Her eyes sparkled with joy.

Chris couldn't move. The responsibility of raising a child in such an environment was daunting, but his mind focused on his wife's happy expression, and he felt an excitement build inside of him. He reached behind her head and drew her into a long kiss. When he broke away, he had only one thought. "I love you, Safira Banks." He drew her in for a tight embrace and lifted her off her feet, twirling her around in the kitchen.

*****

Fay opened the letter from Keilron and smiled as she read. The letter arrived earlier in the week, but she wanted Harris and the kids to be there with her. She'd been dying to open it for three days, but she knew the family wouldn't gather until Sunday, and she was determined to read it with them the first time.

"Come on, Mom, read it to us." Kate rubbed her hands together as she made herself comfortable in the living room."

> *Dear Family,*
>
> *I'm pleased and proud to announce that Safira is going to have a baby around February 10! We're both doing great and are very excited. Translation work is going better than ever with Safira's help. I'm even allowed to write to you now and say that Christ is providing and changing the hearts of kings. Officially, foreign believers are now allowed as long as they follow certain guidelines that make it impossible to share the gospel. But if caught spreading the gospel, a fine of something equal to $300,000 will be charged. If we cannot pay the fine, a time of up to one year is to be served in the Keilronian prison. If a second offense is discovered, rather than a death penalty, they have opted for deportation. Please keep us in your prayers. Safira and I have written letters to everyone. You should be receiving those shortly.*
>
> *Love from both of us,*
> *Chris and Safira Banks*

"Safira's going to have a baby!" Kate said gleefully.

The household erupted in squeals and chatter, not only over the future and a new family member but also over the joy of being able to communicate with Chris more openly and more frequently.

JC rose to answer the knock on the door.

"Hey, Blake, come on in. You are just a few minutes late. We just read a letter from Chris. Good news all the way today!" JC spoke enthusiastically, leading the way into the noisy living room.

Blake entered the living room and smiled as the family greeted him.

"Guess what? Safira's going to have a baby! I'm going to be an aunt!" Kate jumped up and hugged Blake in her excitement.

"Yeah, I know. Safira wrote me. I got the letter yesterday."

"And you didn't call to tell me! I'm insulted," she teased. Backing away from him, she turned her attention back toward her mom and dad. The family continued chatting for several more minutes. JC ditched the family for a planned basketball game with his buddies the moment Fay moved to the kitchen to prepare Sunday dinner. Harris turned on the football game. Kate, still glowing with the news, stared at a picture on the wall for a few minutes before Blake interrupted her thoughts.

"Kate, would you mind taking a walk with me?" he asked quietly.

"No, not at all." She stood and looked at Harris. "Dad, will you let Mom know?"

"Sure thing, you two don't stay out too long. Sounds like dinner will be ready in an hour or so. JC won't be back, so I think she would be glad to have you around, Blake."

"Thanks, Dad." Blake acknowledged. Kate put on her light jean jacket and led the way out the door.

After walking three blocks in silence, Blake finally got the courage to speak up. "Kate, Safira wrote me, but what she said startled me. I guess I hadn't considered it until she brought it to my attention. But what she wrote was true," Blake said. He guided the way to the small memorial park and headed toward a park bench.

"What are you talking about?" she asked casually. Her heart had about jumped out of her chest when he'd requested a private walk with her, and now that he seemed to be talking nonsense, the butterflies in her stomach went into a flutter.

"It's harder than I thought to explain this to you." He was silent for several more steps until he reached the bench and offered her a seat. "Here, read what she wrote me. I don't know how to actually say what I'm feeling right now."

Puzzled by his words, she took the letter Blake handed her. He never had issues speaking his mind to her. Understanding seeped in as she read the letter. She gently handed it back to him. She was doing everything in her power to hold her emotions in check at the words Safira had written. Safira promised not to say anything to him about her feelings for Blake. She hadn't said a word as promised, but what she had done was insinuate that he was in love with her and that he should definitely pursue it because she was the best girlfriend he ever had.

Nervous and completely at a loss how to continue this conversation, Kate stared at her hands. Thankfully, Blake had given some thought to this moment.

Taking her hand in his, he waited until she met his gaze. "Will you allow me to court you, Kate Kleren? It would be a little strange to actually date you, since we've known each other so long, but I want you to know my intentions in the best way I know how. Courting is the most apt description."

"Oh! Yes, Blake!" The tears did come then; unchecked, they ran down her face. "I've been waiting a long time to hear you ask. Yes, I'd be honored." They were happy tears, and Blake smiled as he took his fingers and wiped them away.

They sat on the bench, his arm draped over her shoulder, until Blake checked his watch and suggested they make their way home before the allotted hour. They wouldn't want to miss dinner and certainly wouldn't want to miss the opportunity to share with the family about their new relationship status. Kate smiled, thinking about what her dad might say and even giggled a little at the thought of how her mother might react.

Chapter 24

Last Story

May 2006

Flipping through the mail, Safira glanced at her daughter, Rebekah. Watching her mother intently from her high chair, she cooed when she saw her mom's attention turn back to her.

"Look, sweetheart, we've a letter from your grandma. Let's see," Safira hesitated as she read the letter. "Oh, it seems your aunt Kate is getting married to Blake Marty! And JC is officially making the trip to visit us! You will like your uncle."

Safira picked up her daughter and set her on her hip. The baby gurgled when Safira cooed at her.

Chris opened the door and smiled at his little family. "I like coming home to this sort of scene. It appears both my girls are happy."

Safira's eyes sparkled at him. Chris shut the door behind him, took three steps toward her, and bent to kiss his wife.

"Everything has come together beautifully. Kate and Marty will be married in about ten days. Will we be able to go?" Safira asked hopefully.

Lonika had been helping the orphanage across the city several times a week since Rebekah had been born and was not with them as often as she had been. Their lives were so unpredictable that Safira had learned quickly not to fix dinner until her husband was safe within their walls. She let him take Rebekah and the letter. Grabbing the prepped food and sticking it into the oven, she waited for him to read the letter himself.

As he placed the letter on the table, she heard him sigh. "Well, I've been talking with Pastor Tim about going back for the wedding, and we should know in a few days if we can. I wouldn't hold my breath though. It's been tough to get the plane in and out, and this isn't exactly a necessity. We could use our fake passports and just travel through the airport, but I'd rather keep those papers out of the system as long as possible. Leaving and coming back may not be the best move for us, but I haven't ruled it out. I'd love to be there for the wedding, and I know you would too."

"Yes, I would. But I understand what you are saying. JC will be arriving in a couple of weeks. He's not leaving until after the wedding. Maybe he could bring us pictures and a video of it. His school is not only sponsoring the trip but also giving him credit for it."

"I see that. I think it's a wonderful idea, and we need the extra help."

She heard the dark undertone in his comment, "Bad news?" she questioned.

"Well, Shovak has placed some protection on the American Christians, but our people are still suffering. Some have been returned home after weeks of agonizing pain and torture while others have died during their physical interrogations. I just came from Lotrovik's house. He showed me his wounds and scars. It's not good for our people. Thankfully, the deaths are getting fewer, but without medical attention, many will suffer the effects of their wounds the remainder of their lives."

"Will JC be all right coming here?"

"Yes, but I can't say that he won't have a culture shock. And his student visa will allow him to come legally, without complication."

"I look forward to seeing him." She spoke contentedly as she sat across the table from him, watching him with their daughter.

"I'm sure he'll have to take pictures back with him. Mom would love it."

*****

Lomina's shocked expression had not changed since Narshac had initially broke the news to her. His words had stung her, and yet she knew he was right in his decision.

"I can't lie. It isn't right to lie, and I've learned that I'm a terrible liar when I try."

"I understand, Lomina." With a calm voice he said, "I've already asked Kalita for her help. She has been more than willing to do so. It is long past time for you to leave me, and some are whispering about it. I have Kalita with me most nights now, and I have been calling for you less. Our time is at its end."

"How long will you send me away?" Her voice was childlike and frightened. Life had grown easier with Kalita around to defend her. She was afraid to go to his country estate and face the heat from the women there.

"You will have a miscarriage shortly after you arrive at the country palace. Your shame and my disappointment will keep you from returning to me."

"My lord, may I tell you the most important part of the history, then, before you send me away?"

Narshac nodded his consent, and she immediately dove in where she'd left off.

"Jesus, the son of God, was put on trial."

"Yes, you were at the point where the crowd demanded him to be put to death."

"What would you do? You are a man as Pilate was, a man of power."

"I would've put him to death. The crowd demanded it, and I would have no reason to keep him alive."

"But there was no fault found in this man."

"This was Jehovah?"

"Yes, sir. He was perfectly holy and had committed no wrong."

"It would have been a difficult decision."

"Would you have still done it?"

"Yes."

"As did Pilate, but first, he washed his hands as a symbol that his hands were clean."

"He still gave the order."

"Jehovah, God the Son, was put to death on the Roman cross. Have you studied such a death?"

"Yes, I know how it was done. The whips, the nails, and the bloodiness of it all."

"He died on such a cross."

"He was God. If he created the world, surely he could've delivered himself."

"Yet he didn't because on that cross, He took the sins of all, even yours, Narshac, even yours."

"I've done so many wrongs that I'm not worthy of forgiveness."

"Yet God provided a way to forgiveness that you may live forever."

"He died." Narshac spoke flatly.

"No, that's not the end. Three days later, three women went to mourn at the tomb and found it empty."

"Empty?" Narshac grew interested again.

"Yes, empty. Jesus was not there. A man dressed in white stood before them. 'He is not here, for he has risen,' the man said."

"He lived?"

"He died, but He came to life again, showing that God accepted the death of His son for our payment. He showed Himself before His followers, and they recognized Him. He showed them His scars, and they knew who He was. And when He went back to heaven to prepare a place for those that choose Him, His disciples went out to tell the world."

"What must one do to become His?"

"Believe that it was for you He died and accept the blood of Christ as your payment for the horrid things you have done, for the sins you have committed against Jehovah."

The entire time she had visited with him, she had told him stories and prophesies. She had explained why the Christians felt the way they did. Narshac, after his first wife had returned, had called for her rarely to lessen any suspicion of their meetings, and it had taken them much longer to get to this point than either had originally anticipated.

Narshac turned from her, unable to understand the love this God displayed. He was unable to grasp how one's death could free him from the sins he had committed and the innocent blood that covered his hands. He was not willing to give his heart or his allegiance to a God that may or may not exist. The whole story was too good, too unfathomable, for him to believe without question. He would need time to decide. He would not make such a decision in haste, and he was not the kind of man to make a commitment lightly. Rather than respond to her plea, he changed the subject, and she had no more opportunity to sway him.

"Your things should be packed now. Go to the home in the country. Some of my children and other women are there, so you won't be alone. None of them have met you. There should be no animosity toward you as there was here."

Narshac bent his head toward the door, a sign that she was dismissed.

"Thank you for your kindness and for not taking my honor."

"Your honor is destroyed. No one knows that you are pure." Narshac's voice was almost sad.

"I do, as does my King. If ever you granted my hand to someone else, Narshac, he too would know. I believe in time you will remember me with kindness."

Lomina left the room before Narshac had time to answer. He couldn't believe his ears. She had proven to be good and kind to the core. He understood now that her disposition, though good, was not of her own will, but was rather an attribute Jehovah gave his children. Someday, if he found a man worthy of her, he'd grant her hand to him. But until then, he'd do all he could to protect her. To him, she was a wise teacher, friend, and daughter.

Narshac turned and tried to harden his heart against her last plea that he turn to God. But something inside him couldn't completely block the words out. The truth she had spoken would not relinquish its hold as quickly as he'd like. The words took hold and planted themselves in his conscience. He searched for Safira's face in his mind, and the memory of her desertion to harden his heart as he wished. He stepped out onto his balcony and watched as Lomina's carriage pulled away toward the country.

Lonika was walking the streets calmly with her children when she turned at the sound of a carriage. Moving out of the street, she looked up into the carriage and saw her eldest daughter's calm face as the coachman hurried his horse through the marketplace.

Lonika wanted to cry out, to reach out and touch her daughter's face. There was only one reason Lomina, or any wife was sent to country palace, she was with child. Lonika felt a tear run down her face. Lomina would be sixteen in a week. She was too young to be bearing a child of her own.

Lonika could remember the dreams she and her husband had for Lomina. Dreams that she'd marry a Christian man for love and begin a family centered on Christ. She watched the carriage disappear from sight as a tear ran down her face.

Her son broke through her thoughts, "Mom, are you okay?"

Lonika looked at her two children. She hugged them both before continuing their walk through the market. Brother and sister exchanged confused looks before following their mother.

*****

Zamina had turned her husband in for his decision to become a Christian. She'd hated the man since she'd been given in marriage to him nearly ten years earlier at the age of sixteen. Old enough to be a Keilronian bride years earlier, she'd been spared an early marriage because her mother had needed the help. The only wife of a poor man, her mother had given birth to ten children; Zamina was the eldest daughter. She'd been given to her husband in a twofold advantage agreement for her father. He'd received a substantial sum of money and the added bonus of becoming the father-in-law of the wealthiest merchant in Shemna. Her father had sacrificed nearly half of the marriage price to the gods for making his eldest daughter so beautiful, and her family's life had changed dramatically for the better. But her happiness had been sacrificed. As a child she'd known, this was her fate as a woman.

From the beginning, she'd loathed her husband. He had treated her with no mercy on their wedding night or on any night he had chosen to take his poor but exquisitely beautiful wife. She was his trophy, the one he loved to show his guests and to allow them to drool in desire for her. He'd even been swayed to have her go in with other men if the connection and price was right. She'd known that this too was often a part of life for a Keilronian wife, particularly one with multiple wives and within a wealthy household.

Because she had born no children from the relations she was forced into, she found no end of relief, and although many would condemn her for her barrenness, she'd seen it as a grace.

When her husband returned after a week's journey outside of Shemna on business, he returned with a different perspective on life. He'd not given her to his guests in several months, nor had he called for her himself. He began to take solace in his first wife and left his seven other wives to question the change in him. They were all softened by his changes. Perhaps the new way he began to dote on his children helped them see past the anger and pain he had previously forced on them. For Zamina, the hate had long ago sunk into her very core, and no amount of kindness to the household children would blind her from the kind of man he was. She could still see the scars on some of the wives and children from times when he'd taken his anger out on those closest to him. Zamina had escaped such cruelty only because she was more lucrative for him if she were unscarred.

Searching for meaning behind his changed attitude, she'd found the answers in the strange little book by his bedside while cleaning one day. She could not read, but knew that it had to do with the Christians she'd heard so many rumors about. The book would be presented as evidence. She knew it was her only hope of bringing the wrath of Shovak down on a wealthy merchant.

Presenting the evidence to an officer through a messenger had prompted a thorough investigation. With the evidence she'd found along with other writings discovered in his room, her husband was carried away like the horrible man he was. Instantly, she'd been shunned by the other wives for her disloyalty, but she'd held her head high, knowing she'd done right.

The only question now was what would be done with the man's household.

Shovak was made aware of the situation since the man had been a high-profile Keilronian. Narshac had orders to punish the man as he would any other. It must be known that wealth would not protect against the law of the land nor against disloyalty to the gods. Shovak was concerned with the man's great household. The man had one son who was sixteen who would be given the bulk of the estate and rule over his siblings and his mother. The other wives' lives however were at stake.

Shovak hadn't dealt personally with this type of situation because others would normally be given authority to do so, but the nature of the man's status was significant enough for Shovak to deal with the matter himself. He had decided to bring the women in question before him to determine what was to be done. It was possible for the wives to take the same blame the husband was accused of and be tortured or put to death for the sake of their husband. Shovak could have followed tradition immediately, but he'd heard through the grapevine that one of women in the household was a rare beauty, and he was anxious to see if the rumors were true.

The women stood before him now, and he admitted that the rumors had not done justice to the woman of interest.

"You," he pointed and said to Zamina. "You are the one who reported your husband?"

"I informed them of his infidelity with the foreign god." She spoke with confidence, her head high, unrepentant. She was proud of herself, even as the other women glared at her.

Shovak actually smirked at her piety. She was filled with disdain for the man who was being tortured several floors below her feet.

"You do know I have every right to punish all of you the way your husband is being tortured."

"I'd rather be tortured and die than let the pig ever touch me again!" she spat out.

Shovak recognized at once that she wasn't just another woman and that she was not speaking for the group. The other wives actually looked peeved at her for speaking her mind. He rather enjoyed her ire.

"What of your children? They would become little more than slaves in their brother's household with no more than your husband's other wife to raise them."

"I've no children to worry about."

Shovak was surprised by this. "How long have you been in his household?"

"A little more than ten years."

Shovak considered her response before ignoring her and focusing on the other wives. He knew for certain that they did have children.

"Have any of you chosen to follow your husband's choice?"

The first wife raised her eyes to meet Shovak's gaze. She nodded, her posture stiff with determination. Shovak shook his head at her, and a guard came and escorted her below to remain with her husband. The others remained silent.

"If I found other husbands for you, and they take your children along with you, would you accept those offers?" he asked.

All the women, except Zamina, bowed their head in submissive agreement.

"Very well. Your husband has bequeathed each one of you a generous amount for the men who will take you into their own households. I have five written marriage contracts, and you will be in their households before the week is up. You may return home until your new grooms come for you."

The women calmly left the room accepting their fate, knowing they'd been dealt with kindly. Zamina wanted to cry. Leaving one cruel household for another had not been her hope. She somehow convinced herself she'd either die or be allowed to go home. Her anger dissipated as terror filled her.

"Zamina, you were offered for, but I have turned all offers away." Shovak spoke before she was able to exit the room. Turning toward him, she dared lift a brow at him. He'd declared five offers; she was the one he'd left out. She took a few steps back into the room, knowing she hadn't been dismissed.

"I'm the one who has ordered each wife to be given a stipend, a chance for a different life. You too will receive your portion. But I'm going to ask you, rather than command obedience."

She met his eyes questioningly. "Are you suggesting a choice?"

"I am," he answered pleasantly.

"What choice?" she demanded. Somehow she knew he appreciated her bluntness.

"I want you to marry me," he said kindly. His voice changed, it became tender, enticing her to trust him, "Be under my house."

"You have many wives in your house. Why would I prefer yours any more than I would prefer another?" Her anger was replaced with curiosity. The gentleness that emanated from him touched something inside her.

"I have wives, yes. Perhaps even more than necessary. I have several that I provide for but do not call for anymore. Matters of state often keep me busy, and my household is large enough. I have more than enough children, and it has been a few years since my wives have been around enough to conceive, if you understand me."

She did. She was also shocked that the wealthy and powerful leader would have little desire toward his many wives and had not sought to produce more children.

"I may be older than a young thing like you may prefer, but if we are being honest, the man you may end up with could be twenty years older than me. I'm only fifty-one."

She began to look at the man in front of her as a prospective husband. He was in good shape, strong, and handsome. There was a reason he was attractive to so many outside countries. He was right, of course; most men willing to take a barren wife would be much older than Shovak.

"You are asking me to marry you," she clarified.

"I am. And to make it clear to you, I don't have any wives in the city with me except on rare occasions. You could change that for me. I would be able to have you here with me in the capital. You would be my first wife, and I would no longer have a need to send for my household."

What he said had an appeal, and what was more, his offer making her first wife was a role often given to the woman who'd born his heir. He was offering her the chance to be a queen. She'd never heard even a whisper that the man was a cruel husband. Her attraction to the idea intensified.

One more step toward her, and he was only inches from her face. His voice was like honey, and she felt her body and heart respond to his next words. "I promise to treat you well, and you alone will be mine. No one else will have you, and perhaps no one else will have me."

Shovak knew he'd just hit the nail on the head. He'd known for some time the kind of man her husband had been. He'd also immediately been drawn to Zamina the moment she'd entered the room. The moment she'd spoken, he knew he wanted her, and only her.

"You are choosing me because I'm barren?" Her voice was low and breathless.

"It is definitely a factor, but make no mistake, I find you absolutely beautiful. I also find your strength of character matches my own, and I don't take that lightly. You are my equal."

"You've known me for five minutes, and you are offering me everything."

"I need a woman, and from where I stand, you are the perfect woman I need." He ran his index finger softly down her cheek.

She swallowed. Now, she knew her answer and felt her body tremble at his touch. Her voice was low and accepting. "I will."

Shovak smiled and looked down at her with desire, his eyes filled with tenderness.

"I will draw up the paperwork tonight, and tomorrow, I will have you brought to me. The merchant has provided well for you, but I will give you the world." He lifted her chin and kissed her.

Zamina sighed at the tenderness in the kiss and knew that somehow, she must have found favor with the gods to have been given such a gift.

*****

JC entered the small living space with Chris and Safira.

"I'd make a comment about the small living space, but something tells me this isn't that small."

Chris smiled at his brother who was trying to take it all in at once. "For Shemna, no. This is an average house for a family our size.

Sleeping quarters, the living space, and kitchen are only as big as necessary. We do have a bathroom, which is a little more excessive than some places; but I'm wealthy enough, spoiled enough, and American enough to want to shower and use a toilet. Though the plumbing is a little different, it does the job." Chris wondered if Kindel felt the same when he first introduced him to the world of Keilron.

"Do you hold meetings like we do in the United States?" JC asked.

"Once a month, at least, we try. We have to move locations every time so no one grows suspicious, and so it's hard for any onlookers to recognize the same group coming in."

"Christians are still under great persecution? I thought things were getting better."

"Yes and no. For Americans, yes it has improved, but there is little relief for the natives," Chris said with a note of sadness.

"How's the translating going?"

"We finished the New Testament three months ago and are working on getting it in print and finding a way to smuggle it in. As for the Old Testament, we've only scratched the surface with Proverbs and are about three-quarters of the way through Genesis."

"You're not translating in order?"

"We're translating according to need. With Safira, the translation is moving faster than if we were doing it on our own. In five years, we're hoping to be completely done with the books of Moses. That will give our people a chance to understand more of how the New Testament is relevant, to understand more about prophecies Christ fulfilled."

"Awesome." JC had exhausted his list of inquiries. Perhaps that was okay, considering the long journey and culture shock. After being shown through the house and being able to lay his bags in his own room, they both relaxed in the living room while they waited for Safira to get back from her meeting with a few of the women who needed her help.

"How is Pastor Kindel?"

"He's doing well. He'll be going home to his family at the end of the summer. He's not completely retiring from ministry; rather, he's going home to gather more support for us here, but he will not be returning," Chris said.

JC detected the sadness in his brother's voice but didn't comment.

"Who'll be the ring leader, so to speak? From my understanding, he's the one to get this fire started."

"He has placed Safira and me in charge. We are gaining more men who are able to help ease the burden, but many haven't been here long enough. Those who are native are so young in their faith. Safira and I are the ones who have the most access to our outside sources and are more stable in our ability not to get killed since we are, in fact, still American citizens."

"That's pretty incredible, but I'm guessing that will be a pretty big weight on the two of you."

"Yes, but this is what Kindel has been preparing me for and what God has prepared Safira for."

"I'm glad I'm here. What can I do to help while I'm here?"

"JC, you need to understand how dangerous this is going to be. I won't sugarcoat anything for you. This is going to be rough."

"I know. That's why I'm here, big brother. When I return home, I'm hoping to have gained knowledge of how to pray for you and Safira."

"Well, in that case, welcome aboard." Safira smiled from the doorway. She'd heard only the last bit and was so delighted seeing her brother that she didn't ask for more. She pulled Rebekah from behind her back and introduced her to her uncle.

Chapter 25

The Encounter

July 2006

After living in Shemna for nearly a month, JC was able to move easily through the streets with confidence. He didn't know the city passageways like Chris or Safira, but he knew his way to the market and a few major landmarks.

Zigzagging through the market, his eye caught a glimpse of a brightly colored Keilronian robe. It wasn't uncommon to find bright-colored clothing in the markets, but he found himself interested, rather, in the person wearing the robe. He shadowed the middle-aged woman for a time before realizing why she'd caught his attention. His stride lengthened, and he easily caught up to the lady and touched her shoulder. She turned quickly, and it took her only a moment to recognize the young man.

"Lonika, how are you this afternoon," he asked in her native tongue. Keilronian hadn't come easily, but he was able to communicate, and his time within the country had improved his understanding of the language.

"I'm well. It's good to see a friendly face."

"The children are well?"

"Yes, they're resting, but their schooling has come a long way in the month you've been here. I thank you for teaching them." She spoke slowly so that he would have a chance to sift through her words. Lonika had learned the first couple of nights at the Banks' that JC was not well-versed in Keilronian, so she did her best to be helpful and understanding.

"They're teaching me Keilronian. I teach them English."

"You are improving. I must be going. Give my best to your brother and Safira."

Lonika promptly disappeared in the crowd. JC went back to the main market street and got the things Safira had sent him for. He was still awed at the money exchange. For instance, he could buy a five-pound bag of sugar, a pound of freshly made butter, a loaf of bread, and fish enough to feed all three of them for only two dollars.

To receive the credits for his schooling, he'd been assigned to write a fifteen-page report on the different culture and his brother's impact within that culture. The assignment would be easier done than perhaps his professors expected. To fit all of what he was learning into only fifteen pages would be the true challenge.

"Move, you insolent woman!" he heard a voice shout out.

JC spun around and spotted a woman in the road. The reason for her position appeared obvious. She must have run out in front of the four-horse carriage to retrieve her young child from being trampled by the horses. The driver cared little why she was in his way. The carriage was elaborate, and it no doubt carried a prestigious passenger.

"Let the woman be. She was only trying to protect her son!" JC could not help himself as he pushed through the crowd to aid the woman. Chris had asked him to lay low. Christians in Keilron were not meant to stand out. Why couldn't he keep his mouth shut?

"You are in an extremely crowded part of town. Perhaps the question really is, why weren't you watching the crowd?"

The carriage door was thrust open, and the curious crowd stepped back as closely as possible toward the stone buildings. Everyone's eyes went to the ground. JC saw the crowd's reaction but knew the man was not Shovak. He would've had an entire guard with him or, more accurately, would have been in a vehicle entourage.

"What is your name, boy?" The man's voice was gruff. His dress was that of an upper-class citizen. He was well-built and looked strong like a warrior. Even from the dark interior of the coach, the sight of him made JC hesitate.

"My name is Jeremy Kleren, and you are?"

"You are American," the man stated plainly, ignoring the boy's question.

"I am," he confirmed.

"Let me welcome you to Keilron. I'm Col. Narshac. Come, I'm on my way to my country palace. I'd like the company, and you will benefit by seeing Keilron at its best."

The man's name instantly clicked with JC as Chris had spoken of this man before, and Safira had mentioned his name a dozen times. "I mustn't. I've family that expects me."

"They'll wait. Come." The command was given in such a way JC definitely didn't feel he had a choice.

The man's invitation was spontaneous, and those around whispered in obvious curiosity. JC, however, looked at the woman who'd found her way to the edge of the street. His mission had been successful; the crowd had since forgotten about the woman and child.

JC climbed into the enclosed carriage with the most dangerous man to Keilronian Christians. JC prayed immediately and hoped that others would pray too.

*****

"JC should've been back from the market hours ago," Safira said to herself. She prayed for her brother-in-law as she rocked Rebekah back to sleep.

Minutes after Safira laid Rebekah in the cradle, Chris entered the house, his face strained.

"Safira, love, I've bad news. According to witnesses, JC protected a woman from the whip and found himself face to face with Narshac, and he was invited to the country palace. He wasn't given the chance to decline. Do you know where that place might be?"

"Yes, the country palace is where I grew up. Narshac is the heir, so the palace is his as well as father's. They both keep their households there. I think it best we pray. I have a feeling things will be all right." Her voice sounded calmer than she felt. An invitation to the palace was an honor, but could be turned into a death sentence if JC wasn't careful.

"Mom will kill me if anything happens to him," Chris muttered, remembering how hard it had been to convince Fay to let her other son go, even for the summer.

"No, she wouldn't. Fay already gave her blessing for him to come. She knows the risks involved."

Chris ran a hand through his hair, while he paced the small kitchen. "I'll never forgive myself."

"He's in God's hands. He's always been in God's hands. Maybe there is a plan of great importance that we aren't aware of yet."

Chris stopped midstride to look at Safira standing by the teapot. His expression softened as he walked over to his wife and pulled her into his arms. "God knew what he was doing when he gave me you."

"He'll bless our faith, and JC will return to us unharmed, if it's Jehovah's will. He had a plan for you, and they let you go. We don't know what's been going on in Narshac's heart."

Chris bowed his head and prayed with Safira for their brother's safety.

*****

JC exited the carriage with Narshac close on his heels. His eyes scanned the palace, and Narshac took the lead and led him toward the interior of the home. The building had been aptly described as an estate, and it was an impressive dwelling. When entering the courtyard, the home was designed like a three-sided square. There were three stories, each boasting a balcony that seamlessly connected the different sections of the home. At the center of the large courtyard, an impressive fountain bubbled. Two men immediately greeted Narshac.

"Sir, welcome. How can we serve?" one man asked.

"Bring me Lomina," Narshac demanded. The two men departed down a south corridor while Narshac led JC into a large lounge room.

Narshac sat on a couch and stretched out his legs. He then motioned with his hand for JC to have a seat.

Narshac was at ease here. He spoke warmly to his visitor. "Welcome to my home. This is where I prefer," Narshac said in English. "The reason? Well, I like the orchards, fresh air, quiet, and the woman you are about to meet. She is the reason I come home today."

Obviously, Jeremy had no idea what he was doing here, and Narshac appreciated that the young man hadn't spoken foolishly. He let the silence hang for a minute, while he met the eyes of his guest. Satisfied with what he saw, he broke the silence. "Why did you put yourself between my driver and the woman? Did you know her?" There was no accusation in his tone, only curiosity.

JC measured his words before speaking. "No, it just didn't seem fair that she should be punished for protecting her son. I'm from the United States. We are ingrained with the idea that every life is important." His calm voice surprised himself.

"Every life is important," Narshac agreed. "I also believe that every decision has consequences. Each station in my world keeps my society moving. Example, a woman here has the obligation to wed and have children who will rule and build up our country."

Keeping his tone curious, JC responded. "When you say 'children,' I feel you are really saying 'boys.'"

"To some extent, yes. Our women are not treated as equals as they are in your society. But you will also find that our women are cared for in ways your society does not. Our women are provided for. In America, they often must care for themselves. Both societies have their merits and drawbacks," Narshac conceded.

JC remained quiet. The silence didn't last long. He saw a young girl rush into the room. She knelt on her knees before her master and his guest.

Her words were softly spoken Keilronian, but JC understood. "My lord, you sent for me?"

Changing to his native tongue, Narshac spoke to her. "I have a guest. Take a look at the stranger I've brought with me."

The girl obeyed. In the dark brown eyes that turned to JC, he recognized a light he often saw in fellow believers. Was it possible she was a Christian?

"How old are you?" Narshac asked the girl. The young man's expression was not lost on him.

"I'm sixteen, my lord."

"Jeremy, what is your age?" Narshac asked in English.

"I'm twenty-one."

"Five years," Narshac spoke as if mulling over some decision.

Concerned about what the colonel had in mind, JC spoke with uncertainty, "I'm not sure I understand what you're getting at."

"I'm considering my plan before I make any move. Give me time." Narshac thought quietly for a moment as he looked from one to the other. He decided to tread carefully. "What would you pay for this woman?"

JC's eyebrows raised. "Pay?"

"Yes. What amount of money would you give me for her to be yours?"

Lomina returned her gaze to the young man before her. She understood what Narshac was trying to do. But would the American understand and have mercy on her? It'd take only one day for her to be his. What she feared most was what if this man was one of the Americans who despised Christians?

"I could never put a price on a life, sir. I'm sure a woman of her beauty will get your price, but what of her virtue? What of her soul? Can you put a price on that kind of treasure?" JC's passion was poorly masked, but Narshac took no offense. He'd been to America for a brief time and understood the American culture.

"For Lomina, no. You cannot put a price on such a jewel, which is why I am giving you a gift you could never replace."

JC was sure he'd heard wrong. "Sir, I don't understand. Are you implying that we wed?"

"I would give her to you on no other condition." Narshac folded his hands on top of his chest, appearing satisfied. Jeremy had jumped in front of Narshac's driver to save a stranger, and he knew that Jeremy would care for Lomina. Whether the boy was a Christian or not was debatable, and Narshac wasn't going to ask; he didn't want the answer when Lomina's future was on the line.

JC stammered out his weak protest, "She's not of age."

Narshac leaned forward, realizing the young man didn't understand their customs, and there was some explaining and convincing to be done if he wanted Jeremy to claim Lomina.

"She's been of age for three years," Narshac reasoned. "Between you and me"—Narshac said, angling his body closer to JC and lowering his voice for JC's ears—"she's pure as the skies."

"She's too young," JC said firmly.

"I tell you, she is. She has been for three years, by Keilronian standards. She has been in my household for a while now, and I promise I've not laid a hand on her. You have my word."

Lomina listened silently and motionless on her knees as the two men discussed her future.

"Okay," JC acquiesced. "But why do you want to give her to me?"

"You're American, and you'll take care of her. She's a treasure that ought to be cherished, not wasted here among my wives. She's been my teacher."

JC's curiosity was peaked. "What has she been teaching you?"

"Ask her yourself when she is yours, but I will keep our conversations a secret until you have signed for her hand."

"Why me? You could've chosen any American off the streets."

"She deserves a man of strong character. You've a look about you I think I can trust." Narshac's eyes narrowed as he continued, "If I'm wrong, tell me now, and I'm more than capable of taking your life."

JC was cornered. Her age was an issue, but even Safira had spoken of the young marriage age.

"What of her mother, her father?" JC pressed for more time to make the life-altering decision.

"Her mother is certainly married to another, and her father died in my dungeons some time ago."

"Do you trust me?"

"Yes, lad. For some reason, I do." Seeing victory was near, Narshac relaxed back into the chair.

"I'll return for her hand in two years. If I don't, you may give her to another."

"Waste of time, lad. She could bear you children by then."

"Yes, but it's my time. In America, she won't even be considered an adult until she's eighteen. If we wait until she is of age, then the marriage contract won't be questioned when we return. Will you consent to my terms, or will you take me back to Shemna and forget you offered her to me?" JC was sure that his point had been made. He was hopeful that he'd be immediately returned to Shemna.

Narshac licked his bottom lip and waited only a moment. "I accept." He turned toward Lomina, "This is to be your husband."

JC was dumbfounded. Had he really accepted the hand of Lomina?

Narshac turned toward him. "On Shemna rules, you owe me money, but I've given her to you as a gift. If you do not honor your word, your name will be accursed. If you do not return to Shemna within two years to claim your wife, she returns to me, and you will never again be welcome in Keilron. Do we have an understanding?"

JC nodded and shook Narshac's hand.

"Wonderful," Narshac said lightly and smiling. He clapped his hands loudly twice, and two servants appeared. "Prepare a feast. I've an honored guest to entertain tonight," Narshac said, nodded at JC and escorting him out of the room. Lomina was forgotten.

Alone in the large room, Lomina relaxed on the floor as tears trailed down her cheeks. She prayed as never before to Jesus. Perhaps this American, Jeremy, would do her well. Never before had she felt so alone and so betrayed by all around her.

*****

Safira and Chris were relieved to see JC quite early the next morning. Sitting at the kitchen table with Chris, JC told of his account with Narshac. Safira, who'd been making tea, was the one to speak first.

"You'll have to keep your word. It's trouble you've gotten into, but with the teaching degree you're getting, you could help us so much."

"He's got more to think about than helping our ministry. What was she like?" Chris asked.

"Quiet. Reserved. Narshac spoke of her as his teacher? I'm not sure what he meant. He also told me she was more like a daughter and that he'd never laid hands on her."

"That's rare, Chris," Safira said as she touched her husband's shoulder.

"Which is what I'm worried about. I'm afraid something is wrong with her. You of all people know what men in power are like. Why wouldn't he touch her?"

"Unless she's a spitfire, you mean. Well, that's a thought. JC, what was her name?" Chris inquired.

"Lomina. I think that's what he called her."

"I don't believe it!" Safira gasped.

"Sweetheart, what's wrong?" Chris asked.

"Lomina is Lonika's daughter. She'd be sixteen by now."

Chris's eyes lit with recognition. The stillness surrounding the room was deafening.

"I wonder what the poor girl has gone through and is going through. If Narshac has been honest, then she's been protected under his care, but she's just been given to a complete stranger. She's probably scared out of her mind," Safira said.

"You will return for her, JC," Chris said with finality.

"One more thing. You'll have to marry her. If you return and take her to America only to free her, you'll hurt her worse. Narshac will throw you a party, a feast. And afterward he'll give you a room at the country palace. He'll expect you to marry her in every sense of the word," Safira said.

"I'll return in two years. I graduate in the spring, and hopefully, I'll be able to find a teaching job immediately so that I can support her."

Safira nodded. "Narshac is doing right by her. That's all he wants."

"I'll make sure the papers are in order when I return," JC said.

A heavy silence filled the room for several minutes, each adult in their own thoughts. At last, Chris took a deep breath and said, "Well, you're not leaving tomorrow, so let's get some sleep. We have some work to do tomorrow."

Chapter 26

The Gift

June 2008

Narshac checked his watch and relinquished the bloody whip to the young soldier. The Christian he'd just beaten lay in a heap at his feet. Blood flowed from his back, giving evidence of Narshac's hard heart.

"I'm going home for the night. Put this varmint in a cell. I'll deal with him later. Give him water and a little food," Narshac ordered.

"Yes, sir. Have a good evening." The soldier was barely sixteen, but he was trustworthy.

The moment Narshac entered his city dwelling, he recognized the messenger by his plain forest green tunic and yellow-belted sash. The messenger bent at his waist out of respect, his hand outstretched with an envelope. Narshac took the message, tipped the man, and proceeded to rip the seal. Scanning through it hurriedly, he summoned a nearby servant to fetch his horse.

Once the horse arrived, Narshac lost no time in mounting the black Arab and spurring him toward the country estate.

The horse came to a halt inside the courtyard. Dismounting, Narshac handed the reins to a waiting slave and strode across the courtyard toward his quarters. His guest was easy to spot. The surprise American guest was dressed in trousers and a dress shirt, a distinguished look; but here, he stood out.

"You've kept your promise!" Narshac's face lit up. He took the younger man's offered hand and shook it in greeting. "I'm pleased you have returned. We will feast this night."

"Sir, I'd like nothing more. I do, however, have friends in Keilron. I'd like to visit them before I return to the United States with my new wife," Jeremy spoke respectfully. "Will you allow us to leave in the morning?"

"Only stay this night. Then, I will give you escort in the morning."

"No." Jeremy's voice was firm. "An escort is not necessary."

"Very well," Narshac responded pleasantly. In truth, he'd feared the man would not return. The fact that he had proved Narshac had been right about his character. Nothing was going to dim his happiness tonight, not even a shorter send-off than he'd wanted.

"All right," said Jeremy with resignation. He'd hoped to see Chris and Safira first, but his name immediately caused a stir at the airport, and he'd been escorted to Narshac's home. He was anxious for the visit with his family before returning to his high school teaching job in Colorado, only miles from where he'd grown up. Perhaps, with Lomina's connection with Safira, Chris, and Lonika, coming here first was a good thing.

"This night, Lomina will be your wife," said Narshac as he cupped his hand around Jeremy's shoulder and guided him inside the home.

Narshac signaled with his head to a servant, and five minutes later, Lomina appeared. "Bow before your lord," Narshac ordered. It sounded more like a boast.

Lomina knelt on her knees in front of Jeremy, folded her hands, and bowed her head. Her voice was calm and quiet. "My lord, I'm at your service."

JC saw Lomina shaking fearfully and wished he could comfort her, but he couldn't do so now.

Narshac extended his arm toward the dining hall. "Let's feast!"

"I'm not familiar with your ways. What of the girl?" Jeremy's eyes glanced back at Lomina, still kneeling.

"She'll be prepared and sent to your chambers," Narshac explained. He ushered Jeremy out of the sitting room where Lomina sat kneeling and into a large, expansive dining hall.

JC knew Safira and Chris were praying hard for him at this moment. He prayed to the Lord himself when he was seated at the table filled with food and wine.

"Have a drink," Narshac offered. The colonel offered a bottle of brandy to his guest.

"No, sir. I'd rather not be drunk tonight," JC said, trying to remain anonymous regarding his beliefs.

"Indeed. Wise decision," Narshac chuckled.

*****

Lomina stared at her image in the mirror as the other women prepared her for her husband. Her hands shook, and tears trailed down her cheeks. She'd feared this night for two years. How could she possibly go through with it?

"Don't be afraid, my child. Your new husband looks kind. He will do you well, I think." The woman who'd spoken had taken to mothering Lomina soon after her arrival. She loved the young woman and had heard whispers from the city dwelling.

Lomina squeezed the woman's proffered hand. "May I have a moment alone?"

The room cleared quickly. Gazing into the mirror, she whispered a prayer to her heavenly Father for courage, wisdom, and hope that He'd take care of her. She opened the letter she'd received from Kalita and read it again. The letter had been delivered nearly three weeks ago, and the words often comforted and encouraged her. Narshac had taught his first wife how to read and write, so she would never be cheated while handling household affairs. He'd given the same opportunity to Lomina while she'd been at the country palace.

My Dear Lomina,

Narshac has chosen your husband with care. He wants what is best for you, though he cannot show it in front of others. Take heart and be unafraid. Your husband will be kind and will treat you with tenderness. We both love you, child, and wish there was another way for this to turn out in your favor, but this is the only way our ways will allow. I love you, my friend.

Slipping the note back into her bag that held her few belongings, she wiped the tears from her eyes. She took a few deep breaths and decided to trust in those around her. In Narshac, that he had chosen wisely and in God that He would not leave her.

After a few more moments, she opened her door and allowed the head wife of the country estate to guide her to her husband's chambers.

*****

Safira arrived at her home and thanked Lonika for watching her young children. After giving two-and-a-half-year-old Rebekah a hug and kiss, she picked up her youngest, eight-month-old David. She sat down and smiled at Lonika's own growing children.

"I'll fix supper tonight. You look tired, and your children need your attention." Lonika stood, continuing to speak as she began preparations for dinner. "You and your husband do so much for our people. I'm really glad you've allowed me to help you. I love watching these two. They are so precious."

Safira sighed in contentment. "We're grateful for your help."

Chris walked through the door and straight toward his wife. He bent and kissed her before setting his bag down. "How are you, sweetheart?" he smiled.

"I'm tired, but good." Safira smiled into his eyes still filled with love. Chris bent and kissed her again. Raising Rebekah up and over his head, he swung her around as she giggled. He set her back down on the ground and kissed the top of David's head.

"Again!" Rebekah begged.

Chris grinned. He obliged before setting her up on his shoulders. He walked into the kitchen, reached around Lonika, and grabbed a cookie.

"Out! Both of you. You're going to lose your appetite, Master Banks."

"I could eat a bear. My appetite is never satisfied."

Lonika shook her head. "True enough." She smirked as Chris left the kitchen.

He handed Rebekah over to Lonika's daughter, who was more than willing to entertain the child. He made his way back over to Safira and sat down beside her. With one arm, he pulled Safira closer and kissed her on the cheek.

"I love you, Safira. I'm so glad God put us together." He glanced down at his son and stroked the baby's face with his index finger. "I'm so proud of our family."

Safira's heart was bursting with love for Chris. She kissed him on the cheek. "Let's pray for JC that he learns to open his heart to Lomina. We were expecting him this afternoon, weren't we?"

"I received word while I was out. He was detained at the airport."

"Oh, no," Safira groaned.

"It's all right. Word is he got the royal treatment and an escort to Narshac's estate."

"He may bring her here!" Safira bit her lower lip, excitedly throwing a look toward Lonika, who was busy in the kitchen. Lonika had no idea the surprise the Banks had lined up for her.

*****

JC entered his chambers and saw Lomina sitting on the bed. Taking a deep breath, he leisurely strolled toward her and tried not to intimidate her. He slowly lowered himself beside her on the large bed. He could see her trembling.

"Don't be afraid of me. I've no intention of hurting you." Still, she refused to look at him. JC was desperate for any kind of reaction from her. He lowered his voice, "I've been told you are a Christian." Her eyes flew up to his. She nodded.

"Your mother is well," he said casually. "She is helping my brother and his wife. Narshac isn't aware, but my sister-in-law is his sister, Safira."

"Safira is the reason he will not accept a Savior," she said looking back down at her hands. The initial excitement he'd seen vanished. But at least, she had stopped shaking.

"We'll leave tomorrow for Shemna where we will stay with them for a couple of weeks. Then, we will go to the United States. Do you understand that you will be my legal wife in America as well?"

She looked back up at him. "Leave Keilron?"

"Yes, it is the only way. I'm a teacher in America. I will provide for you, Lomina."

"What of tonight? Will you send me away in shame?" She asked in a shaky voice.

He gave her a small smile. "No. We do not know each other yet. In time, we will build a marriage and a family. Tonight, however, I'll take the floor."

"No! I cannot allow you to be sore." Her voice expressed surprise that he'd even suggested such a thing.

He smiled while looking around the richly furnished room. "I've been in harder conditions since my first introduction to Keilron."

"You are my husband. You must have the better," she argued.

"No, I refuse." JC took a blanket and pillow from the bed and spread it on the floor.

Lomina sighed. "Wait. Let's compromise."

JC spun around to look at her with a lifted brow.

"You are willing to wait for the marriage bed until we know one another. You are a godsend, and I'm grateful. Please, the bed is large enough for both of us," she offered, gesturing toward the massive bed.

"Are you sure?" He studied her expression. She'd been growing more relaxed with every sentence between them.

"Yes," she said firmly.

Taking the blanket and pillow back to the bed, he picked a side and lay down facing the wall. He felt the bed move and knew she'd taken the other side. She was right. There really was plenty of room for both of them.

Lomina relaxed against the softness of the bed, choosing to ignore the man on the other side. What kind of man was this? He'd been so willing to take the floor rather than her virginity. Her mother had suggested long ago that a godly man would treat her as an equal. God truly was at work, and she heard the voice of her Father inside her heart telling her everything was going to work out. This Jeremy was a stranger to her now, but he would not be so for long. Kalita's note came to mind. Narshac had been instrumental in God's plan for her. He'd searched out a man worthy of her, because he'd claimed he cared about her. Now, she believed Kalita's message.

*****

JC and Lomina left the confines of Narshac's home after a large breakfast. Narshac had graciously offered a chauffeured jeep ride to wherever Jeremy was headed. Jeremy helped his new bride out of the vehicle when they'd stopped just outside the main market and thanked the driver. Lomina followed behind him as they swept into the crowded square. Jeremy didn't linger in the crowd or pay any mind to the vendors. They left the market and began moving through the maze of streets toward the Banks' home.

JC knocked once and swept into the home, guiding Lomina in before shutting the door. Lonika, who'd come to help for the day, was relieved to see JC, but she caught her breath at the sight of the young woman behind him.

Tears sprung to her eyes. "Lomina?" she whispered.

Lomina's own eyes began to mist. She took one step toward the mother she'd not seen in four years. Lonika needed no other encouragement. She closed the distance, wrapping her arms around her daughter; she held her tight, afraid this was a dream. The tears gradually subsided. Several times, the women pulled apart long enough to stare into one another's face before clutching each other yet again. JC finally cleared his throat, and Lonika pulled herself together and released her daughter but still touched her arm.

Looking puzzled, she asked, "How did you?"

"Lonika, this is my wife."

Lonika's eyes grew large as they darted between JC and Lomina a few times. She'd been aware of the agreement JC had gotten into with Narshac, but the woman's name had never been mentioned. Choosing to smile, she inwardly thanked God. He had performed a miracle for His glory. Lonika and her husband's prayers had been answered, howbeit not in the way they'd anticipated.

Lonika's gaze softened. With two graceful steps, she'd let go of her daughter and placed her hands on either side of JC's shoulders. Looking him in the eyes, she spoke. "You are the kind of man my husband and I always wanted for Lomina. When you leave, I will find it hard to part with her, but I know she's safe with you."

"I promise she is," he replied solemnly.

"JC?" Safira's excited voice interrupted them as she entered the home with her arms filled with things from the market. She set them on the table and embraced her brother, who quickly made the introductions

*****

The couple had been wed for two weeks, but JC had not laid a hand on Lomina except to aide her. They both enjoyed the time with their siblings, and Lomina loved every moment she had with her mother. The time had passed quickly, and Lomina and JC now sat in the Heathrow Airport awaiting another flight. They had both tried small talk but had soon run out of things to say. There was little to talk about, and both were feeling nostalgic over their goodbyes.

They'd flown from Keilron over the remainder of the Middle East, and Lomina was exhausted, but didn't want to close her eyes. There was so much to see. She'd never seen such wonders as she experienced here in Heathrow. She was fighting between her desire to explore the airport and to curl up against her husband to catch a nap. Both options were intimidating.

"We have another three hours before our flight. You could lean on me and get a little rest," JC offered.

Lomina studied him as she considered his offer. JC's face was compassionate. He encouragingly stretched out his arm around the back of her seat. She leaned in closer, resting her head between his shoulder and chest. Feeling more at ease against him than when she'd been looking at him, she relaxed.

"Why have you not claimed your rights with me?" she asked softly. The question had often surfaced in her mind, but she'd been afraid to voice it. For some reason, the busy airport had faded from her mind when she'd picked up the rhythm of his heartbeat.

"You may be my wife, but you don't know me, and I don't know you very well. The time will come, Lomina, when we will be man and wife in every sense, but not until you are ready to take that step. I'll be patient. I want you to love me, not fear me."

"It is unusual in my country to have a man consider the woman in such matters," she said, her voice fading as her mind began to slow with sleep creeping in.

"God has put us together. I have faith He will bring our hearts together as well. We both need to give it a little time is all."

"Thank you," she mumbled.

Looking down at her, he exhaled slowly. He kissed the top of her head and heard her sigh. She was out. Unwilling to accept Safira's help in preparing her for America, she'd told Safira she wanted to hold onto a piece of home a little longer. So Lomina still wore her Keilronian robes and veil, although the veil had come off shortly after their first flight.

JC had been preparing his mind and heart for two years for this marriage. It hadn't been easy to consider himself engaged when he'd seen Lomina only once. Harder still for him was turning down the girls from church when he had no contact with his betrothed. Gazing down at his bride, he was thankful he'd kept his commitment. She was a beauty, and her heart was made of gold. All he'd witnessed over the last couple of weeks had proven she was a gem. He made a promise in his heart to her in that moment. He was going to shower her with everything he could to give her a reason to love him. With a little time, they'd both find joy in this union God had initiated.

*****

Fay anxiously scanned another group entering the baggage claim for any signs of JC and his bride. When the group began to thin, she sighed and sat back down on a bench, her right leg bouncing in anticipation of the next plane arrival. JC had called right before departing from New York, giving her the flight's ETA. Harris had been unable to join her, and Kate had told her mom they'd see JC at the family dinner on Sunday.

Another group of passengers began to descend on the baggage claim area, and she stood again, scanning the faces. She needn't have worried about not recognizing them. The woman beside her son stood out in familiar clothing. Her robes reminded Fay of another young woman from Keilron she'd been proud to welcome. Bright reds and yellows trimmed in silver, the fabrics that swished around the bride's legs were much richer than Safira's original costume. JC was dressed sharply in his usual dress shirt and black slacks.

JC grinned and waved at his mother. Fay watched the way he gently guided his wife through the crowd. The moment they stood before her, she could see the same vulnerable look in Lomina's eyes that she'd seen in Safira's so many years ago. A soft smile graced Fay's face.

She placed her hands on the young woman's shoulders. She broke the ice, "Welcome, my dear," she said before wrapping Lomina in a hug.

Lomina had heard so much about this woman over the last two weeks from Chris and Safira that she'd been hoping for the same welcome Safira had described. The warm welcome combined with all the emotions she'd felt in leaving her homeland caused her to burst into tears and cling to the motherly woman.

Once Lomina's sobs quieted, JC interrupted. "I see how it is. I bring home a girl, and my mom forgets all about me," JC teased.

Fay smiled broadly. Releasing Lomina, she opened her arms to her son.

"It's so good to have you home and to meet your wife. I see we are starting all over again with the communication thing though."

"Yes. She doesn't speak much English, but thanks to Safira and the time I've spent in Keilron, I can communicate with her. She'll learn more quickly with a translator to help, as long as we keep it basic."

JC excused himself so he could grab their two bags off the conveyer belt. Fay led the way to the car, talking with her son and sending several smiles toward Lomina. Fay had been concerned about this arranged marriage, but seeing the love shining in her son's eyes when he looked at Lomina, trying to translate for her, erased all concerns. Obviously, Lomina was shy and overwhelmed by the things around her, but Fay noticed Lomina was sticking close to JC Fay couldn't wait to tell Harris what she was witnessing. She bit her lower lip to keep herself from grinning when she jumped into the driver's seat of her minivan. She'd been worried about JC for no reason. God had brought these two together, just as He'd done for her other two.

*****

Shovak's head raised when Zamina shuffled soundlessly into his office. She knew he'd be alone. His secretary had given her the best time to interrupt her husband when she'd sought him earlier. Shovak and Zamina had found in each other what they'd not found in anyone else. They were bound together in love, friendship, and respect. The last two years had warmed both their hearts. Shovak had kept his promises toward her. He never called for his other wives nor did he ever send her away. They shared the same quarters, though many talked of how strange it was for the powerful leader to find such constant companionship in just one woman.

After removing the veil she wore so he could see her face, she gave him a shy smile. Her feelings for Shovak had turned from physical desire to an intimate bond she could describe only as love. After a visit with the midwife earlier this morning, who'd confirmed her suspicions, she now feared he would send her away in anger.

He stepped out from behind his desk and reached toward her. "What can I do for you, my love?"

Three graceful steps forward, and she was locked in his embrace. Her eyes openly stared into his. "I'm afraid to tell you. I don't want you to be angry with me."

"Aren't we past such things?" he asked. "I could never be so angry with you as to send you away." He leaned down and kissed her soundly on the lips. She sighed in contentment, wishing his words to be true.

"I spoke this morning with a midwife." She pulled away from his embrace and took a step past him toward the large office window behind his desk.

His brows knit together. Turning toward her, he stared at her back and waited for her to continue.

Now that she was about to actually speak to him, she found the words were difficult to spit out, though she'd practiced a hundred times. She turned to face him, and his look was crying for her to explain.

"My love, I am . . . ," she couldn't say the words, too afraid they would make what she'd been told that morning a reality she wasn't ready for. She took both her hands and placed them over her abdomen and looked down.

Just two seconds passed for him to realize what she was trying to say. "Impossible!" he breathed quietly. "Not only were you barren for ten years before we were married, you have been barren all this time." He wasn't so much trying to convince her as he was himself.

"I had it confirmed this morning."

Shovak stood motionless for several seconds before turning his back to her. He stared at the fireplace mantle. Zamina was afraid to move or speak. Knowing that he was taking it all in and he would need her close when he was ready to speak, she waited. To flee the room was a welcome notion, but she had grown to love him with all of her heart and wanted to be with him for as long as he'd let her.

Had she been able to read Shovak's mind, she might have breathed easier. His mind ran along similar paths as her own. He was sorting through his emotions and the problems and solutions. Five minutes had passed when he slowly turned back to Zamina.

"I will not send you away. You will be given restrictions, of course, but you will remain near me. This is a blessing from Handrel. We will rejoice in this child, and we will raise him or her together. Handrel has given us this child for a reason, even though we don't know why yet. Zamina, we have been blessed, and I will cherish this child for the gift it is. My love, everything will be all right." Shovak moved to his wife and embraced her.

Zamina's relief could not have been expressed. When he wrapped her in a hug, her eyes filled with tears, and her body shook with sobs of relief at her husband's understanding and love. She too would love this child, not because it was a gift, but because this child was Shovak's seed. She knew he had other children, but she could tell he felt a joy and love for this baby that he'd not experienced.

Part 5

The Ultimate Price

Chapter 27

Visit Home

December 2023

Holding Chris's hand with her seven other children trailing behind, Safira strolled toward Fay and Rebekah. Sixteen-year-old David kept his eye on the younger siblings, while they made their way toward the front of the airport where their grandparents waited. Fay hugged each person in turn, welcoming them back. She stood nearby speaking with Safira, while Chris and the boys loaded the fifteen-passenger van with their luggage. She climbed into the heated van and pulled away from the curb.

Safira, sitting beside Rebekah, held her daughter's hand tightly. Seventeen-year-old Rebekah had been in the United States for five months finishing her schooling at the local Christian school Chris had attended. Joseph and Paul were fourteen and excellent tutors for the younger converts who had wanted to learn to read and write. They'd been to the United States only a handful of times and were gazing out their window, mesmerized by the city traffic, though neither would admit it. At eleven, Ruth was like her mother in both looks and temperament. Her eyes kept bouncing from her grandparents in the front seat to the sights outside her window as she joined into the conversation when she had the chance. Daniel, who'd recently had his eighth birthday, and six-year-old Rachel were energetic and talkative from the moment they'd seen their grandparents for the first time that they could remember. Their voices kept getting louder as they began talking over one another, trying to outdo the other one for their grandparents' attention. Four-year-old Maria snuggled closely to her daddy and tried to absorb her new surroundings.

Chris cautioned his two youngest kids, "Daniel. Rachel. That's enough. Bring your voices down. We can all hear you just fine. You need to take turns, or we won't hear either of you."

Neither Fay nor Harris commented while listening to their chatty grandchildren in the back. Finally, Fay glanced into her rearview mirror and smiled.

"You will all have to speak English if you want us to understand you," Fay said as she chuckled a little at the blank expressions on the younger one's faces.

Safira chuckled. "I'm sorry, Mom. It's habit by now. I was just saying how great it is to be home. And I was telling Rebekah how great she looks." Safira cupped her oldest daughter's face in one hand. "I've missed you so much."

Chris spoke up. "I haven't seen Blake and Kate for so long. We were excited to learn they are having a third baby."

"We are thrilled everyone is going to be home this Christmas," Harris said.

"JC and Lomina will be home as well? I guess neither of them mentioned it in their letters," Safira said. The children had grown quiet to give the adults the opportunity to visit and had resorted to awed silence while observing their surroundings.

"Yes, they're going to stay with Blake and Kate for the week they're here. JC got the principal job he applied for. Lomina is excited to see you again, Safira. She wanted their coming to be a bit of a surprise. You should see how the kids have grown!" Fay exclaimed.

Glancing out his window, Chris commented. "It's good to be home. I'm sure I'll have plenty on my schedule after the holidays."

"I hope you enjoy your break from Keilron. Please don't load up your whole schedule before taking a good amount of time to relax," Fay admonished.

Chris's lips turned upward, but he didn't crack a full smile at his mom. Being both missionary and millionaire had its responsibilities.

He knew he was going to be busier than his family with the churches that supported the ministry in Keilron, the media interviews, and his personal business. There was much that needed to be set up legally for his family, and he wasn't going to put it off any longer. Heavy weights were resting on his shoulders lately, and he didn't want his mom aware of just how big his concerns were. He'd brought his family on the presumption of a vacation, but Chris knew exactly why he'd really brought his family home for a visit.

Chris and Safira set their bags down in their upstairs room at the Klerens'. Safira exhaled slowly and took three steps toward the queen-sized bed and plopped down. "I wouldn't mind if this day just ended. I don't care if it is only three in the afternoon here."

Chris's lips split into a smile. He understood her exhaustion and felt the same himself, but she so rarely complained. He found her statement humorous. "We don't live in quarters as nice as my folks' and face the possibility of capture every day, and yet you never voice a word of complaint. But we come home to safety and comfort, and now you complain about a little weariness?"

Safira scowled at him for only a second before she started giggling. What he said was all too true. She just didn't want to admit he was right.

When he stared at her lying on the bed, his heart filled with love. Looking at her would never get old. Over the years, he'd grown to love and appreciate her more. He shed his coat and tossed it over the back of a chair sitting near the door. With two long strides across the room, he was able to sit down beside her. He propped himself up on one elbow, looped an arm around her waist, and gazed into her brown eyes.

After several seconds of silence, Safira softly smiled, "What?"

"Do you know how much I love you?" He bent his head down and kissed her with all the love he had in his heart.

When he pulled away, Safira's look was soft and adoring. "The Lord has blessed me beyond measure. I'd never have thought that I'd have so much or for so long."

Chris smiled and kissed her on the forehead. "He's been good to us. Each day has been a gift."

"Mom! Dad!" Rachel's excited voice sounded from the living room below them.

Chris and Safira both sighed in unison before getting up and heading downstairs to investigate.

Entering the Kleren living room, they saw Blake and JC pushing a Christmas tree through the front door. Maria and Rachel sidled up to their parents. The children had learned Keilronian and English at the same time and were fluent in both, but with all the excitement, the kids slipped into the Keilronian language that had been their most commonly used.

"Mom, what are they doing? Why are they bringing a tree into the house?" Maria whispered up at Safira.

"It's nearly Christmas, and it's an American tradition to bring an evergreen inside and decorate it with lights and small, pretty things," Safira responded in English. It may take some time, but her darlings needed to be reminded to speak in English.

"I've never seen a tree like that before," Rachel said, falling back into English.

"You have. You just don't remember. We don't have evergreens in Keilron," Safira said.

Once the tree was upright in its home for the season, Fay rallied the younger generation into the kitchen to spend some time baking holiday treats with her. Chris, Blake, Kate, Safira, Lomina, and JC were finally given the chance to greet each other properly with hugs, wide grins, and welcoming words. They had all taken a seat when Rebekah and David joined them and began decorating the tree. The two oldest Banks children had been home for Christmas twice that they could remember, and having been in the States for the last few months, Rebekah wanted the chance to get into the holiday spirit

"Lomina, it's so good to see you again." Safira sat close to her sister-in-law and spoke quietly in Keilronian, knowing how much Lomina enjoyed chatting in her native tongue. "Don't you ever miss home? Your mother craves your letters. It would be nice if we could convince you to come for a visit sometime soon."

"I miss her and my siblings too, but not Keilron. I'm happy here. And I know my children are safe here. I'm trying to find a way for her to visit us," she said, looking over at J.C.

"JC, how's Loni doing at the new high school? She's in her freshman year, right? Is she still driving you crazy with the boy talk?" Chris asked.

JC laughed. "I thought a new school would help her break away from the boys and into new groups of friends. Well, I guess this school has just as many doting boys as the last one. It's a good thing I'm the principal. Much to her dismay, my position helps keep them in line."

Conversation drifted through the adventures of JC's three other children before Blake chimed in with his own stories on Kate and their brood. The siblings laughed through the stories of each other's lives. The conversation began to lag an hour later, and Chris stood, catching Blake's eye as he did.

"I think I'm going to put a jacket on and go for a walk. It's a nice day, and I don't get the chance to feel the crisp air anymore."

Safira was enticed by the idea, but knew it would have to wait for another time.

"I'll be back, Kate. I think I'll join him," Blake chimed in. He put on his coat and boots and followed his friend.

Silence hung in the air for two blocks before Chris broke the silence. "I'm not here only for Christmas."

Blake had suspected as much. This was the first time Chris and Safira had come together with their entire clan since Marie's birth. Chris's family usually came to the States in groups rather than as a whole, and the few times they had come together hadn't been near Christmas. The rest of the family refused to see anything suspicious about this holiday gathering with the entire Banks family, choosing instead to rejoice in their presence this Christmas for the first time in nearly two decades.

"I'm wanting to leave my youngest children here in the U.S. for a time," Chris said with reservation. "Things are getting worse in Keilron, and there are stories and rumors of unsanctioned massacres happening. Shovak hasn't done anything because the suspected general is too highly regarded by the people, but something must be done fast. Shovak will not stand as leader if he can't control his general soon."

Chris's voice was passionate and strained at the mention of people falling by the hand of the general. He paused to gain control of his emotions before continuing. "My family has been protected because of their American status, but the tides are changing again. I have a foreboding feeling, and I'm going to listen to my heart. I need your help. I realize you have a nest of your own and you have an unexpected child on the way, but I'd like for you and Kate to take Ruth, Daniel, Rachel and Marie. It's four more kids, but I'm more than capable of getting things in order if you're willing to take them."

"I'll have to talk with Kate. She's the one who would be dealing with them the most. That's a lot of young ones to keep an eye on."

"I'm willing to compensate you for any kind of help you may need. Hire a nanny or housekeeper. I'll be giving you a large stipend that will more than cover their expenses. If Kate agrees and is willing to move, I'd also be willing to buy you a home large enough. I've done some research in your area and have a couple in mind for you to look at."

"I'll present your case to Kate when I get the chance. Do you have other reasons for being here?"

"I sold my grandfather's home and needed to sign some last papers. The tenants who've been living there were willing to purchase it. I have a few news interviews and personal financial business to organize in case anything happens to me or Safira."

Blake stopped walking and put his hand out and grabbed Chris's upper arm, stopping his forward movement and turning him so they could face each other. "I've never seen you get this nervous. To be truthful, you're making me scared to let you go back."

Chris's eyes never wavered from his friend's. He was thankful Blake understood the weight of what he was communicating. "The country is changing. I can feel it. There will be a new general soon, or the country's government will fall to a far worse power than Shovak. The government is shaky as it waits for Shovak to make the next move. Until the government controls the current general, there is a possibility for another civil war. If that happens, we will be caught in the middle, and we will have no way to get out even if we wanted to. Joseph and Paul are a great help to me, and since they are considered men in Keilron, I want to keep them with us. David knows of my intentions and requested to remain here to study and graduate at the Christian school we went to. I've my suspicions that as the oldest son, he also wants to be nearby to keep an eye on the younger ones. Mom and Dad have already agreed to let him stay with them. You can guess how thrilled Mom is. Rebekah has decided to return with us. Safira may need her help with the widows and orphans."

"Isn't Rebekah in danger since she's of age?" Blake asked with concern.

"Not as long as the boys and I are around," Chris said empathetically.

"Does Safira know what you are up to?"

Chris's eyes softened slightly, remembering the conversation he'd had with her several weeks before leaving. The idea of leaving her babies, safe or not, in the United States had been an emotional strain on his wife. Safira hadn't been very good hiding that something was going to change in their household. She'd stay in the girls' room until long after they'd drifted to sleep and was eager to hug each one of the children as often as she could. The boys had received praise at every corner. The older kids grew suspicious and had even sought out their dad to ask him if there was something going on. Chris had only kissed them and hugged them tight in response. The youngest ones thrived under Safira's overbearing attention.

Turning his head to look down the street a moment before responding, he felt his heart ache. He hadn't much liked the necessity of leaving them behind either. He looked back at Blake and at last explained. "Safira's coming with me the weekend after Christmas for our interview with the media in New York, and when we get back, we'll be with the kids. She knows what I'm talking to you about and is hoping you'll agree. It wouldn't surprise me if she speaks with Kate about it too. She swears she's not letting any of her young'uns out of sight when we get back from New York until we leave for home."

The two remained silent, burdened by the harsh realities Chris and his family had to face. They walked the snowy path, each nursing his own thoughts. Although Chris's mind dwelled on Keilron and the dangers he would face when he returned, Blake considered how he'd open the upcoming conversation with Kate and the decision they faced together. He began to pray on the spot for God's will.

*****

"He wants what?" a pregnant Kate exclaimed.

Blake and Kate had come home an hour ago. She had finally said goodnight to her two preteen daughters and was preparing for bed when Blake brought up Chris's request.

"Your brother wants us to care for their four youngest kids."

Kate's voice was clearly overwhelmed at the idea of inviting four more kids on top of their soon-to-be three. "We don't have the room for that many here. What could he possibly be thinking?"

"He said he had an eye on a home if we were willing to move. One large enough for all of us."

"A larger home!" Panic edged its way into her voice. "We will be adding four, make that five"—she rubbed her abdomen—"and you think moving to larger home and all that goes with it is a good idea?"

"Chris isn't dumb, Kate." Blake sat down beside his wife and began to rub her back, trying to get her to relax. "He's willing to pay for a housekeeper who will take some of the burden off you."

"Are they really that worried about this?" Her panic had softened into deep concern for her older brother. "I mean, they've been there for years avoiding suspicion. Why is he so concerned now?"

"Would he make his kids remain here if he wasn't? He loves every one of them as much as we love our three. There is political unrest making him nervous. That's all he could explain to me."

"Can we afford them all?"

Blake held back a chuckle at her question. How long had she known her brother? He knew better than to point at the obvious with laughter. Forcing his face and voice to remain natural he replied, "Chris will take care of that too. It's all part of the stipend I mentioned. He hasn't just let his money sit. Apparently, he's been investing while on the mission field."

"Then we've no reason to say no. If we can do it, how long will we have them?"

"He didn't say, but if he's going to give you a new house, I'm guessing he's preparing for any situation."

"I think this is God's way of letting us help them, our way of being involved in the mission." Her voice had softened, and she was ready to acquiesce.

Blake smiled at Kate. "And maybe it's God's way of giving us the bigger home we needed. That little boy is going to need his own room."

Kate gave him a soft smile. They'd just found out she was carrying a boy and hadn't even told the future grandparents yet.

Blake wrapped his arms around his wife. He was thankful God had given them so many blessings. As an architect, he did well for his family, but to add five more kids would have put them on a tighter budget, but with Chris's help, it would be nothing. They'd even talked about needing a bigger home, despite Blake's attachment to the small two-bedroom home, but hadn't found a home they both agreed on. God was going to bless them for helping his servants, and Blake felt greatly encouraged to be able to help his friend whom he'd felt so helpless to assist in the past and blessed that his friend had become a brother.

January 2024

"Remind me again. You've been in Keilron for nearly twenty years with your family?" the news reporter asked.

"Yes," Chris replied.

"How have you managed to stay alive that long?"

"God's protection and some smart thinking."

"Safira, you were born in Keilron. Why is it you've not been taken back to your family?"

"I'm married. I'd be of no use to my family now. They are also unaware of my presence." She spoke matter-of-factly, but her demeanor was stiff, and the reporter felt it best to skip past his curiosity.

"How did your youngest children enjoy Christmas?"

Chris brought the attention back to himself by responding. "They're amazed at the American traditions. Things like Christmas trees and Santa Claus are fascinating to them. They're still trying to grasp all the stories and traditions. In Keilron, we've always had gifts and the Christmas story, but here, it's like the entire world is celebrating. And they're in awe that everyone knows what Christmas is."

"With the current political and military strains, are you worried about your kids?"

The question brought Safira's mind back to the conversation at hand. "Immensely, but they are God's and only on loan to us. It is up to Him to decide how long they will be with us."

"What if only one of you is killed? Will the other remain in Keilron to keep on, or will you return to the States?"

"Well, that depends on who was killed. If it were Safira, I would more than likely send my children home and continue with my ministry in Keilron."

"But if it were Chris"—Safira interjected—"I'd come home with my children and continue my work here. A widow in Keilron is prey to the men of that country. I'm not protected like Chris is, especially since I'm a native Keilronian. If my sons were willing to remain in Keilron, I could stay, and they would be my protection. I wouldn't ask that of them while they are only teenagers."

Chris cut the interview short.

"I've got a meeting in half an hour, so we'll call it quits. Thank you, Brian for your time."

"No. Thank *you*, Chris."

*****

"When do we go back?" Safira asked Chris on their drive back to the Kleren's home from the Denver airport.

"March, I think. That will make it a twelve-week leave. I really don't want to be gone longer right now." Chris waited, letting the information sink in before continuing. "Kate and Blake are willing to take the kids."

"I'm glad. I'll feel better knowing they're safe. We'll need to tell them soon." Safira cringed at the thought.

"Not yet. Let's wait a couple of weeks or so. I'm going to help Blake and Kate move first. I've signed the paperwork for their new house, so they'll need help. I hired professional movers for Kate's sake, but Blake wants to be in the way, and I should probably be on hand if he needs any help on either end. Once their house is unpacked, we'll tell the kids and go on a shopping spree with them. They will want to make their rooms feel like home."

"And maybe I will feel better about leaving them too knowing they will be happy. Thank you, Chris. You're a gem." She leaned over and kissed him on the cheek as he drove. "I really hate to leave them behind. I'm still going to miss them so much. Rachel and Maria will be grown up before we know it."

"I promise to send you to visit as often as we can. I'm not sure how long this time will be, but if you wanted to stay with the kids, I could handle things for a while," Chris offered.

Safira's face twisted into a scowl at the idea. "You would miss me like crazy, and I you. That last bit isn't an option. I hope coming home to visit often is." She took a deep breath and stared out the windshield. "I'm sure Fay will send us video and letters as often as she can."

Chris was relieved that she'd shot down the idea of staying behind. He really couldn't bear the thought of being without her. But the kids were different. "I'd rather keep them safe than to bring them home." His voice was thick with emotion.

"I know." Safira sounded miserable. Chris reached over and took her hand in an effort to comfort each other as they drove down the road toward the Klerens.

February 2024

"How can you leave us behind? We want to be in Shemna with you, Mom," Ruth said as the tears began to fall.

Chris and Safira had gathered their family in front of the burning fireplace in the large living room at Kate and Blake's new home to break the news. They'd met stunned silence for several heartbeats before reality hit home. Rachel and Marie still stared blankly at their parents, trying to understand why they'd want to leave them behind. The frightened and hurt faces around them were difficult for the two parents to face, knowing they needed to be strong for their children, but wanting to weep with them.

Daniel's voice was strained. "When will we see you again?"

"I'm not sure. I hope to return every three months for a week at a time," Safira said.

Chris tried to lighten the mood. "You'll be able to go to a real school and make many friends."

"But we won't have *you*," Ruth whimpered.

Safira moved to her daughter, wrapped an arm around her and let her cry on her shoulder. "Here in America, you can share Jesus's news with your new friends. You don't have to fear telling them, and perhaps, God wants us to leave you because he has a boy or girl that needs to hear about Him."

"But . . . I just want you, Mama," Rachel said.

Safira's heart broke. She swallowed a few times, fighting the tears and forcing her voice to stay normal. "Honey, you will always have your dad and me, right here." She pointed at her daughter's heart. "God will take care of us all. Remember when you let Jesus take your sins away, and I told you we'd always be together? Even if I was to never see you again on earth, I promise that you will see your dad and me again someday."

Daniel sniffled a bit, and his tears began to get away from him. His lips trembled, and he was doing his best to keep control. Chris walked over to him and put an arm around his small son. "I want you to be brave for me, Daniel. Remember who you were named after. I want you to talk with your sisters in Keilronian when you get the chance, unless you are with other people. I don't want you to forget the language."

"I won't, Dad. I'll remind them every day." His voice trembled, but his dad's words were strengthening his resolve not to cry.

"When will you leave?" Rachel asked quietly.

"Not for three weeks, so we will have many wonderful days together before we say goodbye. Let's not waste them on tears," said Safira as she forced a smile.

"We're not going home?" Little Marie asked, staring up at her mom.

"No, honey. But your dad and I are."

"I have to stay here."

"Yes, dear, but I'll see you again," Safira promised.

Marie had obviously picked up on Safira's earlier words to Ruth. "I need to tell new friends about Jesus."

"Can you do that?"

"Yes, I can be brave like you."

Chapter 28

Comings and Goings

Shovak stood watching his twin sons with pride when Rofisca handed them their first orders. The two boys, Zomak and Shomar, had demonstrated exceptional skill in their initial training. Shovak suggested to Rofisca that he ought to take the boys under his wings and show them how to be great warriors.

Shovak needed witnesses who were willing to stand up against Rofisca and was pleased the suggestion had turned into reality. The general had decided to add them to his ranks. Shovak had promised Zamina years earlier that if the boys proved their worth with Rofisca, they would be more likely to stay in Shemna under Narshac's watchful eye. Shovak hated to be dishonest with her, but he knew his sons were loyal to him, above anyone else, and he'd made his promise long before learning of Rofisca's treachery. He needed witnesses who could prove to the people and political allies that Rofisca was no longer trustworthy, and he had no idea how close the youngest sons of Shovak were to their father.

Shovak didn't linger long at the boys' graduation because he anticipated his wife's desire to speak with him about their twins. Hiding a smirk as he acknowledged Rofisca, Shovak left the ceremonies. The general had no idea he'd just been tricked into taking on two spies. No doubt the general had the audacity to believe that he'd soon control the boys' hearts and would be able to rule in Shovak's stead. Shovak hadn't become the leader of Keilron by being obtuse to people and situations. He was good at the chess-like political game he'd been playing since his youth.

It was no surprise to Shovak when he discovered Zamina waiting patiently for him in his office. She had worried about their two sons, while they underwent the scrutiny and intense training every Keilronian soldier before them had undergone.

The moment she saw him, she spoke. "How did they do?"

A small, patient smile touched his lips when he responded. "They did very well. In fact, because they did so well, Rofisca has requested them to be put under him, personally."

Her face glowed with pride for a moment and then paled at the idea of them under Rofisca. "I thought you were going to have them under Narshac?" she gasped. "Rofisca is dangerous and reckless. He may spend a great deal of time in Shemna, but his endeavors are underhanded, and you are going to allow our sons to be under his command?" Her voice left no doubt she was angry.

"I trust our sons. I need witnesses to Rofisca's disobedience and treachery. Everything we know is only hearsay because no one is willing to stand against him. Our sons are strong, natural-born leaders. They don't know it yet, but I'm depending on them."

"They are just boys!" she exclaimed.

Shovak reached out and grabbed her wrist. "They are men! They are good men I can trust." He spoke through his teeth, glaring at her. He so rarely displayed such aggression that Zamina instantly quieted. The moment she lowered her eyes in submission, his face softened, and he lifted her chin so her eyes would meet his again.

She had been shamed, and her look was apologetic. "We have done well with them, my love." His voice softened. He felt her relax as he gently hugged her.

Zomak and Shomar had proven their father's first impression correct. They were a gift. Zamina had never again conceived, but she had not been disappointed; the boys filled her heart. Shovak too was guilty of favoring his sons, just as Rofisca had been with Safira. The boys had grown up under his own teaching. They worshiped their father and respected their mother. Often, Zamina and the boys forgot that Shovak had other children and wives since he gave his small household in Shemna the majority of his free time.

Shovak experienced a bond with his family that he'd not had from his past relationships. He attended all of his sons' graduations; it had been a matter of honor and pride, but had never intervened with their orders. He'd always allowed Rofisca to choose where best to place them. His other sons had barely known him when they were boys. Zomak and Shomar often spent the evenings playing mind games and learning from their father before they'd gone to train with Rofisca. Shovak often reflected on how different his other sons could have been if they'd had the opportunity to learn from him.

Shovak's promise to Zamina to be with only her had been kept. His children and wives were well-cared for materialistically, but he gave them little thought except when he vacationed at his large country estate. His children from the other wives were mostly grown, with only a handful of daughters left to be married. He'd heard rumors when he visited his estate that none of his wives begrudged his absence. The rumor made sense, and he was grateful they were not brokenhearted about his attachment to the city and the first wife.

Bringing his thoughts back to the present, Shovak kissed Zamina's hair and pulled away from her. He met her gentle gaze for a moment before softly speaking. "I would expect them for dinner tonight. They will have missed you. I've already made the invitation in case they had any misgivings." He placed a kiss on Zamina's cheek and then stepped away from her to his desk.

"Thank you," she spoke wholeheartedly. "I will be seeing you as well?" she asked.

Shovak felt a little guilty about the amount of time he'd had to spend with state affairs of late and the many meals he'd been missing with Zamina.

"Yes, I'll be sure to make a point of it. The evening will be ours, and we will celebrate our sons' achievement together." He was graced with a wide grin filled with happiness from his wife before she left him alone in the large office.

*****

"Kalita, it is good to see you," Narshac said. He'd found her in the city home's garden. She was lovely standing among the flowers in her pink and gold robes hanging delicately from her frame.

She smiled. "It's good to see you too."

He embraced her for a moment.

When he released her, he led her toward the bench in the center of the garden. "I was at the estate for a few days with a colleague, and today, I come home to your lovely face and a well-organized home. I like the changes you've implemented at both homes more than I expected. As a matter of fact, I was told your ideas for my father's orchard have been implemented, and the trees have never produced so much. I'm proud of you."

Kalita blushed deeply as they took a seat. "Thank you. I hope to have some of your time this evening. I wish to speak with you, my lord."

"Kalita, dearest wife, I'll be more than happy to give you your wish, but let's not wait for tonight to talk. Come with me now if you want to speak with me. We can go to my study. I can call for you later this evening for the other." He smiled, drinking in the sight of her.

Nodding in agreement, Kalita followed her husband to his office. Once the door was closed, she said, "I'm coming to you in faith, husband, that what I say is said between husband and wife and will not leave this room." Her voice was formal. She stood with her arms at her sides and eyes searching his in earnest.

"Of course, you have my confidence. What has you troubled?" His voice was soft and his face relaxed.

"I found some of Lomina's things while I was cleaning her old quarters at the country home, and I've gained understanding to what you searched for. Do you still search?" she inquired.

"I've let go of my desires," he said casually. "It brings a soft heart I can ill-afford. I do my work better by not looking at or questioning what I do. I considered all she said, but I couldn't make a leap of faith into the arms of a god I've been offending. What would He do with me, especially since I'm told He knows all?"

Kalita knelt in his office in subjection to him and lowered her head, a stance she rarely took. He came to her and knelt beside her, taking her hands in his. "What are you so afraid to tell me?"

"I wondered at the stories you would tell of the Christians, and when Lomina told me the stories, I didn't understand. But now . . . Lomina left a copy of some of the Christian God's words. I've come to understand what she meant. I've decided to take Him as mine own. I would have remained silent, my lord, but I had no desire to deceive you."

Narshac stood and began to pace.

Several moments passed before he spoke. "Speak to no one else of your decision. I will not be the one to torture you or to betray you. Since you have been dear to me, I'll not make this a known fact. I presume you will do the same."

"Yes, my lord, thank you."

Narshac paused in his pacing and lifted her chin up so she could look at him. "Kalita, I love you. I would protect you, but I beg of you not to bring this up again between us."

"Of course not, my lord."

*****

"Joseph, would you take this to your father?" Safira asked, handing him a basket of food.

Joseph nodded in reply.

Rebekah entered the home just as Joseph squeezed through the door before it shut. She shook her head in good humor at his retreating form as she closed the door behind him.

Safira barely acknowledged her daughter's entrance. "Paul, I need these things from the market. Would you get them for me?" Safira asked, handing him a list and basket. Paul took the proffered items willingly and left.

They were alone at last. Rebekah said, "Mom, Lonika hasn't been feeling well. I think she might need your help."

"I'll go to her tomorrow. I need to visit the new missionaries first. I think they could use some pointers. They just arrived a week ago."

"All right. I'm going to stay here and make sure everyone comes home. I'll cook supper tonight," Rebekah volunteered.

Safira hugged her daughter. "Thank you, dear. You are such a help to me." She wrapped her veil around her face and left the house.

Safira entered the west section of the city half an hour later. She rapped on the door and waited only a moment before letting herself in. The surprise on the couple's faces at her sudden appearance reminded Safira of just how new and unaccustomed they were to missionary life. As leaders in the community, Safira and Chris had grown so accustomed to people coming in with barely two knocks that she'd had no hesitation to do the same to this family.

She spoke hastily to ease their fears. "I'm Safira, Chris's wife."

"Of course, how can we help you?" Jacob asked hesitantly.

"Well, I have come to help you or rather your wife." Safira smiled as she took Ellie's hand and led her to the kitchen table. "I do apologize for the abrupt entrance. You will soon be used to such appearances by many other welcome guests."

"Thank you," said Ellie shyly. "I heard you are native to these parts. Your English is perfect, though."

"I lived in the States for several years before I returned here, but thank you. I've been to America many times, and I've brought some things that you may appreciate." Safira handed the basket to the younger woman. "But I do want to give you a great Keilronian recipe I think you'll like. My husband is American, and he started eating native food with this dish."

"Oh, thank you! I've been going to the market, but our meals have been rather dull. I don't know what to get or how to fix anything here. Truth be told, I barely cooked back home. I used a lot of prepared foods and sometimes even cheated by ordering in."

Safira smiled understandingly. "I learned some while in the United States, but many of the things I can make here my governess taught me. Food isn't the only thing you will need to learn to survive." She looked over at Jacob who had taken a chair at the table and was observing them both.

"When Chris first arrived, he had the help of Pastor Kindel. I'm here to tell you that I'm your guardian angel. Anything you don't understand or anything you need help with, just send Jacob or come yourself. Here, I have a rough description of where we live."

She reached into the heavy basket she'd brought and pulled out a simple drawing illustrating the way to her house. "I didn't just bring you the recipe. I brought you the end result for tonight's meal, and you can give me back the dish and basket when you get a chance."

"We really appreciate this," Jacob spoke up. "Chris said that you guys were here to help, but I assumed he meant getting accustomed to the type of ministry he's wanting us for. Thank you for being such a help to us both. I was growing tired of goat cheese and bread," Jacob grinned unrepentant when his laughing wife threw the towel beside her at his head.

Safira laughed with her. It would be so nice to have another friend, and she could tell that Jacob and Chris would enjoy each other's company.

Safira spent the remainder of the afternoon with the new couple. She finally said goodbye and began heading back to her home. She had just passed the marketplace, though few vendors were still remaining, when a hand reached out and covered her mouth as another arm wrapped around her waist and dragged her into the concealed alley.

"Quiet. I only wish to speak with you."

Her blood ran cold at the familiar voice. Her heart went into overdrive and fear gripped her as she prayed for words and the courage to face her oldest brother she'd not seen in years.

Chapter 29

God's Grace

Paul pulled his mother's list from the pocket of his pants. He glanced around the market. There were few vendors remaining, but he knew his mom wouldn't have sent him had she thought it would be too late. When he recognized a familiar merchant, he moved forward, thankful the man had several items his mom wanted.

A voice behind him halted his approach toward the vendor, "Hey, I didn't know you did women's work." A smile spread across Paul's face, and he spun to face his friend, Zomak.

"Zomak, it is good to see you! It's about time you survived your training," Paul teased, taking note of his friend's uniform.

Zomak's eyes twinkled. "Shomar too has survived," he said of his twin brother. "We've been posted here in Shemna. Turns out, we will see more of each other after all." Zomak grinned. The two friends embraced.

Zomak stood back and asked, "When did your family get back from their visit?"

"A couple of weeks ago."

Zomak's knowledge of Paul's family was limited because Paul had always been a little vague, as his father had taught him to be, but the two still enjoyed one another's company.

Neither set of twins ever gave details about their families. Zomak was aware of Paul's American heritage and knew Joseph too, since the brothers often played together while growing up. They'd met when Zomak and Shomar escaped their home to explore the marketplace. The two sets of twins had bonded effortlessly while playing a game involving a soccer ball.

"Today, we graduated," Zomak continued. "Dad is proud, and Mom is thrilled to have us back at home, even if briefly, and they want to celebrate tonight."

"What brings you here then?" Paul asked.

"I thought maybe I could find some bobble for my mom, though she doesn't need anything."

"We taught you that, didn't we?" Paul asked, smiling at the memory.

Paul and Joseph celebrated American holidays with their family. They went to the market one May morning a few years back, looking for a gift for their mother. Shomar and Zomak had found them looking through the vendors and asked what they were looking for. The two Banks brothers explained Mother's Day and its significance. Their friends instantly liked the idea and not only helped the Banks find a gift for their mother but also bought one for their own. Zomak and Shomar were so impressed by the idea and the reaction of their mother that they had not stopped with a single gift.

Zomak smiled and looked down at his feet briefly and then looked back at Paul. "Yes, I suppose you did. But the way I see it, when I get a wife, I will make her fall in love with me using all your American charms."

Paul smirked, shaking his head.

"I best be going. Grab your brother, and we will meet you here after dark for a game. The market will be empty. It will be like old times!" Zomak spoke over his shoulder while moving away from Paul and toward a merchant selling enticing trinkets.

Paul was grinning when he shouted, "I'll see what we can do!"

*****

"Narshac!" Safira gasped the moment he removed his hand.

His eyes met hers with no hostility. He relaxed his hold on her. When he spoke, his voice was low, "Quiet. I was only recently able to track you down. Please, don't run. I want to speak with you. I have questions I'm afraid only you can answer."

Safira looked unflinchingly into his face. Narshac's eyes were pleading; his troubled expression was not lost on her. He kept glancing around them for any signs of trouble. If her eyes were not deceiving her, God was granting her an opportunity.

Brown eyes finally dropped down to meet hers before he spoke. "Why did you run away without a word?"

Safira knew the time had come for blunt honesty. "Papa would have killed me, Narshac. He discovered I'd been meeting with a Christian and was going to kill me," her voice pleading for him to understand.

"Do you honestly think he'd have killed you, his favorite child and only daughter?"

"He hates the Christians. Do you think he would not have?"

"He hates them now more than ever because you deserted him." Safira's eyes suddenly looked sad. He continued, "I can't say it's made me love them much, either. You left your family and deserted your responsibilities. Is that what Jehovah wants?"

She hesitated, not knowing how to respond. Narshac was being as open and honest with her as he had when she was a little girl. Love and trust overwhelmed her good sense. There was little she wanted more than to show her family Christ, but his words stung and she became defensive. "If you feel Christians are evil like father, why aren't you slitting my throat?"

His eyebrows raised slightly and his voice became soothing, "I told you, I have questions."

After taking a deep breath, she replied smoothly, "You've been searching for me all this time to ask me why I left, when you must have known the answer."

"Your husband, what kind of a man is he? Does he do witchcraft or dark magic with any of the gods?"

The quick change in direction took Safira by surprise, but she followed his trail.

"No. He is a Christian, same as me. We pray to Jehovah and depend on Him for our safety."

"I could have you killed here on the street." His calm stance made his threat weak.

She raised an eyebrow at him. "I realize that, but could you live with yourself killing your only sister?"

"You are no longer my only sister. Father has two other daughters now."

"The fact that you haven't killed me yet proves you still care too much for me." Her voice became a whisper, "Just as I still care for you, brother."

He stood quietly a moment before responding. "You have learned to use words well, but you are the one to defy the gods, and I have every right to take your life."

"Did Lomina's words have no effect on your heart, Narshac?" The moment she'd asked the question she saw she'd reached the heart of the matter. Lomina's words had touched him. She could tell by his hesitation at her name. Safira wondered why, after all these years, was he finally ready to seek answers for questions that had nothing to do with her?

She decided to explain. "The man you gave Lomina to is my brother-in-law. You succeeded in protecting her."

Narshac breathed deeply and shifted his eyes out toward the vacant street. He remembered Safira only as a young precocious child. The woman before him was just as confident and intelligent as ever, and yet something had changed her. She was different from how he'd imagined she would be. Perhaps, there really was something to the God Lomina spoke of so fervently.

"You heard her words. Do you not remember the story of the Savior?" Safira asked.

Still trying to cling to his defensive wall, he was agitated, "If He truly is the God of all other gods, then I've sinned against Him too much to ever hope to be forgiven, which is why I cannot go to Him, even if I wanted."

Her response was softly spoken, "Narshac, were you not told of the Apostle Paul?"

"No," he said flatly.

"He was a man like you. Paul stoned to death many of the earliest Christians, but God spoke to him and told him the truth.

Paul's eyes were opened, and he begged for mercy. Christ forgave him, Narshac, and he became one of the greatest leaders among the Christians. He wrote several books in God's Word."

His eyes bore into hers, "Are you telling me a true account?"

"Yes, I am," she said unflinchingly.

Flustered, Narshac took a step away from her. He ran a hand through his hair and then spun back around to face her.

His voice was low and intense when he spoke. "Your husband was supposed to die, and men in white stopped me." Staring down into her face he continued. "His head was in the guillotine, but a man in white spoke, 'Let my servant go.' How can I deny a God who reveals himself to me? I've more questions, but I want to speak to your husband."

"Come with me. Come to my home, Narshac, and let me make you supper. Chris will welcome you, and he will be pleased to answer all the questions you have. Perhaps, you will find the answers you seek."

He was flabbergasted by her invitation. "Have you no fear for your life? If you take me to your home, you will have no place to run if I decide to turn you in."

"I'm in the hands of the living God, as you should know. You are my brother, whom I love still, and I am inviting you to my home to meet my family."

He lowered his gaze and paused a moment before agreeing. "Lead me to your home, sister. I won't deceive you today."

She smiled. "Follow me." Turning, she led him back into the narrow streets that zigzagged to the Banks' home.

*****

Rebekah's pacing steps echoed inside her family's home. Her mother should have been back by now. The door swung open, and her head whipped around. Her father came into the home, followed by her two fifteen-year-old brothers. Instantly, she sighed with disappointment. Her father's welcoming smile became a teasing grin.

"You look disappointed."

Her tight face did not relax. "Dad, I haven't seen Mom since she went to visit Ellie and Jacob. She should have been home half an hour ago."

"Is supper ready?" Chris asked casually.

"Yes, but . . ."

Turning to his sons, he gave instructions, "Boys, wash up."

Paul hesitated. "Dad, we'd like to meet up with some friends tonight. Can we grab dinner and get going? We'll be home at a decent time, I promise."

Joseph looked at his father expectantly. Chris felt ganged up on. The timing was not ideal for them to disappear and catch up with friends, but neither did he want them affected by Rebekah's obvious concern. "You promise to look after each other?" he asked at last.

The boys nodded in unison.

"Be back before ten."

"Thanks, Dad!" Joseph exclaimed.

They rushed over to the stove and helped themselves, shoveling their food down.

Chris shook his head and started toward the bathroom.

"Dad . . ." Rebekah was appalled at her father's callous attitude. He appeared more interested in dinner than his wife.

He turned. "Reba"—he said with gentle authority—"she's in God's hands. If she's captured, there's nothing I can do. If she's just running late, then our panic would be pointless."

She scoffed at her dad and spun back toward the kitchen just to be away from him. Chris sighed and shook his head. Rebekah had always had a bond with Safira and as a young adult had grown into quite a mother hen. Pushing away the small niggling feeling regarding any harm that could befall his love, he went to wash up. By the time he returned, the twins were gone, and Rebekah was unwilling to converse with him.

The door's squeak caused father and daughter to turn expectantly. With a grateful heart, Chris watched Safira take a step inside. Her eyes silently pleaded with him. Understanding dawned the moment he saw the man stepping in behind her. Chris's mouth went dry, and every memory of his time in prison rushed through his mind like a tidal wave.

Safira did not stop looking at Chris while she spoke softly, "Chris, I think you remember my brother."

Several moments passed before, he choked out, "Yes, Saf." He stepped beside his wife and took her gently by the elbow. "Could we talk a moment in private before dinner? Narshac, would you allow us to slip out for a moment?" His voice was respectful, but his protective stance was obvious.

Narshac lowered his head in respect toward Chris, but spoke to Safira. "Of course. This must be a shock, and perhaps, it would be easier for all of us if you spoke with him for a minute, Safira. I'll wait."

Safira complied with a nod. She extended her hand toward her confused daughter. "This is Rebekah, my oldest. Rebekah, please get your uncle something to drink while I speak with your father."

"Yes, ma'am." She went to obey immediately. Rebekah had never met any of her mother's family, but she knew of General Narshac.

Once Safira and Chris were safe inside their bedroom, Chris stared at his wife in disbelief. Finally, he spoke softly, "What could be going through your head, love?"

"He wishes to speak with you," she calmly replied

"He has proven to be untrustworthy. Tried to kill us both, and you bring him home?" A hardness crept into his tone. He turned away from her and ran a hand through his hair.

Her voice pleaded from behind him, "I think he's looking for Christ, Chris. He wanted to speak with you."

He spun around and his words were bitter, "And if he turns on us?"

"It's a chance I thought well worth risking. I wouldn't have done it if I thought it would place us in immediate danger." Safira came to him, put her hands in his, and looked up into his eyes. "He has done horrible things, but he is my brother, and the only member of my family you've ever met. I said goodbye to them, but it would be my heart's greatest joy to be able to lead at least one of my family to Christ. I want to see them again. How would you feel if the roles were reversed?"

With a deep breath, his body relaxed. "Oh, Saf," he whispered. He pulled her into a hug and kissed the top of her head. "I'll give you my best. And I'm sorry for being concerned. I trust your judgment. If you say he means us no harm, I will trust you. But that doesn't mean I'm not going to be on high alert."

"I understand, and I'm thankful that you care enough about us to worry. This is a chance to change things here. We have to take it, no matter the cost."

Chris knew she was right. He took her hand and prayed for Narshac's soul and for the courage to face, unafraid, the man who had nearly taken his life years ago, and that they would get the chance to see a miracle in Narshac's heart.

They returned to the kitchen table where Narshac sat speaking with Rebekah like an uncle might. When he saw Chris sit down and their eyes locked, all conversation came to a halt. The men stared at one another, remembering a time when they had not been equals. It was Narshac who finally broke the silence.

"I want you to know why I threw you out of my prison," he said bluntly.

Rebekah dished up food onto three plates and served the meal. None of the adults were interested in their plates, but she wanted the chore done with. She desperately wanted to hear her uncle's account of what happened that day.

"I see it as clearly as yesterday. I was going to give the order for your execution when suddenly men dressed in white with long swords held my men captive. For every one of my men, there was a silver sword at their throat. The man behind me, one who was not my captor, told me to let you go. I did so without delay, and the moment you were out of my gate, the men disappeared. I've thought of that moment many times, and I'm beginning to believe it was your God protecting His servant. Tell me, how I can know your God? More importantly, tell me if He will want to know me." Narshac's gaze was intense. His arms rested on the table, and his body angled toward Chris.

Safira caught Rebekah's eye and signaled her to follow. The two women slipped quietly from the room. Rebekah wanted to witness her father's words, but it was wise to allow her dad to do what he did best—share the gospel. Safira held Rebekah's hand, and they prayed together in the next room listening to the muffled voices for an hour.

Narshac sat back in his chair when Chris was done speaking, and Narshac had exhausted his questions. "Thank you. I've much to think on, Mr. Banks. When I've decided what I'll do with this knowledge, I shall give you notice. If I decide to reject Jehovah, I shall give you a twenty-four hour notice before coming for your capture, as a courtesy to Safira. If I choose to follow Jehovah, however, you will have nothing to fear from me."

Narshac stood from the table, shook Chris's hand, and left with no further ado.

Chris, Safira, and Rebekah spent much time in prayer for Narshac that evening. It was well after eleven when Safira offered words of prayer for her two sons who had not yet returned.

Chapter 30

Sparks Fly

Paul and Joseph laughed at the expressions on their friends' faces when they scored the winning point against them. Zomak and Shomar took their loss with good humor and offered Paul and Joseph water from their canteens. The four teens sat down on the steps of a large stone building.

Joseph broke the silence when he recovered his breath, "How was basic training?"

"Well, it wasn't as difficult as I thought it would be, but I figure that's because those men hadn't been raised by our father. He's been preparing both Zomak and me since we were seven, both mentally and physically. We did well. We scored high enough to be on Rofisca's infantry," Shomar bragged.

"That's both good and bad news as far as I'm concerned. I admit I had a rough time dealing with Christians," Zomak confessed.

At Zomak's comment, Joseph looked down at his hands to compose his own anxiety. He looked into Zomak's eyes after a moment and saw for the first time that something was bothering his friend. Joseph found it difficult not to react when their friends spoke openly about common abuse toward believers they accepted as normal. He glanced over at Paul, who'd chosen to gaze across the courtyard, ignoring the comments. Joseph knew Paul was more outspoken than he was; and if his brother refrained from speaking, he ought to keep his mouth shut, but the words were out before he could stop them.

"If your father has been training you for so long, why did you find it difficult when introduced to the Christian prisoners?"

Shomar answered first. "When you look into their eyes and are ordered to beat them, you can see their looks of pity. You expect to see fear or anger, like you would when disciplining a thief or murderer, but what I see is understanding. While training, the idea of defending our nation against assaults is easy to accept, but disciplining men and women for their choice in faith doesn't quite sit with me."

Zomak nodded his agreement.

"You did it though, or you wouldn't have graduated with such high honors," Joseph said. He couldn't quite disguise the hurt and disbelief from his voice.

Paul's eyes focused into the conversation quickly and with one glance shot Joseph a warning to be quiet.

Zomak said quietly. "Of course, it was part of our orders."

"Why do you think Shovak and Rofisca push so hard against the Christians?" Paul asked.

Joseph lifted his eyebrow at his brother. Paul shrugged in response. They were in this conversation now, might as well see where it would go.

"I have no idea. What difference does it make, really, what god a man believes in?" Shomar spat out angrily.

Zomak warned. "Be careful. We can't be heard pitying them."

"These are dangerous times, but since the place is empty, are you willing to hear why it makes a difference?" Paul ventured. Joseph may have started this conversation, but Paul wasn't going to make his quieter brother lead it.

"You are American. You know more about these Christians than we do. Go ahead, tell us. Why is it that these Christians can't just submit to our gods rather than be put through pain and torture?" Shomar questioned.

Paul answered, "It's like this. Jehovah created the world in six days. He created man and woman on that last day of creation. He walked with them and talked with them, and they enjoyed the beauty of a perfect world. God gave them one rule, and they broke that rule. The world has never been the same since. Because of their sin against

God, the rest of mankind could never achieve perfection on their own. So God, in His mercy, sent His Son, who was God, to become man on earth, born of a virgin so that His blood was sinless. He lived and taught many things about His Father and of Himself. He died on a cross to take all the sins of the world away. He was in the grave for three days before He rose from the dead to prove His sacrifice was accepted by the Father. Christians are those who not only believe this account is true but also have accepted the blood of Jesus Christ, God the Son, as payment for their sins. Christians live for the Living God who loves them. For those who are tortured, He gives them strength to endure."

"They believe their God made His own sacrifice?" Shomar asked, his eyes boring into Joseph's. Keilronians understood sacrificing to the gods to bring blessings and favor, but this God who would provide His own sacrifice was a new idea.

Zomak responded with meager conviction, "Surely, you must misunderstand, Shomar."

When Paul nodded his head at Shomar's statement, Zomak asked, "This is the story of Jehovah?"

"Would you like to hear more, understand more, or would you rather I quit this conversation?" Paul inquired, offering his friends a way to drop the subject.

"I want to know of this God," Shomar answered. "How do you know of Him? How can one know of his accounts? Are their stories, a book of this God's teachings?"

Zomak sighed at his brother's eagerness. Paul was right to have inquired whether they wanted to hear and understand. If they understood, it would be impossible to judge the Christians as they had been trained. But Paul's initial introduction had piqued his interest, and he knew he would wonder until he died if he did not hear the two Americans out. One way or another, he knew he would never turn his best friends in just for sharing information.

"Show us what this is about. We will listen," Zomak consented.

Joseph flashed a smile at his brother, and together, the boys shared with their friends all they could about Jesus Christ. He pulled out his small Keilronian New Testament from the satchel he'd brought. Darkness enclosed around the courtyard, so Zomak lit a lantern he'd brought. Shomar pulled out a flashlight so they could read Jehovah's words for themselves.

*****

Across the city, Narshac stood on his balcony. He understood at last what drove the Christians. If their God was willing to save their souls by dying, why should they not feel a desire to live for Jehovah or die standing up for Him? Narshac closed his eyes and listened to the quiet hum of the night.

"Jehovah, if you are truly there, help me understand what I've been told tonight," Narshac whispered to the wind. An image popped into his head of the man who'd spoken the morning of Chris's release.

Narshac fell to his knees and bowed his head. The stars twinkled above him. It had been a long time coming, but now, he understood and allowed the hatred in his heart to be replaced by love. Tears streamed down his face. For five minutes, he begged God on High for forgiveness and then thanked Him for sacrificing His Son so that his sins could be washed away. An overwhelming peace stole through him, and he knew without any doubt that Jehovah forgave him. Narshac continued in thanksgiving toward Jehovah. He remembered many things that led him to fall before the Almighty One. With the help of Safira's husband, a man he'd tried to kill, he would get the chance to learn more of Jehovah, whom he now loved.

He hurried to ask the nearest servant to fetch Kalita. Only a few minutes passed before she entered his room and looked into his eyes. What she saw in his eyes brought tears to her own.

"I'm not alone in my faith now, am I, my lord?"

"No, Kalita. I've been forgiven." He smiled. She leapt into his arms while the tears flowed down their faces. Kalita had prayed for him daily, that somehow his hardened heart would be touched, and it had happened. Her answered prayer gave her more confidence in their new faith.

When they pulled apart, reality settled in. "What will you do about your position?"

"I don't know. I haven't given it any thought. Will you pray with me that Jehovah will give me wisdom in this matter?"

"Nothing, my lord, and I mean nothing could bring me greater joy."

*****

It was extremely late when Joseph and Paul finally slipped into the nearly dark house. Rebekah had obviously gone to bed because her door was shut, and no light glowed from below the door. Still grinning and glowing on the inside from their experience with their friends, the boys silently set their things down. Chris heard the door open, so he got out of bed and slipped into the main room to see who it was. He was relieved to see his two young sons. Safira, he assumed, would soon join him to speak to them.

Chris had been determined that the boys grow up as he had in the States, with rules and curfews. When David had first turned twelve, Safira explained that Chris wouldn't be able to treat them as a dad in the United States could have. Here, the boys grew up faster and were expected to become men at twelve or thirteen. Chris struggled with the idea because they were still so young. But David had proven Safira's theory and had often approached his father for advice. Tonight, looking at his two fifteen-year-old sons, he gestured toward the kitchen table. They both obeyed, still grinning uncontrollably from ear to ear. Chris grabbed four mugs from the open kitchen cabinets and set them on the table. He silently began heating water for tea.

Joseph and Paul were anxious to share their experience, but knew their dad was anticipating the arrival of their mom, so they fidgeted with things on the table and silently exchanged giddy grins. As Chris watched them, he wondered if they even considered that they were in trouble. Obviously, something had detained them, and he looked forward to their explanation, one he would patiently wait for until Safira joined them.

Chris spoke after he sat down with the last full tea mug. "You do realize, if we weren't living in Keilron, I'd probably have both your hides for coming home so late. I find it difficult to accept your mom's view. You are still too young to be set loose on the world, especially here. You promised to be home at a certain time, and you are extremely late. Your mom and I were concerned when you weren't home. Good thing for you, we were otherwise occupied this evening and did not have the time to worry over you two all night. As it is, your mom could still give you an earful, despite her good intentions of letting you be your own men."

Safira came out of the bedroom, her long hair braided over her shoulder.

"He's right," she spoke firmly. "I'm glad you're home, but I hope you both realize there is nothing but trouble to be found after dark."

"Well, Mom, we kicked trouble in the butt tonight!" Joseph exclaimed. He still couldn't stop grinning any more than his brother could.

Safira spoke the moment she sat down and wrapped her hands around the mug. "Okay, I'm listening." She breathed in the sweet smell and sat back to enjoy the moment. The boys were not on her good list; they'd violated the house rule to be home before midnight, but she was also so thankful they were home she couldn't even pretend to be angry.

"You know Zomak and Shomar right?" Paul started.

"Your friends from the market. Of course, we do," Chris said, his gaze darting between the two boys.

"Well, we met them for a quick soccer game in the empty market. It's a great time to do it with great space . . . ," Joseph jumped in.

Paul glared at his brother even though the smile was still in place, "They just got done with basic training and graduated with honors."

Joseph was not discouraged by his brother's glare. "And after the game, we just sort of started talking, asking them about their training time, casual stuff. One thing led to another until we had the opportunity to witness."

"He's being modest. You should have seen the way Joseph led into it. I mean, most of the time, we get friends who talk bad about the Christians, and we just have to keep our mouths shut. But Joseph here couldn't do it."

"I remember you told me once that the best way to gauge if it's safe to open up is by looking into their eyes. I did, and when I saw the struggle going on, I took the opportunity of the empty street," Joseph admitted. "I may have started things, but Paul was awesome when he took charge."

Paul grinned, "And then 'bang,' it happened. They both wanted to know about Christianity, and then, they wanted to know more about Jesus."

"I happened to have my Bible with me, and so we shared a lot of scripture with them," Joseph inserted.

"So, sorry we were late, but we kind of figured you wouldn't mind once you understood," Paul finished.

Silence dominated while Safira took a couple more sips of tea. Finally, she spoke, "Am I to understand you witnessed to these two friends, and they were interested enough to keep you talking long into the night?"

Still grinning, they both nodded.

"And by those grins, I'm going to take a giant leap and say they were receptive," Chris responded. Inwardly, Chris was proud of his two sons. God was leading them. Perhaps, Safira was right after all.

The two nodded.

"It gets better," Joseph said.

"Couldn't let it go, could you," Paul mumbled into his tea.

Safira's small smile belied the pride and joy she felt for her two sons. It hid the laughter inside.

"None of us has ever spoken about who our families are. Turns out, there was good reason for that. You are the head of our Christian circles, and Zomak and Shomar are the sons of Shovak and Zamina."

Chris nearly dropped his mug on the table and stared for several moments at his tea. He looked up at his sons and spoke, "Zamina and Shovak's only children, and you just happen to befriend them and lead them to the Savior, and Narshac opens up to the possibilities, all in one night. God is about to make a mighty big splash."

"General Narshac?" Paul asked, puzzled.

Safira filled in. "Narshac is my brother, your uncle. He found me tonight on my way home from visiting the new couple from

Oregon. He came here tonight to speak with us. Your dad left an impression on him too, though we are less certain of that outcome."

"Wait, wait, wait, General Narshac is our uncle?" Joseph exclaimed. His jaw fell open.

"Man, Mom, we knew you were Keilronian, but you never said anything about being royalty," Paul said.

"I'm from a military family, not royalty," she gave a small smile.

"Here, that is royalty," Paul said shaking his head in awe.

"Dude, this is so cool!" Joseph said excitedly.

Paul shook his head at his twin brother's outburst.

"He had supper with us. He didn't make a decision one way or another. Your news and ours are evidence of the work Christ is doing. Chris, you were right," Safira said, reaching for his hand. The teens didn't understand, and Paul asked their dad what his mom meant.

"I left your siblings in Colorado because I felt things were changing. They are, but only time will tell if it's for the better," Chris stated. "We need to pray, please join me."

They reached for each other's hand and were about to bow in prayer when Rebekah came from her room, and after being briefed on the situation with the boys she too joined their circle of prayer.

Two hours after they'd all finally turned in for the night, there was a pounding on the door. Chris slipped on his pants and coat as had become habit and went to the door prepared to leave if need be. When he opened the door, he found a messenger waiting. Handing him the message, the man left as quietly as he'd come. It was a strange time for a message, which made it all the more peculiar.

Chris went back to the room and opened the letter and read out loud to Safira.

> *Chris and Safira,*
> *I thank you for sharing the truth with me. I now share your beliefs. You are safe from me, but I warn you, Rofisca still wishes to find you, Safira. Chris, you are in danger. Shovak knows your true identity. He has known for a while now, but has felt it prudent to let you be. There are changes in*

government, and you may not be as safe as you once were. What you do with this information is up to you. I will remain in contact with you if I've any further information.

Your brother

Safira's eyes filled with tears. The husband and wife held each other as they lay in bed praising God and asking Him for protection.

Chapter 31

Deception

June 2024

Zomak and Shomar knew they would face new challenges when they returned to their duties the following week. Their new faith placed them in an uncomfortable position because there would be orders given that they were no longer willing to execute. Being placed directly under Rofisca, a man who hated Christians with a passion, was no longer a great honor, but rather an inconvenience. The brothers discussed whether to remain silent about their faith or to reveal their new choice and suffer the consequences. Zomak knew he was not ready to take on the full weight of his decision and had chosen to remain silent. Shomar, always the one to dive off a cliff first, honored his brother's request to stew over his decision a while before making it obvious he had become a Christian.

During their week at home, the brothers took turns reading from the Keilronian Bible Joseph had given them. They hid the book well and discussed what they had read in the evenings.

When they reported to their positions in Rofisca's large infantry, they were told to report directly to Rofisca. Apparently, they were to join Rofisca's group of elite soldiers. The brothers were surprised at the high honor they'd been given and struggled with their mixed emotions. They were proud of each other to have been placed directly under the head of military operations; on the other hand, they were too close to the general.

For two weeks, their main responsibilities had been protecting Rofisca while he went to the different military stations and prisons. Zomak was watchful of the other men; there was something dark and hardened about them. But he could not understand the reason. From what he was experiencing, their duties were relatively relaxed. He warned Shomar to keep to himself, and Shomar willingly obliged after admitting there was something menacing about their small battalion.

The fact that the twins had been stationed together was unusual, and none of the men seemed to trust them. Zomak and Shomar were never far away from each other. Shomar even acknowledged late one evening he suspected Rofisca was intently watching him. Zomak kept his eyes open after that revelation and soon came to realize it was not only Shomar who was being watched. The twins wanted to write to their father, but knew nothing would happen. Shovak might want to defend them, but Rofisca still held a place in the heart of the people. Shomar commented one evening that he felt like a pawn in a chess game being played by Shovak and Rofisca. Zomak agreed. But what purpose did their father have for sending his sons into Rofisca's clutches?

Shomar was on duty, standing guard at Rofisca's base quarters. It was a boring job, and he hoped to join his brother and a few willing soldiers for a game of cards in another hour. The voice inside interrupted his thoughts. Stepping into the office, he acknowledged the general, "Yes, sir."

The general's voice was cold, "I need the entire unit up and ready to move out in thirty minutes. I want the jeeps fueled and ready. Make sure your weapons are loaded."

"Yes, sir!" Shomar responded. He saluted, spun on his heal, and left to execute his orders. Curiosity gnawed at the back of his mind, while he passed the message along to the unit. The men were trained to comply quickly. In less than the allotted thirty minutes, the jeeps were fueled, and every soldier was armed to the teeth with live ammunition. All soldiers were alert and ready when Rofisca marched to his jeep ten minutes later. When the general was ready, the entourage of men and machinery proceeded out of the military compound.

Once en route, the general picked up the radio and began filling in the men. "We're headed to a place ten miles from Shemna called Broshen. I've had my eye on the small village for some time. I have evidence there is a Christian cell growing there. Today, they're meeting at a man's home in the country. We are taking control, even though our prisons are full enough. I have chosen each one of you for your skills and ability to obey orders. These are your orders—when we pull up, and they attempt to scatter, do not let anyone escape."

Zomak and Shomar remained motionless when the radio went silent. Their orders were the kind they'd hoped never to be involved in. Shomar had heard rumors of how ruthless Rofisca could be, but hadn't been expecting complete disregard of his father's orders. Perhaps, many of the men didn't realize orders had been given to cease Christian massacres and outright murder, but they were to be brought to the prison. Zomak followed the same thought pattern, but also questioned why Rofisca would have brought him and Shomar on his unit if he knew the boys were close to their father. Obviously, there hadn't been much communication between the two leaders for some time, or Rofisca would not dare make this kind of mistake. The boys could not disregard direct orders, but they would not stretch out their guns against those of the same faith.

Zomak contemplated speaking to Rofisca to warn him that he knew of his father's orders, and as head of the country, Shovak's orders superseded Rofisca's. There was no time to make such a declaration in private. Perhaps if Rofisca was correct and the prisons were bursting with believers, Shovak had changed his orders. Zomak and Shomar had spent little time with their father since graduation. It was possible Shovak had changed his orders.

The military jeeps and Humvees pulled up fifteen minutes later to the small farm and found exactly what Rofisca had anticipated. The vehicles formed a semicircle around the openly gathering group.

Shomar stood a few paces from Rofisca's right. The group of Christians stood firm, choosing to face their aggressors. The soldiers filed out ready to shoot. Shomar carefully took a few steps closer to Rofisca, unnoticed by the commotion. He got within earshot of Rofisca.

Shomar spoke loudly enough for the general. "Sir, we cannot do this."

The general turned his head toward the younger man, and his eyes bore down into Shomar. "You have no right to say such things to me!" he growled.

Shomar swallowed, but refused to back down, "Shovak has given strict orders against this kind of brutality."

"You think Shovak's ways are more merciful than mine? Have you seen what they do to Christians within the prisons?"

"Perhaps that is why he gave the orders, sir."

"If you do not follow my orders, you will not live past this day, son of Shovak or not." Rofisca turned back toward the group of two hundred souls waiting for a miracle, staring back at his men. A sick smile crossed his face as he gave the signal.

Gunfire filled the air. Red stained the robes of the congregation as they fell to the ground. Several did try to run, but they didn't get far with the bullets raining down on them.

Zomak stood at attention, keeping his gun swung over his shoulder. Shomar stood unflinching, although inwardly his heart broke at the meaningless bloodshed. The gunfire ceased. In a matter of moments, two hundred and five souls met their Savior. Zomak and Shomar used their training to hold back the emotions threatening to overwhelm them. The looks of satisfaction on their comrades' faces while they watched the blood flow from the now-still bodies explained the hardness the boys observed.

Rofisca noticed the boys' insubordination. Although he was able to get around a few of Shovak's orders, he would never convince his men it was legal to gun the two boys down. Even in Rofisca's army, there were protocols.

Facing Shomar and summoning Zomak, he declared, "For disobeying a direct order, you are hereby under arrest and will be court-martialed and suffer the repercussions of your insubordination." Rofisca turned toward Zomak, still standing beside him, and hissed, "Even Shovak can't get you out of this one." Rofisca had the two boys bound and ordered them to be taken to Shemna.

Rofisca considered the situation, while they drove back to the base. The boys were in trouble, but if, or rather when, they opened their mouths to tell why they had disobeyed, there would be a reckoning. Shovak had already begun showing signs that Rofisca had lost favor with the dictator. If he heard of the massacre that had just transpired, the general would be in grave danger.

Rofisca picked up the radio. "I want fifty men to stay behind and bury those bodies. They deserve no ceremony other than to be forgotten. Burry them and conceal their grave so no one will know they ever existed."

*****

Narshac watched the Humvee pull into the prison entrance. He'd been told of two new prisoners, but the familiar fifteen-year-old boys who exited the vehicle surprised him.

"Zomak and Shomar, you were so promising. Your father will be disappointed when he finds out. I hope you know how much pain you will cause your mother." Narshac glanced down at the paperwork the driver handed him. "Disobeying direct orders. Show of blatant disrespect. Well, boys, I will speak with you inside." Narshac dismissed them.

Two guards escorted Shovak's twins into the prison. Once the boys were stripped of their uniforms and given prison garb, Narshac met them in an interrogation room designed for military use.

"What happened out there today?" Narshac asked when he sat down across from them.

"Doesn't the report describe the situation?" Zomak muttered.

Narshac, shuffling through the file, was relaxed, and his response was casual, "I'd rather hear your account."

Shomar volunteered first, "We were given an order that we didn't agree with."

Narshac couldn't find Rofisca's report on his side of what happened, so he sat back and looked directly at Shomar. Something didn't feel right here.

Growing interested, Narshac leaned forward and asked, "What was his order?"

Zomak answered, "He ordered an entire group of people gunned down."

"What had the group done to deserve this kind of punishment?"

"Nothing. They were Christians. That's all." Shomar answered. His brother sent a warning glare, and Narshac knew he was sitting across from two fellow believers. The idea gave him hope.

"He ordered his troops to gun down an entire group?" Narshac clarified.

Zomak didn't give his brother the chance to speak. The fire in the young man's voice left no doubt of the boy's allegiance "Men, women, and children. Rofisca never even offered to arrest them. He just ordered the squad to fire, to kill every last one of them!"

Shomar interrupted Zomak's angry outburst. "I remembered our father saying he'd given orders to prevent this very thing from happening. He wasn't against the torture or the death of Christians, but he knew public displays like this are harmful for the country's foreign negotiations."

"If what you're saying is true, it's not the first time, is it?"

"We wouldn't know, having been with him for a little over two weeks," said Shomar.

"If he's done it today, be assured, he's done it before. The evidence will be well concealed, but he's not the head general for nothing," Narshac commented.

Narshac considered the matter for a moment. He knew he'd have to speak with Shovak immediately on the matter. Shovak would want to know not only of his boys' involvement but also of Rofisca's misconduct. Rofisca was his father, but they'd never been close.

Narshac's eyes were suddenly intense, "I have a personal question for you two. If it hadn't been against your father's orders, would you have obeyed Rofisca?"

The two boys stared back at him silently for several heartbeats. Zomak broke the silence, "No, sir. I would not have. I've found peace with Jehovah, the only God. I count myself among them."

Shomar's eyes were determined when he nodded in agreement.

Narshac smirked. "Nor would I, boys. We will get you out of this, but until then, sit back and enjoy the prison experience. It will be short-lived."

Narshac left the room, the boys gawking at his retreating form, and gave orders to have them put into cells for the time being while their case was under review. They were to be held with no current disciplinary action. Narshac checked his list of things to accomplish and knew there were a few things to be done before approaching Shovak. Writing a quick message to Shovak, he sent a young officer up to the capitol building to deliver it.

Three hours passed before Narshac entered Shovak's office.

"Tell me, what's so urgent?" Shovak insisted.

"Rofisca made a mistake, and I've got proof in my prison that he's overstepped you."

Shovak sighed. "What happened?"

"He's been massacring large Christian groups and then hiding the evidence."

"Who do you have to collaborate this story?"

"Your sons, Zomak and Shomar."

Shovak's gaze intensified. "What?" He spat out the word.

"Rofisca placed them under arrest for disobeying direct orders. They refused to comply with his command. Zomak and Shomar knew you'd ordered the direct killing to stop and the reasoning behind those orders. Your sons honored you."

Shovak closed his eyes and took a deep breath. "I must speak with them. We shall have them released quickly. This is the last time. Rofisca is no longer trustworthy. I've needed witnesses before I could take him down. He's too much of a hero to the people for me to do so without cause. It started with his obsession over your sister, Safira, and has escalated out of control."

Narshac was pleased that the leader had been aware of the situation for some time, but why should that surprise him? After all, Shovak had overthrown the government because of his observation skills. Narshac brought the conversation back to the problem at hand, "Would you like me to take you down to your sons?"

"Yes, I would."

The two wasted no time returning to the prison. Narshac had been absent for barely an hour. The moment he stepped back into the prison walls with Shovak, the soldiers exchanged wary looks. Narshac noticed and demanded to know what was going on.

The higher-ranking officer explained, "Sir, General Rofisca came and demanded to see Zomak and Shomar. He's our superior, so we let him in to see them. He had another man with him. When he left, we saluted and let him pass. Sir, ten minutes ago, the boys would not come to the door to receive their supper. When we opened the door, we found them both dead."

Shovak's composure broke. "Where . . . where are they!" he demanded.

The guard took them to the morgue, where the bodies lay on metal slabs. The two boys looked peaceful. Shovak went first to one and then the other, weeping as he held each one in turn. Narshac and the guard left the room, allowing him privacy to mourn openly. Zamina would not take this well.

Narshac stood at attention guarding the door, praying as he stood there. He didn't understand why Jehovah would allow this to happen and yet would save Chris from the same fate. He prayed for wisdom.

Shovak had no desire to speak when he finally emerged and left the prison to return home. His task was not going to be easy. He'd have to face his beloved wife and mourn with her for the lives of their two children.

While driving back to the large palace that hosted both his home and government center, Shovak vowed he would see the end of Rofisca's reign very soon. He didn't care what it took. Knowing Rofisca intimately would give him the advantage, a plan began forming. Rofisca would not misjudge his men again. Shovak knew his old comrade learned from his mistakes and never repeated them. But he was irrational when it came to his daughter. Safira was the key to bringing him out to the public. The masses would see for themselves the kind of man Rofisca had become, and then, they would eagerly see him removed. Shovak laid his plans aside when he saw Zamina. For now, she was his concern.

Chapter 32

Shadow of Death

United States
August 2024

The dinner table was filled with smiles and laughter. Fay gave a satisfied sigh while watching and listening to her twelve grandkids sharing school stories. They were joking with one another, ignoring the adult conversation going on around them. She knew she was blessed, and her heart was full of gratitude. Fay was grateful for the long dining room table David made for her over the summer. The table could seat up to twenty people when all the center leaves were put in.

The phone rang quietly in the background, and Fay went into the other room, away from the loud family gathering, to answer it. She'd been gone for several minutes when Harris went in search of his wife. He found her collapsed by the phone crying uncontrollably.

His heart pounded. He didn't want to ask. Harris knew of only one reason she would be in such a state. Still, with a weak voice, he asked, "Honey, what's wrong?" Kneeling down beside her, he took her hands in his. She clung to him the moment he touched her.

"It was Safira," She mumbled into his shirt.

He swallowed hard, "What happened?"

"Chris and Rebekah have been captured."

Harris closed his eyes in pain. His heart throbbed the moment the words were out of her mouth. He couldn't imagine what his son and granddaughter were going through. Tears flooded his own eyes.

He fought back the tears and asked, "What of Joseph and Paul?"

"They're with their mom. They weren't at home when the soldiers came."

The joyful sounds of their family drifted in, reminding Harris the family was already gathered.

He stood and lifted Fay to her feet. Guiding her to the living room couch, he helped her sit down. "I'll be back," he whispered. Placing a kiss on her forehead, he returned to their kids.

"I need to speak with the adults. David, that includes you. Please join us in the living room?"

Cold silence followed. The adults quietly stood and followed Harris into the other room.

Siblings and cousins exchanged looks of concern. Their jovial conversation dissolved, and their grandfather's words echoed in their hearts. The youngest cousins slowly began to converse and giggle once again, but the older Banks children could not be persuaded to rejoin the discussion.

"We got a call from Safira. Ladies, you may want to sit down." Harris waited for them to settle before getting to the point. "Chris and Rebekah have been taken prisoner." Harris saw the expressions change from curiosity to mortification in a heartbeat. Kate, who'd declined the suggestion to sit earlier, took his advice and sat down. David, showing no emotion, stared past the group and out the living room window.

Blake was the one to break the silence. "Let's pray."

Harris nodded. The others remained in shock, staring at nothing in particular.

Blake bowed his head. "Lord, you've given us wonderful times with Chris and Rebekah, and for those, we're thankful. Please don't let those times be our last. Give them strength to endure the road ahead. Use them while they are in captivity, and bless them for their service to you. Help Safira and the boys stay strong." Blake's voice broke with a suppressed sob.

David was a silent young man and rarely spoke of his life in Keilron, but he found the strength to finish his uncle's prayer. "Lord, our family knew why we were in Keilron. We understood the dangers of living there, and yet we are shocked and unprepared by this news. Help me and my family to remain strong in our faith. We've tried to prepare for something like this. Help us to lean on you now. Give Rebekah strength and courage. I know she is scared right now. Comfort her. Give my dad the opportunity to share your gospel to one last person. Use both Dad and Rebekah to share your truth with others. Amen."

*****

Narshac entered the prison and received the updated list of prisoners. Glancing through it, he spotted Chris's name. Pointing at the name he ordered, "Clean him up. He's been on the blacklist for a long time. Shovak will want to meet him."

"Yes, sir." The man saluted and left.

Narshac knew of Shovak's plan for revenge and how he planned to use Chris as a pawn in the game being played by the two leaders. Shovak had plans to rile up Rofisca, who never acted rationally when put on the spot, especially when it came to Safira, by publicly giving Chris his freedom. Shovak was counting on Rofisca's retaliation. Narshac willingly went along with Shovak's plan. Narshac had given the orders to have Chris brought in. Unfortunately, Rebekah had been home as well, and she'd been brought in with her father. Shovak needed an opportunity to hear the gospel. It was a rocky idea at best, but Narshac was confident that bringing Chris to Shovak was the right thing to do.

When Chris was brought to Narshac, the soldier took advantage of their time on the way to Shovak.

He spoke quietly, "I promise this won't last long. Shovak has known about your presence since you reentered Keilron years ago. He has a purpose for your imprisonment now. I can't say much more. Trust me, you will not suffer by my hand. Rebekah wasn't meant to be brought here. She was supposed to be with Safira."

Chris's response was calm. "Plans change in a heartbeat. She decided to stay home for a little bit before meeting with some friends. I guess you cancelled her plans."

"She will not be harmed. It may do her well to see the inside of a cell. Jesus has a reason for her coming too. This will not be a long stay as far as I'm aware.

"Why are you taking me to Shovak now?"

Narshac's tone was confident, "Wait and see. Trust in Jehovah, and all will end for His glory."

Narshac's words were meant to reassure, but Chris was finding it difficult to be confident in his brother-in-law's words. He'd been in irons before, and that had been an extremely unpleasant time. Chris hoped Narshac was right, but feared the worst.

*****

"Sir, I'd like to introduce Christian Banks."

The moment Shovak heard Narshac's voice, he turned and, for the first time, laid eyes on the sworn enemy of Rofisca. Shovak understood to some degree why this man drove Rofisca to become the man he was; but he could not comprehend the pure hatred Rofisca harbored for a single man who had nothing to do with Safira's desertion. Knowing Christian's location all these years, and allowing the missionary to remain, was at last going to prove a good move.

Chris's hands were in irons, and his clothes were worn, but the man who'd eluded Rofisca and his army for so long looked nothing like Shovak expected. He'd expected an old man or perhaps a much younger one. Either way, he hadn't expected the middle-aged soldier-like American.

Shovak smiled, "Christian Banks, it is a pleasure to meet you at last."

Chris bowed his head, "It is an honor to meet you, sir."

"You are incredibly polite for a prisoner."

Chris's voice was relaxed. "I've nothing to fear."

Shovak's voice remained conversational. "Narshac has a fear of you that I do not. I don't believe in fairy tales. I'm quite convinced you used witchcraft the morning you were released."

"No, it was my Jehovah God."

Shovak sat down on a plush chair in his office and offered another to Chris. Narshac respectfully left the pair and went into the hall, his heart trembling with hope. He prayed Shovak would get the chance to hear the truth of Jehovah.

Shovak continued to stare at Chris for several moments while considering his next words. He had had no intention of meeting with Chris for another couple of days. He glanced at his watch before he stood and poured himself a glass of brandy.

"Would you care for some?" he offered.

Chris shook his head. "No, thank you."

"I've heard many Christians speak about this strange all-powerful God. I have time today, and you have been greatly influential in the Christian world. I've read much about you in the news. I was surprised you would be so careless. I'm well connected with many countries. It is important I stay up-to-date on the comings and goings of influential people in particularly strong countries. I know you are an educated man and that you would not be deceived by a fairy tale. I've heard bits and pieces from those who have entered Narshac's prison, but I have questions. I'm interested in understanding the psyche of your religion. Please, tell me of your Jehovah."

*****

Zamina knew her husband would be busy for the duration of the day and decided to face her grief alone. She'd put off going anywhere near her sons' room since their death, but today, she felt an ache to touch them. The nearest she could get to that, however, was their shared room. They'd loved the mutual space from a young age and had opted out of separate rooms when they'd gotten older.

The moment she stepped into the large room, tears pooled in her eyes. Taking in deep breaths, she tried to stop the hammering in her chest. It took several minutes before she was able to bring her emotions under some semblance of control before moving into the room toward Zomak's bed. Sitting down, she let her eyes roam the rest of the quarters.

She took in the sight of Shomar's bed across the room and the books piled up by his bed. A smile touched her lips while she soaked in the memories of her son's desire for knowledge. Wanting to feel a part of him, she stood and stepped toward his space and his stack of books. She began to finger through them.

Shomar had taught her how to read, and she smiled as she read the titles. He'd loved history and government. When she set the last book down on the stack, she accidently toppled the book tower. When she reached under his blankets to grab an escaped book, her fingers touched an object that had been tucked further under the bed. She stretched to reach it. Bringing it up, she read the words on the book cover and dropped it instantly. She had seen something similar many, many years ago in her first husband's bed chambers.

Had her son fallen into the Christian religion? Had he forsaken the gods of his father? She had a hard time understanding why Shomar would possess such a book. He had brought books to his room only if he was reading them. If he had read this book, had Zomak known?

Determined to discover if he knew anything of his brother's betrayal, she stood and turned to Zomak's side of the room. It did not take much searching to find Zomak's journal. The boy had kept a journal from a young age and had only grown more faithful to writing as he'd grown older. She began to flip through the pages, scanning the last couple of weeks of his life. He did not write eloquently but rather factually as if writing a log book of his life. She came across the first hints of trouble and slowed her reading, drinking in Zomak's last days all over again.

Tonight, Shomar and I met up with a couple of old friends to enjoy a game of soccer. The empty market lent itself to our fun. After the game, Shomar and I shared with Joseph and Paul the things we experienced during our training. We told them of our misgivings when it came to the way Christians are disciplined for betraying the gods. Paul chose to enlighten us about the God of all Creation, Jehovah, the God the Christians serve. Shomar was more interested than I, but I allowed the conversation. Paul explained so completely in his telling of Jehovah. It was not long before I too was drawn into their explanation. Shomar and I were shown from the book, written by their God, of the love He has for us. Shomar and I have made a decision to follow the one true God, Jehovah.

Zamina slammed the journal shut. Her eyes flashed around the room for any intruders, but she stood alone. Her heart pounded at this new revelation. She did not understand. How could her boys have been fooled? She knew Rofisca had silenced them because of his own actions. They had not been killed for their choice of God. But had they lived, how long would they have been able to keep their convictions a secret? Her sons were both brilliant boys; they would not have made such a choice halfheartedly.

She lowered herself onto Zomak's bed, glaring at the journal she'd thrown aside, and wishing the words were not written. Should she bring the matter up to Shovak, or would it only bring him pain too? She knew he mourned their loss as much as she did, but to keep such a secret would damage the honest communications between them if ever he took the time to read the journal himself. Their openness with one another was what made their marriage work. The question, then, was when?

*****

Rebekah lay in the cell waiting for something, anything, to happen. She hadn't thought being in Keilron would actually come to this. She'd heard of other missionaries and their sacrifices, but had somehow thought her family immune.

She prayed into the night for God's guidance and for her family, especially if she and her father didn't make it out alive. Rebekah had no idea what was transpiring, but she prayed for courage and for the right words for both her and her father.

*****

Shovak stared at Chris who had carefully and effectively laid out the entire Christian faith. Glancing at his watch, Shovak was surprised by the two hours that had passed since they'd begun discussing Chris's God.

"This is all very interesting. I will have to think about and consider your perspective. But right now, I don't see how anything could convince me that changing my allegiance now, at my age, would be the wisest decision."

"What do you have to lose? If I'm wrong and you are right, then there is no heaven or hell, only what we mere mortals can do now to make the gods happy. There would be no consequences. If I'm right, you will have an eternity in hell to consider the truth, but it will be too late then."

Shovak stood abruptly, clearly agitated. "I'm done with this conversation. I will call for Narshac. You may wait outside my office. Thank you for your time." Shovak had ended all conversation and they both knew it.

With a heavy heart, Chris left the dictator. Shovak would have no excuses when he stood before the Lord.

Narshac came for him in short order, and the two began their walk back down to the Jeep waiting to carry them the rest of the way back to Chris's cell.

"How'd it go?" Narshac asked.

"He listened, but he didn't change his will."

"I only hoped."

"How long do you suspect we will be here?"

"I don't know for sure. Long enough for the news to get a hold of this information and long enough for Rofisca to get antsy and come storm the castle, so to speak."

"This is about Rofisca?"

"Yes."

Chris didn't ask any more questions as they drove the five minutes to the prison that had been built by Shovak for the Christian vermin. The original prisons below the large capitol building had not been big enough to hold the large numbers.

*****

A full week passed before Zamina contrived the opportunity to speak with Shovak. He was in his office, as he'd been for the majority of the last two weeks. She never hesitated to enter his office, and with a brief nod to the guard outside the door, she strolled in.

"Shovak, I need to speak with you."

Looking up from his desk, he gestured toward the chairs across from his desk. "All right, have a seat."

She stepped forward and laid the two books down on his desk as she sat down.

"Zomak and Shomar kept secrets before they died. With my history of such things, I felt it wise to bring the matter to you. I know it will make no real difference now, but I thought you would like to know. I found these two items while spending some time in their room."

Recognizing Zomak's journal, Shovak picked it up. He glanced down at the other book, a Keilronian translation of the New Testament. He froze. She'd found these things in their room?

"This must be a fluke," he said. His voice was as unconvincing as his belief in the words.

"Look at Zomak's entry a week before his departure." Tears shined in her eyes. She was keeping them at bay, but he could tell she was having difficulty controlling her emotions.

He did as she asked, but his hands shook. He read the last sentence several times before setting the book down. She wanted a response, but his mind was in complete shock. He'd trained his boys to honor the gods, to give gifts to them, and to live to be men of honor. He had hoped that everything he'd taught them would have had some bearing on their decisions. But it was written so decisively, the decision made without hesitation. No mention was made of any guilt for such a complete change of heart.

"Joseph and Paul are the boys behind this. They would know more of our sons' feelings on this than we do. We never got the chance to discuss this with them. We had dinner with them that night before they left to meet these two friends. That was the last time we had dinner as a family."

She nodded her understanding and agreement.

"We both ought to have closure to this part of our lives. How can we do that when we now wonder whether they even found favor with the gods so that they were able to find rest in their deaths? Names such as these boys have must be American or English." Shovak picked up his phone and dialed a few numbers. After waiting a few moments, he spoke, "Narshac, I need you to find out if there are any Americans or Englishmen who have sons around the age of fifteen. I'm seeking a Joseph and a Paul. Once you have them, I want to see them." He paused long enough to hear the man comply before hanging up the phone and staring at his wife.

"We will have an end to this nightmare."

Narshac hung up the phone and closed his eyes in pain. He had promised Chris that this was about him. He had told his brother that Rebekah's capture had been an accident. What would his brother say now? Narshac knew exactly who Shovak was looking for and where to find them. He also knew that the imprisonment of the two boys was going to break his little sister's heart. He didn't want to bring his nephews in before Shovak. The man had sounded angry and hostile regarding the two unknowns. What would he do when he met them? Narshac knew that the time was coming for him to reveal his alliance with Jehovah. He would not harm his fellow brethren any longer. For the moment, neither death sentence nor orders of torture had been given. He turned to his right-hand man and gave the order, even as he felt the pain he'd soon be causing his favored sister. He would not be there for this raid. His heart wouldn't bear it.

*****

Safira lay in bed, thankful her two sons remained with her, yet still tearful over her husband's absence. She knew it wouldn't be long before she'd need to head back to the States with her boys, but the thought of deserting her husband before she knew for sure if he had been martyred was unfathomable. God had protected him before; He would do it again, wouldn't He?"

Down the hall, Joseph and Paul prayed quietly together for their father and sister. They knew circumstances were difficult for their mother and prayed for strength, courage, and comfort. The house was silent, so when the knock came hard against the door, it startled them all.

The boys dressed quickly and rushed out to meet their mom at the door. Before they got there, however, they heard flesh strike flesh; and when they rounded the corner, they saw their mother knocked out on the floor. Immediately, the boys rushed toward her, but they were forced down to the ground by four soldiers. Their arms were forced behind them, and their hands were clasped in irons. The boys tried to pull away from the soldiers' grasp to no avail. They were told she'd be fine, as long as they stopped fighting. They immediately stopped struggling, realizing the soldiers were not interested in Safira. The soldiers cursed at them several times as they shoved the two boys out the door and into the waiting Jeep outside. They were driven from their home and into the middle of the city, down into the pits where so many Christian soldiers before them had been tortured and killed.

Safira regained consciousness only to have her eyes fill with tears as she huddled against the cold floor, staring out the open door into the streets of Shemna. She prayed for them to be all right, as she'd never prayed before as she felt the bitter loss of her family members, but she also prayed for herself, seeking the Lord with all her heart. She needed His comfort in a way she'd never needed before. Just as she'd experienced the night she was eighteen and hopelessly running from her father, the arms of the Savior wrapped around her, and she felt His peace surround her.

*****

The Banks brothers were escorted into the prison and brought before Narshac, who looked down at the boys with indifferent eyes.

"These are the boys we've been expecting. They have an appointment with Shovak. It's time they face what their father already has."

The soldiers nodded and escorted the boys to the dressing area where they were given prison garments, and their hair was combed by a rather intimidating man.

Narshac came for them once they'd been made presentable and spoke to the guard, "I think I can handle them both. They're just boys and gentle Christians at that," he sneered. The brothers exchanged uncertain glances, not knowing what to expect from this uncle they'd never met.

They moved forward when Narshac put his gun to their backs. Once they were out of earshot, Narshac spoke.

"I took your father to Shovak only days ago. I knew Chris would share the truth with him. Shovak was not sure what to think, so he chose to stick with the gods of his father. Late last night, I received a rather intense call from Shovak requesting your presence by name. You wouldn't know anything about that, would you?"

"Only thing I can think of is if Zomak and Shomar let it slip that we are Chris Banks' kids."

"Boys, I hate to be the one to break this to you, but Rofisca murdered your friends. Shovak has kept it quiet because he's been preparing his revenge."

Paul and Joseph silently mourned their friends on the drive to Shovak's office. They were now more confused than ever as to why Shovak would want to see them.

Chapter 33

Persuaded

Shovak watched Narshac enter the room behind the two boys. He looked them over and instantly realized they must be Joseph and Paul. His look was the only acknowledgment they received. Shovak picked up his phone and spoke. "You may join me. The boys are here."

The phone was set back into its cradle, and his eyes bore into the two young men. Several minutes of silence passed before a woman entered the room and stood behind Shovak.

Shovak began his inquisition. "How did you meet Zomak and Shomar?"

Joseph and Paul had expected a great many things, but after only hearing of their friends' death only moments earlier, this was not the line of questioning they'd anticipated.

"We met them four or five years ago at the market," Paul answered.

"You have been friends for years?" Zamina gasped. Shovak gave her a warning glance, and she sent him an apology with her eyes.

"You played together often?"

Joseph took the initiative this time. "Yes."

"Who are your parents?"

With their father in prison, there was no need for secrecy. "Christian and Safira Banks," Paul declared.

Shovak's next question had been at the tip of his tongue, but he hesitated. He swallowed and leaned back into his office chair, gazing intently at the two as if seeing them for the first time. Zamina shot her husband a confused look, but he paid her no attention.

His voice became more personable, "When was the last time you saw my boys?"

"Um, I'm not sure. Three months ago I think, maybe more," Joseph responded.

"I'm going to ask you a direct question. And I'm begging for a direct answer. Did my boys speak to you about your Jehovah?"

"Yes," Paul answered.

"Did they accept what you told them? Did they believe in Him?"

"Yes," both boys answered.

Zamina's hand covered her mouth in a gasp.

Shovak leaned forward in his chair, folding his hands in front of him on the desk, his eyes narrowed and his voice, though quiet, was intense. "Give me one good reason why I shouldn't just have you killed right now for your treason."

"Whether you do or not, you will be brought to your knees for the deeds done against His people," Paul said.

"I've been killing those of your kind for quite some time without a problem."

"Your arrogance and pride will soon destroy you," Joseph said.

"Wait, aren't you going to try and tell me about your Jehovah?"

"Sir, I believe my father has told you enough. You've heard all you've needed. If you were to accept the gift, we would be more than honored to be here for that, but I think perhaps that is not the case," Joseph said.

Shovak chanced a glance at Narshac who gave him a slight nod of assurance that indeed he was on the boys' side.

Catching the exchange, Paul felt emboldened. "If, sir, my brother is wrong, we would be honored to help you open the door to Jehovah."

Shovak's disposition changed completely when he'd realized Narshac, his most trusted general, was on the boys' side. He glanced up at his wife and saw her look of confusion. Shovak could tell she wanted to know what Chris had already told him. He was ready to lean on the God who had proven Himself real and loving. His wife may not be ready, but he was no longer willing to risk turning his back on Jehovah. He'd been persecuting God's people, and he'd felt the conviction of doing so, but he'd always covered such feelings of disgust with anger and hate, derived from his youth. The time had passed when he could blindly follow his father's footsteps. His own sons had seen the light, and now, it was his turn to experience the living God and His mercy.

They remained in Shovak's office for some time. Paul and Joseph reiterated what their father had already told Shovak, and he accepted the sacrifice of Jesus Christ to cover all of his sins, to make his heart white before the living God.

Zamina stood silently observing everything going on. As she watched her husband bow his head to the all-present God and offer his filthy heart to be cleansed, she was confused because she had not been taught or made to understand this God. Shovak finished his inward prayer before looking up with a smile. Zamina hadn't seen him smile outside their bedroom for many years, and even then, it had been reserved for her. Shovak glanced over at her, his eyes shining with joy.

"I have made the right decision!" he said confidently.

Narshac and the boys knew Zamina would have to be told the whole story, but it would have to be another time. There were pressing issues to discuss.

"My plan for Rofisca has not changed. The only difference is revealing all my news. You must go back with Narshac to the prison, boys. I promise you will not be there long," Shovak said.

"Sir, their mother remains at the house in which they've lived. May I inform her about the situations at hand?" Narshac asked.

"Not just yet. Safira is still the key to bringing this country back to order. For now, your orders are to hold the Christians who are brought in, but cease the tortures."

"As you wish, sir," Narshac said, and he led the boys from the room.

*****

Rebekah quickly sat up straight when she saw Narshac enter the cell with her two brothers. She reached for them, and they embraced one another. Narshac was touched by the family's open affection. He turned and left, locking the cell before going home for the night and taking the only set of keys with him. There was no way he was going to chance Rofisca discovering them.

Rebekah looked at her younger brothers. "How did you guys get here? Is Mom here too?"

"No. They left Mom. I think Narshac had something to do with that. The soldiers stormed into our house. Narshac ordered our arrests. Shovak wanted to speak with us, and Mom was left alone," Paul said.

"Shovak! What is going on around here?"

Joseph answered in an excited whisper so the guards could not overhear. "Shovak spoke with Dad earlier, and then I guess Shovak figured out his boys got saved and that their decision had something to do with us. Shovak was not happy about us, but then after he figured out we were Banks, his entire line of questioning changed. He started off attacking us for being Christians and threatened to kill us, but I kind of bad-mouthed him. And Paul, as usual, covered my butt. And then the most shocking of news, Shovak just put his faith in Jesus Christ!"

"That's amazing! What about Dad? Do you know anything about him?" Rebekah asked.

"No, but this is Narshac's prison, so he must be alive yet," Paul said.

"I hope so." Rebekah sat down on the prison bench and allowed her brothers to follow suit as they all fell into silent prayer.

Meanwhile, Chris sat in a prison cell only five feet away from his children on the other side of the brick wall. He sat silently, waiting as many other fellow Christians before him. He stared at the guard in front of his cell. Tears fell as he thought of his children and wife. Leaving them behind in such a cruel world was almost too much to bear, but his own words echoed in his memory, "They're in God's hands and always will be."

Curling up against the wall, he started remembering the Apostle Paul's letters from prison. He felt a song deep within his being and began singing.

> *"Almost persuaded" now to believe;*
> *"Almost persuaded" Christ to receive;*
> *Seems now some soul will say,*
> *"Go spirit, go Thy way,*
> *Some more convenient day on thee I'll call."*

The children heard their father's voice echoing somewhere nearby and raised their voices with his.

> *"Almost persuaded," come, come today;*
> *"Almost persuaded," turn not away;*
> *Jesus invites you here,*
> *Angels are ling'ring near,*
> *Prayers rise from hearts so dear;*
> *O wand'rer, come!*

The other Christian prisoners joined in as the Banks family began singing the Keilronian version of *What a friend we have in Jesus*. The guards didn't know what to do and remained silent while they listened to the music surrounding the dungeon walls.

It was a relief for the children to hear their father's voice and feel the strength of Jehovah's comfort. Tears rolled down each Banks' face as the family sang hymn after hymn early into the morning.

*****

David stared out his window at Blake's house. He feared for his family a great deal, but he knew his responsibility was to care for his siblings. Getting up from his spot by the window, he moved out of his room and meandered to his sisters' room.

Rachel and Marie shared a room. David opened their door and stared at their sleeping forms. He would do anything to protect his sisters. He loved them and had been taught through the Keilronian culture how to be the man of a household. He moved to his brother's room and watched Daniel sleeping for several moments before going to Ruth's room. She was nearly twelve and was as kind as their mother.

Gently closing her door, he proceeded to the front porch. He stared up at the moon, praying for his imprisoned family and his worried mother on the other side of the world. He often regretted not staying in Keilron with his family, but was also thankful he was in Colorado caring for his younger siblings.

The opening door behind him caused him to turn quickly. Blake closed the distance to stand beside his nephew.

"Easy," Blake said. "I didn't mean to spook you. I couldn't sleep, so I came out here, hoping some fresh air might help."

David, as usual, remained silent, looking up into the evening stars. Blake set his hand on David's shoulder.

"Sometimes, it's hard to understand what God's plan is. David, be strong like your biblical namesake. God will work everything out for His glory, no matter the outcome."

"I know, Blake. I'm grateful to be here so I can look after my family. If I weren't here, Daniel would have to take the responsibility, and he is far too young to care for our sisters. I'm exactly in the right spot, but I'm still concerned for the rest of my family. They're not here, and the young girls need my mother. Ruth is nearly of age, and she will need our mother most now."

"In time, you will be together again, I promise. If not in this world, at least in heaven."

"Thanks, Blake."

No more words were spoken. No more were needed. They both understood the other. Blake felt a deep compassion for the young man before him. They remained in silence for some time before Blake went back into the house, leaving David to his own thoughts.

David knew his uncle had meant well, but as much as he knew it was all for God's glory, he couldn't help but selfishly want his family all home safe and sound, despite the good they were doing now. What did their lives mean to the rest of the world? How could sacrificing them to a darkened world bring more light? He was frustrated, and he knew it. Taking a deep sigh, he sat down on the porch swing, staring into the darkness. He began to speak with his heavenly Father about his frustrations.

*****

Halfway around the world, Safira watched as the crowd grew outside the courtyard of the capitol building. Among them were friends and Christian converts, while others she recognized as reporters from other countries. Her eyes scanned the yard looking for something of interest to so many people. In the center of the courtyard, she noticed the guards standing ready at The Altar, a raised monument used for sacrificing the vilest traitors, criminals, and enemies of Keilron.

The crowd suddenly grew quiet. Safira watched her husband and three children being led to The Altar. Standing them side by side, Narshac looked directly at Safira with regret. Rofisca entered the courtyard and stood beside the Banks on The Altar. Safira pushed her way to the front of the crowd.

Rofisca's voice boomed over the crowd. "Today, I will sacrifice my own blood as many have done with fellow family members who've turned from the gods. I give you my grandchildren and son-in-law." He stretched out his hand indicating the four people kneeling at the top of The Altar with their arms tied behind them. No sound was made, no cheering, no booing, only silence followed. Shovak entered the courtyard and ascended the steps to stand on the opposite side of The Altar from the head general.

Rofisca had been told earlier this morning of the capture of Chris and his three children, all part of Shovak's plan. Rofisca had come out to the prison, as expected, and demanded his right to execute his family for their treachery. Shovak knew Rofisca well, and

Narshac gave the leader props for such a skilled outward show of authority. Rofisca was a proud man, and Narshac had seen and heard enough to know that Rofisca had been treading deep waters for too long.

Shovak's voice carried through the quiet crowd, "My friend, I've known you many years. But today, I use my authority against you. I forbid this execution."

A stir began to pass through the people in the courtyard.

Narshac stood beside the dictator and heard Shovak speak quietly to Rofisca. "These are now my friends. You have disobeyed me long enough."

Rofisca ignored the quiet rebuke and responded in a loud growl, defying his sovereign. "I will have these lives, my lord. This man stole my daughter, and these children are no better than pigs."

Rofisca hoped to rile the crowd as he once had, but his voice was filled with anger, and the crowd had grown to respect their ruler and were no longer willing to follow a general who long ago abandoned his loyalty to the people in his quest for revenge.

"We have struggled against their God in vain. It is time to let them be." Shovak didn't need to shout for the reporters and nearby soldiers to hear his orders.

"If you give me these lives, I will never ask for anything again. I will resign willingly." Rofisca was now inches from Shovak's face, pleading for his only desire to end the lives of those who had, in his eyes, taken the life of his daughter.

"You will not defy me anymore. We must begin a new chapter," Shovak declared to the crowd.

"I will have my way," Rofisca shouted, his face flushing bright red.

Safira took the last few steps forward to stand on the steps of The Altar. Bowing low before Shovak and Rofisca, she looked into the eyes of her father.

"I beg you, if you've any compassion left toward me, spare the lives of my family. Please, Papa."

Rofisca stared at the woman before him. Could this be his small child, the spoiled child he'd raised, now a grown woman of such beauty? He looked back at her family and then back at her. His face calmed, and he looked almost proud. He stood straighter, sure now that he had gained the victory after so many years of battling her insolence.

"I forgive you for your insolence and for the way you disgraced me. Now that we are together again, you must not be so defiled."

"I'm not coming back to you, Papa. I desire only the life of my husband and children."

Rofisca's face grew red with rage again. He pulled his long sword from his belt and with a catlike motion, slit the throats of Chris, Paul, and Joseph. Narshac pushed forward and caught Rofisca's arm before he could reach Rebekah.

Safira watched as if in slow motion. Her husband and two sons leaned forward before their bodies collapsed on The Altar. They lay motionless, their blood flowing from their precious bodies. Never had she felt such a gripping pain and a depth of hurt. She fell to the ground in shrieks of pain and grief as if her own life had been taken from her. The crowd watched helplessly, awed and shocked by what had just happened.

Shovak had anticipated a show from Rofisca, but had not expected he'd go so far. To disobey him so completely and openly was a death sentence to the general. Shovak motioned for the guard, and they swept in and placed Rofisca in chains. Even so, Rofisca fought against his captors.

Ellie, the wife of the young couple Safira had helped, came toward Safira as she wept on the steps of The Altar only inches from her husband and sons. Safira's hand was stretched out toward Chris's head in a last effort to touch him. Her other hand reached out to touch Paul's still hand. Her hands became red and sticky from the blood that seeped down the stone monument.

The crowd fell into a mournful cry. Those who had known the Banks family as their leader, guide, and friend were at long last able to express the pain they felt, not only for this man but also for those they themselves had lost for the great cause of Christ. The reporters had been taking pictures since the moment Shovak had shown up, and they remained focused on the scene before them.

General Rofisca was led away toward the prison, and Shovak raised his voice against the cry. "This day, you've seen what kind of man Rofisca has turned into. Today, I free all men from my prison who were arrested under conviction of Christianity. No more prisoners of this kind shall be taken!" Glancing down at the bodies before him, he spoke again. "Take these bodies and prepare them for burial. Get them off this platform. This is meant for traitors, not heroes."

Shovak turned from the crowd with a heavy burden on his chest. He had not meant for these men to die. He had every intention of releasing them to their mother and wife. How had he underestimated Rofisca's obsession? He went to Ellie as she held Safira back from her husband's blood.

"She is welcome here. She will need time to register what just happened. She is in shock now. My guard will show you where to take her for privacy. My wife will see to your needs." Shovak left only after he'd witnessed Ellie following the guard and guiding Safira off The Altar toward a side entrance.

Chapter 34

God Watches Over Me

Safira cried herself to sleep, and when she woke two hours later, Rebekah sat beside her. While looking up at her daughter, tears welled up as she sat up to embrace her. Safira was thankful to hold her daughter, but she also felt the hole in her heart. The pain felt like a knife lodged into her chest. She had no words to send to her heavenly Father, only the broken and painful emotions. She knew He heard her inaudible cries. The door opened, and Safira recognized Shovak entering the room. She swung her feet off the couch, releasing Rebekah as she did so. Rebekah turned to face the intruder.

"I know something of your pain as my own twin sons were murdered only months ago. I wish I could do something to help, but I know that I can't. I will make sure they receive heroes' burials. The nation is indebted to you. They were all very courageous men."

"Thank you, Shovak. Their hearts were for Shemna, but I do wish to take my boys back to the States with me. Chris would've wanted that for his family."

"You want them taken back to Colorado?"

Tears filled her eyes as she nodded.

"Very well. It will be done. I will have the bodies embalmed immediately. I'm willing to make the arrangements for their bodies to be shipped as soon as they are prepared."

"Thank you, Shovak, for what you tried to do and for sparing my daughter." Safira squeezed her daughter's hand as the young lady stood silently.

Shovak nodded, wishing he could comfort the two women, but knowing such a thing would be impossible. "Before I leave you, I'd first like to tell you that it was Joseph and Paul who led me to the cross of Christ. I have put my trust in Him. They were also the ones who boldly spoke with my sons. I was honored to have met them. And your husband was a great teacher. I'd also like to introduce you to my wife Zamina before you leave for home. Later this evening perhaps?"

"Yes. Of course."

Safira was soon left alone when her daughter requested a chance to use the bathroom and find some water for both of them. Bowing her head in the quiet, she prayed silently allowing the Spirit to translate her prayer because she had no idea how to even form coherent thoughts in the midst of this storm. She considered what would become of her father, but she knew Shovak would never tolerate such blatant disobedience and felt only pity for him.

She picked up the phone on the nightstand and dialed Colorado, for a single sound of happiness. Surely, this tragedy would be all over the news by now, but this moment, she wanted only the joyful sounds of her living children, to know they were safe.

*****

The phone rang at the Klerens early that Thursday morning; everyone had just gotten up and was preparing for school when Fay answered. The Banks siblings had been staying with their grandparents that week to give Kate a break because Blake had business out of town. Safira was always in communication and knew exactly where her children would be. She was grateful they were at Fay's. Kate was much too perceptive, and Safira had no desire to be confronted with what she had witnessed—not yet.

"Fay, I've good news. Rebekah is here with me, and the men were all freed from prison." The words rolled off her tongue easily enough. The words were true.

"Oh, Safira, how exciting!" she said happily, missing the strangeness of her daughter-in-law's usually spirited tone. "You sound tired dear, but then, it is late afternoon there. Is Chris with you, or would you like to talk to the children."

"I'd like to speak with my babies."

"Of course, hold on." Fay had never heard Safira call her children her babies. She suddenly realized something was horribly wrong, but it was obvious Safira did not wish to share just now.

Safira waited only a moment before she heard Ruth's voice. "Hey, Mom. It's so good to hear from you. I'm loving school! How is everyone?"

Avoiding the question Safira responded, "Rebekah's here with me, but she just went into the other room. Do you like it better there than in Shemna?"

"Yes. I mean the people aren't the same, but the classes are great."

"I'm glad to hear that. Can you pass the phone on so I can talk to everyone before school?"

"Hold on."

Safira talked to each child for a few minutes before the phone was passed on. When David got on the phone, however, he heard the same thing Fay had. Something wasn't right.

"What's wrong, Mom?"

Tears filled her eyes, and her voice cracked as she spoke to her eldest son. She knew he would at least be able to be a beacon to the family if he knew before the rest.

"Your father and Paul and Jo . . . ," she couldn't finish immediately. After several swallows, she spoke again, "Your grandfather had them executed this afternoon, four hours ago. It's going to be all over the morning news. Perhaps, you shouldn't go to school today. Keep the kids away from the news until I get there."

David's voice was barely audible enough for his mom to hear, "Mom, when are you coming home?"

"As soon as we can get a flight out."

"I love you, Mom. I'm going to get everyone to school. They won't ask any questions that way. I'll pass the word on here. Come home safe."

"You're driving. I'd forgotten. I'll be home within a few days if all goes well."

David didn't stay on the phone much longer before signing off. He drove his siblings to school as normal, but it was Ruth who noticed something was wrong. When she asked him, he simply said he'd talk to her after school; and with a look that said, "Whatever you say big brother," she leapt out of the car and ran toward her school.

*****

Blake glanced at his phone and excused himself as he answered it.

"What's up? Aren't you supposed to be in school?"

"We need to talk." David's hard voice got his uncle's attention.

"Just a minute," Blake turned toward his client as he muted his phone. "I really need to take this. My nephew doesn't call unless it's important."

"Let's make it a half-hour break. I skipped breakfast this morning, so I could use the break myself."

Blake thanked the man before returning his attention back to David.

"Have you seen the news this morning?" David asked.

"No, I usually wait till evening to catch up."

"There is news from Keilron."

Blake waited through several seconds of silence. "You're skipping school to tell me that?"

"It's going to be about my family." David was hesitant, and his voice was strained. It was obvious he was having difficulty trying to explain.

"What's really going on here, Dave?" Blake asked, his heart pounding with fear.

David was not a boy of emotion. In fact, he was the very glue that kept the youngest Banks together, so when Blake heard the sob escape when David tried to speak, Blake instantly knew there was bad news. The words had not been uttered, but Blake knew in his heart that Chris was gone.

"Dad . . . the boys . . . killed." David was having difficulty saying the words out loud for the first time since his mother had told him. The reality of what he was saying settled on him. He let the tears fall and listened to the silence at the other end for some moments before he was able to collect himself enough to finish. "Mom and Rebekah will be flying home as soon as possible."

Blake couldn't move. He had no idea how to respond when images of his college buddy thumping him on the back popped into his head. His own eyes grew misty thinking back to the years he'd spent growing up with Christian Banks.

"Dave, are you sure?"

"Yes. Mom spoke to me this morning."

"It must be getting late in Keilron. I'm in Chicago, but I'll cancel the remainder of my business and be home on the next flight. Don't even think about trying to tell anybody else. Let me. I'll be home for supper. Get everyone gathered, but you don't need to be worried about how to tell them."

"Thanks." David could say no more, so he hung up the phone knowing Blake would be home shortly to help everyone understand. Blake had always been the rock in the family when it came to things concerning his father. The two men had always had each other's backs. Blake had always known that he would tell the Klerens if anything happened, but it would be just as hard on him as it would be on the rest of the clan.

That afternoon after the kids were sent to their rooms inside the Marty's home, the adults of their family gathered in Fay's living room. Blake looked into the faces of curious family members.

"What's this all about, Blake?" Fay asked as she handed him a glass of water.

"Fay, please take a seat next to Harris." He waited a moment for her to comply. "David received a disturbing message from Safira this morning."

Fay knew at that moment something really had been wrong. It hadn't been her imagination at all.

*****

Safira held Rebekah's hand as they waited in the London airport for their flight. They had made it to London two hours earlier from the Keilronian airport. They had a five-hour delay before they'd board a plane for New York City, where they would have another long delay before they would fly to Denver International. It would be a long couple of days for the two Banks women. They were exhausted from the journey and the emotional roller-coaster they were unable to get off of.

"Excuse me, ma'am, are you Mrs. Christian Banks?" Safira looked up at the woman who stood before her, dressed in a customary navy blue suit for the airport staff.

"Yes, I am."

"Would you follow me please, with your daughter, of course?"

Safira was exhausted as she stood, took Rebekah's hand, and followed the woman to a VIP lounge. When she entered the lounge, she stopped abruptly. She found herself staring into the face of Shovak and four Keilronian guards.

"Shovak, what brings you to London?" her voice was quizzical. She met the leader's gaze unflinchingly. "You did give us permission to leave," she confirmed.

"Of course. I knew you were planning on leaving as soon as possible, but I'd assumed you'd have waited for your men. I promised to make the arrangements, but it seems we were on two different wavelengths. I may have let you go without hesitation, but then, I was told how lengthy your trip would be. Instead, I have my private plane waiting for us to board and a limo in Denver prepared to take you to your husband's family. I was also able to load the bodies. You will be able to return with your whole family."

"In Keilron, I know that women are not respected, but your deeds have proven your worth. Let me do this for you. It's the least I can do after everything that's happened," Shovak said. He saw her eyes fill with tears and knew she was grateful.

"Zamina, after meeting you the other night, insisted on joining me. She's waiting for us," Shovak added. Zamina had not only taken to Safira as a person, but had also bonded with her over their shared grief. Safira had been unable to speak with her on the subject of salvation, but Shovak knew that the way Zamina accepted Safira, it would only be a matter of time before his wife learned of Jehovah and all He had to offer her.

He stood before Safira waiting for her response with his hands humbly folded in front of him. Shovak was not the man Safira remembered when she was a child. She began thanking God silently for giving her this small grace as Shovak escorted her and Rebekah to his waiting luxury private jet.

Safira had called Fay while in the air so her mother-in-law met them at the airport. Shovak and Zamina said their goodbyes to Safira while still in the plane. They didn't want to intrude on the family's time at the moment. Zamina and Safira exchanged contact information and promised to e-mail one another. Rebekah shook hands with their hosts and then deplaned.

The moment Fay saw them, she ran to meet them both with open arms. She had held her tears in check on the way to the airport. Safira had warned her that the boys' bodies were on board with her. Fay had even called a funeral home. A vehicle met them at the airport to transfer the bodies to the local funeral home. The moment she let go of Safira, her eyes caught the movement behind her daughter-in-law as the airport personnel and funeral home assistants unloaded, one by one, the boxes holding her son and two of her grandchildren. Their deaths became real at that moment. Fay reached out and clung to Safira as she sobbed.

Hours later, Safira, Rebekah, and Fay entered the Kleren's home. The three of them were exhausted emotionally and, the two younger women, physically as well. The ride home had been somber and silent as they all tried to gather their composure.

"Rebekah, why don't you go take a bath upstairs and then take a nap," Safira said. Rebekah hadn't yet been able to fully clean off all the filth from the prison because they'd left Shovak's home immediately after their meal and hadn't taken the time to clean up before departing.

"Where are my children?" Safira asked after Rebekah had willingly gone her way.

"They're at Blake's house."

"What do they know?"

"We left that up to David. I think he was waiting for you to be home. Because the media's going crazy with the live footage, we thought it best to pull them from school. All of us have been avoiding the news."

Safira nodded. Her voice was exhausted when she said, "I'm going to take a nap for an hour or so. Would you call Kate and ask her to bring the kids here?"

"Get some rest, dear. I'll take care of it."

*****

It turned out David, not Kate, was the one to bring the family over. Fay made herself scarce after letting her grandchildren in.

"Mom," David whispered as he entered her room.

Hearing her eldest son's voice, her eyes filled with tears as he came in. Embracing his mom, he sat down beside her on the bed. Several minutes passed before she spoke.

"David, it's so good to have you here. It's a blessing in so many ways that you grew up in Keilron."

David understood what she meant. His dad had warned him before he'd gone to Keilron for the last time that anything was possible and that he needed David to step up and take care of the family.

"I want to see all of you. Please bring in the younger ones. I think we need to talk."

David left for only a moment. Her children came to Safira with a mixture of smiles and tears. She held them one by one as they joined her on the bed. Safira forgot for a moment that they didn't know why she was home. It was Marie who brought her to the sad reality.

"Where's Joe, Paul, and Daddy?"

David reached for Marie, and she came easily into his arms. He glanced at his mother.

"They went home to Jesus. They're not coming back," said Safira, tears streaming down her face.

"Never?"

"Marie, we'll see Papa and Joe and Paul again," said David.

"How long?"

"I don't know, but we'll see them when we see Jesus."

"But I thought you don't get to see Jesus unless you die."

"That's right, Marie," David said as he looked into her eyes.

Marie started crying as the pieces fell together in her young mind. David held her closer as she wept. Ruth and Rachel wrapped their arms around their mom and cried. Daniel sat close to his mom with tears running down his face as he looked at his big brother. David laid his hand on Daniel's shoulder. The contact was more than Daniel could take. He scooted himself closer to his brother, and David wrapped his arm around him in comfort.

Ruth, Daniel, Rachel, Marie, and David stayed in the bedroom together for over an hour, comforted by each other's presence. Rebekah woke from her nap at last and found her family gathered around their mom. She joined them, taking Marie from David and cuddling her little sister close. They were all soon reminiscing. Another hour passed before they went downstairs in search of food. Grandma Fay found beds for them all, and the kids were soon tucked into bed. David kept his mom in the living room for a bit longer once the younger ones had dispersed.

"Mom, what's going to happen with their bodies?"

"Shovak has taken care of it. Keilron has given them a memorial fit for a king. And we brought their bodies home, so we could have a proper burial with the whole family. Shovak's the one who got me home today. I'd be in the New York airport right now if it hadn't been for him meeting me in London."

"Shovak?"

Safira filled David in on the details.

"Then there is a purpose for all this," he said in awe.

"David, there are much bigger things going on in that country, and some of those great changes are due to our family's influence. God used your father in an unusual way, a way that we should all be proud of. Narshac and Rofisca were only the cherry on top of the work your father and I started there a long time ago. The New Testament we completed and smuggled in was due to your father's fortune. There are many sparks flying around we still aren't aware of. A fire has begun, and there will be no stopping its influence."

"I know, but it's hard to let him go," David said as a tear crept down his face.

Safira knew he was hurting just as they all were.

She had one plea, "David, don't turn your heart away from God."

"I won't, Mom." He grasped her hand and squeezed it before turning and going upstairs.

After the family buried their loved ones and those that comforted the grieving family returned to their homes, the true healing began. Every night was difficult for Safira. The empty spot beside her was a constant reminder of Chris's absence. David often reminded her of her husband in his mannerisms, and Daniel in his looks as he began to mature into a handsome young man. Each holiday and special event brought anew the sharp pain, the absence of Chris and the twins. But with time and faith, the hurt became less intense and more bearable. The ache in her heart was a constant reminder of the life she'd shared with her husband and sons.

The next six months passed quickly. Safira bought a home for herself and her children to live in, rather than remaining with the Klerens. The children found their new home a safe place to remember their dad and brothers without bringing more pain to anyone else. As life began to pick up a rhythm once again, David approached his mom.

"I want to go back to Keilron, Mom, and I've been praying about it. I want to go to school this fall to prepare for full-time service. I've already talked with the Admissions Office at Dad's college. I can get my four years done in two years, if I take all the summer classes and load up with credits."

"That's a lot of work."

"We need to go back as soon as we can. I want to be prepared biblically before we go. And I'll keep talking to the kids in Keilronian so the transition won't be so strange to Marie and Rachel."

"We'll return together. I've been praying God would work in your heart toward Keilron. I wouldn't go alone, nor would I force a ministry on you that wasn't yours."

"What about the younger ones?"

"They can return with us. Rebekah and probably Ruth will have their own say. Rebekah will still be in college, you know."

"I'm getting my GED, and I'll be going to college starting this summer."

"All right, do you think you'll live on campus then?"

"Yes, I'll be taking as many credits as I can because I want to leave as soon as possible."

Safira smiled. He truly was like his father. Keilron was home, not only for her but also for her children.

May 2027

"Do you have everything, kids?" Safira asked again. David picked up Marie's suitcase and hauled it to the car. They were all going home to Keilron. The flight and travel would be once again long and hard, but the reward of returning home would be gratifying. David had spoken little English with his family since the day he'd talked to his mother two years earlier. His speech had affected the younger ones, forcing them to remember the Keilronian language as well.

Rebekah decided to stay in America with her new boyfriend. Ruth, at fourteen, was excited to return, for it was a new adventure. Daniel, now twelve, anticipated seeing his old neighborhood. Rachel, just turned nine, anticipated meeting her old friends again. And Marie, now seven, could remember just a little about the inside of the Keilronian home.

David, nineteen, had much on his mind as he guided his family to the road that would lead back home.

When they reached the airport, they were amazed to find that the airline returned their money and retrieved their tickets. Safira was confused, but her inquiries were ignored. When she was escorted to the VIP lounge, she began to understand. It wasn't Shovak as she'd suspected, however, but several Keilronian guards.

"We were instructed to escort you and your family to Keilron. His greatness asks forgiveness for not being able to escort you himself, but he had other responsibilities," said the officer.

"Thank you kindly for your help. We will need to get our bags."

Nodding, the four men followed David.

An hour later, her family was relaxing in the Keilronian luxury plane.

"Mom, this is great. How'd you do this?" David asked, sitting beside her.

"All the papers and most all of the media were covering our departure. I did send Zamina an e-mail that we would be home soon. Shovak probably put two and two together and sent us the escort."

"Look!" Daniel said excitedly pointing out the window as the plane reached its altitude.

A fighter plane appeared on either side of the plane. The symbols on their wings were Keilronian.

Ruth smiled, "Mom, when they said escort us, I think they were quite serious."

When they reached the Keilronian airport, Safira exited the private plane and found reporters waiting with cameras to take pictures of the Banks family returning to their adopted homeland.

Shovak and Zamina, who'd only days earlier accepted Christ for her own salvation, appeared beside the stairs of the plane, and Shovak held out his hand to Safira as she touched Keilronian dirt once again.

He smiled welcomingly. "My lady, welcome home."

Safira smiled in return. "Thank you, Shovak. I'd like you to meet my other children. This is David, Ruth, Marie, Daniel, and Rachel."

"It is a pleasure to meet you all."

Turning to the cameras, he spoke in a loud voice for all to hear.

"She left the first time as a runaway, returned a fugitive, left a widow, and returns home a welcome citizen!"

Shovak turned and shook David's hand. "It is an honor to meet the eldest son of such a great man."

"Thank you, sir. With your permission, I desire to remain in Keilron for many years."

Shovak smiled. "As long as you remember to visit me occasionally."

David nodded and thanked him.

Safira looked at the crowds, tears coming to her eyes. God had worked a miracle. She and Chris had prayed for Keilron for years, hoping that many would choose Christ. They had prayed for the doors to open. She only wished Chris was standing with her now to witness the transformation that was so beyond either of their dreams. The people applauded Safira and her children surrounding her. As she gazed across the welcoming crowd, Safira knew God's work was just beginning.

Epilogue

"David stayed in Keilron and eventually married Angie's daughter, Penny. It is a small world," Safira's gentle smile gave hinted at the humor she found in that situation. "As this account is directed to my family, you know how my children became wonderful men and women who continue to give God the praise for everything. I remained in Keilron for twenty-eight more years until I had to return here for health reasons. My life has been one used of God, and for that, I'm thankful beyond measure."

"I don't feel as if I'm going to die right now, but I have asked Marie to wait until my passing to share this account with you. I want to give you words to live by. Serve Christ with all you have, and you will be rewarded with blessings beyond your imagination. Give to others all you can, love others as if you've nothing to lose, and the love that you feel, I hope, will compare to the love and joy I feel when looking at my family who have trusted Christ. I'm so proud of the men and women you have become. I don't get a chance to say it often enough. I love you."

Soft music played in the background as the camera once again slowly panned over the items behind Safira.

Sophie looked at her surrounding family when Marie finally hit the stop button. None of the Banks family sitting in the room had a dry eye. Many of her cousins sat in awe at the story Safira had told. They had no idea their great-grandparents had been so bold. They had not known the tremendous role their family had played to make it safe for the missionaries there. They had heard so little about their grandfather Christian Banks.

David, Ruth, and Marie lived in Keilron still with their spouses, although most of their children now resided in the United States.

Having come to visit from her home in Minnesota, Rachel sat with her husband, tears still in her eyes. Rebekah had remained in Colorado after marrying her college sweetheart who sat beside her, his arm wrapped around her shoulders. Daniel's two children had come with their native Keilronian mother. Sophie wished she could remember more of her late Uncle Daniel who'd gone home to be with the Lord more than a decade earlier.

"This is not the end. This is just the beginning," Sophie said quietly from her spot on the floor. She looked over at Marie. "Where was this taken?"

"Here, of course. Would you like to see the room?"

Sophie's eyes lit up, "Yes."

The other grandchildren were less curious than Sophie and were soon engaged in conversation. Sophie followed her grandmother down a series of halls before they reached the small room. Marie opened the door and let Sophie drink it in.

Sophie didn't waste time entering the small space. It was tiny compared to the rest of the mansion's rooms. Perhaps it had originally been meant as a large walk-in closet. She touched the items as her hands glided over them. She picked up several photos and news articles as she investigated.

She saw a picture of Safira and Chris smiling for their first newspaper man, the family gathered at the airport, hands held while they prayed, just as Grandma had said. She read the articles of Safira's return. The pictures from Keilronian newspapers of Narshac, embracing his sister as Shovak shook David's hand told a story of their own.

Startled, Sophie looked toward the door as Ruth walked in to stand beside Marie.

"I didn't know Mom had made a special room. I recognized the small space from when we first bought the house. When we were looking for a place, it was this room she fell in love with. I didn't understand at the time why she'd care for such an awkward space. Now, I understand. Mom always had her mind set on us, on Keilron.

It was more than her native home, though. You could tell when you talked to her that Keilron was her passion."

Marie spoke to Sophie, "I thought that this would make it more real for you. Our family's been in the press a long time."

"Who kept all these articles? Did Grandma Safira do all this?" Sophie inquired.

"For many years, it was Chris's sister, Kate, who collected the articles and captured moments that she saw as special. When she passed, Blake found them and continued to gather the material until he died, and Mom found the scrapbooks. She added things from there. Her old journals, her first English Bible, and Keilronian New Testament. I gave it all to her when she made Colorado her permanent home. She'd occasionally ask us for trinkets when we came home. It's really neat to see what she's done," Ruth said.

Marie nodded her agreement.

David spoke as he too stood near the doorway. "Sophie, you have shown the most interest in Keilron, more than any of the other grandchildren, and you have the biggest heart for Shemna."

"I want to go to Shemna and see the places she talked about and meet the people who stole her heart. I want to make a difference. I want to write her story just as she's told it," said Sophie.

"I know that someday you will," Marie encouraged.

"My mother's story was true, every bit of it," said David.

"Her story will be told in an extraordinary way that will not soon be forgotten," Sophie vowed as she looked at her aunts and uncle. She realized the children Grandma Safira had spoken so lovingly of, children of courage and strength, were the ones standing before her. It was not just Safira's story—it was also her nation's and her children's story. Sophie glanced back into the small room, this was *her* family and *her* legacy to carry on, and she would share all of their story that, by God's grace, some would be saved.

About the Author

Hannah Beth began this story while attending a small Bible college and going through trials of her own. Her heart for missions both foreign and domestic fueled the passion of each character. Although she now resides in Conneautville, Pennsylvania, with her husband and daughter, she has lived in several states in her young adult life including her home state of Minnesota, Illinois, Michigan, Tennessee, and Kansas. The debut of this, her first novel, has been a journey she wouldn't have traded for the world.